RICHMOND PUBLIC LIBRARY, CA 94804-1659

3 1143 00605 2048

Richmond Public Library

D0058413

ALSO BY ANNE RICE

Interview with the Vampire
The Feast of All Saints
Cry to Heaven
The Vampire Lestat
The Queen of the Damned
The Mummy
The Witching Hour
The Tale of the Body Thief
Lasher
Taltos
Memnoch the Devil

UNDER THE NAME ANNE RAMPLING

Exit to Eden
Belinda

UNDER THE NAME A. N. ROQUELAURE

The Claiming of Sleeping Beauty
Beauty's Punishment
Beauty's Release

Servant
of the Bones

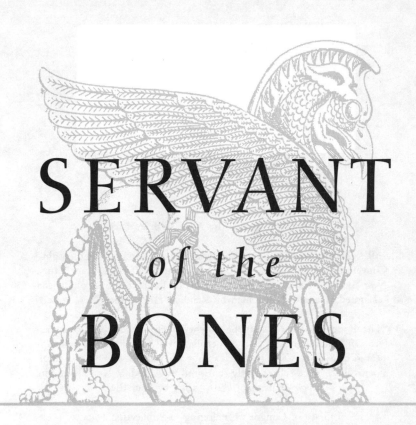

SERVANT
of the
BONES

Anne Rice

ALFRED A. KNOPF
New York   1996

31143006052048
Fic Ric
Rice, Anne, 1941-
Servant of the bones

THIS IS A BORZOI BOOK
PUBLISHED BY ALFRED A. KNOPF

Copyright © 1996 by Anne O'Brien Rice

All rights reserved under International and Pan-American Copyright
Conventions. Published in the United States by Alfred A. Knopf, Inc.,
New York, and simultaneously in Canada by Random House of Canada
Limited, Toronto. Distributed by Random House, Inc., New York.

"The Bones of Woe," "Aesthetic Theory," "How Keep Dark and Pattern Off," and "Lament" used by permission of Stan Rice originally appeared in *Some Lamb*, copyright © 1975 by Stan Rice. The first three
poems listed were subsequently reprinted by Alfred A. Knopf, Inc., in
Singing Yet, copyright © 1992 by Stan Rice.

Library of Congress Cataloging-in-Publication Data

Rice, Anne.
Servant of the bones / Anne Rice. — 1st ed.
p. cm.
ISBN 0-679-43301-5
1. Jews—History—Fiction.   2. Time travel—Fiction.   3. Spirits—
Fiction.   I. Title.
PS3568.I265S47   1996
813'.54—dc20   95-49357
CIP

Manufactured in the United States of America
First Edition

This book

is

dedicated

to

GOD.

By the rivers of Babylon, there we sat
down, yea, we wept, when we
remembered Zion.

    We hanged our harps upon the willows
in the midst thereof.

    For there they that carried us away
captive required of us a song; and they
that wasted us *required of us* mirth,
saying, Sing us *one* of the songs of Zion.

    How shall we sing the Lord's song in
a strange land?

    If I forget thee, O Jerusalem, let my
right hand forget *her cunning*.

    If I do not remember thee, let my
tongue cleave to the roof of my mouth;
if I prefer not Jerusalem above my chief joy.

    Remember, O Lord, the children of
Edom in the day of Jerusalem; who said,
Rase *it*, rase *it, even* to the foundation
thereof.

    O daughter of Babylon, who art to be
destroyed; happy *shall he be*, that
rewardeth thee as thou hast served us.

    Happy *shall he be*, that taketh and
dasheth thy little ones against the stones.

PROEM

Murdered. Her hair was black and so were her eyes.
It happened on Fifth Avenue, the murder, inside a fine clothing store, amid hustle and bustle. Hysteria as she fell . . . perhaps.

Soundlessly I saw it on the television screen. Esther. I knew her. Yes, Esther Belkin. She'd been a student once in my class. Esther. Rich and lovely to behold.

Her father. He was the head of that worldwide temple. New Age platitudes and T-shirts. And the Belkins had all the money human beings could ever want or dream of, and now Esther, sweet Esther, that flower of a girl who had always asked her questions so timidly— was dead.

On the news, "live," I think I saw her die. I was reading a book, not paying much attention. The news went on in silence, mingling movie stars and war. It made slow garish flickers on the walls of the room. The silent leap and flare of a television watched by no one. I read on after she died "live."

Now and then in the days that followed I thought about her. Some horrors followed her death, having to do with her father and his electronic church. More blood shed.

I never knew her father. His followers had been detritus on street corners.

But I remembered Esther pretty well. She wanted to know everything, one of those kind, humble, ever listening, and sweet, yes, very sweet. I remembered her. Sure. Ironic, that doe of a girl slain and then the tragedy of her father's delusions.

I never tried to understand the whole story.

I forgot about her. I forgot that she'd been murdered. I forgot about her father. I guess I forgot that she'd ever been alive.

There was news and news and news.

It was time to stop teaching for a while.

I went away to write my book. I went up into the mountains. I went to the snow. I hadn't so much as offered a prayer in Esther Belkin's memory, but I am a historian and not a praying man.

In the mountains, I learnt everything. Her death came after me, vivid and lush with meaning, through the words of another.

Part I

THE BONES OF WOE

Golden are the bones of woe.
Their brilliance has no place to go.
It plunges inward,
Spikes through snow.

Of weeping fathers whom we drink
And mother's milk and final stink
We can dream but cannot think.
Golden bones encrust the brink.

Golden silver copper silk.
Woe is water shocked by milk.
Heart attack, assassin, cancer.
Who would think these bones such dancers.

Golden are the bones of woe.
Skeleton holds skeleton.
Words of ghosts are not to know.
Ignorance is what we learn.

Stan Rice, *Some Lamb* 1975

1

This is Azriel's tale as he told it to me, as he begged me to bear witness and to record his words. Call me Jonathan as he did. That was the name he chose on the night he appeared in my open door and saved my life.

Surely if he hadn't come to seek a scribe, I would have died before morning.

Let me explain that I am well known in the fields of history, archaeology, Sumerian scholarship. And Jonathan is indeed one of the names given me at birth, but you won't find it on the jackets of my books, which the students study because they must, or because they love the mysteries of ancient lore as much as I do.

Azriel knew this—the scholar, the teacher I was—when he came to me.

Jonathan was a private name for me that we agreed upon together. He had plucked it from the string of three names on the copyright pages of my books. And I had answered to it. It became my name for him during all those hours as he told his tale—a tale I would never publish under my regular professorial name, knowing full well, as he did, that this story would never be accepted alongside my histories.

So I am Jonathan; I am the scribe; I tell the tale as Azriel told it. It doesn't really matter to him what name I use with you. It only mattered that one person wrote down what he had to say. The Book of Azriel was dictated to Jonathan.

He did know who I was; he knew all my works, and had painstakingly read them before ever coming. He knew my academic reputation, and something in my style and outlook had caught his fancy.

Perhaps he approved that I had reached the venerable age of sixty-five, and still wrote and worked night and day like a young man, with no intentions of retiring ever from the school where I taught, though I had now and then to get completely away from it.

So it was no haphazard choice that made him climb the steep forested mountains, in the snow, on foot, carrying only a curled newsmagazine in his hand, his tall form protected by a thick mass of curly black hair that grew long below his shoulders—a true protective mantle for a man's head and neck—and one of those double-tiered and flaring winter coats that only the tall of stature and the romantic of heart can wear with aplomb or the requisite charming indifference.

By the light of the fire, he appeared at once a kind young man, with huge black eyes and thick prominent brows, a small thick nose, and a large cherub's mouth, his hair dappled with snow, the wind blowing his coat wildly about him as it tore through the house, sending my precious papers swirling in all directions.

Now and then this coat became too large for him. His appearance completely changed to match that of the man on the cover of the magazine he'd brought with him.

It was that miracle I saw early on, before I knew who he was, or that I was going to live, that the fever had broken.

Understand I am not insane or even eccentric by nature, and have never been self-destructive. I didn't go to the mountains to die. It had seemed a fine idea to seek out the absolute solitude of my northern house, unconnected to the world by phone, fax, television, or electricity. I had a book to complete which had taken me some ten years, and it was in this self-imposed exile that I meant to finish it.

The house is mine, and was then, as always, well stocked, with plenty of bottled water for drinking, and oil and kerosene for its lamps, candles by the crate, and electric batteries of every conceivable size for the small tape recorder I use and the laptop computers on which I work, and an enormous shed of dried oak for the fires I would need throughout my stay there.

I had the few medical necessaries a man can carry in a metal box. I had the simple food I eat and can cook by fire: rice, hominy, cans upon cans of saltless chicken broth, and also a few barrels of apples which should have lasted me the winter. A sack or two of yams I'd also brought, discovering I could wrap these in foil and roast them in my coal-and-oak fire.

I liked the bright orange color of yams. And please be assured, I was not proud of this diet, or seeking to write a magazine article on it. I'm simply tired of rich food; tired of crowded fashionable New York restaurants and glittering party buffets, and even the often wonderful meals offered me weekly by colleagues at their own tables. I am merely trying to explain. I wanted fuel for the body and the mind.

I brought what I needed so that I might write in peace. There was nothing that peculiar about all this.

The place was already lined in books, its old barn wood walls fully insulated and then shelved to the ceiling. There was a duplicate here of every important text I ever consulted at home, and the few books of poetry I read over and over for ecstasy.

My spare computers, all small and very powerful beyond any understanding I ever hope to acquire of hard drives, bytes, megabytes of memory, or 486 chips, had been delivered earlier, along with a ludicrous supply of diskettes on which to "back up" or copy my work.

Truth is, I worked mostly by hand, on yellow legal pads. I had cartons of pens, the very fine-point kind, with black ink.

Everything was perfect.

And I should add here that the world I had left behind seemed just a little more mad than usual.

The news was full of a lurid murder trial on the West Coast having to do with a famous athlete accused of slitting his wife's throat, an entertainment par excellence that had galvanized the talk shows, the news shows, and even that vapid, naive, and childlike connection to the world that calls itself E! Entertainment.

In Oklahoma City, a Federal office building had been blown sky high—and not by alien terrorists, it was believed, but by our own Americans, members of the militia movement they were called, who had decided in much the same manner of the hippies of years before that our government was a dangerous enemy. Whereas the hippies and the protesters of the Vietnam War had merely lain on railroad tracks and sung in ranks, these new crewcut militants—filled with fantasies of impending doom—killed our own people. By the hundreds.

Then there were the battles abroad, which had become regular circuses. Not a day went by when one was not reminded of atrocities committed among the Bosnians and the Serbs in the Balkans—a region that had been at war for one reason or another for centuries. I had lost track of who was Moslem, Christian, Russian ally, or friend. The city of Sarajevo had been a familiar word to television-watching Americans for years now. In the streets of Sarajevo people died daily, including men they called United Nations peace keepers.

In African countries, people starved as the result of civil strife and famine. It was a nightly sight as common as a beer commercial to see on television fresh footage of starving African babies, bellies swollen, faces covered with flies.

Jews and Arabs fought in the streets of Jerusalem. Bombs went off; protesters were shot at by armies; and terrorists destroyed innocent people to strengthen their demands.

In the Ukraine, remnants of a fallen Soviet Union made war on mountain folk who had never given in to any foreign power. People died in the snow and cold for reasons that were nearly impossible to explain.

In sum there were dozens of places raging with suffering in which to fight, to die, to film, as the parliaments of the world tried in vain to find answers without bullets. The decade was a feast of wars.

Then there was the death of Esther Belkin, followed by the scandal of the Temple of the Mind. Caches of assault weapons had been found in the Temple's outposts from New Jersey to Libya. Explosives and poisonous gases had been stockpiled in its hospitals. The great mentor of this popular international church—Gregory Belkin—was insane.

Before Gregory Belkin, there had been other madmen with great dreams perhaps but smaller resources. Jim Jones and his People's Temple committing mass suicide in the jungles of Guyana; David Koresh, who believed himself the Christ, perishing by gun and fire in a Waco, Texas, compound.

A Japanese religious leader had just recently been accused of killing innocent people on the country's public subways.

A church with the lovely name of the Temple Solaire had not so long ago staged a mass suicide coordinated at three different locations in Switzerland and Canada.

A popular talk show host gave directions to his listeners as to how they might assassinate the President of the United States.

A fatal virus had only recently broken out with stunning fury in an African country, then died away, leaving all thinking individuals with a renewed interest in the age-old obsession: that the end of the world might be at hand. Apparently there were more than three kinds of this virus, and numerous others equally as deadly lurking in the rain forests of the world.

A hundred other surreal stories made up each day's news, and each day's inevitable civilized conversation.

So I ran from this, as much as anything else. I ran for the solitude, the whiteness of snow, the brutal indifference of towering trees and tiny winter stars.

It was my own jeep which had brought me up through "the leather stocking woods," as it is sometimes still called, in honor of James Fenimore Cooper, to barricade myself for the winter. There was a phone in the jeep by which one could, with perseverance if possible, reach the outside world. I was for tearing it out, but the truth is I'm not very handy and I couldn't get the thing loose without damaging my car.

So you see, I am not a fool, just a scholar. I had a plan. I was prepared for the heavy snow to come, and the winds to whistle in the single metal chimney above the round central hearth. The smell of my books, the oak fire, the snow itself whirling down at times in tiny specks into the flames, these things I love and need now and then. And many a winter before this house had given me exactly what I asked of it.

The night began like any other. The fever took me completely by surprise, and I remember building up the fire in the round pit of a fireplace very high because I did not want to have to tend it. When I drank all the water nearest the bed, I don't know. I couldn't have been fully conscious then. I know that I went to the door, that I myself unbolted it, and then could not get it closed; this much I do recall. I must have been trying to reach the jeep.

Bolting the door was simply impossible. I lay for a long time in the snow itself before I crawled back inside, and away from the mouth of the winter, or so it seemed.

I remember these things because I remember knowing then that I was very much in danger. The long journey back to the bed, the long journey back to the warmth of the fire, utterly exhausted me. Beneath the heap of wool blankets and quilts, I hid from the whirlwind that entered my house. And I knew that if I didn't clear my head, if I didn't recover somehow, the winter would just come inside soon and put to sleep forever the fire, and take me too.

Lying on my back, the quilts up to my chin, I sweated and shivered. I watched the flakes of snow fly beneath the sloping beams of the roof. I watched the raging pyramid of logs as it blazed. I smelled the burnt pot when the soup boiled dry. I saw the snow covering my desk.

I made a plan to rise, then fell asleep. I dreamed those fretful stupid dreams that fever makes, then woke with a start, sat up, fell back, dreamed again. The candles were gone out, but the fire still burned, and snow now filled the room, blanketing my desk, my chair, perhaps the bed itself. I licked snow from my lips once, that I do recall, and it tasted good, and now and then I licked the melted snow I could gather with my hand. My thirst was hellish. Better to dream than to feel it.

It must have been midnight when Azriel came.

Did he choose his hour with a sense of drama? Quite to the contrary. A long way off, walking through snow and wind, he had seen the fire high on the mountain above, sparks flying from the chimney and a light that blinkered through the open door. He had hurried towards these beacons.

Mine was the only house on the land and he knew it. He had learnt that from the casual tactful remarks of those who had told him officially and gently that I could not be reached in the months to come, that I had gone into hiding.

I saw him the very moment he stood in the door. I saw the sheen of his mass of black curling hair and fire in both his eyes. I saw the strength and swiftness with which he closed and locked the door and came directly towards me.

I believe I said, "I'm going to die."

"No, you won't, Jonathan," he answered. He brought the bottle of water at once and lifted my head. I drank and I drank and my fever drank, and I blessed him.

"It's only kindness, Jonathan," he said with simplicity.

I dozed as he built up the fire again, wiped away the snow, and I have a very distinct and wondrous memory of him gathering my papers from everywhere, with great care, and kneeling by the fire to lay them out so that they might dry and some of the writing might be saved after all.

"This is your work, your precious work," he said to me when he saw that I was watching him.

He had taken off the big double-mantled coat. He was in shirt sleeves which meant we were safe. I smelled the soup cooking again, the bubbling chicken broth. He brought the soup to me in an earthen bowl—the sort of rustic things I chose for this place—and he said drink the soup, and I did.

Indeed, it was by water and broth that he brought me slowly back. Never once did I have the presence of mind to mention the few medications in the white box of first-aid supplies. He bathed my face with cold water.

He bathed all of me slowly and patiently, turning me gently, and rolling under me the new fresh clean sheets. "The broth," he said, "the broth, no, you must." And the water. The water he gave me perpetually.

Was there enough for him, he had asked. I had almost laughed.

"Of course, my friend, dear God, take anything you want."

And he drank the water down in greedy gulps, saying it was all he needed now, that once again the Stairway to Heaven had disappeared and left him stranded.

"My name is Azriel," he said, sitting by the bed. "They called me the Servant of the Bones," he said, "but I became a rebel ghost, a bitter and impudent genii."

He unfurled the magazine for me to see. My head was clear. I sat up, propped by the divine luxury of clean pillows. He looked as unlike a ghost as a man can look, muscular, brimming with life, the dark hair on the backs of his hands and on his arms making him appear all the more strong and vital.

Gregory Belkin's face stared forward from the famous *Time* magazine frame. Gregory Belkin—Esther's father—founder of the Temple of the Mind. The man who would have brought harm to millions.

"I killed that man," he said.

I turned to look at him, and then it was that I first saw the miracle. He wanted me to see it. He did it for me.

He had grown smaller in size, though only slightly; his mane of tangled black curls was gone; he had the trimmed hair of a modern businessman; even his large loose shirt was changed for the supremely acceptable and impeccably tailored black suit, and he had become . . . before my very eyes . . . the figure of Gregory Belkin.

"Yes," he said. "It was the way I looked on the day I made my choice, to forfeit my powers forever; to take on real flesh and real suffering. I looked just like Gregory when I shot him."

Before I could answer, he began to change again, the head to grow larger, the features to become broader, forehead stronger and more distinctive, the cherub mouth of his own to replace the thin line of Belkin's. His fierce eyes grew large beneath the thick eyebrows that tended to dip as he smiled, making the smile and immensity of the eyes seem secretive and seductive.

It was not a happy smile. It had no humor or sweetness in it.

"I thought I would look this way forever," he said, holding up the magazine for me to see. "I thought I would die in that form." He sighed. "The Temple of the Mind lies in ruins. The people will not die. The women and children will not fall on the road as they breathe the evil gas. But I didn't die. I am Azriel again."

I took his hand. "You're a living breathing man," I said. "I don't know how you made yourself look like Gregory Belkin."

"No, not a man—a ghost," he said, "a ghost so strong that he can wrap himself in the form he had when he was alive; and now he cannot make it go away. Why did God do this to me? I am not an innocent being; I have sinned. But why can't I die?"

Suddenly a smile came over his face. He was almost a boy, the tangled curls making their dark frame for his low cheeks and the large beautiful cherub mouth.

"Maybe God let me live to save you, Jonathan. Maybe that's all it was. He gave me my old flesh back so I could climb this mountain and tell you all this, and you would have died had I not come here."

"Perhaps, Azriel," I said.

"You rest now," he said. "Your forehead is cool. I'll wait, and I'll watch, and if you see me, now and then, turn into that man again, it is only that I'm trying to measure each time the difficulty of it. It was never so very hard for me to change my shape—for the sorcerer who called me up from the bones. It was never so hard for me to throw an illusion to trick my master's enemies or those he would rob or cheat.

"But it's hard now to be anything but the young man I was when it started. When I bought their lies. When I became a ghost and not the martyr they promised. Lie still now, Jonathan, sleep. Your eyes are clear and your cheeks have color."

"Give me more of the broth," I said.

He did.

"Azriel, I *would* be dead without you."

"Yes, that much is true, isn't it? But I had my foot on the Ladder to Heaven, I was on it this time, I tell you, when I made this choice, and I thought when it was all over, the Temple destroyed, the Stairway might come down for me again. The Hasidim are pure and innocent. They are good. But battles they must leave to monsters like me."

"Lord, God," I said. Gregory Belkin. A lunatic plan. I remember fragments . . . "And there was that beautiful girl," I said.

He put down the cup of broth, and wiped my face and my hands.

"Her name was Esther."

"Yes."

He opened the curled and damp magazine for me. It was now badly creased as it was drying out in the warm room. I saw the famous photograph of Esther Belkin, on Fifth Avenue. I saw her lying on the stretcher just before they had put her into the ambulance, and just before she had died.

Only this time I focused on a figure in this photograph which I had noticed before, yes, in television broadcasts, and in the larger cover photographs of this very scene. But I hadn't until now paid any real attention to the figure. I saw a young man by Esther's stretcher, with his hands raised to his head, as though crying out in grief for her, a young man blurry and indistinct as all the other crowd figures in the famous photograph, except for his heavy beautifully shaped eyebrows and his mane of thick black curly hair.

"That's you," I said. "Azriel, that's you there in the photograph."

He was distracted. He didn't reply. He put his finger on the figure of Esther. "She died there, Esther, his daughter."

I explained that I had known her. The Temple was new then, and controversial rather than solid and immense and indefatigable. She had been a good student, serious and modest and alert.

He looked at me for a long time. "She was a sweet, kind girl, wasn't she?"

"Yes, very much so. Very unlike her stepfather."

He pointed to his own shape in the picture.

"Yes, the ghost, the Servant of the Bones," he said. "I was visible then in my grief. I will never know who called me. Maybe it was only her death, the dark horrible beauty of it. I'll never know. But you see now, you feel now, I have the solid shape of that form which was nothing before but vapor. God has wrapped me in my old flesh; he makes it harder and harder for me to vanish and return; to take to the air and to nothingness and to reassemble. What is to become of me, Jonathan? As I grow stronger and stronger in this seeming human form, I fear I *can't* die. I will never."

"Azriel, you must tell me everything."

"Everything? Oh, I want to, Jonathan. I want to."

Within an hour, I was able to walk about the house without dizziness. He'd found my thick robe for me, and my leather slippers. Within a few more hours I was hungry.

It must have been morning when I fell asleep. And then waking in the later afternoon, I was myself, clearheaded, sharp, and the house was not only safely warmed by the fire, but he had put a few candles around, the thick kind, so that the corners had a dusty soft nonintrusive light.

"Is it all right?" he asked me gently.

I told him to put out a few more. And to light the kerosene lamp on my desk. He did these things with no trouble. A match was no mystery to him, or a cigarette lighter. He raised the wick of the lamp. He put two more of the candles on the stone-top table by the bed.

The room, with its wooden windows bolted shut as tight as its door, was softly, evenly visible. The wind howled in the chimney. Again came the volley of flakes dissolving in the heat. The storm had slackened but the snow still fell. The winter surrounded us.

And no one will come, no one will disturb us, no one will distract us. I stared at him in keen interest. I was happy. Uncommonly happy.

I taught him how to make cowboy coffee by merely throwing the grinds into the pot, and I drank plenty of it, loving the smell of it.

Though he wanted to do it, I mixed up the grits for a good meal, showing him again how it came in little packets, and all one had to do was boil the water on the fire, and then stir the grits to a thick delicious porridge.

He watched me eat it. He said he wanted nothing.

"Why don't you taste it?" I said. I begged.

"Because my body won't take it," he said. "It's not human, I told you."

He stood up and walked slowly to the door. I thought he might open it on the storm and I hunkered my shoulders, ready for the blast. I would not even consider asking him to keep it shut. After all he had done, if he wanted to see the snow, I wouldn't deny him anything.

But he lifted his arms. And without the door being opened, there came a blast of wind and his figure paled, seemed to swirl for a moment, its colors and textures mingled in a vortex and then vanished.

Spellbound, I rose from my place by the fire. I held the bowl to my chest in a desperate childlike gesture.

The wind died away. He was nowhere to be seen, and then, when the wind came again, it was hot: a blast as if from a furnace.

Azriel stood opposite the fire, looking at me. Same white shirt, same black pants. The same dark black hair of his chest thick beneath his open collar.

"Will I never be *nefesh*?" he asked. "That is, body and soul together."

I knew the Hebrew word.

I sat him down. He said he could drink water. He said that all ghosts and spirits could drink water, and they drank up the scents of sacrifice and that was why all the ancient talk of libations and of incense, of burnt offerings and of smoke rising from the altars. He drank the water, and it seemed to relax him again.

He sat back in one of my many cracked and broken leather chairs, oblivious to its worn crevices and rips. He put his feet up on the stone hearth, and I saw his shoes were still wet.

I finished my meal, cleared it away, and came back with the picture of Esther. At this round hearth, six people could have sat in a circle.

We were near to one another, near enough, him with his back to the desk and beyond it the door, and I with my back to the warmer, smaller, darker corner of the room in my favorite chair, of broken springs and round fat arms, stained from careless wine and coffee.

I looked at her. She was half a page, in this the recurrent story of her death which had been retold only because of Gregory's downfall.

"He killed her, didn't he?" I said. "It was the first assassination."

"Yes," Azriel answered. I marveled that his eyebrows could be so thick, beautiful and brooding, and yet his mouth so gentle as he smiled. There was no double to die in her place. He killed his own stepdaughter.

"That's when I came, you see," he went on. "That's when I came out of the darkness as if called by the master sorcerer, only there was none. I appeared fully formed and hurrying down the New York street, only to witness her death, her cruel death, and to kill those who killed her."

"The three men? The men who stabbed Esther Belkin?"

He didn't answer. I remembered. The men had been stabbed with their own ice picks only a block and a half away from the crime. So thick was the crowd on Fifth Avenue that day that no one even connected the deaths of three street toughs with the slaughter of the beautiful girl inside the fashionable store of Henri Bendel. Only the next day had the ice picks told the story of blood, her blood on three, their blood on the one chosen by someone to do away with them.

"I suppose I thought it was part of his plot, then," I said. "She was killed by terrorists, he said, and he had disposed of those henchmen so that he might make the lie bigger and bigger."

"No, those henchmen were to *get away*, so that he could make the lie of the terrorists bigger and bigger. But I came there, and I killed them." He looked at me. "She saw me through the window before she died, the window of the ambulance that came to take her away, and she said my name: 'Azriel.'"

"Then she called you."

"No, she was no sorceress; she didn't know the words. She didn't have the Bones. I was the Servant of the Bones." He fell back in the chair. Quiet, looking at the fire, his eyes fierce and thick with dark curling eyelashes, the bones of his forehead strong as the line of his jaw.

After a long time he cast on me the most bright and innocent boy-ish smile. "You're well now, Jonathan. You're cured of your fever." He laughed.

"Yes," I said. I lay back enjoying the dry warmth of the room, the smell of burning oak. I drank the coffee until I tasted the grounds in my teeth, then I put the cup on the circular stone hearth. "Will you let me record what you tell me?" I asked.

The light shone bright in his face again. With a boy's enthusiasm, he leant forward in the chair, his massive hands on his knees. "Would you do it? Would you write down what I tell you?"

"I have a machine," I said, "that will remember every word for us."

"Oh, yes, I know," he said. He smiled contentedly and put his head back. "You mustn't think me an addlebrained spirit, Jonathan. The Servant of the Bones was never that.

"I was made a strong spirit, I was made what the Chaldeans would have called a genii. When brought forth, I knew all that I should know—of the times, of the language, of the ways of the world near and far—all I need to know to serve my Master."

I begged him to wait. "Let me turn on our little recorder," I said.

It felt good to stand up, for my head not to swim, for my chest not to ache, and for most of the blur of the fever to have been banished.

I put down two small machines, as all of us do who have lost a tale through one. I checked their batteries and that the stones were not too warm for them, and I put the tape cassettes inside and then I said, "Tell me." I pressed the buttons so that both little ears would be on full alert. "And let me say first," I said, speaking for microphones now, "that you seem a young man to me, no more than twenty. You've a hairy chest and hair on your arms, and it's dark and healthy, and your skin is an olive tone, and the hair of your head is lustrous and I would think the envy of women."

"They like to touch it," he said with a sweet and kindly smile.

"And I trust you," I said for my record. "I trust you. You saved my life, and I trust you. And I don't know why I should. I myself have seen you change into another man. Later I will think I dreamt it. I've seen you vanish and come back. Later I won't believe it. I want this recorded too, by the scribe. Jonathan. Now we can begin your story, Azriel.

"Forget this room, forget this time. Go to the beginning for me, will you? Tell me what a ghost knows, how a ghost begins, what a ghost remembers of the living but no . . ." I stopped, letting the cassettes turn. "I've made my worst mistake already."

"And what is that, Jonathan?" he asked.

"You have a tale you want to tell and you should tell it."

He nodded. "Kindly teacher," he said, "let's draw a little closer. Let's bring our chairs near. Let's bring our little machines closer so that we can talk softly. But I don't mind beginning as you wish. I want to begin that way. I want for it all to be known, at least, to both of us."

We made the adjustments as he asked, the arms of our chairs touching. I made a movement to clasp his hand and he didn't draw back; his handshake was firm and warm. And when he smiled again, the little dip of his brows made him look almost playful. But it was only the way his face was made—brows that curve down in the middle to make a frown, and then curve gently up and out from the nose. They give a face a look of peering from a secret vantage point, and they make its smile all the more radiant.

He took a drink of the water, a long deep drink.

"Does the fire feel good to you, too?" I asked.

He nodded. "But it looks ever so much better."

Then he looked at me. "There will be times when I'll forget myself. I'll speak to you in Aramaic, or in Hebrew. Sometimes in Persian. I may speak Greek or Latin. You bring me back to English, bring me back to your tongue quickly."

"I will," I said, "but never have I so deeply regretted my own lack of education in languages. The Hebrew I would understand, the Latin too, the Persian never."

"Don't regret," he said. "Perhaps you spent that time looking at the stars or the fall of the snow, or making love. My language should be that of a ghost—the language of you and your people. A genii speaks the language of the Master he must serve and of those among whom he must move to do his Master's bidding. I am Master here. I know that now. I have chosen your language for us. That is sufficient."

We were ready. If this house had ever been warmer and sweeter, if I had ever enjoyed the company of someone else more than I did then, I didn't recall it. I wanted only to be with him and talk to him, and I had a small, painful feeling in my heart, that when he finished his tale, when somehow or other this closeness between us had come to an end, nothing would ever be the same for me.

Nothing was ever the same afterwards.

He began.

2

I didn't remember Jerusalem," he said. "I wasn't born there. My mother was carried off as a child by Nebuchadnezzar along with our whole family, and our tribe, and I was born a Hebrew in Babylon, in a rich house—full of aunts and uncles and cousins—rich merchants, scribes, sometime prophets, and occasional dancers and singers and pages at court.

"Of course," he smiled. "Every day of my life, I wept for Jerusalem." He smiled. "I sang the song: 'If I forget thee, Oh Jerusalem, may my right hand wither.' And at night prayers we begged the Lord to return us to our land, and at morning prayers as well.

"But what I'm trying to say is that Babylon was my whole life. At twenty, when my life came to its first—shall we say—great tragedy, I knew the songs and gods of Babylon as well as I knew my Hebrew and the Psalms of David that I copied daily, or the book of Samuel, or whatever other texts we were constantly studying as a family.

"It was a grand life. But before I describe myself further, my circumstances, so to speak, let me just talk of Babylon.

"Let me sing the song of Babylon in a strange land. I am not pleasing in the eyes of the Lord or I wouldn't be here, so I think now I can sing the songs I want, what do you think?"

"I want to hear it," I said gravely. "Shape it the way you would. Let the words spill. You don't want to be careful with your language, do you? Are you talking to the Lord God now, or are you simply telling your tale?"

"Good question. I'm talking to you so that you will tell the story for me in my words. Yes. I'll rave and cry and blaspheme when I want.

I'll let my words come in a torrent. They always did, you know. Keeping Azriel quiet was a family obsession."

This was the first time I'd seen him really laugh, and it was a light heartfelt laugh that came up as easily as breath, nothing strangled or self-conscious in it.

He studied me.

"My laugh surprises you, Jonathan?" he asked. "I believe laughter is one of the common traits of ghosts, spirits, and even powerful spirits like me. Have you been through the scholarly accounts? Ghosts are famous for laughing. Saints laugh. Angels laugh. Laughter is the sound of Heaven, I think. I believe. I don't know."

"Maybe you feel close to Heaven when you laugh," I said.

"Maybe so," he said. His large cherubic mouth was really beautiful. Had it been small it would have given him a baby face. But it wasn't small, and with his thick black eyebrows and the large quick eyes, he looked pretty remarkable.

He seemed to be taking my measure again too, as if he had some capacity to read my thoughts. "My scholar," he said to me, "I've read all your books. Your students love you, don't they? But the old Hasidim are shocked by your biblical studies, I suppose."

"They ignore me. I don't exist for the Hasidim," I said, "but for what it's worth my mother was a Hasid, and so maybe I'll have a little understanding of things that will help us."

I knew now that I liked him, whatever he had done, liked him for himself in a way—young man of twenty, as he said, and though I was still fairly stunned from the fever, from his appearance, from his tricks, I was actually getting used to him.

He waited a few minutes, obviously ruminating, then began to talk:

"Babylon," he said. "Babylon! Give the name of any city which echoes as loud and as long as Babylon. Not even Rome, I tell you. And in those days there was no Rome. The center of the world was Babylon. Babylon had been built by the Gods as their gate. Babylon had been the great city of Hammurabi. The ships of Egypt, the Peoples of the Sea, the people of Dilmun, came to the docks of Babylon. I was a happy child of Babylon.

"I've seen what stands today, in Iraq, going there myself to see the walls restored by the tyrant Saddam Hussein. I've seen the mounds of sand that dot the desert, all of this covering old cities and towns that were Assyrian, Babylonian, Judean.

"And I've walked into the museum in Berlin to weep at the sight of what your archaeologist, Koldewey, has re-created of the mighty Ishtar Gate and the Processional Way.

"Oh, my friend, what it was to walk on that street! What it was to look up at those walls of gleaming glazed blue brick, what it was to pass the golden dragons of Marduk.

"But even if you walked the length and breadth of the old Processional Way, you would have only a taste of what was Babylon. All our streets were straight, many paved in limestone and red breccia. We lived as if in a place made of semiprecious stones. Think of an entire city glazed and enameled in the finest colors, think of gardens everywhere.

"The god Marduk built Babylon with his own hands, they told us, and we believed it. Early on I fell in with Babylonian ways and you know everybody had a god, a personal god he prayed to, and beseeched for this and that, and I chose Marduk. Marduk himself was my personal god.

"You can imagine the uproar when I walked in the house with a small pure-gold statue of Marduk, talking to it, the way the Babylonians did. But then my father just laughed. Typical of my father, my beautiful and innocent father.

"And throwing back his head, my father sang in his beautiful voice, 'Yahweh is your God, the God of your Father, your Father's Father, the God of Abraham, Isaac, and Jacob.'

"To which one of my somber uncles popped up at once, 'And what is that idol in his hands!'

" 'A toy!' said my father. 'Let him play with it. Azriel, when you get sick of all this superstitious Babylonian stuff, break the statue. Or sell it. You cannot break our god, for our god is not in gold or precious metal. He has no temple. He is above such things.'

"I nodded, went into my room, which was large and full of silken pillows and curtains, for reasons I'll get to later, and I lay down and I started just, you know, calling on Marduk to be my guardian.

"In this day and age, Americans do it with a guardian angel. I don't know how many Babylonians took it all that seriously either, the

Babylonian personal god. You know the old saying, 'If you plan ahead a god goes with you.' Well, what does that mean?"

"The Babylonians," I said, "they were a practical people rather than superstitious, weren't they?"

"Jonathan, they were exactly like Americans today. I have never seen a people so like the ancient Sumerians and Babylonians as the Americans of today.

"Commerce was everything, but everybody went about consulting astrologers, talking about magic, and trying to drive out evil spirits. People had families, ate, drank, tried to achieve success in every way possible, yet carried on all the time about luck. Now Americans don't talk about demons, no, but they rattle on about 'negative thinking' and 'self-destructive ideas' and 'bad self-image.' It was a lot the same, Babylon and America, a lot the same.

"I would say that here in America I have found the nearest thing to Babylon in the good sense that I have ever found. We were not slaves to our gods! We were not slaves to each other.

"What was I saying? Marduk, my personal god. I prayed to him all the time. I made offerings, you know, little bits of incense when nobody was watching; I poured out a little honey and wine for him in the shrine I made for him in the deep brick wall of my bedroom. Nobody paid much attention.

"But then Marduk began to answer me. I'm not sure when Marduk first started answering me. I think I was still fairly young. I would say something idly to him, 'Look, my little brothers are running rampant and my father just laughs as though he were one of them and I have to do everything here!' and Marduk would laugh. As I said spirits laugh. Then he'd say some gentle thing like 'You know your father. He will do what you tell him, Big Brother.' His voice was soft, a man's voice. He didn't start actually speaking questions in my ear till I was nearly nine and some of these were simply little riddles and jokes and teasing about Yahweh . . .

"He never got tired of teasing me about Yahweh, the god who preferred to live in a tent, and couldn't manage to lead his people out of a little bitty desert for over forty years. He made me laugh. And though I tried to be most respectful, I became more and more familiar with him, and even a little smart mouthed and ill behaved.

" 'Why don't you go tell all this nonsense to Yahweh Himself since you are a god?' I asked him. 'Invite him to come down to your fabulous temple all full of cedars from Lebanon and gold.' And Marduk would fire off with 'What? Talk to your god? Nobody can look at the face of your god and live! What do you want to happen to me? What if he turns into a pillar of fire like he did when he brought you out of Egypt . . . ho, ho, ho . . . and smashes my temple and I end up being carried around in a tent!'

"I didn't truly think about it till I was perhaps eleven years old. That was when I first came to know that not everybody heard from his or her personal god, and also I had learnt this: I didn't have to talk to Marduk to start him off talking to me. He could begin the conversation and sometimes at the most awkward moments. He also had bright ideas in his head. 'Let's go down into the potters' district, or let's go to the marketplace,' and we would."

"Azriel, let me stop you," I said. "When all this happened, you spoke to the little statue of Marduk or you carried it with you?"

"No, not at all, your personal god was always with you, you know. The idol at home, well, it received the incense, yes, I guess you could say that the god came down into it then to smell the incense. But no, Marduk was just there.

"I did, stupidly enough, imitate the habit of other Babylonians of threatening him sometimes . . . you know, saying, 'Look, what kind of god are you that you can't help me find my sister's necklace! You won't get any incense out of me!' That was the way with the Babylonians, you know, to bawl out the god fiercely if things didn't go right. They would yell and scream at their personal gods: 'Who worships you like I do! Why don't you grant my wishes! Who else would pour out these libations for you!' "

Azriel laughed again. I was considering this whole question which was not unfamiliar to me as a historian naturally. But I laughed too.

"Times haven't changed that much, I don't really think," I said. "Catholics can get very angry with their saints when the saints don't get results. And I think once in Naples, when a local saint refused to work a yearly miracle, people stood up in the church and yelled 'You pig of a saint!' But how deep do these convictions go?"

"There's an alliance there," Azriel answered. "You know, there are several layers to that alliance. Or shall I say, the alliance is a braid of many strands. And the truth lies in this: the gods need us! Marduk needed . . ." He stopped again. He looked suddenly utterly forlorn. He looked at the fire.

"He needed you?"

"Well, he wanted my company," said Azriel. "I can't say he needed me. He had all of Babylon. But these feelings, they are impossibly complex." He looked at me. "Where are the bones of your father?" he asked.

"Wherever the Nazis buried them in Poland," I said, "or in the wind if they were burnt."

He looked heart stricken at these words.

"You know I'm speaking of our World War II and the Holocaust, the persecution of the Jews, don't you?"

"Yes, yes, I know so very much about it, only to hear that your father and mother were lost to it, it hurts my heart, and it makes my question pointless. I meant only to point out to you that you probably have superstitions about your parents, that's all, that you wouldn't disturb their bones."

"I have such superstitions," I said. "I have them about photographs of my parents. I won't let anything happen to them, and when I do lose one of them, it's a deep sin to me that I did it, as if I insulted my ancestor and my tribe."

"Ah," said Azriel, "that's what I was talking about. And I want to show you something. Where is my coat?"

He got up from the hearth, found the big double-mantled coat, and took out of the inside pocket a small plastic packet. "This plastic, you know, I rather love it."

"Yes," I said, watching him as he came back to the fire, sank down on the chair, and opened the packet. "I dare say all the world loves plastic, but why do you?"

"Because it keeps things clean and pure," he said looking up at me, and then he handed me a picture of what looked like Gregory Belkin. But it wasn't. This man had the long beard and forelocks and the silk black hat of the Hasidim. I was puzzled.

He didn't explain the picture.

"I was made to destroy," he said, "and you remember, don't you, the beautiful Hebrew word before so many of the old Psalms, telling us to sing it to that certain melody: 'Do Not Destroy.' "

I had to think.

"Come on, Jonathan, you know," he said.

"Altashheth!" I said. " 'Do Not Destroy.' "

He smiled and his eyes filled with tears. He put back with shaking hands the picture and he laid the plastic packet aside on the small footstool between our chairs, far enough away from the fire for it not to be hurt, and then he looked again at the flames.

I felt the most sudden overwhelming emotion. I couldn't talk. It wasn't only that we had mentioned my mother and father, killed in Poland by the Nazis. It wasn't only that he had reminded me of the mad plot of Gregory Belkin which had come perilously close to success; it wasn't only his beauty, or that we were together, or that I was speaking with a spirit. I don't know what it was.

I thought of Ivan in *The Brothers Karamazov* and I thought, Is this my dream? I am dying actually, the room's filling with snow, and I'm dying, imagining I'm talking to this beautiful young man with curling black hair, like the carvings on the stones from Mesopotamia in the British Museum, those stately kings never feline like the Pharaohs but with hair that was almost sexual on their faces, dark hair, hair as thick as the hair around their balls must have been. I don't know what was coming over me.

I looked at him. He turned slowly, and just for one moment I knew fear. It was the first time. It was the way he moved his head. He turned towards me, obviously listening to my thoughts, or reading my emotion, or touching my heart, or however one would say it, and then I realized he had done a trick for me.

He was dressed differently. He wore a soft tunic of red velvet, tied loosely at the waist and loose red velvet pants and slippers.

"You're not dreaming, Jonathan Ben Isaac, I'm here."

The fire gave off an incredible burst of sparks. It gave off sparks as if things had been tossed on it.

I realized that something else about him had changed. He had now his heavy smooth mustache and his beard curling exactly as the beards of kings and soldiers in those old tablets, and I saw why God had given him the large cherubic mouth because it was a mouth you could see in spite of all that hair, a mouth that talked to you, a mouth developed by nature at a time when mouths had to compete with hair.

He started. He reached up. He touched the hair and then he

scowled. "I didn't mean to do that part. I think I shall give up on it. The hair wants to come back."

"The Lord God wants you to have it?" I asked.

"I don't think so. I don't know!"

"How did you make the clothes change? How do you make yourself disappear?"

"There's little to it. Science will one day be able to control it. Today, science knows all about atoms and neutrinos. All I did was throw off all the tiny particles smaller than atoms which I had drawn to myself, through a magnetic strength you might say, to make my old clothes. They weren't real clothes. They just were clothes made by a ghost. And then to banish them, I said, as the sorcerer would say, 'Return until I call to you again.' And then I called up new clothes. I said in my heart with the sorcerer's conviction:

" 'From the living and the dead, from the raw earth and from that which is forged and refined, woven, and treasured, come to me, tinier than grains of sand, and without sound, unnoticed, hurting no one, at your greatest speed, penetrating whatever barriers surround me that you must and clothe me in red velvet, soft garments the color of rubies. See these clothes in my mind, come.' "

He sighed. "And it was done."

He sat quiet for a moment. I was so mesmerized by this new red attire, and by the way it seemed to change him somewhat, give him a sort of regal air, that I didn't speak. I pushed another big log into the pyramid of the fire, and threw some more coal on it from the scuttle, all of this without leaving the sanctuary of my rotting and crunched old chair.

Then and only then did I look at him. And at that same moment, when his eyes were utterly remote, I realized he was singing in a very low voice, a voice so low I had to strain to disentangle it from the soft devouring rush of the fire.

He was singing in Hebrew but it wasn't the Hebrew I knew. But I knew enough of it to know what it was: It was the Psalm "By the Rivers of Babylon." When he finished, I was awestruck and even more shaken than before.

I wondered if it was snowing in Poland. I wondered if my parents had been buried or cremated. I wondered if he could call together the ashes of my parents, but it seemed a horrible, blasphemous thought.

"That was my point, that we have things about which we are superstitious," he said. "When I blunderingly asked about your parents, I meant to say, you believe certain things but you don't believe them. You live in a double frame of mind."

I reflected.

He looked at me deliberately, eyebrows curving down, though his cherubic mouth smiled. It was a respectful, sincere expression. "And I can't bring them back to life. I can't do that!" he said.

He looked back at the flames.

"The parents of Gregory Belkin perished in the Holocaust in Europe," he said. "And Gregory became a madman. And his brother a holy man, a saint, zaddik. And you became a scholar, and a teacher, with a gentle gift for making students understand."

"You honor me," I said softly. There were a thousand little questions buzzing around me like bees. I wasn't going to cheapen things.

"Go on, Azriel, please," I said. "Tell me what you want to tell me. Tell me what you want me to know."

"Ah, well, as I indicated we were the rich exiles. You know the story. Nebuchadnezzar came down on Jerusalem and slew the soldiers and littered the streets with bodies, and left behind a Babylonian governor to rule over the peasants who would tend our estates and vineyards and send the produce home to his Court. Customary.

"But rich men, tradesmen, scribes like the men of my family? We weren't slain. He didn't come sharpening his sword on our necks. We were deported to Babylon with everything that we could carry, I might add, wagons of our fine furniture which he allowed us to have, although he had thoroughly looted our temple, and we were given fine houses in which to live so that we might set up shop and serve the markets of Babylon and serve the temple and the Court.

"This happened a thousand times over in those centuries. Even the cruel Assyrians would do the same thing. They'd put to the sword the soldiers and then drag off the man who knew how to write three languages, and the boy who could carve perfectly in ivory, and so it was with us. The Babylonians, they weren't as bad as other enemies might have been. Imagine being dragged back to Egypt. Imagine. Egypt, where people live just to die, and sing night and day of dying, and of being dead, and there was nothing but village after village and field after field.

"No, we didn't have it bad off.

"By eleven years old, I had been to the temple itself, a page, as many a rich Hebrew boy was, and I had seen the great statue of Marduk himself, the god, in his high sanctuary atop the great ziggurat of Etemenanki. I had entered into the inner shrine with the priests, and the strangest thought had occurred to me! This big statue looked more like me than the little one I had which I had always thought bore a distinct resemblance.

"Of course I didn't chirp this out loud. But as I looked up at mighty Marduk, the great gold Marduk, the statue in which the god lived and ruled, and should have been carried each year in the New Year's Procession, the statue smiled.

"I was too clever to say anything to the priests. We were in the process of preparing the inner sanctuary for the woman who would come and spend the night with the god. But the priests noticed something. And they saw me look at Marduk and one of them asked, 'What did you say?' and of course I'd said nothing. But Marduk had said, 'Well, what do you think of my house, Azriel? I've been so often to yours.'

"From that moment, the priests were on to it. Yet things might still have gone differently. I might have had a long human life. I might have had a different path. Sons, daughters. I don't know.

"At the time, I thought it was hilarious and wonderful, and loved Marduk for this little trick. But we continued to ready the chamber, which was truly magnificent in plated gold, and the silken couch where the woman would lie to be taken by the god that night, and then we left, and one of the priests said: 'The God smiled on you!'

"I was stiff with fear. I didn't want to answer.

"Rich Hebrew hostages or deportees like us were treated very well, as I said, but I didn't really talk to the priests, you know, as if they were Hebrews. They were the priests of the gods we were forbidden to worship. Besides, I didn't trust them and there were too many of them and some were very stupid and others very sly and smart. I said simply that I had seen the smile too and thought it was sunlight.

"The priest was quaking.

"I forgot about that for years. I don't know why I remember it now, except to say that that might have been the very moment when my fate was sealed.

"Marduk started talking to me all the time then. I'd be in the tablet house, working hard, you know, learning thoroughly every text we possessed in Sumerian so that I could copy it out, read it, even speak it, though by then nobody spoke Sumerian. Ah, I must tell you a funny thing I heard only recently here in this twentieth century world. I heard it in New York in the days after it was all over, finished with, Gregory Belkin I mean, and I was wandering around trying to make my body take the form of other men—and it kept changing back. I heard this funny thing . . ."

"What?" I asked at once.

"That nobody even now knows where the Sumerians came from! Not even to this day. That they came out of nowhere the Sumerians, with their language which was different from all others, and they built the first cities in our beautiful valleys. Nobody knows more about them even to this day."

"That's true. Did you know then?"

"No," he said, "we knew what was written in the tablets, that Marduk had made people from clay and put life into them. That's all we knew. But to find out two thousand years later that you have no long archaeological or historical record for the origin of the Sumerians— how their language developed and how they migrated into the valley and all of that—it's funny to me."

"Well, haven't you noticed that nobody now knows where the Jews came from either?" I asked. "Or are you going to tell me that you knew for a fact in those days, when you were a Babylonian boy, that God called Abraham out of the city of Ur and that Jacob did wrestle with the angel?"

He laughed and shrugged. "There were so many versions of that story! If you only knew. Of course people wrestled all the time with angels. That was beyond dispute. But what do you have today in the Holy Books? Its remnants! The whole story of Yahweh defeating the Leviathan is gone, gone! And I used to copy that story all the time! But I get ahead of myself. I want to describe things in some order.

No, I am not surprised to hear that no one knows where the Jews came from. Because even then there were just too many stories . . .

"Let me tell you about my house. It was in the rich Hebrew quarter. I've explained what exile meant.

"We were to be citizens of quality of a city filled with people of all nations. We were booty, set free to increase and multiply and make wealth. By my time, as you can guess, Nebuchadnezzar had died, and we were ruled by Nabonidus, and he was not in the city and everybody hated him. Just hated him.

"He was thought to be mad, or obsessed. This is told in the book of Daniel though he is given the wrong name. And true, our prophets did go try to drive him crazy with their predictions about how he ought to let us go home. But I don't think they got anywhere with him.

"Nabonidus was driven by secret ideas of his own. Nabonidus was a scholar for one thing, a digger into the mounds, and he was determined to keep Babylon in glory, yes, but he had a mad love for the god Sin. Well, Babylon was Marduk's city. Of course there were many other temples and chapels even in Marduk's temple, but still, for the King to fall crazy in love with another god?

"And then to go running off for ten years, ten years into the desert, leaving behind Belshazzar as the ruler, well, that made everybody hate Nabonidus even more. The whole time that Nabonidus was gone, the New Year's Festival couldn't happen, and this was the biggest festival in Babylon where Marduk takes the hand of the King and walks through the street with him! That couldn't happen with no King. And the priests of Marduk, by the time I came to serious work in the temple and palace, were really despising Nabonidus. And so were many other people too.

"To tell you the truth, I never knew the whole secret of Nabonidus. If we could call him up, you know, as the Witch of Endor called up the dead prophet Samuel, disturbing his sleep, remember, so that Saul the King could talk to him . . . if we could call up Nabonidus he might tell us wondrous things. But that is not my mission now, to become a necromancer or a sorcerer, it's to find the stairway to heaven, and I am done with the fog and the mist in which the lost souls linger begging for someone to call a name.

"Besides, maybe Nabonidus has gone into the light. Maybe he's mounted the stairs. He didn't live his life in cruelty or debauchery but devotion to a god who was not the god of his city, that's all.

"I only saw him once, and that was during the last days of my life, and he was all caught up in the plot of course, and he seemed to me a dead man already, a King whose time had passed, and he seemed also blessed with an indifference to life. All he wanted, on that last day when we met, or that night, was that Babylon would not be sacked. That's what everybody wanted. That's how I lost my soul.

"But I'll come to that awful part soon enough.

"I was talking about being alive. I didn't give a damn about Nabonidus. We lived in the rich Hebrew quarter. It was filled with beautiful houses; we made the walls then about six feet thick, which I know sounds mad to you today, but you cannot imagine how effectively it kept our houses cool; they were sprawling affairs, with many anterooms and big dining rooms, and all these rooms surrounded a large central courtyard. My father's house was four stories high and the wooden rooms above were full of cousins and the elderly aunts, and they often didn't come all the way down to the yard, but merely sat in the open courtyard windows taking the breeze.

"The courtyard was Eden. It was like a small portion of the hanging gardens themselves, and the other public gardens all over the city. It was big. We had a fig tree, a willow tree, and two date palms, and flowers of all kinds, grape vines covering the arbor where we could take our evening meal, and fountains that never stopped sending their rivers of sparkling water down into the basins where the fish darted about like living jewels.

"The brickwork was glazed and beautiful, and had many figures in it, having been built by some Akkadian before us, before the Chaldeans came, and it was full of blue and red and yellow and flowers, but there was also plenty of grass in the courtyard, and then the room off it where the ancestors were buried.

"I grew up playing among the date palms and flowers, and I loved it till the day . . . the day I died. I loved lying out there in the late afternoon listening to the water of the fountains, and ignoring everybody who kept telling me I ought to be in the scriptorium copying psalms or some such. I wasn't lazy by nature. I just sort of did what

I wanted to do. I got away with things. But I wasn't bad by any stretch; in fact, I was far and away the best scholar of the family, at least as I saw it, and many times, my uncles, though they didn't want to admit it, would bring to me three versions of a Psalm by King David and ask me which I thought was the most nearly correct, and then they'd follow my judgment.

"We had no official gathering place for prayers, of course, because we had such grandiose plans for going home and building the Temple of Solomon all over again; I mean no one was going to throw up any little street-side temple in Babylon. The temple would have to be done according to sacred dimensions, and after I was dead and cursed and had become the Servant of the Bones, the Jews did go home and build that temple. In fact, I know they did, because I saw it once . . . once, as if in a fog, but I saw it.

"In our Babylonian life we gathered at private homes for prayers, and also for the elders among us to read the letters we received from the rebels still hiding on Mount Zion, and also the letters coming from our prophets in Egypt. Jeremiah was imprisoned there for a long time. I don't remember anyone ever reading one of his letters. But I remember a lot of mad writing by Ezekiel. He didn't write it down himself. He walked about talking and predicting and then other people wrote it down.

"But so we prayed, in our homes, to our invisible and all-powerful Yahweh—reminded always that before David promised him a temple, Yahweh and the Ark of the Covenant had been housed only in a tent, and that had its meaning and its value. Lots of the Elders thought the whole temple idea was Babylonian, you know. Go back to the tent.

"On the other hand, our family had for nine generations been rich merchants, city men, living in Nineveh before Jerusalem, I think, and we had little concept of the nomad life or carrying about shrines in tents. The story of Moses didn't make a great deal of sense to us. For instance, how could the people be so lost in the desert for forty years? But, I repeat myself, don't I? . . . What am I saying . . .

"A tent to me was all the silk over my bed, the red-tinged light in which I lay with my hands cupped under my head talking to Marduk about the prayer meetings and listening to his jokes.

"At some of these prayer meetings we had our own prophets,

whose books are lost now, who did a great deal of ranting and screaming. I was frequently pointed to, and told that I had found favor in the
eyes of Yahweh, though what this meant nobody was certain.

"I guess they all knew in a way that I could see farther than others,
look into souls, you know, see like a zaddik, a saint, but I was no saint,
only an obstreperous young man."

He stopped. The sharpness of memory seemed to cut him off and
hold him.

"You were happy," I said. "By nature, you were happy, truly
happy."

"Oh, yes, I knew it, and so did my friends. In fact, they often
teased me about being too happy. Things never seemed all that difficult, you see. Things never seemed dark! Darkness came with death,
and the worst darkness for me was right before it, and maybe . . .
maybe even now. But darkness. Oh, to take on the world of darkness, that is like trying to chart the stars of heaven.

"What was I saying? Things were easy for me. I enjoyed them.
For example, to be educated I had to work in the tablet house. I had
to get a real Babylonian education. This was wise, this was for the future, this was for trade, this was to be a man of learning. And they
beat the daylights out of us if we were late, or didn't learn our lessons,
but usually it was easy for me.

"I loved the old Sumerian. I loved writing out the whole stories of
Gilgamesh and 'In the Beginning' and copying all kinds of records so
that fresh tablets could be sent to other cities in Babylonia. I could
practically speak Sumerian. I could now sit down and write for you
my life in Sumerian—" He stopped. "No, I couldn't do that. I
couldn't because if I could have written my life, I wouldn't have
climbed up this snowy mountain to commit it to you . . . I can't . . .
I can't . . . . write it in any tongue. Talking lets the pain flow . . ."

"That I understand perfectly, and am here to listen. The point is,
you know Sumerian, and you can read it, and you can translate it."

"Yes, yes, yes, and Akkadian, the language that had been used after,
and the Persian which was creeping up on us all then, and Greek—I
could read that well—and Aramaic which was taking the place of our
own Hebrew in daily life, but then I wrote Hebrew too.

"I learnt my lessons. I wrote fast. I had a way of plunging the stylus into the clay that made everybody laugh but my writing was good. Really good. And I also loved to stand up and read out loud, so whenever the teacher took sick, or was called out, or suddenly needed some medicine, otherwise known as beer, I'd stand up and start reading Gilgamesh to everybody in an exaggerated voice, making them laugh.

"You know the old myth of course. And it's important to our story, stupid and crazy as it is. Here is this king Gilgamesh and he is running wild around his city—on some tablets he is a giant, on others he is the size of a man. He behaves like a bull. He has the drums beaten all the time, which makes everybody unhappy. You're not supposed to beat the drums except for certain reasons—to frighten spirits, to call to nuptials, you know.

"Okay, so we have Gilgamesh tearing up the city of Uruk. And what do the gods do, being the Sumerian gods, being about as smart as a bunch of water buffalo—they make an equal for Gilgamesh in a wild man called Enkido, who is covered with hair, lives in the woods, and likes to drink with beasts—oh, it is so important in this world with whom one eats and drinks and what!—anyway, here we have wild Enkido coming down to the stream to drink with the beasts, and he is rendered tame by spending seven days with a temple harlot!

"Stupid, no? The beasts wouldn't have anything to do with him once he knew the harlot. Why? Were the beasts jealous because they didn't get to lie with the harlot? Don't beasts copulate with beasts? Are there no beast harlots? Why does copulating with a woman make a man less of a beast? Well, the whole story of Gilgamesh never made any sense anyway except as a bizarre code. Everything is code, is it not?"

"I think you're right, it's code," I said, "but code for what? Keep telling me the story of Gilgamesh. Tell me how your version ended," I asked. I simply couldn't resist the question. "You know we have only fragments now, and we don't have the old script that you had."

"It ended the same way as your modern versions. Gilgamesh couldn't resign himself that Enkido could die. Enkido did die, too, though I don't remember quite why. Gilgamesh acted as if he'd never seen anybody die before, and he went to the immortal who had survived the great flood. The great flood. Your flood. Our flood. Everyone's flood. With us it was Noah and his sons. With them it was an immortal who lived in the land of Dilmun in the sea. He was the great survivor of the flood. And off to see him, to get immortality, goes this genius Gilgamesh. And that ancient one—who would be the Hebrew Noah for our people—says what? 'Gilgamesh, if you can stay awake for seven days and nights, you can be immortal.'

"And what happens? Gilgamesh instantly fell asleep. Instantly! He didn't even wait a day! A night. He keeled over! Smash. Asleep. So that was the end of that plan, except that the immortal widow of the immortal man who had survived the flood took pity on him, and they told Gilgamesh that if he tied stones to his feet and sank down in the sea he could find a plant that, once eaten, gives you eternal youth. Well, I think they were trying to drown the man!

"But our version, as yours, followed Gilgamesh in this expedition. Down he went and he found the plant. Then he comes up again. He goes to sleep. His worst habit apparently, this sleeping . . . and a snake comes and takes the plant. Ah, what utter sadness for Gilgamesh and then comes the old advice to all:

" 'Enjoy your life, fill your belly with wine and food, and accept death. The Gods kept immortality for themselves, death is the lot of man.' You know, profound philosophical revelations!"

I laughed. "I like your telling of it. When you would stand up in the tablet house, did you read it with that same fervor?"

"Oh, always!" he said. "But even then, what did we have? Bits and pieces of something ancient. Uruk had been built thousands of years before. Maybe there was such a real king. Maybe.

"If I have a point in all this right now, let me make it. Madness in kings is common. In fact, I think sanity in kings must be rare. Gilgamesh went crazy. Nabonidus was crazy. You ask me, Pharaoh was crazy in every story I ever heard about him.

"And I understand this. I understand it because I have looked into the face of Cyrus the Persian and into the face of Nabonidus, and I know that kings are alone, utterly alone. I have looked into the face of Gregory Belkin, a king in his own right, and I saw this same isolation and terrible weakness; there is no mother, there is no father, there is no limit to power, and disaster is the portion of kings. I have looked into the face of other kings, but that we will pass over quickly later on, because what I did as the evil Servant of the Bones does not matter now, except that every time I killed a human life, I destroyed a universe, did I not?"

"Perhaps, or you sent the evil flame home to be cleansed in the great fire of God."

"Ah, that is beautiful," he said to me.

I was complimented. But did I believe this?

"So, let's go on with my life," he said. "I worked at the Court as soon as I left the tablet house, and then my writing and reading were of the utmost importance. I knew all languages. I saw many strange documents and old letters in Sumerian and was useful to the King's regent, Belshazzar. No one much cared for Belshazzar, as I said. He couldn't hold the New Year's Festival, or the priests didn't want him, or Marduk wouldn't do it, who knows, but he wasn't destined to be loved.

"Yet I can't say this made for a bad atmosphere in the palace. It was fairly congenial and of course the correspondence was endless. Letters were pouring in from the outlying territories complaining about the Persians being on the march, or about the Egyptians being on the march, or about the stars as seen by various astrologers predicting very bad or good things for the King.

"I became acquainted in the palace with the wise men who advised the King on everything, and liked listening to them, and realized that when Marduk spoke to me, sometimes the wise men could hear it. And I also came to know that the story of the smile had never been forgotten. Marduk had smiled on Azriel.

"Well, what secrets I had.

"So look. I am walking home. I am nineteen. I have very little time left to live and I don't know it. I said to Marduk, How could the wise men hear it when you talk to me? He said that these men, these wise men, were seers and sorcerers just as were some of our Hebrews, our prophets, our wise men, though nobody wanted much to admit it, and they had the power as I did to hear a spirit.

"He sighed and he said to me in Sumerian that I must take the utmost care. 'These men know your powers.'

"I'd never heard Marduk sounded dejected. We had long ago passed the foolish point of me asking him for favors or to play tricks on people, and now we talked more about things all the time, and he frequently said that he could see more clearly through my eyes. I didn't know what this meant, but on this day when he seemed dejected I was worried.

" 'My powers!' I said sarcastically. 'What powers! You smiled. You are the god!'

"Silence, but I knew he was still there. I could always feel him, like heat; I heard him like breath. You know, the way a blind person knows that someone is there.

"I got to my front door and was ready to go in, and I turned around and for the first time I actually laid eyes on him. I saw Marduk. Not the gold statuette in my room. Not the big statues in the temple. But Marduk, himself.

"He was standing against the far wall, arms folded, one knee bent, just looking at me. It was Marduk. He was completely covered in gold as he was at the shrine but he was alive and his curly hair and beard seemed not made of solid gold as they were on the statue but living gold. His eyes were browner than mine, that is, paler, with more yellow in the irises. He smiled at me.

" 'Ah, Azriel,' he said. 'I knew it would happen. I knew it.' And then he came forward and he kissed me on both cheeks. His hands were so smooth. He was my height, and I was right, there was a great resemblance between us, though his eyebrows were set just a bit higher than mine and his forehead was smoother, so he didn't look so mischievous or ferocious by nature as I did.

"I wanted to throw my arms around him. He didn't wait for me to say it. He said, 'Do it, but for that moment maybe others will see me too.'

"I hugged him as my oldest friend, as the dearest to me in the world next to my father, and it was that night I made the mistake of telling my father that I talked with my god all the time. I should never have done it. I wonder now what would have happened if I had not done that."

I interrupted. "Did anyone else see him, to the best of your knowledge?"

"Yes, as a matter of fact, they did. The doorkeeper of our house saw him and all but fainted dead away to see a man all covered in gold paint, and one of my sisters looking down from the lattice above saw him too, and an elder of the Hebrews got a glimpse of him for a moment and came flying at me later that night with his staff, claiming he had seen me with a devil or an angel, and he did not know which.

"That's when my father, my beloved, sweet, good-hearted father said, 'It was Marduk, Babylon's god, whom you saw.' And maybe that is why . . . that is why, we are here now. My father never meant to hurt me. Never. He never meant to do a cruel thing to anyone in his life! He never meant it! He was . . . he was my little brother.

"Let me explain. I have figured it out. I was the eldest son, born when my father was young, because the deportation from Jerusalem had been hard on our people and they married quickly to have sons.

"But my father was the baby of his family, the little Benjamin beloved by everyone, and somehow or other in our family I fell into being his elder brother, and treating him as such. As eldest son I bossed him about a bit. Or rather, we became . . . we became as friends.

"My father worked hard. But we were close. We drank together. We went to the taverns together. We shared women together. And I told him, drunk that night, how Marduk had talked to me for years, and how now I had seen him, and my personal god was the great god of Babylon himself.

"So foolish to have done it! What good could have come of it! At first he laughed, then he worried, then he became engrossed. Oh, I never should have done it. And Marduk knew this. He was in the tavern but so far from me that he had no visibility, he was vaporous and golden like light, and only I could see him, and he shook his head 'no,' and turned his back when I told my father. But you know, I loved my father, and I was so happy! And I wanted him to know. I wanted him to know how I had put my arms around the god!

"Stupid!

"Let me return to the background. The foreground is suddenly too hot for me and it hurts me and stings my eyes.

"The family. I was telling you what we were. We were rich merchants and we were scribes of our Sacred Books. All of the Hebrew tribes in Babylon were in one way or another scribes of the Sacred Books and busy making copies for their own families at all times, but with us it was a very large business because we were known for the rapid and accurate copy. And we had a huge library of old texts. I think I told you, we had maybe, I don't know, twenty-five different stories about Joseph and Egypt and Moses and so forth, and it was always a matter of dispute what to include and what not to. We had so many stories of Joseph in Egypt that we decided not to give all of them credit. I wonder what became of all those tablets, all those scrolls. We just didn't think all those stories were true. But maybe we were wrong. Oh, who knows?

"But to return to the fabric of my life. Whenever I left the court of the palace, or the tablet house, or the marketplace, I came right home to work all evening on the Holy Scriptures, with my sisters and my cousins and uncles in the scriptoria of our houses, which were big rooms.

"As I told you, I was never very quiet, and I would sing the psalms out loud as I wrote them, and this irritated my deaf uncle more than anyone. I don't know why. He was deaf! And besides, I have a good voice."

"Yes, you do."

"Why should a deaf uncle get so upset? But he knew I was singing the psalms not as I just sang that one for you, but as one would sing, with cymbals, dancing, you know, with a little bit of added dash, shall we say, and he wasn't so happy about it.

"He said that we were to write when we were to write and to sing the Lord's songs at the appropriate time. I shrugged and gave in but I was one for cutting up all the time. But I'm giving the wrong impression. I wasn't really bad . . ."

"I know what kind of man you are, and were then . . ."

"Yes, I think by now you do, and maybe if you thought me bad you would have thrown me out in the snow."

He looked at me. His eyes weren't ferocious. The brows were low and thick, but the eyes were plenty big enough beneath them to give him a pretty look. And, it seemed to me that he was warmer and more relaxed now than earlier, and I felt drawn to him and wanting to hear everything he said.

But I wondered: Could I throw him out in the snow?

"I've taken many lives," he said, plucking the thought right from me, "but I would not hurt you, Jonathan Ben Isaac, you know that. I wouldn't hurt such a man as you. I killed assassins. At least when I came to myself that was my code of honor. That is my code now.

"In my early days as the Servant of the Bones, as the bitter, angry ghost for the powerful sorcerer, I killed the innocent because it was my Master's will and I thought I had to do it, I thought that the man who had called me up could control me, and I did his bidding, until the moment came when I suddenly realized that I did not have to be a slave forever, that maybe though my soul had been taken from my spirit, and my spirit and soul from my flesh, that perhaps I could still be pleasing to God. That somehow all could come and be united once more in one figure! Ah!"

He shook his head.

"But Azriel, maybe it's happened!"

"Oh, Lord God, Jonathan, don't give me consolation. I cannot bear it. Just hear me out. Make sure your tapes record my words. Remember me. Remember what I say . . ."

His confidence broke suddenly. He looked at the fire again.

"My family, my father," he said. "My father! How it hurt him what he finally did, and how he looked at me. Do you know what he said about hurting me? He said, 'Azriel, who of all my sons loves me as you do? No one else could ever forgive me for this but you!' And he meant it. He meant it, my father, my little brother, looking at me full of tears and sincerity and absolute conviction!

"I'm sorry. I jump ahead. I'll die soon enough. It won't take too many more pages, I don't think." He shuddered all over. And again the tears stood in his eyes. "Forgive me, and recall again that for those thousands of years, I didn't remember these things. I was the bitter ghost without memory. And now it has all come back to me and I pour it out to you. I pour it out to you in tears."

"Continue. Give me your tears, your trust, and your hurt. I won't fail you."

"Ah, you are the rare thing, Jonathan Ben Isaac," he said.

"Not really, I'm a teacher and a happy man myself. I have a wife and children who love me. I'm not very special."

"Ah, but you are a good man who will talk to someone who is evil! That is what is rare. The Rebbe of the Hasidim, he turned his back on me!" He laughed suddenly, a deep bitter laugh. "He was too good to talk to the Servant of the Bones."

I smiled. "We are all Jews, and there are Jews, and there are Jews."

"Yes, and now Israelis, who would be Maccabees! And there are Hasidim."

"And other Orthodox, and some 'reformed,' and so on it goes. Let's go back to your time. You were a big and happy family."

"Yes, true, and it was regular—I was explaining—it was regular for the rich Hebrews to work at the palace as I said, my father worked there too, and many of my cousins. We were scribes, but also merchants, merchants of jewels, silks, silver, and books. My father's gift in trade was choosing the very finest vessels for the King's table and for the Table of the Gods in Marduk's temple and for Marduk himself.

"Now at the time, the temple was full of chapels, and every day a meal was set out for each deity, including Marduk, so the temple had a huge stock of gold and silver vessels for this. And my father was the one who put aside those vessels not fit.

"I went down with him to the docks all the time to meet the ships coming in from the sea, with the finest new work from Greece or Egypt, and I learned from him how to judge the carving on a goblet, and how to know the heaviest and finest mixture of gold. I learned to know a true ruby or diamond and pearls—pearls, I loved the pearls, we dealt in pearls of all kinds, we didn't call them pearls, you know, we called them eyes of the sea.

"This is how we made our living—in the marketplace and in the temple and in the palace.

"My family had stalls all through the marketplace where they dealt in gems of all kinds, in honey, and in cloth dyed purple and blue, the finest of all silk and linen, and they sold the incense too, though they sold it to idolaters who would burn this incense for Nabu and Ishtar, and for Marduk, of course.

"But it was our living, it was our source of power, it was our way of staying together, of being strong so that one day we could go home. It was as important as the copying of the Sacred Books."

"It's an old tale," I said.

"This whole trade, by the way, gave to my own house a sumptuous quality that it might not have had, had we been camel breeders. And that you must understand because the richness around us colored my father's values as much as mine.

"What I mean is, not only did we make money, but the house was always full of merchandise passing through. You know. Here would be a magnificent cedar statue of the goddess Ishtar just come from

Dilmun, and my uncle would keep it at home for a week or two, gracing the living room, before the sale was made. The place was full of beautiful footstools, delicate furniture from Egypt, the fine black and red urns and pots of the Greeks, and just about anything portable and ornamental and lovely to behold."

"You grew up on beauty, didn't you?"

"Yes," Azriel said. "I did. I really did. And I grew up, for all my smart talking and carrying on and flirting with Marduk, I grew up with love. My father's love. The love of my brothers. My sisters. The love of my uncles even. Even my deaf uncle. Even once the prophet Azarel said to me, 'Yahweh looks at you with love.' So did the old witch Asenath. Ah, such love."

He had come to a natural pause. He sat there, resplendent in the red velvet, hair glossy and natural, and the pure skin of his young man's cheeks as soft as a girl's I suppose. I must be getting old. Because young men look to me now as beautiful as girls. Not that I desire them. It's only that life itself is lush.

He was confused. In pain. I hesitated to press him. Then he parted his lips, only to be quiet.

3

"What was it like, roaming in the temple? The palace?" I asked. "The beautiful house, I can envision. But the palace, was the palace plated in gold? Was the temple?"

He didn't respond.

"Give me pictures, Azriel. Take your time by means of images. The temple, will you tell me what that was like?"

"Yes," he said. "It was a house of gems and gold. It was a world of the deep vibrant gleam of the precious, of lovely scents and the sounds of harps, and pipes playing; it was a world for the bare feet to walk on smooth tiles that were themselves cut in the shapes of flowers." He smiled.

"And," he said, "it was a hell of a lot more fun than you might think. Not all that solemn. The two buildings were huge, of course, you know Nebuchadnezzar built the palace to the full glory of the past, or so he thought, and greatly expanded the private gardens; and the temple was the great building known as Esagila, and behind the building itself stood the big ziggurat, Etemenanki, with its stairway to heaven, and then its ramps going up to the very topmost temple of my great and favorite smiling god.

"The temple and the palace were full of locked and sealed doors. Some of these seals had not been broken in a hundred years. And of course, as you probably know, we had contracts made in this way too . . . in that a contract would be written out on a clay tablet, dried, and then enclosed in a clay envelope with the same words on it, which was then dried, so that one could not get to the original tablet inside without breaking the envelope. So if some corrupt individual had made a change on the outer envelope, the sealed inside tablet would tell the truth.

"There was a lot of that at court, people bringing in contracts, breaking open the envelopes, discovering some wily bastard had made a change in the contract, and the King and his advisors and wise men passing judgment. I never followed out any condemned man to see him executed. As you said, I grew up on beauty.

"In the streets of Babylon I never saw the hungry. I never saw a wretched slave. Babylon was the city people dreamed of living in; everyone was happy in Babylon and under the protection of the King.

"But to return to your question. One could roam in the temple. One could just roam. I could creep in my fine jeweled slippers into the chapels where the other gods were—Nabu and Ishtar and any god or goddess who had been brought from another city for sanctuary.

"You know, that was happening. Cyrus the Persian was on the march most definitely, taking the Greek cities along the coast one after another. And so from all over Babylonia, frightened priests were sending their gods to us for protection, to the great gateway, and we had set up these visiting deities in chapels and these chapels were full of twinkling light.

"This fear for the god, that the enemy would get him, it was very real. Marduk himself had for two hundred years been a prisoner in another city, stolen and taken there, and it had been a great day for Babylon, long before my birth, when Marduk had been recovered and had been brought home."

"Did he ever tell you about it?" I asked.

"No," he said. "But I didn't ask him. We'll come to such things . . .

"As I was saying, I liked roaming about the temple. I took messages to the priests; I waited at table when Belshazzar dined, and I made friends of all the palace crowd, you might say, the eunuchs, the temple slaves, the other pages, and some of the temple prostitutes who were, of course, beautiful women.

"Now all of this work I did in the temple and the palace, there was a Babylonian point to it. The government had a sensible policy. When rich hostages like us, rich deportees, were brought in not only to enhance the culture, young men like me were always picked out to be trained in Babylonian ways. That was so that if or when we were sent back to our own city or some distant province we would be good Babylonians, that is, skilled members of the King's loyal service.

"There were scores of Hebrews at court.

"Nevertheless, I had uncles who went into a fury that my father and I worked at the temple, but my father and I, we would shrug our shoulders and say, 'We don't worship Marduk! We don't eat with the Babylonians. We don't eat the food that the gods have eaten.' And a good deal of the community felt the same way as we did.

"Let me note here, this eating of food. It's still important for the Hebrews. No? You don't eat with heathens. You didn't then. And you didn't eat anything ever that had once been put before an idol. It was a big thing.

"As good Hebrews, we broke bread only with one another, and our hands were always washed carefully with ritual prayer before we took the food, and afterwards there was not one thing in our lives that was not permeated by our desire to praise Yahweh, our Lord God of Hosts.

"But we had to survive in Babylon. We had every intention of returning rich to our homeland. We had to be strong. And that meant what it has always meant to the Hebrews. You must be powerful enough to disperse without being destroyed."

Again came one of the inevitable pauses. He leant forward and stirred the fire, as people do when they want to think, and want to have the feeling of doing something. Stirring fires can give you that feeling, especially if you aren't drinking anything, clutching your coffee as if that were a full-time job, the way I was doing.

"You looked then exactly as you look now, didn't you?" I said, though this was a repeat question. It was one of those soft verbal signals: God gave you all the right gifts, young man.

"Yes," he said. "I wanted now to be smooth-faced. I think I told you. But it doesn't seem to be in my luck.

"I came as myself this time, and I don't know even to this moment who called me. Why now? Why has my body come back around me? Why? I don't know.

"In the past when I was called forth by sorcerers, they made me look the way they wanted, and that could be quite horrible. Seldom if ever did they wait, or take a deep breath, to see what I might look like on my own. I would be summoned in a specific form: 'Azriel, Servant of the Golden Bones which I hold in my hand, come forth in a blaze of fire and consume my enemies. Make of them cinders.' That sort of chant.

"Whatever the case, in answer to your question I looked exactly the same when I died as I do now except for one salient characteristic which had been added to me before my murder, which I will recount later. I am as I died."

"Your father, why was it a mistake to tell him about Marduk? Why? What did all that mean? What did he do to you, Azriel?"

He shook his head. "This is the hardest part for me to tell you, Jonathan Ben Isaac, but I have never told anyone, you know. I never told any master. Does God never forget? Will God deny me forever the Stairway to Heaven?"

"Azriel, let me caution you, simply as an older human being, though my soul may be newborn. Don't be so sure of Heaven. Don't be any more sure of the face of our god than Marduk was sure."

"This means you believe in one and not the other?"

"This means I want to blunt your pain in the telling of what happened. I want to blunt your sense of fatality, and that you are destined for something terrible because of what others have done."

"Wise of you," he said. "And generous in spirit. I am a fool still in so many ways."

"I see. I understand. Let's go back to Babylon, shall we? Can you explain the plot? What did your father have to do with it in the end?"

"Oh, my father and I, what friends we were! He didn't have a better friend than me, and my best friend was Marduk.

"I was the leader on our drinking jaunts, and it was he . . . it was only he who could have ever made me do what I did . . . the thing which made me the Servant of the Bones.

"Strange how it all comes together." He fell to murmuring. He was distracted. "They choose ingredients and they blend them, because the potion won't work unless you have everything. The priests alone, they could never have gotten him to do it. Cyrus the Persian? I trusted him as much as any tyrant. And old Nabonidus, what was his advice? He was only there out of some sort of kindness on the part of

Cyrus, and cleverness. Everything with the Persian empire was cleverness. Perhaps it's so with all empires."

"Take your time," I said. "Catch your breath."

"Yes . . . let me give you pictures of my family. My mother died when I was young. She was very sick, and she cried that she wouldn't live to see Yahweh lift His Face to us again and take us back to Zion. Her people had all been scribes. She herself was a scribe and at one time, I heard, had been something of a prophetess, but this had ceased when she had sons.

"My father missed her unbearably until the last day I ever knew him. He had two Gentile women and so did I; in fact, we shared the same two women most of the time, but this was not for having children or marriage, this was just for fun.

"And at home in the family my father was a hard worker at writing down the psalms and trying to get exact the words we remembered from Jeremiah over which we all argued night and day. My father seldom if ever led the prayers. But he had a beautiful voice, and I can still remember him singing the Lord's praises.

"When we worked in the temple, it was secret between him and me that we thought all idolaters were completely crazy, and why not work for them and humor them?

"As I was explaining, we set the meal out for the god Marduk himself from time to time with the priests. I had many, many friends among the priests, and you know, it was like any group of priests; some believed it all, and some believed nothing. But we drew the veils around the god's table, and then afterwards we took away the food, which of course the god Marduk in his own way had actually savored and fed upon—through fragrance and through the moisture that he could feel—and we helped set up that meal for the members of the royal family, the royal hostages, and the priests and the eunuchs who would eat the god's food, or eat at the King's table.

"But again, as good Hebrews we didn't eat that food ourselves. No, we would never have done that.

"We kept to the laws of Moses in every way that we could. And days ago, when I found myself pitched down into New York, and I began my journey to find the killers of Esther Belkin, when I happened upon the grandfather of Gregory Belkin, the Rebbe in Brooklyn, I saw that many of those Jews, strict as they were, had made a living in the big city of New York in *handel* as we would call it, just as we did in Babylon.

"And I saw also that there were Jews at all levels of devotion, as you yourself said."

He stopped again. He was not anxious for the pain to come.

"But let me get back to Babylon. Look, I'm dancing in the tavern with my father. All men are dancing there together, you know. No harlots there that night. Just a man's place. And I tell him, 'I saw my god with my own eyes. I saw him and I held him to my heart. Father, I am an idolater, but I swear to you, I saw Marduk and Marduk walks with me.'

"And there in the far corner, look, Marduk turns his back on me deliberately and he shakes his head.

"And hours later my father and I were still arguing. 'You are a wise man, you are a seer, and you have misused your powers,' he said. 'You should have used them for us.'

" 'I will, Father, I will use them for us, but tell me, what do you want me to do? Marduk asks nothing of me. What do *you* want me to do?'

"The following day Marduk appeared just a few blocks from the house, vaporous, gold, visible however. He cautioned me: 'Don't touch me or we will have a religious spectacle on our hands.'

" 'Look, are you angry with me for telling my father?' I asked him straight away. We were walking just like friends, and to have him visible was such a comfort to me.

" 'No, I'm not angry with you, Azriel, it's just I don't trust the priests of the temple. There are many, many old and conniving priests, and you never know what they will want of you. Now listen to me. I have some things to tell you before we get deeper into this, before you do, that is, for I am as deep as I can get. Let's go to the public gardens. I like to see you eat and drink.'

"We went to his favorite place, a huge public garden right on the Euphrates, down away from all the docks and the shipwrights and the commotion. In fact it was where one of the many canals came in, and it was more on the canal than the river itself which was always busy. This garden was filled with big drooping willow trees, just like in the psalm, you know, and there were a few musicians out there playing their pipes and dancing for trinkets.

"Marduk sat down opposite me and folded his arms. We really did look so much alike that we could have been brothers. It occurred to me that I knew him better than I knew any of my brothers. And by the way, I didn't hate my brothers the way Hebrews are always hating their brothers in the stories. Forget that. I loved my brothers. They were a little tame, when it came to drinking and dancing. I had more fun with my father. But I loved them."

He stopped. It seemed out of respect for the dead brothers. He was now beyond beautiful in the red velvet, and these pauses brought me back visually to him in a way that was seductive. But then he began to talk again:

"Marduk started in on me right away. 'Look, I am going to tell you the truth and you pay attention. I have no memory of my beginnings. I have no memory of slaying Tiamat the great dragon and making the world out of her belly and the sky out of the rest of her. But this does not mean that it didn't happen. I walk most of the time in a fog. I see the spirits of the gods and the roaming spirits of the dead and I listen for prayers and I try to answer them. But this is a dreary place where I live. When I retreat to the temple for the banquet it's a great pleasure because the fog clears. You know what clears it?'

" 'No, but I can guess . . . that the priests see you, that powerful seers see you.'

" 'That is it, Azriel, I can become solid and visible for witches, for sorcerers, for those who have eyes to see, and then I drink up the libations of water, I inhale them and inhale the fragrances of food and this puts me in the mood of life. Then I go into the statue, and I rest in darkness and time means nothing to me, and I listen to Babylon. I listen. I listen. But the myths of the beginning, I don't remember, you see what I'm saying?'

" 'Not entirely,' I confessed. 'Are you telling me that you aren't a god?'

" 'No, I am a god and a powerful one. Were I to draw on my will, I could clear this marketplace, this garden now, with a great forceful wind. Easy to do. But what I am saying is that gods don't know everything, and this story of how Marduk became the leader of the gods, how he slew Tiamat, how he built the tower to heaven . . . well, I've either forgotten it, or I am growing weak, and I can't remember. Gods can die. They can fade. Just like Kings. They can sleep and it takes much to wake them up. And when I awake and am fully alert, I love Babylon and Babylon loves me back.'

" 'Look, my Lord,' I said, 'you're weary because the New Year's Festival hasn't been held in ten years, because our King Nabonidus has neglected you and your priests. That's all. If we could get the addlebrained old idiot to come home and hold the Festival, you would revive; you would be filled with the life of all of those in Babylon who would see you on the Processional Way.'

" 'That's a nice idea, Azriel, and there's some truth in it, but I have no love for the New Year's Festival, for residing in the statue and holding hands with the King. I get tempted in the very middle of it, to knock the King down and away from me and right to the gutters of the Processional Way. Don't you see? It's not what they tell you! It's not!'

"He then went silent with a gesture to me to ponder these words and then he said he wanted to try something. These next few moments were to have a crucial influence over my own destiny as a spirit, but I couldn't have known it then.

" 'Azriel,' he said. 'I want you to do this. Look at me, and strip me in your mind of this gold, and see me pink and alive as you are, with my beard black and my eyes brown, and then reach out and touch me with both your hands. Let the god out of the gold. Let's try it.'

"I was trembling.

" 'Why are you so scared! Nobody will see anyone across from you but a noble in fine dress, that's all.'

" 'I'm scared because it might work, my Lord,' I told him, 'and the most troubling thought has come to me. You want to escape, Marduk. You want to get away. And if this works, if my eyes and my touch can render you a visible body, you can escape, can't you?'

" 'And why the hell does that frighten a Son of Yahweh!' He took in his breath. 'I'm sorry I was angry with you. I love you over all my worshipers and all my subjects. I'm not going to abandon Babylon. I will be here as long as Babylon needs me. I will be here when the sands come to bury us all. And then maybe I will escape. But yes, this would give me freedom. It would teach me that as a god I could slip into a visible human body and walk about. It would teach me something about what I can do, you see? I can make storms, I can heal sometimes though this is very very tricky, and I can make wishes come true because I know things, and I know the demons the people fear are just the restless dead.'

" 'This is true?' I asked him. But let me say here that in Babylon getting rid of demons was a big business. I mean men made fortunes getting rid of demons from houses and sick people and so forth. There were rituals and charms for it, and you went to the exorcist and you did what he said. So I wanted to know if there were no demons. But he didn't answer me right away.

"Then he spoke up, 'Azriel, *most* of the demons are the restless dead. But there are strong spirits, spirits as strong as gods and some of them are full of hate, and like to hurt. But most of the time they don't bother with making a milkmaid sick or cursing a little house. That's the mischief of the restless dead! And the restless dead need to make mischief so that the fog and the smoke in which they wander will lift.'

"I didn't wait any further. I was impressed with his generosity and patience with me—and you must realize how splendid he looked sitting there, covered and permeated with gold, this beautiful noble creature—that I loved him with a beating heart. I loved him with tears. I loved him with laughter.

"I reached out, and as I touched him, I asked that all the gold covering him be stripped and that he have the freedom of a man to walk amongst us. Can you guess what happened?"

"He became visible as real," I said.

"He did, and I learnt something then about spirits that I was later to use to my advantage and used up till not very long ago. He did. He became visible, a great noble gentleman in festival dress sitting opposite me at the marble table with the wine cup in front of him, and he smiled. There was a stir all around as people saw him, and took notice. I don't think they had seen him materialize as we would say in this day and age. They just noticed him. For he was beautiful."

"Was it clear that he was Marduk?" I asked.

"No. Without the gold he could have been a King, an ambassador.

You know. The statue, you see, it was more stylized, remember. But everybody saw *him*. Even the musicians stopped their piping until he turned his head and gave a gesture for them to go on. And they saw him! And they went on.

"I was frozen with anxiety. 'Come on, friend,' he said. 'I see more clearly than ever, and though this body is light, I like the form of it, and it draws eyes to me which give me power such as the New Year's Procession itself gives. They see me! They don't know who I am but they see. Come on, friend, let's walk, I want to walk up on the walls and through the temple with you, I want to see things clearly now with you. You don't have to take me into your home. Your uncles will all go crazy. Unfortunately, I can hear with this god's ears that they are already gathering the wise men of Judea to talk about you, and that you can see and hear the pagan gods. Come on, let's go, I want to walk.'

"He stood up and put his arm around me and we strolled out of the garden. We walked all afternoon. I asked him, 'What happens if you don't go back to the temple for the morning feast?'

"'Idiot!' he said laughing. 'You know perfectly well what happens. I just smell the food. I don't eat it. They'll lay it down before the statue and take it away and bring it to all the temple personnel who are to eat from the table of God. Nothing is going to happen!'

"We walked all over the quarters of Babylon, along the canals, the river, over the bridges, through different districts and through the marketplace and through the many open gardens and parks. He was staring wildly at things, and now, of course, spirit that I am, I know what it was like for him to see these vivid colors. I understand better what he had endured.

"Suddenly, near the Ishtar Gate, he stopped in his tracks. 'Can you see that?' And I did see it; it was the goddess herself. She was glowering at both of us. She was caked with gold and jewels and invisible. In fact I could see through her angry face.

"'Ha, she doesn't like it, what I'm doing, that I escaped!' He stopped and began to worry. He then took on for the first time the look of fear. No, not fear. Apprehension. He became guarded. And I saw why. Many spirits were now around us, looking at him, and envying him and challenging him with their furrowed brows, and gods were there. The god Nabu was there! I saw him. And suddenly I saw the god Shamash. Now all of these were Babylonian gods and they had their own temples and priests. But I could see they were angry at us.

" 'Why aren't you afraid of them, Azriel?' Marduk asked me in a confidential breath.

" 'Should I be, my Lord? First of all I am with you, and second of all I am Hebrew. They are not my gods.'

"This struck him as hilarious and he began to laugh and laugh. I hadn't heard him laugh since he had become visible. 'That's a perfect Hebrew answer,' he said.

" 'Yes, I think so too,' I said. 'My Lord, would I offend them if I tried not to see them. Would you offend them if you banished them!'

" 'No, I am the great god here.' And he did make a decisive and angry and bold gesture, and the spirits turned pale and like smoke, even the angry angry Shamash, and they vanished. But what lingered was the dead, everywhere the restless dead. He opened his arms and he conveyed blessings on them. He began to talk in Sumerian, and he gave blessing after blessing, 'Return to your slumber, return to your rest in the Mother Earth, return to the peace of your graves, and to the safety of the memories of you in the hearts and minds of your children.'

"And thank God these dead people all went away. Of course he and I were standing there, plainly visible, and attracting much attention, this noble Lord who made extravagant gestures to people nobody could see, and this rich Hebrew overladen with jewelry, standing there like his page, or companion or whatever.

"But the dead did fade. My heart sank. I remembered the ghost of Samuel when he had been called forth by the Witch of Endor for King Saul. He had said, 'Why do you disturb my rest?' Oh, but the woe of this rest. I didn't want to be dead. I didn't. I didn't want to be dead. I reached out and clutched his hand. Marduk was of course stronger now, from having been seen for so long by so many. I don't have to tell you the cosmology, it's simple, he would grow stronger and stronger the more he appeared.

"I was confused, however, on every other score. For example. Why did he not let the priests bring him to life in gold and walk in gold, the god himself, about the city? Of course I'd never heard of any god doing that, but then I'd never met a god before Marduk. He read these thoughts for me. He still looked apprehensive.

" 'Azriel, first off the priests are not strong enough to make me solid and visible in gold. They cannot move the statue! They cannot make an image of me in gold as you can and then make it walk. They don't have the power. They don't have your gift. And even if they did, what would be my life? An endless New Year's Festival, surrounded by worshipers? I've seen gods fall for this! And in the end they have nothing, they belong to everyone who can touch their garments or their skin or their hair, and they flee into the fog, finally, screaming like the confused dead. No, such a thing I would only do if Babylon needed it of me, and Babylon does not. But Babylon needs something and soon, and you know why.'

" 'Cyrus the Persian,' I said. 'He draws closer every day. He'll sack Babylon. And . . . and . . .' I said. 'He will either slaughter my people with all the inhabitants or he will maybe let us stay.'

"Marduk put his arm around me and we walked bravely through the enormous crowd that had gathered to stare at us and our strange activities, and we went on into another great garden, one of my favorites where the musicians were always playing the harps. In fact, here the Hebrews played their music and the Hebrew men often gathered to dance. I hadn't meant to come to my people directly, but as it turned out it didn't matter. He said quite quickly,

" 'Azriel, I think we took the wrong turn.'

" 'Why, they won't notice us any more than anyone else. They see me with a rich man. I'm a merchant. I'll say I sold you your beautiful girdle of gold and these jewels.'

"He laughed at that, but he made us sit down together and we were once again whispering. 'What do you know about the Persians!' he asked me. 'What do you know about the cities that Cyrus conquers! What do you know?'

" 'Well, I know the lies the Persians spread, that Cyrus brings peace and prosperity and leaves people alone, but I don't believe it. He is a murdering King like any other. He is on the march like Assurbanipal. I don't believe the Persians will peacefully accept the surrender of this city. Who would believe them? Do you?'

"I realized that he was no longer listening to me. He pointed ahead. 'This is what I meant,' he said, 'when I said we took the wrong turn. But they would have found us anyway. Be calm. Say nothing. Give away nothing.'

"I saw what he saw, a great mass of the Hebrew elders storming towards us, clearing back the crowd and thickening it on all sides. And at the head of this crowd was the prophet Enoch in a fury with his white hair streaming in all directions, and he gazed on Marduk, and I knew he saw Marduk, whereas all those around him, uneasy and unsure, and not wanting to provoke a riot, only saw a Noble Man and their slightly crazy Azriel, whom they already knew to be a troublemaker of a mild, powerful, and obedient sort.

"Marduk looked the prophet in the eye! So did I. He came to a halt not far from us. He was half-naked, as prophets often are. He was covered with ashes and dirt and he carried a staff, and I knew for the first time since I had ever heard of him—he wasn't a favorite of mine—that he was a real prophet because of the way he beheld Marduk with flaming indignation and violent faith.

" 'You!' he declared, lifting his staff and pushing it at Marduk. The crowd fell back in fear. I mean, this figure did look like a rich man! But then the most terrible of all things happened. The prophet opened wide his eyes, and said, 'Bring to yourself your loot, the gold that your soldiers took from our temple in Jerusalem, clothe yourself with it, you stupid, useless idol, go on, you were made to be metal!'

"And before I could think to act, the gold did come down upon Marduk and enclose him, but he resisted it, and I tried to banish it, and between us we made it a light covering only, and it did not have the deep vitality of the visions I had so long had. But the gold was all over Marduk, and the streets were filled with the sounds of running feet. I looked up at the distant houses that enclosed the garden, and the rooftops were thronged with onlookers.

"My father suddenly pushed his way to the fore, and threw his arm in front of Enoch. 'You hurt us with this, don't you see!' he declared, and then he too saw Marduk standing there now dusted with gold, and Enoch hit my father with his staff.

"I was enraged, but my brothers surrounded the prophet, and Marduk took my arm. 'Stay with me,' he said imploringly in a soft whisper. 'Am I all gold?' I explained he was covered over with it, and it was getting thicker but he was not the moving idol that he had seemed to me at first. He merely smiled and he looked up at the people on the rooftops and turned round and round, and people began to scream.

" 'Silence,' shouted Enoch, stamping the bricks with his staff, his beard shuddering. You should have seen him. He was in his glory. I tell you, prophets are murderous, a murderous breed. 'You, Marduk, God of Babylon, are nothing but an impostor sent out from the temple!' he roared.

"Marduk laughed under his breath. 'Well, he's giving us a way out, Azriel, what a relief!'

" 'Do you want them to believe in you, my Lord? All you need to do is vanish and reappear. I'll help you.'

"He gave me a devastating look.

" 'I know,' I said, 'I disappoint you. You don't want to be the god.'

" 'Who in the hell would want it, Azriel? No, I shouldn't say that. Let me say, who would give up life for it? But there's no time. Your prophet here before us is about to bellow like a bull.'

"And Enoch did just that. He raised his powerful voice, though how such a thunder could come from such a scrawny rib cage, it's hard to imagine, and he declared:

" 'Babylon, your time is come. You will be humbled. Even as we speak, the anointed one comes, Cyrus the Persian, the scourge whom the Lord God Yahweh has sent to punish you for what you have done to his Chosen people and to lead us back to our own land!'

"Roars came from the Hebrews, roars and prayers and chants and bowing and bowing to the Lord God of Hosts, and the Babylonians looked on in amazement, some of them even laughing, and then Enoch made his prophecy again:

" 'Yahweh sends a saviour in the person of Cyrus to save this city . . . aye, even you Babylon, you yourself will be delivered out of the hands of mad Nabonidus into the hands of a liberator.'

"There was a beat of silence. Only a beat. And then the roar rose from all—Hebrew, Babylonian, Greek, Persian. The whole crowd cried up for joy. 'Yes, yes, the anointed one, Cyrus the Persian, may he liberate us from a mad king who has left the city.'

"Hordes began to bow to Marduk, bow at his feet and stretch out their arms and then back away . . .

" 'All right, impostor, savor your moment!' cried Enoch. 'It is the will of Yahweh that your city be surrendered without bloodshed. But you are no true God. You are an impostor and in the temples there are nought but statues. Statues, I tell you. You and your priests will see us leave in triumph and you will thank us that we have saved Babylon for you!'

"I was truly speechless, no joke. I couldn't figure this out! But Marduk only nodded his head and took the insults of the prophet, and then he turned and threw up his arms. 'I'm leaving you now, Azriel, but take care and do nothing until you have my advice! Be on guard against those you love, Azriel. I feel dread, not for Babylon, Babylon shall conquer, but for you. Now comes my moment of pride.'

"He then began to blaze with gold light, and I could see by his maddened eyes that it was coming from him, and as the Babylonians and the Jews saw it, he had the strength from them to grow brighter and then he said in a huge voice, more huge than a man's, and rattling the lattices and echoing off the buildings:

" 'Get away from me—Enoch and all your tribe. I forgive you your rash words. Your God is faceless and merciless. But I call down the wind now to scatter you all!'

"And the wind came. The wind came with huge ferocity over the rooftops, lifted off the desert and filled with sand. The gold figure of Marduk suddenly grew immense before me, but I knew now this was illusion, for it was paling, and as I stood looking up at him, he exploded into a shower of gold, and the people went completely wild.

"Everyone ran. Panic drove them. What they had seen drove them. What they had heard and, if nothing else, the wind salted with sand drove them.

"Only I stood there, my brothers now rushing to my side, and the prophet, Enoch, laughing, just laughing and throwing out his arms! Then he bore down on me, shoving my father to one side with his staff. He gave me the evil eye! He looked at me and he said, 'You will pay for eating the food of the false gods. You will pay! You will pay.' And he spat at me, and reached down for the sand that was gathered and threw it at me. My brothers begged him to stop, but he laughed, and he said, 'You will pay.'

"I got furious, truly furious. My happy nature left me. I felt the first anger that would soon become common to me after my death. I leant forward and I said,

" 'Call on Yahweh to stop this sandstorm, you fool!' and then my brothers literally dragged me away.

"A host of devoted elders rushed out to shelter Enoch and they picked him up and carried him away like a madman thrashing and screaming and gradually, gradually . . . as we ran to the shelter of our own house, the wind died away."

4

I was almost sick by the time we reached the house. My brothers were carrying me. And outside the gate, what should we see?

"First were two of the other prophets, the more quiet ones who merely echoed the old words of Jeremiah sent from Egypt, and with them an old woman whom everyone feared and despised. Her name was Asenath, and she was one of our tribe but she was a necromancer, everybody knew, and such things were forbidden, whether the great King Saul had ever called up Samuel with the Witch of Endor or not.

"Also, everybody went to her for help from time to time. So you know, it wasn't so great to see her outside our gate, but she had known my mother and my grandparents, and she wasn't the enemy, just someone with an unsavory reputation who could mix up poisons to kill people and potions to make people fall in love.

"She had straggling hair, very white, and eyes which had turned a perfect brighter blue with age, rather than pale, and a withered long face and a great triumphant expression, and she wore all scarlet, defiant scarlet, silks all over her, as if she were some Egyptian whore or something, and she carried a crooked staff, with a snake on the end of it, not so unlike the staffs of the prophets, and she said to me:

" 'Azriel, you come to me. Or you let me in.'

"By this time all the household was in the courtyard inside screaming and yelling at her to get away from our house, old witch, and my brothers told her to go, but to my surprise my father said, 'Come inside, Asenath, come inside.'

"Next I remember lying on my bed, and listening to people talk.

My brothers wanted to know how in the hell I had gotten into this, and how could I believe this demon was Marduk when he was obviously a demon, and why had I not told them that I was conversing with other gods! My sisters kept saying, 'Oh, leave him alone,' and for a moment I thought I saw the ghost of my mother, but this might have been a dream.

"All the uncles and elders were gathered in the long rooms of the scriptoria which flanked the courtyard for half its distance . . . it was quite big, as I told you. And I didn't know where my father was.

"At last, he sent for me, and my brother propped me up, and got me on my feet and took me to him. I didn't like the door through which we passed. This was a small antechamber off the chamber of the ancestors, that is, the little room in which earlier Assyrians and Akkadians of this very house had buried their dead. This little room was part of their old pagan worship and we had never cleaned the paintings of priests and priestesses and ancestors of other people off the walls. Superstition stopped us, and after all, heathens that they were, their bones lay under the floor.

"There were three chairs in the room, simple chairs, you know the kind, of leather and crossed painted legs, but they were our very finest, and also there were three lamp stands, and in each the wick was burning the olive oil brightly, so the room had a splendid but frightening look.

"Old Asenath sat in one chair, and my father in the other, and they were whispering, which they stopped when I came in. I sat down in the free chair, and my brothers left us, and there we were among painted Assyrians, in the flicker of these lamps, in an airless place. I closed my eyes. I opened them. I deliberately tried to see the dead. I tried to see them as I had seen them when Marduk was with me. And for a moment I did. I saw them as wraiths throughout the room, sort of shuffling and mumbling and pointing, and then I shook my head and said, 'Be gone.'

"Asenath, who had a very young voice for such an old hag, laughed at me.

" 'You learnt your imperial ways from the great god Marduk, didn't you?'

"Silence from me.

"Then she said, 'What? Won't you own up to your loyalty to your god in your father's presence? It doesn't surprise. You think you are the first Hebrew who has worshipped the Babylonian gods? The hills around Jerusalem are filled with altars where Hebrews still worship pagan gods.'

" 'Which means what, old woman?' I said, surprised at my own anger and impatience. 'Get to the point. What do you have to say to me?'

" 'Nothing to you. It's all said to your father. You make your choice. You make it. Ten years since the Festival has been celebrated but many, many more years since the true miracle of the Festival has been brought about. And the old priests; they know how to do it; but they don't know everything; and for this, this which I hold here'—and she drew a cumbersome package out of her garments—'they would give me anything and they will.'

"I looked at it. It was an ancient Sumerian clay envelope which meant that the ancient Sumerian tablet was untouched inside. It had never been tampered with. I could see that.

" 'What do I want with that? What do I care about the true miracle of the Festival?' I said.

"My father motioned for me to be quiet.

"She put the clay envelope with its secret tablet hidden inside it into my father's hands. 'Hide it here with the bones of the Assyrians,' she said. She laughed. 'And remember what I said, they will give you Jerusalem for it! Do as I say! They've already sent for me. They don't know clearly even how to mix the gold without me. I will help them, but when they demand the tablet of me, it will be safe with you.'

" 'Who gave you this all-precious tablet, Asenath?' I asked sarcastically, becoming ever more anxious and impatient at this whole thing. I'd never seen my father so serious! I didn't like it.

" 'Look at it, scribe, scholar, smart one!' she said. 'How old do you think this is?'

" 'A thousand kings have reigned since then,' I said. 'It's as old as Uruk.' And really this was the same as saying to you in English, this thing is two thousand years old.

"She nodded. 'Given me by the priest they put to death, just to spite them,' she said.

" 'I want to read the outside,' I said.

" 'No!' she said. 'No!' Then she stood up and leaned on her snake staff or whatever the hell she called it, and she said to my father, 'Remember, there are two ways to do this. Two ways. I give you my counsel. Were he my son, I would give them this tablet. I would give it into the hands of the most ambitious. I would give it into the hands of the most dissatisfied and eager to be gone from here, and that is the young priest, Remath. Be clever. You hold your people in your hands.'

"Then she turned and threw out her staff, and lo, the doors opened of themselves and she turned to me and she said, 'You are most privileged for I give you my one chance at immortality. Were I to keep it, were I to abide by it, I might rise above this world and the stumbling dead, with the strength of a great spirit.'

" 'And why don't you?' said I.

" 'Because you can save your people. You can save us all. You can take us back to Jerusalem and then, for that you deserve something, yes, you deserve something for that . . . to be an angel or a god.'

"I was on my feet, trying to stop her and demand more of her, but she went out directly, scattering the family with wild threats, and strode through the anterooms, and the gate opened for her staff, and on she walked, a blaze of red silk into the street and away.

"I looked at my father. He sat still holding this enveloped tablet and looking at me with large tear-filled eyes. I had never seen his face so frozen. It was as if the muscles of his face didn't know grief or pain or fear well enough to form a face for it. He was at a loss.

" 'What the hell is she talking about, Father?' I asked him.

" 'Sit down here close to me,' he said, the tears spilling now as freely as they might from a woman, and he held my hand.

" 'Will you let me read that damned thing?' I asked.

"He didn't respond. He held it close to his chest. And he was thinking. The door lay open and I saw my brothers out there, all peering in and then my sister came and said, 'Father, brother, do you want some wine?'

" 'There isn't wine in the world enough to get me drunk now,' said my father. 'Shut the door.' My sister did.

"He turned to me suddenly, his lips pursed and then he swallowed and he said, 'It was Marduk with you, wasn't it? Or a spirit who claimed that he was Marduk. It was true.'

" 'Yes, I would say that is precisely the truth, Father. I've talked to him since I was a child. Am I to be punished now for this? What's to happen? What's this about Remath, the priest? You know him? I don't know that I do.'

" 'You know him,' he said. 'You just don't remember him. The day that Marduk smiled at you, when you were a boy, Remath was standing in the corner of the banquet chamber. He's young, ambitious, full of hatred of Nabonidus and enough hate of Babylon to want to go away.'

" 'What's this to me?'

" 'I don't know, my son, my beautiful and beloved son. I don't know. All I know is that all Israel is begging for you to do what the priests of Marduk want you to do. As for this enveloped tablet here? I don't know. I just don't know.'

"He cried for a long time. I was tempted to snatch the enveloped tablet from him and suddenly I did. I read the Sumerian.

" 'To make the Servant of the Bones.'

" 'What is that, Father?' I said. He turned, his tears disfiguring his face somewhat, and he wiped at his wet beard and lips and he took the tablet back. 'Leave that to my judgment,' he said in a low voice, and then he stood up and he went along the wall, looking for loose stones, for bricks that might come out, and he found what he wanted, a hiding place, and he put the tablet inside.

" 'To make the Servant of the Bones,' I repeated. 'What can it mean?'

" 'We have to go up to the temple, my son, to the Palace. Kings are waiting on us. Deals have been struck. Promises have been exchanged.' Then he embraced me and he kissed me slowly all over my face, he kissed my mouth, my forehead, my eyes.

" 'When Yahweh told Abraham that he was to bring Isaac and sacrifice him,' he said, 'you know our great Father Abraham did as he was told.'

" 'So the tablet and the scrolls tell us, Father, but have you been told by Yahweh that I must be sacrificed? Yahweh has come to you now, along with Enoch and Asenath and all the others? Is that what you expect me to believe? Father, you are grieving for me. I am dead already in your mind. What is this? What, why am I to die? For what? What's wanted, that I personally renounce the god, that I tell the King the god has wished him well, what! If it's a performance I'll do it! But, Father, don't cry for me as if I were dead!'

" 'It's a performance,' he said, 'but it takes a very very strong one to perform it, one with endurance and conviction, and one with a great heart filled with love. Love of his people, love of his tribe, love of our lost Jerusalem and love of the Temple to be built there to honor the Lord. If I thought I could do it, that I could see the performance through to the finish, I would do it. And you can turn on us, you can say no, you can flee.

" 'But the priests of Marduk want you, my son, they want you. And so do others even more powerful than they. They want you. And they know you are stronger than your brothers.' His voice broke.

" 'I see,' I said.

" 'And you are the only one who could ever forgive me for condemning him to such a fate.'

"I was thunderstruck. I just looked at him, at his tearful eyes, and I said, 'You know, Father, you are perhaps right, at least insofar as this. I could forgive you anything. Because I know you, and you wouldn't do evil to me, you wouldn't do that.'

" 'No, I wouldn't. Azriel, do you know what it means to me that you are to be taken from me, you and your future wife and future sons and daughters? Oh, it doesn't matter. Forgive me, son, for what I do. Forgive me. I beg you. Before it begins, before we go to the palace, and hear the lies and look at the map, forgive me.'

"He was my father. He was sweet and kind and overcome with grief, terrible grief and pain. It was an easy thing for me to put my arms around him as if he were my little brother and say, 'Father, I forgive you.'

" 'Never forget that, Azriel,' he said. 'When you are suffering, when the hours are dragging by, when you are in pain, forgive me . . . not just for my sake, son, but for yours!'

"A knock came. Priests were here from the Palace.

"We got up at once, wiped our faces, and then we went into the courtyard.

"Remath was standing there, and as soon as I saw him, I did re-member him as my father had said. I had never spoken much with him as he was a real malcontent; I mean he hated Nabonidus beyond belief for not giving Marduk's temple what it should have, but he also hated everybody else. He usually stood around the palace and the temple, doing nothing. But he was clever. I knew that. And he was very restless. He was young and smart.

"He studied us now, his eyes very deep set and seemingly better sculpted in his white skin, and his long thin nose gave him a disdainful look. All the rest was the usual mass of curly black hair . . . and priestly robes very fine, down to his jeweled sandals, and then he drew near my father and he said, 'Did Asenath give it to you?'

" 'Yes,' said my father. 'But that does not mean that I will give it to you.'

" 'You're stupid not to. Your son goes into the earth otherwise. What good is that?'

" 'Don't call me names, you heathen,' my father said. 'Let's get on with it. Let's go.'

"In the anteroom stood other priests waiting for us, and as we went outside, we found that there were brightly adorned litters for us and we were taken to the palace, each alone in his own litter, and I lay back trying to figure this out.

" 'Marduk, are you going to help me?' I whispered.

"Marduk answered, 'I don't know what to tell you, Azriel. I don't. I can see what is bound to happen. I don't know! I know this, that when it is over, one way or another, I will still be here. I will be walk-ing the streets of Babylon in search of eyes that can see me, and prayers and incense that can arouse me. But where will you be, Azriel?'

" 'They're going to kill me. Why?'

" 'They'll tell you. You'll see it all. But I can assure you of this much. If you refuse to do what they want, they'll kill you anyway. And they'll probably kill your father, because he knows the plot.'

" 'I see. I should have realized that. They need my cooperation and if I don't give it, well, then it would have been better for me had I never been asked.'

"There came only silence from him but I could feel his breath and

I knew he was close. He wasn't material, but it didn't matter; we were even closer in the darkness of this litter, being carried with the curtains drawn through Babylon's hollow paved streets.

" 'Marduk, can you help me get out of this?' I asked.

" 'I have been thinking of that for hours and hours, hours since your prophet spewed out all his filth at me. I have been asking myself, "Marduk, what can you do?" But you see, Azriel, without your strength, I cannot do what I want to do. I can't. I can be the gold god on his throne and that is all. I can be the standing statue carried in procession. Those objects or encasements they already have. And if I were to run with you . . . if we were to escape, where would we go?'

"A strange sound filled the little curtained compartment. He was weeping. Then suddenly, 'Azriel, tell them no! Refuse their filthy designs. Refuse them. Don't do it, not for Israel, not for Abraham, not for Yahweh. Refuse.'

" 'And die.'

"He didn't answer.

" 'Well, either way I shall die, no?'

" 'There's a third way,' he said.

" 'You're speaking of Asenath and the tablet.'

" 'Yes, but it is terrible, Azriel. It's terrible. And I don't know if there's truth in it. It is older than I am. It is older than Marduk and older than Babylon, that tablet; it came from the city of Uruk. Maybe from before. It is very old. What can I tell you? Know your own mind. Take your chance!'

" 'Marduk, don't leave me,' I said. 'Please.'

" 'I won't, Azriel, you are the dearest friend of my heart that I have ever had. I won't leave you. Make me appear if you need me to frighten them or stop them. Make me appear and I will try. But I won't leave you, I am your god, your own god, your god, and I'll be with you.'

"We had come to the palace. We were being brought in by a private gate, and now we were welcomed out of our little compartments so that we might walk on the grand stairway of gold and glazed brick, through the magnificent veils that separated one giant room from another, and we did, we walked, in silence, my father and I, we walked, following the priest, and they took us into the royal chamber where Belshazzar, listening to cases, made a farce of justice every day, and where his wise men told him hour after hour what the stars were saying to them, and we went beyond that into small and fine apartments that I had never seen.

"I saw that a seal had been broken, an ancient seal, as the doors had been opened. But the servants had come. For everywhere was luxury, fine carpets, pillows, the usual veils, and everywhere the lamps hung from the beams of the ceiling and the oil was sweet and the light was bright.

"A table stood in the middle of the room. Men were seated at it. And behind them stood my uncles, two of them, including the one who was deaf, may he have no name, and the Elders of Israel in Captivity, and Asenath and Enoch the prophet as well.

"Only gradually did I let myself look down at those seated at the table, though we were being placed opposite, the servants hustling to draw back the golden chairs.

"I saw our miserable regent, Belshazzar, and he looked stupid with drink and terrified, and was mumbling to himself something about Marduk, and then I realized I was looking at Nabonidus, old Nabonidus, our true King who had been gone almost half my life. Our true King sat there in his full raiment, though not on a throne, merely at a table, and his big watery eyes were dead and empty already, and he merely smiled at me, and he said, 'Pretty, pretty . . . you have chosen one that is so pretty . . . pretty as the god.'

" 'Pretty enough to be a god!' said a voice, and I looked directly opposite at this fine handsome man, taller than anyone there, thinner in build than any of us, with black curling hair but hair that was cut shorter than ours, and a trimmed mustache and a shorter trimmed beard.

"This was a Persian! The men beside him were Persians. They were in Persian robes, very like our own, but in royal blue, and they were crusted with jewels and gold embroidery, and their fingers were covered with rings, and the goblets before them were our temple goblets!

"These were men from the Persian empire which was conquering us, which was killing us. All the strange predictions of Enoch came back to me and I saw him glaring down at me, with a near impish smile, and Asenath seemed filled with wonder.

" 'Sit down, young one,' said the tall robust man with the big laughing eyes, the handsomest man, the man who gleamed with power. 'I'm Cyrus, and I want you at your ease.'

" 'Cyrus!' I said. Cyrus was the conqueror.

"The full details of the man's accomplishments were sharpened in my mind. This was Cyrus the Achaemenid King who already ruled half the world. He had united the Medians with the Persians, the man who meant to take Babylon. The man who had scared all the cities around us. This was no longer tavern talk of war. This was Cyrus himself sitting here before us.

"I should have prostrated myself before him but no one was doing anything like that before anyone, and he had said in a clear voice with an excellent command of Aramaic that I was to be at ease.

"Very well. I looked at him directly. After all, I thought, I'm going to die. So what. Why not?

"My father took the empty chair beside me.

" 'Azriel, my boy, my beautiful boy,' said Cyrus. The voice was crisp, full of good humor. 'I have been in Babylon for days. There are thousands of my soldiers throughout Babylon. They have come in by many gates over a long time. The priests know. Here, your beloved King—and may the gods keep him well always—Nabonidus himself knows.' He gave a generous nod to the suspicious and dying old King. 'All your King's regents and his officials know that I am here. Your Elders, you see. Don't feel fear. Feel joy. Your tribe will be rich and they will live forever, and they will go home.'

" 'Ah, and this depends then on what I do?' I asked.

"I wasn't sure then and am still not today sure why I was so cold and disdainful of him. He was compelling but he was human, and young. And also, no matter what he'd done so far, he was a heathen to me, and he wasn't even Babylonian. So, I was cold to him.

"He gave a silent measuring smile.

" 'So it depends then on what I do?' I repeated the question. 'Or your will, Lord, has your will already been decided?'

"Cyrus laughed, with crinkling cheerful eyes. He had the vigor of kings all right, and not yet the total madness. He was too young and he'd been drinking up the blood of Asia. He was full of strength. Full of victory. 'You speak boldly,' he said to me generously. 'You look with a bold eye. You are your father's eldest, aren't you?'

" 'For the three days required,' said one of the priests, 'he must be very strong. To be bold is part of it.'

" 'Put another chair at this table,' I said, 'with your permission, My Lord King Cyrus, and My Lords, King Nabonidus and Lord Belshazzar. Put it here at the end.'

" 'Why, for whom?' asked Cyrus politely.

" 'For Marduk,' I said. 'For my god who is with me.'

" 'Our god is not at the beck and call of you!' roared the High Priest. 'He won't come down off the altar for you! You have never seen our god, not really, you are a lying Jew, you are—'

" 'Close your mouth, Master,' said Remath in a small voice. 'He has seen the god and he has spoken with him and the god has smiled at him, and if he invites the god to this chair, the god is most likely to come.'

"Cyrus smiled and shook his head. 'You know,' he said, 'this is truly a marvelous city. I am going to love Babylon. I wouldn't hurt a stone of such a place. Ah, Babylon.'

"I might have laughed at that, at his wiliness, his disrespect for the elders and the old priests, his ruthlessness and his wit. But I was past laughing. I looked at the light of the lamps and I thought, 'I am going to die.'

"A hand touched mine. It was vaporous. No one could see it. But it was Marduk. He had taken this chair to my left; invisible, transparent, golden, and vital. My father sat to my right and my father just put his hands up to his face and cried and cried.

"He cried like a child. He cried.

"Cyrus looked with patience and compassion at my father.

" 'Let's get on with it,' said the High Priest.

" 'Yes,' said Enoch, 'let's get on with it now!'

" 'For these men, these elders, these priests, this prophetess, get stools for them to be comfortable,' said Cyrus amiably and cheerfully. He smiled at me. 'We are all in this together.'

"I turned to look at Marduk. 'Are we?'

"They all watched me in silence speaking to my invisible god.

" 'I can't tell you what to do,' said Marduk. 'I love you too much to make a mistake, and I have no right answers.'

" 'Stay then.'

" 'Throughout,' he said.

"The stools and chairs were quickly brought in and the Elders allowed in very casual fashion to sit all about us and this conquering Persian King, this monarch who had driven the Greeks crazy all over the world and now wanted our city and had everything we had but the city.

"Only the priest Remath remained standing, at a distance against a gilded column. The High Priest had told him to leave, but he had ignored this command and apparently been forgotten. He was watching me and my father, and then I realized that he could see Marduk. Not so clearly. But he could see him. Remath moved his position slightly so that he could see all three of us, going to a farther column behind Cyrus where Cyrus's soldiers, by the way, stood poised to become butchers. And there Remath stared at the seemingly empty chair with cold and conniving eyes, and he looked at me."

5

ell, my lord, what do you want of me?' I asked. 'Why am
W I, a Hebrew scribe, so important so suddenly?'
" 'Listen, child,' said Cyrus. 'I want Babylon without a
siege, I want it without a death. I want it the way I have taken the
Greek cities when they have been smart enough to let me do it. I
don't want ashes behind me and ruins galore! I don't come with a
torch, and a bag for loot, a thief. I will not rape your city and deport
your populations. On the contrary, I will send home to Jerusalem all
of you, with the blessing to build your own temple.'

"Enoch now stood up and laid down before us a scroll. I reached
for it, and read it. It was a proclamation freeing all the Hebrews to go
home. Jerusalem would be under Cyrus's benevolent protection.

" 'He is the Messiah,' said Enoch to me. And what a change of
tone from the old man. Now that Cyrus the Great was talking to me,
my own prophet was talking to me. Now, by Messiah he meant
'anointed one.' Later on the Christians made a big deal of this word,
but that's all it meant then. But still, it was a strong word.

" 'Add to that proclamation,' said Cyrus, 'gold, gold beyond your
imagining,' he said, 'and permission to take all that you possess with
you, to reclaim your vineyards, your lands, and be loyal to a powerful
empire that will let you build your Temple to Yahweh.'

"I looked at Marduk. Marduk sighed. 'He's speaking the truth,
that's all I can tell you. He's going to conquer one way or another.'

" 'I can trust him, then?' I asked my god.

"Everyone was shocked. 'Yes,' said Marduk, 'but to what degree . . . keep listening. You have something they want, your life,
there may be a way, who knows, for you yet to escape with it.'

" 'Ah no,' cried Asenath, 'God Marduk, you are wrong. There is but one path for him to escape and he should take it for it is better than life itself.'

"I realized she could see him, at least partially, and hear his words.

"He turned to her. 'Let him be the judge. Death may be better than what you have in store for him.'

"Cyrus watched all this in amazement. Then he looked at the priests gathered all around, the High Priest of Marduk, and the wily Remath standing over by the pillar.

" 'I need the blessing of your god,' said Cyrus, 'you are right, you are more than right,' he said humbly, but also rather cleverly, since this was just what these priests wanted to hear.

" 'You see, Azriel,' said Cyrus, 'it's this simple. The priesthood is strong. The temple is strong. Your god, if he sits with us, and I must confess I am prepared to worship him, is strong. And they can turn the city of Babylon against me. All the rest of Babylonia, I hold, but this is the jewel, this is the Gate of Heaven.'

" 'But how could you hold all the rest!' I said. 'Our cities are safe and secure. We knew you were coming, but someone is always coming.'

" 'He's telling you the truth,' said Nabonidus, and when he spoke all eyes turned to him. He wasn't addled or stupid. Just very old and tired. 'The cities are taken, every one has collapsed into Cyrus's arms. The fire-signal towers have all fallen to him, and the signals being sent are sent by Cyrus's men, to lull Babylon, but the cities are fallen and the signals are false.'

" 'Look,' said Cyrus, 'I'll send back to those cities all the gods which have been sent here for refuge. I want your temples to thrive. Don't you see? I want to embrace you! I didn't lay waste Ephesus or Miletus! They are Greek cities still and their philosophers are arguing in the agora. I want Babylonia in my embrace, not her destruction.'

"He then turned sharply and stared at the 'empty' chair. 'But your god Marduk must take my hand,' he said, 'if I am to conquer this city without fire. And then I shall send home all the gods of Babylonia as I promised.'

"Marduk, unseen by him, only listened to him and said nothing. But the High Priest lost his temper. 'There is no god in that chair!

Our god is neglected by our king and has gone into a deep sleep from which no one can wake him.'

" 'Look,' I said, 'why call me into this? What have I to do with it? You have right here in Esagila the statue of Marduk that you need for the procession. You ride with him on the great wagon, and you hold his hand, and he holds your hand and you are King of Babylon. If the priests will let you take the statue, what's it to do with me? Have you heard some rumor, Majesty, that I can control the god or turn him against you? You need a golden idol for your work! It's there, over there in the chapel.'

" 'No, my son,' said Cyrus, 'all that might have worked just fine if you had had a procession year after year with the god, and if the people had seen the golden idol, as you call him, and they had cheered him and your King Nabonidus, but those processions were not held, and the precious statue is not going to enter into any procession with me now, even if I wanted it to. What I need is the ceremony as it was done of old.'

"A chill passed through me. Marduk looked at me and said, 'I know little of what he is talking about, but all spirits see far, and I see horror for you. Don't speak. Just wait.'

"Meantime the priests were in a commotion. They had brought in on a bier a great heap of something, which was draped in linen and, now bringing it near to our table, with several torchbearers, they drew away the linen and we all gasped at what we saw.

"It was the processional statue and it was broken, and out of its rotted inside stuck bones which appeared to be those of a man, rotted, too, and half the skull showed where the thick gold-plated enamel had turned to dirt, and the whole mess lay a disgrace and an insult.

"The High Priest glowered at me. He folded his arms. 'Did you do this, Hebrew?' he asked. 'Did you cause Marduk to leave the statue! To leave this city? Was it you rather than our King here whom we have so accused?'

"I understood a great deal in a moment. I looked at my god who sat staring coldly at the heap of ruin.

" 'Are those your bones, my Lord?' I asked Marduk.

" 'No,' he said, 'and I only vaguely remember when they were put there. The spirit of that young one was weak, and I vanquished it and continued my reign. Perhaps it invigorated me that I was to be replaced? *I don't know*, Azriel! Remember, those are the wisest words I have for you. I don't know. Now they mean to put *you* in my place, that much we both know.'

" 'What do you want, Lord?' I asked Marduk.

" 'For you not to be hurt, Azriel,' he said. 'But do you want to become what I am? Do you want your bones encased three hundred years in that! Until it then crumbles and another young man must be lured for the sacrifice? But let me get to your point.' He leaned towards me.

" 'I forget how large your heart is, Azriel. You ask for my sake. I can tell you this, I can come and go as I wish. I banished the last replacement with a wave of my arm, and back into the fog he went. For a mortal man to be murdered in this fancy way does not necessarily make him either a god or a strong spirit.' He shrugged. 'Think of yourself and yourself only. What I am is . . . is what you know.' Then the sadness of his face shocked me. 'I don't want you to die!' he whispered.

"The High Priest could stand this dialogue no longer. He couldn't see or hear Marduk. He was sputtering with fury. But Asenath was hearing it all and looking from me to the god with great curiosity, and Remath the sly one wouldn't give himself away, but he knew something sat in the empty chair. He knew it. He understood something of what it said also.

" 'You're speaking of a statue of gold,' my father spoke up. 'You can't make a statue of gold without my son?' he asked.

" 'The bones are the bones of the god!' declared the High Priest. 'This is why our city is as it is, why we need the Persian deliverer. The god is old, the bones are rotten, the statue will not stand, and there must be a new god.'

" 'But the statue in the High Sanctuary?' my father asked, which was a childish question.

" 'That can't be carried through the streets,' said the priests. 'That's a mere hunk of—'

" 'Metal!' said the prophet Enoch with a cruel smile.

" 'You are wasting time,' said Cyrus. 'The ceremony has to be done in the old way,' he said, looking at me. 'Explain to him, Priests, don't just stand there. Explain. And you, my brave Azriel, what does Marduk say to you?'

"It was old white-haired Asenath who spoke up, stamping the floor first with her serpent staff to let everybody know they had better shut up for her. 'The god says he will go or stay as he pleases, that the bones inside the statue do not matter to him, they are not his bones, that's what he says!' Then she looked directly at Marduk, 'Well, isn't that what you say, you miserable little god who trembles in the light of Yahweh!'

"The Priests were thoroughly confused. Were they to defend the honor of their Marduk, who wasn't even supposed to be there?

" 'Look, my boy,' said Cyrus, 'become the god. Walk in the procession. You will be delicately covered in gold, though the old formula seems somehow to be . . . missing?' He cast a glance at the High Priest. 'You will be alive beneath the covering. You must live long enough to hold my hand, and to raise your other hand to your subjects. And you will live the three days it will take to fight off the forces of chaos, and then return here with me to the Courtyard of Esagila, where I shall be proclaimed King by you. We shall do it faster if we can think of some way to make that acceptable.'

" 'Alive, covered with gold.' I was amazed. 'And then?'

"Asenath spoke up. 'By then the gold will have hardened and you will be dead. You will see and hear for a while, but you will die inside, and when they see that your eyes are rotting, they will take out your eyes and replace them with jeweled eyes, and the statue of Marduk will be your shroud.'

"My father put his face in his hands and then looked up. 'I never saw it done in the old way,' he said quietly. 'But my father's father saw it once, or so he said. And the poison in the gold is what will kill you. You'll die slowly as the gold penetrates, as it reaches your heart and lungs, and then . . . as they say, you will at last be at peace.'

" 'This,' said Asenath, 'after you have been carried the full length of the Processional Way, gold and gleaming, raising your hand, even turning your head ever so slightly as the thick coating gets harder and harder.'

" 'And for this!' said Enoch. 'We will return to Jerusalem, all of us, including those in prison, and we will have the means to build the Lord God's Temple again according to the measurement of King Solomon.'

" 'I see,' I said. 'So in the old days, it was a real man! And when the statue finally crumbles . . .'

" 'You blaspheme!' said the High Priest. 'Those are the bones of Marduk.'

"This was too much for Marduk. Invisible or not, he stood up, throwing over the chair, and with a great thrust of his left hand sent the bones swirling in all directions. They shattered and crumbled against the walls. Everyone cowered. Even I lowered my head. Cyrus did not but stared with wild, childlike eyes, and old Nabonidus put his head down on his arm as if he would go to sleep. The prophet Enoch sneered.

"Then Marduk turned to me. He looked hard at me and then at Asenath. 'I know your wiles, old woman. But tell him everything! Tell him the full truth of it all. You know the dead. What do they say to you when you call them up? Azriel, do what you want to do for your people and your tribe. I will be here afterwards as I am now, and whether you can see me then and give me strength, and whether I can see you and give you strength, no one knows. Whether I can talk to you, no one can say. Your soul will be tested by this grand procession, this fight with chaos, this courtyard coronation, this torment! But this torment will not necessarily give you spiritual life. And you may fade in the mist with all the other weary and wandering dead. The dead of the whole world, regardless of gods or angels or demons or Yahweh. Do what you will as an honorable man, Azriel. For after it is done, I don't know that even I, strong as I am, will be able to find you or help you.'

"Asenath was overcome with excitement. 'I would worship you, Marduk, were you not an evil, worthless god. You're clever.'

" 'What does the god say!' demanded Cyrus.

"Enoch looked at Asenath. 'We must tell him now what will happen to him, that is all. Azriel, you resemble the statue of Marduk. Encased with gold, you will fool all of your friends. No one will know that you are not a god, you will seem a man of living gold, and you will feel numbness and some pain, yes, the slow pain as life ebbs, but it's not terrible. Even as you walk the Processional Way, all your people will be preparing to go out of Babylon!'

" 'Well, it's simple enough,' I said. 'Let the entire Hebrew population leave now, and I'll do it.' I felt a tightening in my throat. I knew that this was youthful stupidity and that soon horror would come on me that was damn near unbearable.

" 'Cannot be done, my son,' said Cyrus. 'We need your people and we need your prophets. We need them proclaiming Cyrus the Persian is the anointed of your god. We need all the city to roar in one voice, and I will not deceive you, I don't believe in your god, Marduk, and I don't believe that you will become a god if you do this.'

" 'Tell him all of it!' said Marduk.

" 'Not now, and that part doesn't matter,' said Asenath. 'He may say no to that, you know as well as I do.'

" 'Azriel,' Marduk said turning to me and embracing me. 'I love you. I will be with you in the procession. They are speaking the truth. They will let your people go. I can stand this mortal company no longer. Asenath, be kind to the dead whom you call so often for they are desperate to be near to life, you know. Desperate.'

" 'I know, god of the heathens,' she said. 'Will you come to me now and talk to me!'

" 'Never,' screamed the High Priest. Then he quieted down. He looked at two other priests, men I scarcely remember. It was Remath, the sly one, who spoke up. 'She is the only one who knows how to mix the gold, remember.'

"I laughed. I couldn't stop myself. I laughed.

" 'Ah, I see,' said Cyrus. 'So you turn to the Canaanite sorceress because your own wise men no longer know the secret.'

"My laughter—unshared—finally left me in peace.

"It took great courage for me to turn to my father. He sat as one broken and finished, his eyes wet and his face still. You might have thought I was already buried.

" 'You must come too, Father, you and all my brothers.'

" 'Oh, Azriel—'

" 'No, that's the last thing I ask of you, Father. Come. When we are led down the Processional Way let me see your upturned face and the faces of my family. That is, of course, if you believe in these men and you believe in this proclamation.'

" 'Money has already changed hands,' said Cyrus. 'Messengers are already on the way to Jerusalem. Your family will be great among the tribe, and you will be remembered for your sacrifice.'

" 'Like hell, great King,' I said. 'Hebrews don't remember those who pretend to be Babylonian gods. But I'll do it. I'll do it because my father wants me to do it . . . and I . . . and I forgive him.'

"My father looked at me. His eyes said it all, his love, his broken heart. Then he looked at Enoch and Asenath and the Elders of our tribe, who had sat silent all this while, and then he said in the simplest words, 'I love you, my son.'

" 'Father, I want you to know this,' I said. 'There is another reason why I do this . . . I do it for you, for our people, for Jerusalem, and because I have talked with a god himself. But I do it for one more reason, and that is simple. I wouldn't have anyone else suffer this. I wouldn't wish it on another.'

"Surely there was vanity in my words, but no one seemed to think so. Or if they did they forgave it. The Elders rose, they had their Proclamation in their hands. All were satisfied. It was done. Cyrus the Persian was the Messiah.

" 'Tomorrow morning, the trumpets sound,' said the High Priest. 'It will be announced that Marduk has brought Cyrus to liberate us from Nabonidus! The Processional Way is already being prepared. By the time the sun is high everyone will be in the street. The boat waits in the river to take us to the garden house where you will slay the dragon Tiamat, and that, by the way, will be nothing to you. We will return the following day, with you. We will hold you, and do all we can to ease your pain.'

" 'On the third morning, in the Courtyard, you must have life enough in you to rise and to put the crown on the head of Cyrus. That is all. After that, you may stand, held straight by the gold that kills you, warmed by it, numbed by it, and you may die in it. All the rest, the reading of the poems, the Destinies, all you need do is keep your eyes fixed and open.'

" 'And if I don't make the three days?'

" 'You will. The others always did. It is after that we may have to ease your death with a little more of the gold perhaps, in your mouth. But it will be painless.'

" 'I'm sure,' I said. 'Do you know how I despise you?'

" 'I do not care,' said the High Priest. 'You're a Hebrew. You never loved me. You never loved our god.'

" 'Oh, but he does!' said Asenath, 'that is the pity! But don't fear,

Azriel, your sacrifice is so great for Israel that the Lord God of Hosts will forgive you, and your flame will be joined in death with the great fire that He is.'

" 'I vow it,' said Enoch.

"I laughed contemptuously. I looked up, meaning only to look away in disdain, but I could see now that the room was thick with spirits. Like smoke they hovered all around, ghosts. I didn't know what they were or had been, their clothes were gone to such simplicity. Nothing remained except a tunic here or a robe there, sometimes there was not even a real form, only a face looking at me.

" 'What is it, son?' asked Cyrus kindly.

" 'Nothing. Only I see the lost souls and I hope that I do find rest in the fire of my god. But . . . it's foolish to even think of it.'

" 'Leave us now, all of you, leave the boy with us,' said Remath. 'We must groom him and dress him to be the finest Marduk who has ever been carried down the Processional Way, and you, old woman, will keep your promise, and tell us how to mix the gold and how to put the gold on him, on his skin, his hair, his clothes.'

" 'Go on, Father,' I said. 'But do let me see you tomorrow. Know that I love you. Know that I forgive you. Make of us a powerful house, Father, make of us a powerful nation.' I bent over and kissed him hard on the mouth and on both cheeks and then I looked to King Cyrus.

"After all, he had not dismissed me. But my father left, and the Priests took out old Nabonidus, who had in fact fallen asleep, and the miserable mumbling Belshazzar, who was drunk and confused and seemed ready at any moment to be murdered. I didn't care what happened to either of them. I listened to my father's steps until I couldn't hear them anymore.

"Enoch went out with the Elders, making some big fine speech then, of which I don't remember a single word, except that it sounded like a bad imitation of Samuel.

"Cyrus stared at me. His eyes spoke, they spoke respect, they spoke forgiveness for my rudeness, my lack of servility, my lack of courtesy.

" 'There are worse ways to die!' said the High Priest. 'You will be surrounded by those who worship you; as your vision dims you will see rose petals fall before you, you will see a king kneel at your feet.'

" 'We need to take him now,' said Remath.

"Cyrus beckoned for me to come to him. I stood up, went round the table and bent down to receive his embrace, and he rose with me, embracing me man to man. 'Hold my hand for those three days, my son, hold steady, and I promise you, Israel will live under me forever in peace, as long as there is Cyrus and Persia, and Yahweh will have his temple. You are braver than I am, son, and I consider myself the bravest man in the world, you know. But you are braver. Now go, and tomorrow we will begin our journey together. You have my love, you have my unbounded love, the love of a King who was a King before he came to you and will be a greater King because of you.'

" 'Thank you, My Lord,' I said. 'Be good to my people. I am a poor spokesman for my God, but he is powerful.'

" 'I honor him,' said Cyrus, 'and all the beliefs and all the gods of those I take under my protection. Good night, child. Good night.'

"He turned and his soldiers closed in around him and he walked very straight and calm out of the chamber. No one remained now but me and the priests and Asenath.

"I looked about. The dead had faded. But Marduk had come back and watched with folded arms. Marduk had sent them scurrying perhaps.

" 'Parting words for me?' I said.

" 'I'll be with you,' he said. 'I shall use all my power to be with you and ease your pain and help you. As I told you, I remember nothing of any such procession, or birth, or death. And maybe when your flame has gone into the great fire of your god, I will be here still for Babylon. If you love your people so much, maybe I can love my people a little more.'

" 'Oh, you needn't doubt him, he's a fine demon,' said Asenath.

"Marduk glared at her and disappeared.

"The old priest raised his hand as if he would strike her, and she laughed in his face.

" 'You can't do this without me, you fool,' she said. 'And you had better write down everything I tell you. You're a laugh, all of you, you pious priests of Marduk. It's a wonder any of you can even read the prayers!'

Remath came up to her.

" 'Remember your promise to me,' said Remath under his breath.

" 'In time, in the right time,' said Asenath, 'the Father has the tablet hidden where you will never find it, and when the three days are concluded, when the army has entered through all gates, and when the Hebrews are on the march, I will see that you have its contents.'

" 'What is this other tablet you speak of?' I asked. 'What part does it play?' Of course I knew where it was, where my father had hidden it in our house.

" 'A prayer for your soul, son,' she said, 'that you may see god, and of course you know I'm lying to you.' She shook her head. The mirth went out of her, even the hate. 'It's an old charm. You can choose then. You'll be dying. It's nothing to worry you now. Just a charm, such as the ancients believed, that's all, nothing else. The rest that we do here is medicine, not magic.'

"They led me through the palace and now we broke another ancient seal and entered together a large chamber. Servants moved swiftly past us to place the tables and the lamps. I saw a great cauldron brought in. I saw a brazier for fire that would lie on the floor beneath the cauldron. I felt for the first time total fear. Fear of pain and hurt and burning.

" 'If you've lied to me about the pain, tell me the truth, it will make it easier for me.'

" 'We haven't lied to you about anything!' said the High Priest. 'You will stand in the temple of Esagila for centuries and you will receive our libations. Be our god! If you ever saw him, then be him! How did he become what he was, if it wasn't for us?'

"They brought a couch for me, and I lay down on it and shut my eyes. Who knows? Maybe I was home and dreaming. But I wasn't. They began to groom me. I lay there with my eyes closed, turned towards the wall, or towards them, and I felt their hands on me, clipping my hair and my beard, and trimming my nails to the perfect length, and when I had to, I lifted my limbs so that they could undress me and bathe me. And then it was dark. Only the fire beneath the cauldron burned.

"I could hear the old woman reciting the words in Sumerian. It was a formula, a mixture of gold and lead and other herbs and potions, some which I knew and many which only an enchantress might know, but I knew enough to know it would kill anybody.

"I also realized it had in it, this brew, the seeds that people chew to see visions, and a great deal of the potions they drink to make them have wild dreams, and I knew those intoxicants would ease my pain and blur my thoughts. 'Who knows? Maybe I'll miss my own death,' I thought.

"Remath came to me. His face was very simple and there was no meanness in him. He spoke almost sorrowfully.

" 'We won't put on the final garments until dawn,' he said. 'They are ready in the other chamber. The gold boils but it will cool, you needn't fear, it will be cool and thick when we apply it to your skin. Now, what can we bring you, lord God, Marduk, what can we bring you to make you happy tonight?'

" 'I think I want to go to sleep,' I said. 'I fear that boiling gold.'

" 'No, it will be cooled,' said Asenath. 'Remember you must live long days whilst this gold eats into you. It will be cooled. You must be a smiling god as long as you can, and then a god with his hand lifted as long as you can, and then a seeing god as long as you can.'

" 'Yes, all right, leave me.'

" 'You don't want to pray to our own god?' asked Asenath.

" 'I wouldn't dare,' I whispered.

"I turned my back, and closed my eyes. And strangely enough I did sleep.

"They covered me with the softest blanket. That was sweet.

"I slept from sheer exhaustion, as though the ordeal lay behind me rather than ahead. I slept. And what I dreamed I don't know. What does it matter? I do remember being puzzled that I didn't want to see Marduk again; I remember thinking, Why is that, why am I not weeping on his shoulder? But that was just it, I didn't want to weep on anyone's shoulder. I had been dealt the mortal blow. I didn't know what lay ahead. The smoke, the fog, the flame, or power such as his. I couldn't know. And neither could he.

"I think I began to sing the psalm I loved so much of home and then I thought, The hell with it, Jerusalem will be theirs, not mine.

"A vision came to me. I think it was from Ezekiel, whom we were always copying at home, always fighting about, and arguing about . . . it was a vision of a valley of bones, the bones of all the dead, the bones of all mortal men and women and children. And I didn't think of the bones rising, I didn't think of them called to life. I simply saw them, and I thought, 'For that valley, I do this, for that valley, for all of us who are merely human.'

"Was I too proud? I don't know. I was young. I wanted nothing. I slept. And too soon, too soon indeed, came the lamps and the light and the distant shine of the sun on marble floors far from the doors of the chamber."

6

I was dizzy. I think it was the fumes. All night the kettle had cooked its immense blend of golden glaze, such a huge amount of gold and lead and whatever else went into it. The perfume was rich and delicious and I reeled.

"They stood me on my feet.

"I shook myself all over to waken more, to make the lamps stop hurting my eyes. That was sunlight, wasn't it? Asenath was there, and then the priests began to apply the gold. They began at my feet, telling me to stand straight and firm, and they covered my legs all over with the gold, painstakingly, in motions that were almost soothing. It was warm, but it didn't hurt. It held no sting whatsoever. They painted my face slowly. They brought the paint up into my nostrils, and they covered my eyelashes, one by one, and then they took the ringlets of my hair and my beard and one by one made them golden.

"By now I was fully awake.

" 'Keep your eyes wide,' said Asenath.

"Then they brought all the fine robes of Marduk. Now these were real clothes which were put on the statue every day, but I saw now what they meant to do, not trim them with gold but to coat them, so that indeed I would seem a living statue.

"They dressed me, and this they began to do, painting each fold of the long robe, the long full sleeves, and asking me again and again to raise my arms and to walk as they did their work.

"I stood before a mirror. I saw myself and I looked like the god. I saw the god.

" 'You *are* the god!' said a young priest to me. 'You are our god and we will serve you forever. Smile on me, Lord God Marduk, please.'

" 'Do it,' said Asenath. 'You see, the enamel must not harden too fast. We can't have it become brittle. And each time it does become too hard, the priests will add more to that place so that you can move the muscle. Smile, open your eyes and close them, that's right, my beautiful boy. That's right. Do you hear that noise?'

" 'It sounds like the entire city roaring,' I said. I heard the trumpets too, but I didn't speak of that.

" 'I am dizzy!' I said.

" 'We will hold you,' said the young priest. 'Cyrus himself will hold you, your attendants will hold you. Remember, take his hand, hold his hand. Turn to him often, and kiss him. The little gold from your lips will not harm his skin. You must do it.'

"Within seconds we were high on the wagon, and all around me I saw the layers of flowers—every fine flower that can be grown inside or out in Babylonia, and flowers brought in from places far away, the blooms of Egypt and southern islands.

"We were in a war chariot atop this wagon, but the chariot's wheels were fixed, and the attendants stood lower and behind us, and holding me firmly by the waist. And one on the side held me also by the waist. And Cyrus mounted the chariot.

"Screams and cries came from everywhere. The gates had been open all the time. The people flooded in. The Procession had begun. I blinked. I tried to see. I saw the petals flying through the air, pink and red and white, and I smelled the incense rising. I looked down, feeling a stiffness in my neck and I saw all the priesthood and all the women of the temple prostrating themselves on the great tiled floor of the courtyard. The white mules began their slow march forward.

"In a daze I turned and looked at the King! How splendid and beautiful he looked.

"Just as we passed through the gates, there came the loudest shrieks and cries. The Hebrews were on the rooftops. I looked. It was a haze. But I could hear them singing the psalms of Zion. The faces were small and distant.

"The wagon picked up speed, as much speed as a giant wagon can get, which is not much, but we were rolling steadily, you might say, and I held to the edge of the chariot with one hand, letting my golden fingers curve around it, and then I reached out as if by instinct, for no one told me, and I put my hand into Cyrus's hand and gave him the first kiss.

"The crowd was in ecstasy. Every house along the Processional Way seemed a living thing in itself, with life screaming from its windows and its roof, and life pressed up against its door, and in every side street people sang and waved palms and again and again I heard the Hebrew music. The Hebrew music followed us.

"I don't remember when we crossed the great canal, though I think I did see the dazzle of the water. The attendants were holding me firmly and telling me harshly to be strong.

" 'You are my god, Marduk,' said Cyrus. 'Bear with them, they are fools. Hold my hand, my god. For now, we are King and god and no one can deny it.'

"I smiled, and again I bent forward to kiss his cheek and again the screams of joy surged through the crowd. We were approaching the river. We would now be placed in the boat, and taken to the House of the Ordeal with Tiamat, the god's great battle with chaos. And what would that be?

"I was as one so drunk it simply didn't matter. I could feel the gold hardening all over me. And I could feel it caressing me as they said it would. I had anchored my feet fairly well at last and the attendants had their grip, and Cyrus's living hand held warm and tight to mine, and he waved and bowed and shouted a thousand greetings to the eager citizens of Babylon.

"A funny thought came to me as the boat moved up the river. There were crowds on all sides. And I thought, 'He thinks this is all for him, Cyrus. And it's really just Babylon. Babylon having a big party or festival like it does so often, but he's never seen the city going crazy with dance and drink, and so he is very impressed. Well, let him enjoy it.' Only dimly did I realize, I had not seen my family. They had been there, I was sure, but I had not seen them.

"The House of the Ordeal was splendidly plastered in silver and emerald and rubies. The pillars were gold and made to look like great lotus blossoms at the top. The middle of the roof was wide open, and all around us were crowded hundreds upon hundreds of noble Babylonians, the rich, great officials from other cities, priests who had come with their gods to Babylon for safety, and also hundreds upon hundreds of Cyrus's court, so like us, yet so different. Taller, leaner, more trim, and more sharp of eye.

"Suddenly I stood alone in the midst of the open court. Everyone had backed away. Remath stood beside me, and on the other side, the young compassionate priest.

" 'Lift your arms,' said the priest. 'Take your sword from the scabbard.'

" 'Sword, I didn't know I had one.'

" 'You do,' said the young priest eagerly. 'Ah, yes, raise it high.'

"I scarcely knew whether I obeyed. The world was swimming before me. The nobles were chanting and harps were playing, and then I heard a sound I knew, knew from many spectacles of the past, and from the hunts with my father and brother. I heard the roar of lions, caged lions.

" 'Don't fear,' said Remath. 'These animals are satiated and filled with potions that make them sluggish and they will come one by one as they are released, and they will rise as they have been trained to lick the honey from your lips, which I will put there now, honey and blood, and when they do, you will drive your sword into them.'

"I laughed. 'And you, where are you going to be?' I asked.

" 'Right here, beside you,' said the young priest. 'This is nothing, Lord God Marduk, these lions want to die for you.'

"He lifted a chalice to my lips. 'Drink the honey and the blood,' he said.

"I did, barely able to feel myself swallowing. I realized suddenly that almost all sensation had left my skin, I was as one in bitter cold night desert wind. But I swallowed and he gave me more until my tongue and lips were coated with blood and honey.

"A terrible excitement ran through the crowd. I could see the fear. The first lion had been released and came towards me. The Persians were backing up against the walls, I think. I could feel the fear, smell it. And I laughed again. 'This is so funny,' I said. 'I'm half-dead and this lion is staggering towards me.'

"Suddenly, the lion sprang, and the two priests had to hold me so that the lion's weight didn't throw me backwards. I lifted the sword. I called on the gold enamel to give me strength and I drove the sword into the lion's heart. His hot foul breath blew into my nostrils and his tongue touched my lips, and then he fell over, awkward, dead, and the crowd sang and sang and sang of courage.

"Now the King came to my side, and he too had his sword, and I saw that as the second lion and third lion were released that we were to kill them together. The King's face was as rigid as mine, and he narrowed his eyes at the beast. 'They have plenty of life in them, it seems to me,' he said.

" 'Ah, but you're a King and I'm a god, so let's kill them.'

"Behind them the priest cracked the whip which made one lion jump for Cyrus first and he staggered back as he drove the sword and then kicked the animal away from him. The lion rolled on its back roaring, dying. The second beast was in my face. I felt the priest lift my wrist. 'Thrust now!' I did. I thrust more than once wanting the thing dead and off me.

"And once again, all sang, and cheered, and I could hear the crowds outside singing and cheering. I saw the lions lifted and carried out. I heard the song of the priest of the slaying by Marduk of the evil Tiamat.

" 'And from her hide he made the heavens and the earth and the seas . . .' the words rang out in the old Sumerian. And then in Akkadian, and then in Hebrew, and it was like overlapping waves of sound, and I swam in them.

"I stood alone in the court. The priests were painting me with the blood and honey. 'They cannot hurt you,' said Remath.

" 'What?' I asked. But I knew. I could hear them as distinctly as the beasts. It was the bees. And now as a great silken dragon proceeded towards me, tightly sewn with spindly gold ribs and controlled by those who worked it on sticks, I saw it was full of bees. The dragon was wrapped around me, and I was enclosed in a silken tent. Its tail even covered my head. I heard the sound of ripping fabric. The bees were loosed on me and covered my body over. I was filled with loathing. But my feet were frozen in place. And the stings of the bees did not penetrate the gold, and when they came near my eyes I only closed my eyes, and gradually I realized the bees were dying. They were dying from their own sting and from the poison perhaps in the gold. I heaved a great sigh.

" 'Keep your eyes open,' cried Remath.

"And when all the bees had fallen, and the great silken dragon, now collapsed, had been offered to me to rip with my sword there came the cries again.

"I was being carried up the stairs, to the roof. I could see out over the open fields. I could see the crowds going on and on forever. I lifted my arm with my sword, I lifted it again and again, turning to the east, and the west, and the north, and the south, and lifting it and smiling, and the crowds sang back to me. All the earth sang back to me.

" 'It is so very beautiful,' I said, 'so indescribably beautiful.' But there was no one to hear me. The fresh air waked me a little, touching my nostrils and my throat, and cooling my eyes. The priestesses of the temple surrounded me, throwing flowers in the air, and then I knew I was being led away to the royal couch.

" 'You can have as many as you want, but I advise you to sleep,' said Remath.

" 'Yes, good idea. And how do you keep me from dying?'

" 'I can hear your heart. You will live long enough to make the journey home. You are stronger than anyone imagined.'

" 'Then give me a harlot,' I said.

"Everyone was upset. 'Well?' I said.

"The harlots screamed with delight. I beckoned for them to come. But I couldn't do it with them. I could only take each one in my arms and plant a poison kiss on her grateful upturned sweet little mouth and send her away in swoons, to wipe off the kiss, I hoped, as soon as she could. I laughed deep in my chest with my lips closed.

"Other things were done that night, but I slept. Fire, poetry, dances, things I never saw.

"I slept. I stood, resting back at a tight angle so that I seemed to be supporting myself, and with my eyes open, painted open now with fresh gold, so that I could not close them, but I slept.

"The world seemed a pit of madness. Now and then I woke to see the flames and the dancing figures. Now and then I heard some whisper or sound. Or heard running feet and felt human hands clasp me.

"Once I think I saw the King dancing below. I saw the King dancing with the women in a great strange slow dance, figures turning ceremoniously and then the King threw up his arms and bowed down to me. But nothing was required of me. The smile was fixed on my face now by the hardened gold. And only when I laughed did I feel the flesh tingle.

"At noon, the following day, as we began the procession back into the court of Esagila, I knew for sure I was dying. I could scarcely move at all. The attendants, under the cover of silk scarves and robes, fiercely painted the gold fluid on my knees to keep them flexible, but they didn't want the people to see. And I was not tired so much as stunned, staring at those before me.

"We came now to the gates . . . we went into the courtyard, where the great poem 'In the Beginning' would be read, and the actors would begin their pageant. I felt a sadness suddenly, a terrible sadness and confusion. Something was wrong.

"But all of a sudden as if it were the answer to a prayer, the thing was made right. I heard my father singing. I heard him and my brothers:

> *'I will make a man more precious than fine*
> *gold; even a man than the golden*
> *wedge of Ophir.'*

"I struggled to hear it more clearly, their blessed familiar voices:

> *'Thus saith the Lord to his anointed, to*
> *Cyrus, whose right hand I have holden,*
> *to subdue nations before him . . .'*

" 'Turn your head to them, Lord God Marduk,' said Cyrus. 'It is your father, singing with all his heart.'

"I turned. I saw nothing but a blur of waving arms, of garlands tossed in the air, of flowers falling, but I heard my father:

> *'I will go before thee, and make the*
> *crooked places straight. . . .*
> *And I will give thee the treasures of*
> *darkness, and hidden riches of secret*
> *places, that thou mayest know that I, the*

Lord, which call thee *by thy name,* am
the God of Israel.'

"The singing went on and on, following us to the gates of the temple. And then came the shouts, 'Messiah, Messiah, Messiah!' And Cyrus waved and threw them his kisses, and at last it was time for the coronation.

"We were taken down from the chariot and the wagon, and walked on a bed of flowers up and up the seemingly endless stairway of the great ziggurat Etemenanki, so that the people from far off could see us through the wide gates. I thought I might die before I reached the top; I couldn't look above, only at the golden stairs before me and I thought of the stairway to Heaven which Jacob had seen in his dream with the angels coming and going.

"At last we stood on the summit, the mountain made by and for the god, and I was given the crown. By now it seemed I did not control my limbs at all. I felt nothing. I smiled because it was easiest to smile, and my arms ached suddenly with tiredness as I lifted the big Persian crown of gold and placed it on the head of the Living King.

" 'Now may I die,' I whispered. Exhaustion overcame me. My knees were in pain, my feet, all of me that could no longer move or stand with any freedom.

"Distinctly I saw the loving eyes of Cyrus, I saw the solemnity in his face, I saw . . . the dedication to Kingship in him. I saw perhaps a little of a King's madness.

"Slyly and cleverly the priests crowded around me and painted me over and over that I might move my limbs, and some vitality came back to me. 'Keep your eyes open,' Remath said. 'Keep your eyes open.'

"I did. We were taken down to the courtyard. The banquet lasted for hours. I know the poets came and they sang, and I know that the King dined and all the nobles dined. But I sat rigid staring. My eyes wouldn't close now whatever I did. They had been stupid to add paint. They only softened the lids when they did, I thought to myself, and I looked down at my hands lying on the table, and I thought, 'Marduk, I have never once called on you.'

"His voice came in my ear. 'You have had no need of me, Azriel. But I'm with you.'

"Finally it came to an end. Darkness had fallen. It was finished. The King was crowned, Babylonia was Persia, the city was drunk beyond the palace gates and the temple gates, and within these two buildings others drank and sang.

" 'Now,' said the young priest, 'we will carry you up to the shrine. You need walk no more. You need only take your place at your banquet table there, and if you do not die within a few hours we will give you the gold in your mouth.'

" 'Not quite yet,' said Remath. 'Follow me and quickly, for we have one more ritual to perform and it must be done properly.'

"The young priest was confused. So was I but I didn't care. I didn't give a damn. I didn't care at all. I was slumbering already, and when I saw the vague shapes of the dead hovering about, staring at me in fear, I was pleased. I would have thought they would have come thundering down upon me like an army and dragged me out of my gold clothes and said, 'Come stumble through eternity with us!' but they didn't.

"Suddenly I felt an unbearable heat. I saw a huge fire. I thought I heard my father's voice, but I wasn't sure, and then I heard Asenath say,

" 'It is powerful powerful magic! Do you want him to die! Give it to me!'

"For one brief second I saw my father, and in confusion, he gave over to her the old tablet, in its clay envelope. 'Azriel!' he called out. He reached beyond her, towards me.

"I wanted to speak but I was past it. I couldn't do anything.

"The doors were slammed shut on my father and on the world.

"We were in a chamber with a hot, hot fire, the cauldron full of gold boiling, and the air almost impossibly hot. And Asenath then broke the clay envelope of the old tablet. She just smashed the outer clay as if it was nothing, and then she held up the secret tablet to the light of the torch.

"I was standing on my own, too rigid to move, too rigid to fall, staring at them. I wasn't even too horribly afraid of the fire. What were they doing, Remath and the old woman? Where was the High Priest? Hadn't I glimpsed him now and then?

"And then Asenath began to read, but this was not Sumerian, it was Hebrew, old old Canaanite Hebrew.

" '. . . and that he should see his own death and that he should see his soul, his tzelem and his spirit and his flesh all boiled together in the bones, to live in the bones, forever, only to be called forth by the Master who knows his name, and calls his name . . .

" 'No!' I screamed. 'That is not a charm! That is Hebrew. That's a curse. You lying witch.'

"The gold covering on me cracked all over as I sprang with all my drunken strength at her, but she backed up like a dancer and Remath had me by the throat. I was as stupefied and weak as those lions who had come against it.

" 'You witch, that's a curse,' I said.

" 'That he shall see all of him that is visible and invisible and all fluids of his body boiled down into the bones, and that he shall be bound to those bones and whoever is Master of those bones, and that he shall not be taken into the darkness of Sheol nor the eternal life of God forever and ever.

" 'Marduk!' I screamed.

"I felt myself heaved backwards, and thrown into the boiling gold. I screamed and screamed. It was unthinkable. It was not possible that I could know such pain. It was not possible that such a thing could happen to me, that boiling gold should choke my mouth and cover my eyes!

"And when I thought I would go blank mad, blank mad with horror and pain, with nothing of human thought left, I shot upwards out of the cauldron, free-floating above the body that was slumped and boiling in the pot, with only one open eye above the bubbling gold. The body that had been mine! And I was not in it.

"I was there above, arms outstretched, staring down. And I saw the face of Asenath upturned.

" 'Yes, Azriel,' she screamed, 'watch, watch the gold boil, watch the flesh fall from your bones, watch the bones become the gold, don't take your eyes off it, lest you be drawn back down into agony and death.'

" 'Marduk,' I cried.

" 'It's your choice,' he said. 'Go back down into that cauldron of pain and you die.' His voice was broken or sad. I realized that he was below me. He stood looking up.

"And for the first time he looked small to me and simple. Not grand or godly. And Asenath was just an old fool of a woman. And Remath staring at the body sinking into the bubbling pot was jumping up and down and making his hands into fists and cursing and screaming.

"There was no time. There was no decision. Or maybe it was pure cowardice. I could not go down into that pain. I could not be boiled alive. I could not bear that such a thing would happen to any human being. I watched and I watched, and the flesh floated loose in the golden muck and the skull floated to the top, and the pot boiled and boiled and boiled and the room grew denser and denser with steam.

"Asenath was choking. She could not breathe, and she fell forward on her face. Remath stood staring at the pot. And Marduk merely looked up at me with wonder.

"At last the pot was empty save what was left of me. Remath kicked and poked at the fire to put it out. He drew as close as he could to the hot metal and he looked down at the heap of golden bones that lay in the bottom of the pot. The cloth was gone, it had dissolved, the flesh was gone, it had dissolved, the liquid was gone, it had dissolved. Only the bones were left and in this sealed chamber all the fumes and particles of what had been my body. And the bones were all gold.

" 'Call it to you, spirit,' said Remath. 'Call the flesh to you, call it to you now from all the world, call it from the depth of the bones and from the air to which it has tried to flee, call it.'

"I moved downwards and stood on my feet. In the thick torturous steam, I saw I had a body. It was vapor. But it was mine, and then it grew denser and denser.

"Marduk took a step backwards, shaking his head.

" 'What is it? Why do you do that?' I asked.

" 'Oh gods of old, Remath,' said Marduk, 'what have you and the witch wrought?'

"Remath roared, 'You are mine, Servant of the Bones, for I am the Master of the Bones. You will obey me. You will obey.'

"Marduk backed up against the wall, staring at me in perfect fear.

"Remath grabbed a heavy bunch of cloth from the couch to protect his hands and with this he managed to throw over the cauldron.

The bones spilled out and what did not spill he reached for, hurt by the heat until he had all the bones on the floor.

" 'Wake up, old woman!' he screamed. 'Wake up! What do I do now!'

"I stood beside him. My body was dense as if it were living. It was pinkish and vivid as his body, but it wasn't real. It didn't feel real. It had no heart, no lungs, no soul, no blood; it had only the shape that my spirit gave to it, down to the last detail.

" 'Look, fool,' I said, 'Asenath is dead. If you want to know what to do, you'd better bring that tablet to me, I am the only one here who can read the old Canaanite words.' "

7

Remath did not move. He was far too frightened to move. He even let go of the bones. They lay gleaming on the glazed floor. Scattered, hideous, teeth among them, and the tiny bones of my hands and feet like pebbles.

"Marduk remained still.

"There was a low howling sound gathering round us. I could hear it as if a wind moved through the rest of the palace and temple, slowly, corridor by corridor, alcove by alcove, and then I looked up and saw the dense world of spirits as I had never seen it before.

"The walls and the ceiling of this cell were gone. The whole of the world was the lost mumbling souls staring and pointing and leaping towards me with grasping hands, yet afraid.

" 'Get away!' I roared. And at once the entire cloud dispersed, but the howling pierced my ears and hurt me, and when I looked again I saw that Marduk's face was alien to me, and no longer afraid, but neither trusting nor gentle as always before.

"I turned, walking easily and light as a man would walk to the body of the fallen Asenath, and I took from her the tablet. The text wasn't easy for me. It was a form of Hebrew, yes, but a dialect from the time before my time. I stood reading to myself.

"I turned around. The priest had withdrawn to the farthest corner and the god merely stared. I read the words as best I could:

" 'And having seen his death, and having seen the fluids of his body, and the flesh and the spirit and soul boiled into the bones, and sealed in the bones in gold forever, let him be called down into the bones, made to enter them, and made to remain in them, until his Master should call him forth.'

" 'Do it,' Remath cried. 'Go into the bones.'

"I looked down at the tablet. 'And once these bones are assembled, they shall forever contain his spirit, passing from one generation to another, to serve the Master by ownership and by power, to do the Master's bidding, and roam only at the Master's will. When the Master shall say, "Come," the Servant of the Bones will appear. When the Master says, "Take on flesh," the Servant of the Bones will take on flesh, and when the Master says, "Return to the bones," the Servant of the Bones will obey him, and when the Master says, "Kill this man for me," the Servant of the Bones shall kill that man, and when the Master says, "Lie quiet and watch, my slave," the Servant of the Bones shall do it. For the Servant and the Bones are now one. And no spirit under heaven can rival the strength of the Servant of the Bones.'

" 'Well,' I said, 'that is quite a story.'

" 'Into the bones,' he declared. 'Go into the bones.' He stood trembling, clenching his fists and bending his knees. 'Return to the bones!' he declared. 'Lie quiet and watch, my slave!' he declared.

"I did nothing.

"I studied him for a long moment. Nothing changed in me.

"I saw the linen he'd pulled from the couch. There was a sheet, fresh, changed from when I'd last slept here, and I picked it up now, and formed a sack out of it, and into it I put the tablet, and then the bones. I picked up the thigh bone, and the leg bone, and the arm bones, and the skull, my very own skull, still hot and gleaming with gold, and I gathered every tiny fragment of what had been Azriel, the living man, the fool, the idiot. I gathered the teeth, I gathered the bones of the toes. And when I had all of this in a small sack, knotted, I slung it over my shoulder and then I looked at him.

" 'Damn you into hell, go into the bones!' he roared.

"I went forward towards him and I put out my right hand and broke his neck. He was dead before he hit his knees. I saw a spirit rise blundering and in terror, gauzy and soon shapeless and then dispersed and gone.

"I looked at Marduk.

" 'Azriel, what will you do?' he asked. He seemed utterly confounded.

" 'What can I do, Lord? What can I do, but find the strongest Magician in Babylon, the one strong enough to help me learn my destiny and my limitations, or shall I simply wander as I am? I am nothing, as you see, nothing, only the semblance of the living. Shall I wander? Look, I am solid and visible, but I am nothing, and all that is left of me is in this sack.'

"I didn't wait for his answer. I turned and I left. I turned my back on him as it were. I dismissed him, sadly, I think, and rudely and thoughtlessly and I had a sense of him hovering near me, watching me, as I went on.

"I went through the temple, in the convincing shape of a man, challenged again and again by guards whom I threw off with my right hand. A spear passed through my back. A sword passed through my body. I felt nothing, but merely looked at the perplexed and miserable assailant. I walked on.

"I walked into the palace and I walked towards the chambers of the King. His guards fell on me and I stepped through them, feeling this no more than a shudder and saw them stumble behind me, and then I looked up and saw Marduk watching from afar.

"I went into the King's chamber. Cyrus was in bed with a beautiful harlot, and when he saw me, he leapt up naked from the bed.

" 'Do you know me?' I said. 'What do you see?'

" 'Azriel!' he declared, and then with genuine joy he said, 'Azriel, you've cheated death, they've saved you, oh, my son, my son.'

"This was so heartfelt and honest that I was stunned. He came towards me but as he put his arms around me he realized I was nothing, only the appearance of something solid, as a shell more or less, or even lighter than that, a bubble on the surface of the water so light it could explode. But it did not. I did not. I merely felt his heavy strong arms around me and then he backed away from me.

" 'Yes, I am dead, Lord King,' I said. 'And all that is left of me is here in this sack, and covered with gold. Now you must repay me.'

" 'How, Azriel?' he asked.

" 'Who is the greatest sorcerer in all the world? Surely Cyrus knows. Is the strongest and wisest of wise men in Persia? In Ionia? Or is he in Lydia? Tell me where he is. I am a horror. I am a horror! Even Marduk fears me now! Who is the wisest man, Cyrus, to whom you would trust your own damned soul if you stood here as I do!'

"He sank down on the side of the bed. The harlot meantime had covered herself with the sheets and merely stared. Marduk came silently into the room, and though his face was no longer cold with suspicion it lacked the warmth we'd always shared.

" 'I know who it is,' said Cyrus. 'Of all the wizards ever paraded before me, only this man had true power and simplicity of soul.'

" 'Send me to him. I look human, do I not? I look alive? Send me to him.'

" 'I will,' he said. 'He is in Miletus, where he roams the markets daily, purchasing manuscripts from all the world, he is in the great Greek port city, gathering to himself knowledge. He says the purpose of all life is to know and to love.'

" 'You are saying then that he is a good man?'

" 'Don't you want a good man?'

" 'I hadn't even thought of it,' I said.

" 'What about your own people?'

"The question confused me. In one instant I knew a whole list of names and I could smell skin and hair, and then the identity of these beings was gone. 'My own people? Do I have people?' I tried desperately to backtrack, to recover my memory. How had I come to this room! I could remember the cauldron. I could remember that woman but what was her name, and the priest I'd slain, the god, the good gentle god who stood there, invisible to the King, who was he?

" 'You are Cyrus, King of Persia and Babylonia, King of all the world,' I said. I was horrified that I did not know the names of those I loved, for surely I had only moments ago. And that old woman who had died, I had known her all my life! I turned and looked around the room in confusion. It was filled with offerings, gifts from noble families of all Babylonia. I saw a casket, made of cedar and gold. It wasn't big. I went to it, and opened it.

"The King watched speechless. Inside were plate and goblets.

" 'Take them if you wish,' said Cyrus, very well masking his fear. 'Let me call my Seven Wise Men to me.'

" 'I want the casket only,' said I. I emptied out the contents gently, so as not to dent these precious things and then I held the cedar box and I could smell the cedar beneath the red silk padding that lined it. I tore open the poor linen sack and into this casket I first put the tablet with all its writing, including words I hadn't even read aloud yet, and then I laid down gently my bones.

"I wasn't even finished when the beautiful harlot had come, and she put out a golden silk veil. 'Here, to wrap them,' she said. 'To cushion them.' I took it and it wrapped the bones, and she brought me another of deep purple, and I accepted that and wrapped them more securely so that when the casket moved now they wouldn't make any sound. I had scarcely looked at them.

" 'Send me into them, Cyrus,' I said. 'Send me into the bones!'

"Cyrus shook his head.

"Marduk spoke up. 'Azriel, go yourself into them and then come out again, do it now or you will never be able to do it, or you will never know. This is the advice of a spirit, Azriel. Cast aside all the particles that make up your form and seek the darkness and if you cannot come out, I will call you forth.'

"The King who could neither hear nor see Marduk was confused. Once again he mentioned his Seven Wise Men, and indeed, I could hear men outside the chamber, I could hear their whispering.

" 'Don't let them enter, Lord,' I said. 'Wise men are liars; priests are liars; gods are liars!'

" 'I understand you, Azriel,' said Cyrus. 'You are an angel of might or demon of might. I don't know which, but no ordinary wise man can guide you.'

"I looked to Marduk.

" 'Go into the bones,' he said. 'I promise to use all my power to bring you out. See if you can seek refuge there as I do in my statue. You must have refuge!'

"I bowed my head. 'Into the bones, until I will myself to return; all of you that are parts of me, you are to remain near and wait for me till I summon you.'

"A huge wind caught the bed hangings. The harlot ran to the King and he quietly enfolded her in his arms. And I felt immense and airy—indeed I touched the walls and the ceiling and the four corners of the painted room and then the whirlwind tightened around me, and I felt the intolerable press of the howling, screaming souls. 'No, you don't, damn you!' I shouted. 'The bones, I have the refuge of my own bones. I go into my bones.'

"There was darkness. Perfect darkness and stillness. I drifted. It was the sweetest rest I had ever known. Only I should do something now, should I not? But I couldn't. I couldn't. And then came the voice of Marduk,

" 'Servant of the Bones, rise and take form.'

"Of course, that was what I had to do, and I did it. It was like a deep intake of breath and then a soundless shout. I found myself again a tolerably perfect replica of Azriel standing beside the open casket and the golden bones. My body shimmered in my own eyes and then grew steady. I felt the cool air as if I had never known it before.

"I looked at Cyrus. I looked at Marduk. I knew now that if I entered into the bones, I didn't have the power to return. But what did it matter? There was velvet sleep. There was the sleep you sleep when you are a boy and lie on the warm grass of a hill and the breeze strokes you, and you have no cares in all the world.

" 'Lord King,' I said, 'I beg you. I will go now back into the bones. Send them in this casket with the tablet to your wise man in Miletus. Do that for me, and if you do betray me, what of it? I won't know. Someone else . . . has betrayed me, but I can't remember who it is . . .'

"He came forward to kiss me. The kiss was on the lips in the Persian style of kings and equals. I turned and looked at Marduk.

" 'Marduk, come with me, I can't remember what is between us except that it was always good.'

" 'I haven't the power, Azriel,' he said calmly. 'It's as the Lord King Cyrus says. You are what the Magi call an angel of might or a demon of might. I have no such power. The tender flame of my thoughts is fed by the people of Babylon who believe in me and pray to me. Even in captivity, the devotion of my captors sustained me. I can't go with you. I don't even know how.'

"His brow became furrowed. 'But why trust any man, even a King?' he asked. 'Take the casket yourself and go where you would . . .'

" 'No. Look, even now the body quavers. I am newborn and not that strong. I can't. I have to trust in . . . Cyrus, King of the Persians, and if he would get rid of me, if he would be as vile to me and as cruel to me as all those whom I loved, if he would do that, I will find a way for vengeance, won't I, great King?'

" 'I won't give you cause,' said Cyrus. 'Turn your hatred from me. It wounds me. I can feel it.'

" 'So can I,' I said. 'And it feels divine to hate! To be angry! To destroy!'

"I took a step towards him.

"He didn't move an inch. He stared at me, and I felt myself gently transfixed, unable to do anything really but look into his eyes. I didn't try very hard to oppose him, but I felt his domination, rooted in fearlessness and victory, and I stood still.

" 'Trust in me, Azriel, for today you made me King of the World, and I will see that you are taken to the Magus who will teach you all a spirit can be taught.'

" 'King of the World? Did I do that for you, beautiful man?' I asked. I shook myself all over. Of course, I knew him. I knew the drama. The lion's breath.

"But then I didn't. I knew nothing.

"Marduk spoke up, but by now Marduk was merely a spirit standing there, friendly and good.

" 'Azriel, do you know who I am?'

" 'A friend, a spirit friend?'

" 'What more?'

"I was anguished. 'I don't remember,' I said. I told him that I could remember the cauldron, murdering that nameless priest and the dead old woman. I knew the King. I knew him. But I couldn't really remember. I caught the sudden scent of roses. I looked down and saw the floor was littered with petals.

" 'Give them to him,' said Cyrus, pointing to the petals as he spoke to the harlot.

"And the sweet gentle harlot gathered up the petals in handfuls.

" 'Put them in the casket for me,' I said. 'What is this city? Where are we?'

" 'Babylon,' said Cyrus.

" 'And you are sending me to Miletus to a great wizard. I must know and remember his name.'

" 'He'll call you,' said Cyrus.

"I took one last look at them. I walked to the windows which were open to the river and I looked out and I thought, What a beautiful city this is, it is so filled with burning lights tonight, and so much laughter and merriment.

"Without raising my voice, I dissolved my form once more, raging at the souls as they surrounded me and plunged again into the velvet blackness, only this time I could smell the roses, and with the roses there came a memory, a memory of a procession, and people cheering and crying, and waving, and a handsome man singing with a beautiful voice, and petals tossed so high they showered down on us, on our shoulders . . . but the memory faded.

"I was not to remember these moments, these things, what I have told here for two thousand years."

Azriel sat back.

It was almost daylight.

He closed his eyes.

"You have to rest now, Jonathan," he said, "or you'll be sick again, and I must sleep, and I fear what will happen. But I'm tired, tired!"

"Where are the bones, Azriel?" I asked.

"That I'll tell you when we wake. I'll tell you everything that happened with Esther, with Gregory and the Temple of the Mind. I'll tell you . . ."

He seemed too weary to continue.

He stood up and then very firmly helped me up from the chair. "You must drink more broth, Jonathan."

He gave it to me, from a cup by the hearth, and I drank it, and then he helped me into the small bathroom of the cabin and politely he turned his back as I made water, and then he helped me to bed.

I was shaking badly. My throat was thick, my tongue swollen.

I could see that he was in great anxiety. The telling of the tale had been an ordeal.

He must have read my sympathy. "I'll never tell it again to anyone else," he said. "I don't ever want to say it again, I don't ever want to see the boiling cauldron—" His voice dried up.

He shook his head and his thick hair to wake himself, and then he helped me into the bed. He made me drink more cool water, which was very good.

"Don't fear for me," I said. "I'm well. Only a little tired, a little weak." I took one last deep drink of water then offered the bottle to him and he drank more deeply. And he smiled.

"What can I do for you now?" I asked. "You're my guest and my protector."

"Would you let me sleep beside you?" he said. "As if we were just boys together in the field, so that . . . that . . . so that . . . if the whirl-wind comes for me, so that if the souls come, I can reach out and touch your warm hand."

I nodded. He put me under the covers, and then he climbed in be-side me. I turned towards him and he faced away. I put my arm over him. The red velvet robe he wore felt comfortable and thick and warm. I had my arm around him. He went limp, as it were, in the covers, his head deep into the pillow, the big mass of black curls close to my face, and smelling of the clean air outside and the sweet smoke from the fire.

The sunlight was just creeping under the door. And I could tell by its brightness and the warmth of the room that the snowstorm had slacked off. The fire was healthy. The morning was quiet.

I woke once at noon.

I was hot and mumbling and having a horrible dream. He lifted me up and gave me a big drink of cool water. He had put snow in it, and it tasted clean. I drank and drank, and then I lay back down.

He seemed to shimmer, a figure clad in red with deep black eyes. His beard and hair looked silky, and I thought of all the old texts that tell of ointments and oils and perfumes for hair; his hair was worthy of all that, I thought. There came back to me a panorama of the wall carvings I'd seen all over the world.

I saw the great Assyrian carvings in the British Museum. I saw the pictures in books. "The black-headed people," that was what the Su-merians had called themselves. And we had come from them, or somehow mingled in them, and I knew now that those strange carv-ings of bearded kings in robes were nearer to me than European emblems I'd cherished as familiar when in fact they mattered very little at all.

"You slept well?" I asked, but I was already drifting off.

"Yes," he said. "You sleep now. I'm going out into the snow to walk. You sleep, you hear me? I'll have your supper for you when you wake."

8

In the very late afternoon I awoke. I could tell again by the light beneath the door that we must have a blue sky and a brightly dying sun.

He wasn't in the house, which was little more than one room. I got up, wrapping my heaviest robe around me, a cashmere robe, and then I looked for him—in the little rooms off the back, the bathroom, the pantry. He wasn't there. I remembered what he said about walking in the snow, but his absence unnerved me.

Then I stared down at the hearth, and I saw the large pot of broth filled with potatoes and carrots he'd put in it, and that meant I hadn't dreamt all this. Someone had come. I also felt very faintly sick. My head wasn't wondrously clear yet, the way it would feel when the illness was completely flown away.

I looked down at my feet. I had on thick wool socks with leather soles. He must have put these on me. I went to the door. I had to find him, find out where he was. I was in terror suddenly that he was gone. Utter terror.

I was in utter terror for a whole series of reasons, and I don't know what they were.

I put on my big boots, and my greatcoat, which is an enormous bulky garment, weighing a ton and made to cover the thickest sweaters, and then I opened the door.

The dying sun was still gleaming on the distant snow of the mountains, but otherwise the light was gone from the sky. The world was gray and white, metallic and growing dim.

I didn't see him anywhere. The air was still and tolerable as it can be in the worst winter, when for a moment there is no wind. Icicles hung from the roof above me. The snow showed no tracks. It looked fresh, and it wasn't impossibly deep.

"Azriel!" I called out to him. Why was I so desperate? Did I fear for him? I knew I did. I feared for him, for me, for my sanity, for my wits, for the security and peace of my entire life . . .

I shut the door, and walked out some distance from the house. The cold began to hurt my face and hands. This was plain stupid and I knew it. The fever would come back. I couldn't stay out here.

I called to him several times, and heard nothing. It was a beautiful snow-laden scene around me in the dusk. The firs wore their snow with dignity, and the evening stars were beginning to shine. The sun had gone. But it was twilight.

I noticed the car some distance away; I had been looking at it all this time, more or less, but had not noticed it because it was all covered with snow. A thought came to me. I hurried to the car, realizing that my feet were already numb, and I opened up the back of it.

There was an old television set there, a portable, the kind they make for fishermen to take on boats. It had a tiny screen, and it was long and with a built-in handle, rather like a giant flashlight. It ran on D-cell batteries. I hadn't used it in years. I picked it up, closed the jeep, and ran back to the house.

As soon as I shut the door, I felt like a traitor to him. I felt as if I wanted to spy upon the world he'd spoken of—the Belkin world, the ugly, ugly world of terrorism and disgusting violence spawned by the Temple of the Mind.

I shouldn't need this, I thought. Well, perhaps it won't even work. I sat down by the fire, took off my boots, and warmed my hands and feet. Stupid, stupid, I thought, but I wasn't shivering. Then I went to the big stash of batteries and I filled up the little television, which I held by its handle, and brought it back so that I could sit in my chair.

Pulling up the aerial, I turned the dial. I had never used this thing here. It had been in the car forever. If I'd remembered it before I had left, I would not have taken it out.

But in a boat I'd used it, fishing five summers ago, and now, as then, it worked. It brought in flashes of black and white, zigzag lines, and then finally a "news voice," very distinct, with the authority of a network, summing up the latest events.

I turned up the volume. The picture danced and wiggled and then flipped, but the voice was coming clear. War in the Balkans had taken another terrible turn. Shells heaved into Sarajevo had killed people in a hospital. In Japan, the cult leader had been arrested for conspiracy to commit murder. A murder had happened in a nearby town. It went on and on, the packing of fact into swift crisp sentences . . . the picture was steadying. I saw an anchorwoman, a news face, not distinct, but I could focus now more clearly on the voice.

". . . horrors of the Temple of the Mind continue. All members in the Bolivian temple are now dead, having set fire to the compound themselves rather than surrender to international agents. Meanwhile, arrests of Gregory Belkin's followers continue in New York."

I was excited. I picked up the little thing and held it close to look at it. I saw blurry fast coverage of those arrested, handcuffed, and chained.

". . . enough poisonous gas in New York City alone to have killed the entire population. Meantime, Iranian authorities have confirmed to the United Nations that all members of Belkin's Temple are in custody, however the question of extradition of the Belkin terrorists to the United States will, according to officials, take considerable time. In Cairo, it has been confirmed that all Belkin's followers have surrendered to authorities. All chemicals in their possession have been impounded."

More pictures, faces, men, shooting, fire, horrid fire reduced to a tiny flash of black and white in my hands. Then the bright face of the newswoman, and a change of tone, as she looked directly in the eyes of the camera and into mine.

"Who was Gregory Belkin? Were there in fact twin brothers, Nathan and Gregory, as those closest to the mogul–cult leader suspect? Two bodies remain, one buried in the Jewish cemetery, the other in the Manhattan morgue. And though the remnants of the Hasidic community in Brooklyn, founded by Belkin's grandfather, refuse to talk to authorities, the coroner's office continues to investigate the two men."

The woman's face vanished. Azriel appeared. A photograph of him, coarse and remote, but unmistakable.

"Meantime the man accused of the murder of Rachel Belkin, the man who might in fact be deeply involved in the entire conspiracy, is still at large."

Then came a series of still pictures, obviously gleaned from video surveillance cameras—Azriel beardless and without his mustache walking through the lobby of a building; Azriel in the crowd crying out over the body of Esther Belkin. Azriel in close-up, beardless without his mustache, staring directly in front of him as he went through a door. There was a string of shots, almost too blurry to mean anything, obviously taken from other surveillance cameras, including one of the beardless Azriel walking with Rachel Belkin herself, mother of Esther, wife of Gregory, or so the commentator informed me. Of Rachel, all I saw was a slender body, impossibly high-heel shoes, and mussed hair. But there was Azriel, no doubt.

I was enthralled.

The face of a bald male official, also suffering in freezing weather, probably that of Washington, D.C., appeared suddenly with the reassuring assertion:

"There is no reason at all to fear the Temple or its grandiose schemes. Every single location has been either raided by police, burned during the raid by its own members, or thoroughly cleared, with all members under lock and key. As for the mysterious man, we have no eyewitnesses to him at all after the night of Rachel Belkin's death, and he may very well have perished in the New York Temple along with hundreds of others during the fire that lasted a full twenty-four hours before police could get it under control."

Another man, even more authoritarian and perhaps angry, took the microphone. "The Temple is neutralized; the Temple has been stopped; even as we speak, banking connections are being investigated and arrests have already been made in the financial communities of Paris, London, and New York."

There was a crash of static, of glittering white lights on the little screen. I shook the tiny television. The voice talked again, but this time it was about a terrorist bomb in South America, about drug lords, about trade sanctions against Japan. I put down the little thing. I turned it off. I might have cruised a while for another channel, but I had had enough.

I coughed a couple of times, caught off guard by how deep the

cough sounded and by how much it hurt me, and then I tried to remember: Rachel Belkin. Rachel Belkin murdered. That had happened
only days after Esther Belkin. Rachel Belkin in Miami. Murdered.

Twins. I remembered the picture Azriel had shown to me—the
Hasid with the beard and locks and the silk hat.

From some giant filing system in my mind it came to me that Rachel Belkin had been the socialite wife of Gregory, a conspicuous
critic of his Temple, and the only time I had even noticed the woman's
name, reputation, or existence is when I'd caught a fragment of the
funeral of Esther. And the cameras had followed her mother to a black
car, voices clamoring for her opinions. Had Belkin's enemies killed her
daughter? Was it a Middle Eastern terrorist plot?

A wave of dizziness came over me. It threatened to get worse. I put
down the television and went back to the bed. I lay down. I was tired
and thirsty. I covered up, then sat up enough to drink more of the water. I drank it and drank it and drank it and then lay back and I
thought.

What seemed real was not the television set and its cryptic reports.

What seemed real was this room, and the way the fire danced, and
that he had been here. And what seemed real was the image of the
cauldron filled with boiling liquid and the unspeakable, unimaginable
idea of being cast into such a thing. Cast into boiling liquid. I closed
my eyes.

Then I heard him singing again:

"By the rivers of Babylon, there we sat down, yea, we wept, when
we remembered Zion."

I heard myself singing it.

"Come back, Azriel, come back! Tell me what else happened!" I
said, and then I slept.

The sound of the door opening woke me. It was completely dark
outside now, and it was deliciously warm in the room. All the chill was
gone out of my bones.

I saw a figure standing by the hearth looking down at the flames.
I let out a little cry before I could catch myself. Not exactly manly or
courageous.

But a steam rose from the figure, or a mist, and the figure appeared
to be Gregory Belkin, to have that man's head at least and hair, and

then to be shifting back into the massive curls of Azriel, and Azriel's scowl. Another attempt was made. A putrid smell filled the room, as foul as the smell in a morgue. Then it grew faint.

Azriel, restored to himself, was there, with his back to me. He spread out his arms and he said something that was probably Sumerian but I don't know. He called for something, and the something was a sweet fragrance.

I blinked. I could see rose petals in the air. I felt them fall on my face. The morgue smell was gone.

Before the fire, he stretched out his arms again and he changed; it was a pale image of Gregory Belkin; it flickered, and at once his own form swallowed it. And he let down his arms with a sigh.

I climbed out of bed and went to the tape recorder.

"May I turn it on?" I said.

I looked up and saw him in the full light of the fire now, and I realized he was wearing a suit of blue velvet trimmed in an old gold motif around the collar, the ends of the sleeves, and the pant legs. He wore a thick belt of the same color embroidered in gold and his face looked slightly older than it had before.

I stood up and came close to him as politely as I could. What had changed, precisely? Well, his skin was slightly darker, like that of a man who lived in the sun, and his eyes definitely bore more detail, the lids having softened and become less than perfect and perhaps more beautiful. I could see the pores of his skin and the small random hairs, dark, fine, at the edges of his hair.

"What do you see?" he asked.

I sat down, near to the tape recorder. "Everything is a little bit darker and more detailed," I said.

He nodded. "I can no longer summon the shape of Gregory Belkin at will. As for the semblance of anyone else, I cannot hold it very long. I am not a scientist enough to understand it. Someday it will be understood. It will have to do with particles and vibration. It will have to do with things mundane."

I was in a fury of curiosity.

"Have you tried to take any other form, the form of someone you like perhaps a little more than Gregory Belkin?"

He shook his head. "I can make myself ugly if I want to frighten you, but I don't want to be ugly. I don't want to frighten anyone. Hate has abandoned me, and it's taken some power with it, I imagine. I can work tricks. Watch this."

He put his hands up round his neck, and slowly drew them down the embroidered front of his coat, revealing as he did a necklace of engraved gold disks, like ancient coins. The entire house rattled. The fire flared for an instant, and then became smaller.

He picked up the necklace, to demonstrate the solidity and the weight of it, and then he let it drop.

"You have a fear of animals?" he asked me. "A distaste for wearing their skins? I see no skins here, warm skins, like bearskins."

"No fear at all," I said. "No distaste."

The temperature of the room rose dramatically, and once again the fire exploded as if someone had fanned it, and I felt myself surrounded by a large dark bearskin blanket, lined in silk. I put my hand up and felt the fur. It was deep and luxurious and made me think of Russian woods, and men in Russian novels who are always dressed in fur. I thought of Jews who used to wear fur hats in Russia, and maybe still do.

I sat up, adjusting the blanket more comfortably around me.

"That's quite wonderful," I said. I was trembling. So many thoughts were racing in me that I couldn't think what to say first.

He gave a deep sigh and rather dramatically collapsed in his chair.

"This has exhausted you," I said. "The changes, the tricks."

"Yes, somewhat. But I'm not exhausted for talking, Jonathan. It's that I can only do so much and no more . . . but then . . . who knows? What is God doing to me?

"I just thought that this time, after this ordeal was completed, you know, that the stairway would come . . . or there would be deep sleep. I thought . . . so many things.

"And wanted a finish."

He paused. "I've learnt something," he said. "I've learnt in these last two days that to tell a story is not what I thought."

"Explain to me."

"I thought to talk about the boiling cauldron would send the pain out of me. It didn't. Unable to hate, to muster anger, I feel despair."

He paused.

"I want you to tell me the whole story. You do believe in it. That's why you came, to tell it all."

"Well, let's say that I will finish, because . . . someone should know. Someone should record. And out of courtesy for you because you are gracious and you listen and I think you want to know."

"I do. But I must tell you how difficult it was to imagine such cruelty, to imagine that your own father gave you up to it. And to imagine a death so contrived. Do you still forgive your father?"

"Not at the moment," he said. "That's what I was talking about, that telling it did not produce forgiveness. It drew me close to him, to tell it, to see him."

"He wasn't as strong as you, on that he was right."

A silence fell between us. I thought of Rachel Belkin, the murder of Rachel Belkin, but I said nothing.

"Did you like walking in the snow?" I asked.

He turned to me in surprise and smiled. It was very bright, and kind.

"Yes, I did, but you haven't eaten your supper which I warmed for you. No, sit there, I'll get it, and one of your silver spoons."

He was as good as his word. I ate a bowl of the stew, as he watched with his arms folded.

I put aside the empty plate and at once he took it and then the spoon. I heard the sound of water running as he washed them. He brought back to me a small clean bowl of water and a towel, as someone might have done in another country. I didn't need it. But I dipped my fingers, and I used the cloth to wipe my mouth clean, which felt rather comforting, and he took these things away.

It was now that he saw the little boat television set with its built-in handle and tiny screen. I'd probably left it too near the fire. I felt a surge of embarrassment, as though I had spied upon his world while he was gone, as if to verify things he said.

He looked at the thing for a long moment and then away.

"It works? It talked to you?" he asked without enthusiasm.

"News from some local town, network I think, coming through the local channel. The Belkin Temples have been raided, people arrested, the public is being reassured."

He waited a long time before he answered. Then he said,

"Yes, well, there are some others, perhaps, that they haven't found yet, but the people in them are dead. When you come upon these men with their gun belts, and their vow to kill themselves along with the entire population of a country, it's best just to . . . kill them on the spot."

"They showed your face," I said, "smooth shaven."

He laughed. "Which means they'll never find me under all this hair."

"Especially not if you cut the long part but that would be rather a shame."

"I don't need to," he said. "I can still do the most important thing of all."

"Which is what?"

"Disappear."

"Ah! I'm glad to hear it. Do you know they are looking for you? They said something about the murder of Rachel Belkin. I hardly know the name."

He seemed neither surprised nor insulted nor upset in any way.

"She was Esther's mother. She didn't want to die in Gregory's house. But I'll tell you the strange part. When he looked at her dead body, I think he was grief-stricken. I think he actually loved her. We forget that such men can love."

"Do you want to tell me . . . whether or not you killed her? Or is that something I shouldn't ask?"

"I didn't kill her," he said simply. "They know that. They were there. That was early. Why would they bother to look for me anymore?"

"It's all to do with conspiracy, and banks, and plots, and the long tentacles of the Temple. You're a man of mystery."

"Ah, yes. And as I said, I am one who can, if necessary, disappear."

"Go to the bones?" I asked.

"Ah, the bones, the golden bones."

"You ready to tell me?"

"I'm thinking how to do it. There's a little more that I should tell before I come to the moment of Esther Belkin's death. There were masters I did love. I should explain a little more."

"You won't tell me about all of them?"

"Too many," he said, "and some are not worth remembering, and some I can't remember at all. There are two I want to describe to you. The first and the last master whom I ever obeyed. I stopped obedience to any master. I slew when called—not only the man who had called me or the woman, but everyone who had witnessed the calling. I did that for years and years. And then the bones were encased with warnings in Hebrew and German and Polish and no one took the risk to call the Servant of the Bones.

"But I want to tell you about the two—the first and the last masters I obeyed. The others which I do recall we can dismiss with a few words."

"You look more cheerful now, more rested," I said.

"I do?" He laughed. "How is that? Ah, well, I did sleep and I am strong, very strong, there's no doubt of it. And the story has a way of calling me back."

He sighed.

"I don't know much life in death without pain," he said. "But that I deserve, I imagine, being a demon of might. The last Master I obeyed was a Jew in the city of Strasbourg and they burned all the Jews there because they blamed them for the Black Death."

"Ah," I said. "That must have been the fourteenth century."

"The year 1349 of the current era," he said with a smile. "I looked it up. They killed the Jews then all over Europe, blaming them for the Black Death."

"I know. Yes, and there have been many holocausts since."

"Do you know what Gregory told me? Our beloved Gregory Belkin? When he thought he was my master and that I would help him?"

"I can't guess."

"He told me that if the Black Death had not come to Europe, Europe would be a desert today. He said that the population had grown rampant; that the trees were being cut down so fast that the entire forests of old Europe were gone by that time. And the forests of Europe we know now date back to the fourteenth century."

"That's true," I said. "I think. Is that how he justified the murder of people?"

"Oh, that was one of just many ways. Gregory was an extraordinary man, really, because he was an honest man."

"Not mad, to found this worldwide temple and fill it with terrorists?"

"No," he shook his head. "Just ruthless and honest. He said to me at one point that there was one man who had utterly changed the history of the world. I thought he would say that that man was Christ or Cyrus the Persian. Or perhaps Mohammed. But he said no. The man who changed the entire world was Alexander the Great. That was his model. Gregory was perfectly sane. He intended to break a giant Gordian knot. He almost succeeded. Almost—"

"How did you stop him? How did it all come about?"

"A fatal flaw in him stopped him," he said. "Do you know in the old Persian religion, one legend is that evil came into the world not through sin, or through God, but through a mistake. A ritual mistake?"

"I've heard of it. You're talking of very old myths, fragments of Zoroastrianism."

"Yes," he said, "myths the Medians gave to the Persians and the Persians passed on to the Jews. Not disobedience. Bad judgment. It's almost that way in Genesis, wouldn't you say? Eve makes a mistake in judgment. A ritual rule is broken. That must be different from sin, don't you think?"

"I don't know. If I knew that, I would be a happier man."

He laughed.

"What undid Gregory was a flaw in judgment," he said.

"How?"

"He counted on my vanity being as great as his. Or maybe he just misjudged my power, my willingness to intervene . . . No, he thought I would be swept up with his notions; he thought they were irresistible. It was an error in judgment. Had he not told me things, key things right at the appropriate moment, even I could not have stopped his plan. But he had to tell, to boast, to be recognized by me, and to be loved . . . I think, even be loved by me."

"Did he know what you were? The Servant of the Bones? A spirit?"

"Oh, yes, we came together without any question of credibility, as you would say today. But I'll get to that."

He sat back. I checked the tape recorders. I removed the small cassettes and replaced them with fresh cassettes, and then made markings on the labels so that I wouldn't confuse myself. I laid both machines back on the hearth.

He was watching me with keen interest and an agreeable look.

Yet he seemed reluctant to begin, or to be finding it difficult, yet yearning to do it.

"Did Cyrus the Persian keep his word to you?" I asked. I had been thinking of this on and off since we'd broken off. "Did he actually send you to Miletus? I find it hard to believe that Cyrus the Persian would keep his word—"

"You do?" He looked at me and smiled. "But he kept his word to Israel, as you know. The Jews were allowed to leave Babylon and they went home and they made the Kingdom once again of Judea and they built the Temple of Solomon. You know all this from history. Cyrus kept his word to his conquered peoples and particularly the Jews. Remember, the religion of Cyrus was not so terribly different from our religion. At heart, it was a religion of . . . ethics, wouldn't you say?"

"Yes, and I know that under Persian rule Jerusalem prospered."

"Oh, indeed, always, for hundreds of years, up until the time of the Romans, actually, when the rebellions started, and then the final defeat of Masada. We speak of these things to remind ourselves. At the time, I knew nothing of what was to come. But even I knew that Cyrus would keep his word, that he would send me on to Miletus. I trusted him from the first moment I ever laid eyes on him. He wasn't a liar. Well, not as much as most men."

"But if he had his own wise men," I said, "why would he let something so powerful . . . I mean, someone so powerful . . . as you slip from his grasp?"

"He was eager to get rid of me!" Azriel said. "And frankly, so were his wise men! He didn't let me slip from his grasp. Rather he sent me to Zurvan, the most powerful Magus whom he knew. And Zurvan was loyal to Cyrus. Zurvan was rich and lived in Miletus which had fallen to Cyrus and the Persians without even a skirmish as Babylon had. Later on, of course, the Greeks of those Ionian cities, they would rise against the Persians. But at this time, when I stood there, glaring at the great King and begging that he send me to a powerful magician, Miletus was a thriving Greek city under Persian rule."

He studied me. I started to ask another question but he stopped me.

"You went into the cold, you shouldn't have. You're warm now, and the fever has risen just a little. You need cold water. I'll get it for you. You drink it and then we'll go on."

He rose from the chair and went to the door. He brought a bottle from near the door. It was very cold, indeed, I could see that, and I was thirsty.

I looked down and saw that he was pouring the water into a silver cup. It wasn't an ancient silver cup. It seemed rather new even, machine-worked perhaps, but it was beautiful, and of course it got cold all over with the water. It was like the Grail, or a chalice or something a Babylonian would drink from. Or perhaps Solomon.

There was another cup just like it in front of the chair.

"How did you make the cups?" I asked.

"Same as I make my garments. I call together all the particles that are required, to come unobtrusively and without disturbance. I am not such a good designer of cups. If my father had designed these cups, they would be gorgeous. I merely told the particles that they were to make ornate cups of the style of this time . . . There are many, many more words to it than that, much more energy, but that is the gist."

I nodded. I was grateful for the explanation.

I drank all the water. He filled it again. I drank. The cup was solid enough. Sterling. I studied it. It had a common Bacchanalian design to it, clustered grapes carved around the rim, and a simple pedestal foot. But it was very fine indeed.

I was holding it in both my hands, lovingly, I suppose, admiring the fluted shape of it, and the deep carving of the grapes, when I heard a faint sound emerge from it, and felt a tiny movement of air beneath my nostrils. I realized that my name was being written on the cup. It was in Hebrew. Jonathan Ben Isaac. The writing went all around and was small and perfect.

I looked at him. He lay back in his chair with his eyes closed. He took a deep breath.

"Memory is everything," he said softly under his breath. "Don't you think we can live with the idea that God is not perfect, as long as we are assured that God remembers . . . remembers everything . . ."

"Knows everything, that's what you mean. We want him to forget our transgressions."

"Yes, I suppose."

He poured another cup of water for himself into his goblet, nameless but identical to mine, and he drank it. Again he rested, drifting, staring at the fire, his chest heaving.

I wondered what it would be like to live in a world of figures such as his.

Was that what Esagila had been like? Robed and bearded men dripping with gold ornament, and shining with purpose.

"Do you know," he asked me, smiling, "that the old Persians, they thought that . . . during the last millennia before the final Resurrection men would gradually turn away from the eating of meat and milk, and even plants, and that they would be sustained only on water? Pure water."

"And then would come the Resurrection."

"Yes, the bony world would rise . . . the valley of bones would come to life." He smiled. "So I think sometimes, when I want to comfort myself that angels of might, demons of might, things such as me . . . that we are simply the last stage of humans . . . when humans can live on only water. So . . . we're not unholy. We are simply very far advanced."

I smiled. "There are those who believe our earthly bodies are only one biological stage, that spirits constitute another, that it's all a matter of atoms and particles, as you've said."

"You pay attention to those people?"

"Of course. I have no fear of death. I hope that my light will rejoin the light of God, but perhaps it won't. But I pay attention, lots of attention to what others believe. This isn't an age of indifference, though it may seem so."

"Yes, I agree with you," he said. "It's a practical, pragmatic time, when decency is the prime virtue—you know, decent clothes, decent shelter, decent food—"

"Yes," I said.

"But it's also a time of great luxurious spiritual thinking, maybe the only time when such thinking carries no penalty, for after all, one can preach anything and not be dragged away in chains. There is no Inquisition in the heart of anyone."

"No, there's an Inquisition, alive in the hearts of all fundamental-ists of all sects, but they don't in most parts of the world have the power to drag away the prophet or the blasphemer. That's what you've observed."

"Yes," he said.

There was a pause.

He sat up, obviously refreshed and willing to talk again. He turned slightly towards me, his left elbow back a bit, his arm outstretched on the arm of the chair. The gold on the blue velvet ran in loops and circles, which no doubt had a venerable history as a pattern, perhaps even a name. It was thick gold thread. It was twinkling in the light of the fire.

He glanced at the tapes. I made the gesture that we were all ears, all of us, the tapes and me.

"Cyrus kept his word," he said, with a shrug. "To everyone. He kept his word to my father's family, to the Hebrews of Babylon. Those Hebrews that wanted to, and not all did, by the way, but those that wanted to, went back to Zion and rebuilt the temple and the Persians were never cruel to Palestine. Trouble came only centuries later with the Romans, as we've said. And you know too that many, many Jews stayed in Babylon and they studied there and wrote the Talmud there, and Babylon was a place of great learning until some horrible day in later centuries when it was burnt and then destroyed. But that came much later. I wanted to tell you first of the two masters who taught me everything that would be of use."

I nodded. He let a silence fall and I didn't disturb it.

I looked into the fire, and for a moment I felt a dizziness, as if the pace of life, my heart, my breath, the world itself, had gradually slowed. The fire was made of wood I hadn't brought here. The fire was full of cedar as well as oak and other wood. It was perfumed and crackling, and for a moment I thought again that perhaps I was dead, that this was some kind of mental stage. I could smell incense, and a feeling of ineffable happiness came over me. I knew I was sick. I had a pain in my chest and my throat, but these things were of no impor-tance at all. I merely felt happy. What if I am dead, I thought.

"You're alive," he said in a soft, even voice. "May the Lord God Bless you and Keep you."

He was watching me. He said nothing.

"What is it, Azriel?" I asked.

"Only that I like you," he said. "Forgive me. I knew your books, I loved them, but I didn't know . . . that I would like you. I foresee now what my existence is going to be . . . I see something of what God has planned, but never mind on that. We talk of the past, not God and the future . . ."

Part II

AESTHETIC THEORY

Contrive a poem out of ears.
Tell it
so that its petals unchocolate
like a brain in a jar.
Wax walnut, melting with thought.
Make it a poem almost
lewdly knowledgable
and make its knowledge
ooze, syrup from the punched trunk.
Make it snake up to the molecule whorey
and put its mouth
atomic against the mouth of its core.
Pull on its stem
to expose its foetus. Make it
have children with sleek ginger jaws,
make the dogs moan when it passes,
let it out of its jar,
make it lie with our corpse, our chaos.
Make it hungry, evil, enemy of Death.
Put it on paper. Read it. Make surgery
its sigh, and of such sting
the scorpions call it Jehovah & Who.
Make it now before you crap out.
Contrive it, sperm it, stroke it,
make it efficient, make it fit,
make it more poem than Poem can survive.

Stan Rice, *Some Lamb* 1975

9

Now, I begin the story of my two masters and what they taught me. And I assure you that this will be the briefest part of my tale. I am eager to get on to the present. But I want this known and written down by you, if you will be so kind. So . . .

"Zurvan announced himself to me dramatically. As I told you, I had gone into the bones. I was in darkness and sleep. There was an awareness in me, and there always is, but I can't express it in words, this awareness. Perhaps I am like a tablet in my sleep upon which history is being written. But that image is too clumsy and concrete.

"I slept, I knew neither fear nor pain. I certainly didn't feel trapped. I didn't know what I was or where. Then Zurvan called me:

" 'Azriel, Servant of the Bones, come to me, invisible, your tzelem only, fly with all your might.' I felt I had been sucked up into the sky. I flew towards the voice that called me and as before, I saw the air full of spirits, spirits in all directions, and spirits through which I moved with great determination, trying not to hurt them, yet deeply dismayed by their cries and the look of desperation in their faces.

"Some of these spirits even grabbed onto me and tried to stop me. But I had my command, and I threw them off with wondrous strength, which made me laugh and laugh.

"When I saw the city of Miletus below me, it was midday; the air was clearing of spirits as I neared the earth, or at least I was now moving at a different rate of speed and they weren't visible to me. Miletus lay on its peninsula, the first Ionic or Greek colonial city that I had ever beheld.

"It was beautiful and spacious, containing wondrous open areas and colonnades and all the perfection of Greek art even at that early age. The agora, the palaestra, the temples, the amphitheater . . . it seemed all of it to be like a hand open to catch the summer breeze.

"And on three sides of it was the deep sea, filled with Greek and Phoenician and Egyptian merchant ships, and the harbor swarming with traders and with long lines of slaves in chains.

"The lower I dropped, the more I saw the beauty of it, which of course was not entirely unfamiliar to me in Babylon, but to see a city with so much splendid marble, to see it white and shining and not barricaded against the desert winds, that was the spectacle. It was a city where people went outdoors to talk and walk and gather and do the business of the day, and the heat was not unendurable, and the desert sands did not come.

"Into the house of Zurvan I came immediately and found him sitting at his desk with a letter in his hand.

"He was Persian, maybe I should say Median, black-haired, though with plenty of gray on his head and in his beard, though not too old, and with large blue eyes that looked up at me at once, perceiving my invisible shape perfectly, and then he said,

" 'Ah, make yourself flesh; you know how to do it. Do it now!'

"This was exactly the tack to take, I guess, because I took great pride in calling for a body. And I didn't really know any words then other than what had been on the tablet. But I had the body made and well made within seconds, and he sat back laughing with delight, his knee up, looking at me. I suppose I looked as I do now.

"I remember being too astonished by this lovely Greek house with its courtyard and doors open everywhere, and paintings on the wall of slender, big-eyed Greek persons in sinewy flowing garments that made me think of Egypt, but were definitely Ionic, unto themselves.

"He put his foot down on the floor, turned his folded arms, and then stood up. He was dressed in the looser, more naked Greek manner of clothing without fitted sleeves as we always wore, and he wore sandals. He studied me fearlessly as my father might have studied a piece of the silversmith's craft.

" 'Where are you fingernails, spirit?' he asked. 'Where is the hair on your face? Where are your eyelashes! Be quick! Hereafter you need only say "Bring to me all those details which I require at this moment" and nothing more. Fix an image and you've finished your work. That's it. That's it.'

"He clapped his hands.

" 'Now you are plenty complete enough for what you have to do. Sit there. I want to see you move about, walk, talk, lift your arms. Go on, sit down.'

"I did. It was a Greek chair, graceful with high arms and no back. Everywhere around me the light seemed glorious and different; outside, the clouds were piled higher. The air was clearer.

" 'That's because you are on the shores of the sea,' he said. 'Do you feel the water in the air, spirit? That will always aid you. That is why the addle-headed ghosts of the dead and the demons like damp places, they need the water, the sound of it, the smell of it, the coolness creeping into them, in whatever form they possess.'

"He made a long stroll about the room. Arrogantly I just sat there, showing him no respect. He didn't seem to care.

"A Babylonian or Persian full suit would have been more flattering to him with his thin old legs and feet. But it was too warm.

"I drifted from looking at him. I was marveling at the mosaic floor. Our own floors at home had often been as colorful and as well crafted, but this floor was not full of stiff rosettes or processional figures, but with frolicking dancers and great clusters of grapes for ornament, and there was every kind of inlaid marble around its borders. The designs were fluid and jubilant. I thought of all the Greek vases I had handled in the marketplace, and how I had loved their graceful work. The murals on the walls were equally lovely and lively, and there were the repeated bands of color which utterly delighted my eye.

"He stopped in the middle of the room. 'So we admire the beautiful, do we?' I didn't answer him. Then he said: 'Speak, I want to hear your voice.'

" 'And what shall I say?' I answered without rising. 'What I want to say? Or what you tell me to say? What my true thoughts are, or some servile nonsense—that I am your spirit-slave!'

"I broke off suddenly. I lost all confidence in myself. I realized I didn't know quite why I was saying these things. I struggled to remember. I had been sent to this man. This man was a great magician. This man was supposed to be a Master of his craft. I was a Servant. Who had made me that?

" 'Don't make yourself dissolve with all this petty worry,' he said. 'You speak well and clearly, that's what I wanted to know, and you think, and you are most powerful. You are perhaps the greatest angel of might I've ever seen, and nothing I've ever conjured has had your strength.'

" 'Who sent me? It was a King,' I said, 'But my mind is muddled suddenly, and it's agony not to know.'

" 'It's the trap of spirits, it's what keeps them weak, it's the hobbling of them provided by God, you might say, so that they don't ever gain strength enough to hurt men and women too much. But you know who sent you. Think! Make yourself come up with the answer. You are going to start remembering things now, you are going to start paying attention. And first, let go of the raging scream in you. I had nothing to do with those who hurt you and killed you. And I suspect there was much bungling to the whole affair, which a weaker spirit than you might never have overcome. But you did overcome it. And the man who sent you? He did as you asked him to do, remember? He did what you asked.'

" 'Ah, yes, King Cyrus, he did send me to Miletus as I asked.' It came clear and it was all the more clear when I tried to let the anger pass from me like so much air out of my lungs. I even felt my lungs. I felt myself breathe.

" 'Don't waste your time on that,' he said. 'Remember the questions I put to you? Your fingernails? Your eyelashes? Details that are visible. You need no inside organs. Your spirit fills up the perfect shell that you are, which no one can tell from a real man. Don't waste your strength making hearts for yourself, or blood or lungs, just to feel human. That's stupid and foolish. Only now and then you'll need to make a little blood flow from your body. That's nothing, but don't go hungering after your human form. You're better now!'

" 'Am I?' I asked, still slouching in the chair, ankle on my knee, as this older wiser man put up with my arrogance. 'Am I good, or am I something to do evil? You said angel of might. I heard the King use those words. But then he also said demon. Or was it someone else?'

"He stood in the middle of the room, rocking a little, and composed, studying me through narrow eyes.

" 'I suspect you will be what you want,' he said, 'though others may try to make you what they will. You have such hatred in you, Azriel, such hatred.'

" 'You're right. I do hate. I see a boiling cauldron and I feel terror and then hate.'

" 'Nobody's ever going to be able to hurt you like that again. And remember, you rose above the cauldron, did you not? Did you feel the scalding gold!'

"I shuddered all over. I gave way to tears. I can't even stand to talk now of it, and I didn't want to talk to him. 'I felt it for an instant,' I said, 'one instant I felt it and what it would mean to remain in it and die in that pain. I felt it . . . I felt it piercing through some covering on me, some thick numbing armor, but where it hurt me . . . was my eyes.'

" 'Ah, I see. Well, your eyes are fine now. I need the Canaanite tablet that brought you into being. I need the bones.'

" 'You don't have them here?'

" 'Hell, no,' he said. 'A pack of fools stole them. Desert bandits. They set upon Cyrus's party, slew them for every bit of gold they wore, and went off with the casket. They think the bones are solid gold. Only one Persian lived to reach the nearby village. Messages were sent. Now, you have to go and find the bones and the tablet, the whole casket, and bring it to me.'

" 'I can do this?'

" 'Certainly. You came when I called you. Go back to that place, or to the place from which you came. See, this is the secret of magic, my son. Be specific. Say I wish to return to the very place from which I came. That way, if the bandits have wandered ten miles from where you were when you heard my summons, you'll apprehend them. Now when you reach that place, remain corporeal and kill these thieves if you can. If you are not strong enough to do this, if they combat you with physical weapons which make you stagger, if they hurl charms at you that frighten you—and I warn you there isn't a charm on earth that ought to frighten the Servant of the Bones—then become incorporeal, but take the bones with you, gather them to yourself as though you were a funnel of desert wind, gather them and bring them to me. I will deal with these thieves later. Go, bring the bones to me.'

" 'But you do prefer that I kill them?'

" 'Desert bandits? Yes, kill them all. Kill them easily with their own weapons. Don't bother with magic. It would be a waste of strength. Grab their swords and cut their heads off. You'll see their spirits for a moment, shout at them to frighten them, believe me you won't have any trouble. Maybe that will soothe your pain. Go on, get the bones for me and the tablet. Hurry.'

"I stood up.

" 'Do I have to tell you what to say?' he prodded. 'Ask that you be returned to the place from which you came, and that all the articles of your present body wait at your beck and call to surround you and make you visible and strong when you reach the location of the bones. You'll love it. Hurry. I estimate this will take you until suppertime. I will be dining when you get back.'

" 'Can anything happen to me?'

" 'You can let them frighten you so that you fail and I can laugh at you,' he said with a shrug.

" 'Could they have powerful spirits?'

" 'Desert bandits, never! Look, you'll enjoy it! Oh, and I forgot to tell you, when you begin your return, of course become invisible. They'll all be dead, you'll hold the casket tightly inside your spirit body, like so much wind surrounding it. I don't want you walking back here in a body with that casket. You have to learn to move things. If anyone sees you, ignore that person because you'll be gone from the sight of that being before he begins to make sense of what he's seen. Hurry.'

"I rose to my feet and with an immense roaring in my ears, I re-appeared with the whole shell of the body in a small thick desert house, where a group of bedouins were gathered around a fire.

"At once they leapt to their feet and screamed at the sight of me and drew their swords.

" 'You stole the bones, didn't you?' I said. 'You killed the King's men.'

"I had never felt such pleasure in all my human life; I had never felt such prowess or such utter freedom. I think I gnashed my teeth with happiness. I took a sword from one of them and hacked them all, every one, to pieces, easily cutting off the hands that tried to defend them and slicing some heads from some bodies and kicking their limbs about. I stared at the fire. I dropped the sword and I walked into the fire, and then back out of it. It didn't hurt this body, or its appearance of humanity! I gave out a roar that must have been heard in Hell. I was hysterically happy.

"The place stank of blood and sweat. The death rattle came from one of them, and then he lay still. The door came open, two armed bedouins flew at me, and I grabbed one of them and twisted his head off his neck. The other was now on his knees. But I killed him the same way too—easily. I could hear the noise of the camels outside and shouting.

"But the room was now empty of living beings, and I saw a great heap there covered by rude wool blankets. Throwing them back I discovered the casket of my bones and looked inside. This I have to admit was not a pleasure. It broke the stride of my lusty killing. I looked and saw the bones, and then I sighed and thought, 'Ah, well, you knew you were dead. So what?' There was much other treasure there, too. Sacks of it.

"I gathered everything up into the blanket, clutched it with both arms, and said, 'Leave me, particles of this body. Allow me to be invisible, swift, and strong as the wind, and keep these precious articles safe in my arms, and take me to my Master in Miletus from whom I was sent.'

"The great treasure was like an anchor, a stone, which made my travel slow but delicious. I felt the ascent with exquisite pleasure as I reached the clouds and then came down over the shimmering sea. I was so stunned by the beauty I almost dropped everything, but then I got stern with myself and said, 'Go to Zurvan now, idiot! Return to the man who sent you *now*.'

"I and the casket landed in the courtyard. Dusk. The sky was filled with a glorious fresh-colored light. The clouds were tinged with it. I was lying there, in manly form, apparently simply by wishing it, and the treasure was there, the casket, now broken from my having crashed, and another box of letters, thrown open.

"Out into the garden came my new Master, who at once started to pick up the letters. 'These miserable bastards; all this is from Cyrus to me! I hope you killed them.'

" 'With great joy,' I said. I stood up, lifted the half-broken casket of the bones, and stood ready for any help he would need. He piled my arms with a few soft sacks that apparently held jewels, I wasn't sure, it felt like it, and that was all I'd brought with me, other than the casket and the letters, and he cast aside the blanket.

"To my utter amazement the blanket just drifted off, as if wafted on a draft, and then went over the walls, snarling in the breeze, and disappeared.

" 'Some poor hungry person will find it, and do something with it,' he said. 'Always remember the poor and the hungry when you cast aside what you don't want.'

" 'Do you really care about the poor and the hungry?' I asked. I followed him. We went back into the great room, which was now lighted by many oil lamps. I noticed for the first time shelves of tablets and lightly built wooden racks for the scrolls which the Greeks preferred. This had all been behind my back when I'd been slouching about before.

"I set down the broken casket on the floor, and opened it. There were the bones, all right.

"He took the letters and the sacks of jewels to his desk, sat down, and at once began to read all the letters, quickly, leaning on his elbows, and only now and then reaching for a grape from a silver disk beside him. He opened the sacks, dumped out great clumps of jewelry, most of it looking Egyptian to me, some of it Greek obviously, and then he went back to reading.

" 'Ah,' he said, 'here is the Canaanite tablet with the ritual that created you. It's in four pieces, but I can put it together.' He assembled the four pieces and he made the tablet whole.

"I think I was relieved. I'd forgotten all about it. It had not been in the casket. It was small, thick, covered in tiny cuneiform writing, and seemed perfect, as if it had never been broken.

"He looked up suddenly and then he said, 'Don't just stand about. We need to work. Look, lay out all the bones in the form of a man.'

" 'I will not!' I said. My wrath came up so hot I felt it even in this shell. It didn't make me melt. But it gave me a shimmer of heat which I could almost see. 'I will not touch them.'

" 'All right, suit yourself, sit down and be quiet. Think, try to think of everything you know. Use your mind which is in your spirit, and never was in your body.'

" 'If we destroy these bones, will I die?' I asked.

" 'I said for you to think, not talk,' he said. 'No, you won't die. You can't die. Do you want to end up a tottering idiot of a spirit mumbling in the wind? You've seen them, haven't you? Or a stupefied angel roaming the fields trying to remember heavenly hymns? You're of this earth now, forever, and you might as well forget any bright ideas of simply dispatching the bones. The bones will keep you together, literally. The bones will give you a badly needed resting place. The bones will keep your spirit formed in a manner that will allow it to use its strength. Listen to what I'm telling you. Don't be a fool.'

" 'I'm not arguing with you,' I said. 'Have you finished reading the Canaanite tablet?'

" 'Hush up.'

"I sighed angrily and sat back. I looked at my fingernails. They were splended. I felt my hair, thick and the same. What was this like? Being alive in perfect health at a perfect moment of wakefulness and energy, untouched by hunger, fatigue, the remotest discomfort . . . a seemingly perfect physical statue. I smacked the floor with my slippered feet. I had on my favorite embroidered robes, naturally, and velvet slippers. The slippers made a good noise.

"Finally he put all the tablets aside and said, 'All right, since you are so reluctant to touch your own bones, finicky, cowardly young spirit, I'll do the work for you.'

"He came to the center of the room. He dumped all the bones out on the floor. He stood back and he stretched out his hands and then he lowered himself slowly, bending his knees, and out of his mouth came a long series of Persian incantations, murmurings, and I saw from his hands something coming forth, like heat perhaps from a fire, but nothing more visible than that.

"To my amazement the bones assembled themselves in the form of a man laid out for burial, and now he continued his exhortations, and making a whipping gesture with his hand, as though sewing, he brought to him an immense spool of heavy wire, copper, or gold, or what, I couldn't tell, and now with the gesture repeated over and over he made the wire thread the entire skeleton together as if it were beads. He hooked bone to bone with this wire, without ever touching anything, merely making the motions, and he let his hands linger long over the hands and feet of the body which had so many little bones.

Then he moved to the ribs and the pelvis, and finally, with a long sweeping gesture of his right hand, he laid out the spine of this skeleton and connected it to the skull. He now had it all threaded together. One could have hung it from a hook to jangle in the wind.

"I saw a skeleton laid there as though in an open grave. I pushed aside all memory of the cauldron, of the pain, and I merely looked at it.

"Meantime he had rushed into another room and now returned with two short little boys, boys about the age of ten, which I realized in an instant were not real, but spirits, barely corporeal. They carried with them another casket, smaller than the first, rectangular, smelling of cedar, yet heavily plated in gold and silver, thick with jewels. He opened this casket. I saw a bed of folded silk. He told the little boys now to take this skeleton and to arrange it as if it were a child in its mother's womb, with its arms drawn up, and its head bent down, and its knees to its chin.

"The little ones obeyed these commands. They both stood up and looked at me with ink-black eyes. The bent-up skeleton just fit into the casket. It hadn't an inch to spare.

" 'Go!' he said to the little ones, 'and wait for my next command.' They didn't want to. 'Go!' he roared.

"They ran from the room, and stood peeping at me from the far door.

"I stood up and came towards the casket. It was like an old burial now, one found in the hills, from the ancient times when they buried men like this, in the womb of Mother Earth. I looked down at it.

"He was brooding. 'Wax,' he said. 'I want a great deal of melted wax.' He stood up and turned. At once I felt a shock of fear. 'What's wrong with you?' he demanded.

"His two servants appeared again, eyeing me cautiously and carrying a big bucket of the melted wax. He took the kettle from them, for that's what it was, more or less, and he poured the wax all around the bones, so that as it hardened before my eyes, it fixed them in place. It was a soft, white fixture for them. And then he told the little ones to go again, get rid of the kettle, and that they could play in the garden for an hour in their bodies if they didn't make noise. They were overjoyed.

" 'Are they ghosts?' I asked.

" 'They don't know,' he said, still staring at the bones now fixed in wax. Obviously the question didn't interest him. He shut the casket. It had strong hinges and a strong lock. He tested this and opened it. 'In time,' he said, 'though I won't wait too long, being as old as I am, I will make a tablet of silver to go with this, containing all that is needed from the Canaanite tablet, but for now, the bones are as they should always be. Go into them and come back out.'

"Naturally I didn't want to do it. I felt a loathing for the bones, and a rebellious temper. But he waited me out like a wise teacher, and I did it, dissolving, feeling the smooth calm darkness, and then being sucked out of it in a whirl of heat and finding myself standing beside him, embodied again.

" 'Excellent,' he said. 'Excellent. Now tell me all you remember of your life.'

"Now that request on his part began one of the most unpleasant arguments of my entire immortal existence. I couldn't remember anything of my life. No matter how he badgered me I couldn't remember. I knew I feared a cauldron. I knew I feared heat. I knew I feared bees and the wax had made me think of them. I knew that I had seen Cyrus, King of Persia, and that the favor I had asked of him had not been unreasonable. Other than that? I knew only general things.

"Over and over he demanded I try. Over and over I failed. I wept. Finally I told him to leave me alone, what did he want of me, and he touched me on the shoulder and said, 'There, there, don't you see, if you don't remember your life, you can't remember its moral lessons.'

" 'Well, what if there were none!' I said ominously. 'What if all I saw was treachery and lies.'

" 'That is simply impossible,' he said. 'But you do remember Cyrus, and you do remember what you did today?'

"All that I could remember—coming to him, all he'd said, being sent to slay the bedouins and enjoying it, and coming back to him and all that had happened since. He threw at me a few random questions about details . . . such as what had the fire been made of round which the bedouins camped: camel dung was the answer. Had there been any women? No. Where was the place? I had to think and extract an answer, as I had taken no note, but it came to me to his satisfaction, fifty miles from where the desert begins due east of Miletus.

" 'Who is King now?'

" 'Cyrus of Persia,' I said. He then went into a whole series of questions. I answered them all. Who were the Lydians, the Medians, the Ionians, where was Athens, who was Pharaoh, what was the city where Cyrus had been declared King of the World. I answered and answered and answered.

"He asked practical questions about colors and food and air and warmth and heat. I knew all the answers. I knew everything general, but nothing pertaining to my own life. I knew lots about silver and gold and could tell him that—he was impressed. I looked at the emeralds the King had sent him and told him they were most precious and especially beautiful and which was better than another. I told him the names of flowers in his garden. Then I felt tired.

"A strange thing happened. I began to weep. I began to weep like a child. I couldn't stop myself from it and any sense of being humiliated before him didn't matter to me. Finally I looked up and saw him waiting with his bright, curious, and rather merciless blue eyes.

" 'Did you really mean it when you said, always remember the hungry and the poor?' I asked.

" 'Yes,' he said. 'I'm going to tell you the most important things I know now. Listen. I want this repeated back to me whenever I ask you for it. Very well? You call it the lessons of Zurvan and long after I'm dead, you demand of your masters that they tell you what they know, and you keep it in your memory even if it is something stupid, and you'll know when it's stupid. You are a clever, clever spirit.'

" 'All right, bright-blue-eyed Master,' I said angrily. 'Tell me all you know.'

"He furrowed his brows at the sarcasm and insult. He sat brooding. He put one knee over the other. He looked bony in his tunic. His gray hair came to his shoulders and there broke off, but his face was most alert.

" 'Azriel,' he said, 'I could punish you for your impertinence. I could make you feel pain. I could pitch you into the cauldron you fear so that you do not know that it is not real! I can do that at any time.'

" 'And if you do, I will climb out of that cauldron and I will rip you limb from limb, magician!'

" 'Yes, that's more or less why I haven't done it,' he said. 'So let me put it to you this way. I want and expect courtesy from you, in return for all that I teach you. I am your Master at your pleasure.'

" 'Sounds all right,' I said.

" 'All right. Now this is what I know. Don't ever forget it. As long as you hate, and you roast in a hell of anger, there will be a limit to what you can do. You will be at the mercy of other spirits now and then and magicians. Anger is a confusing force, and hatred is blinding. So. You cripple yourself with this, you see, and that is why I would like to discipline it out of you, but that can't be done.

" 'But here are the lessons. Accept what your hatred and anger will allow you to accept. First and foremost, there is one God, and his name does not matter. Yahweh, Ahuramazda, Zeus, Aten, it does not matter at all. How he is worshipped, how he is served, by what ritual, it doesn't matter at all.

" 'There is one purpose to life and one only: to bear witness to and understand as much as possible of the complexity of the world—its beauty, its mysteries, its riddles. The more you understand, the more you look, the greater is your enjoyment of life and your sense of peace. That's all there is to it. Everything else is fun and games. If an activity is not grounded in "to love" or "to learn," it does not have value.

" 'Thirdly, be kind. Always, if you have a choice, be kind. Remember the poor, the hungry, and the miserable. Always remember the suffering, and those who need. The greatest creative power you have on earth, whether you are an angel, a spirit, or a man or a woman or a child is to help others . . . the poor, the hungry, the oppressed. To ease pain and give joy are your finest powers. Kindness is a human miracle, so to speak. It's unique to us humans, and our more developed angels or spirits, *to be kind*.

" 'Fourth, on the subject of magic. All magic of all lands and all schools is the same. Magic is an attempt to control the unseen spirits, and the spirit within the living, or to bring back the spirits of the dead which still surround the earth. That is all that magic is. Making illusions, doing tricks, bringing wealth, it's all done through spirits, that is, beings without bodies who can move swiftly, unseen, steal, spy, transport, etc. That's all magic. The words differ from country to country, from Ephesus to Delphi, to the northern steppes. But it's all the same. I know all magic that can be known, and I continue my search for more. To learn a new incantation teaches me a new possibility. Now listen to me! It teaches me a new possibility, but it doesn't increase my power, my power increases with understanding and will. All magic is the same. What I'm saying is, you can do most anything whether you know the words or not!

" 'Magicians are born for the most part, but some men become magicians . . . incantations school and direct them, but ultimately the words don't count. To God all languages are one. To the spirits all languages are one. Incantations help the weak magician more than the strong. But you can see why, can't you? You are very strong. You can do things without incantations. I've seen that today. So have you. Don't let anyone ever convince you by any incantation that they can have power over you. A magician can have power over you, yes, but don't ever be fooled by mere words. Confront the power if you would resist it. Rouse yourself and make an incantation of your own. Incantations frighten spirits and humans alike. Make a song of strength, a song of might, when you would have your way. Doors will open.'

"He snapped his fingers. He waited a moment, then proceeded.

" 'Lastly, no one human ever knows what lies beyond true death. Spirits can come very close to knowing; they can see bright stairways to heaven, they can see the fruit trees of paradise, they can talk to the dead in various forms, they can glimpse the light of God, oh, that is forever happening, these glimpses and glimpses of light, but they can't really know what lies beyond true death! No one who really escapes the earth and its earthbound spirits ever comes back. They may appear to you. They may talk to you. But you can't make them come from beyond death. Once they are dead, it is in their hands or God's hands whether they appear here or not. So don't ever believe anyone who tells you he knows all about Heaven. All of the realms of the spirits and angels that will ever be known to you or to me are of the Earth, not beyond Death. You understand?'

" 'Yes, I fear I do,' I said. 'But to love and to learn, why? Why is that the purpose of life? I mean how did it become so, why would one set out to do only those things with such dedication?'

" 'You're asking a stupid question,' he said. 'Doesn't matter why it's that way; it's that way: the purpose of life is to love and to learn.' He sighed. 'Let's imagine answering the question for others . . . why is it so important to love and to learn? For a cruel, stupid man this would be a sufficient answer: "It is the safest way to live life." For a great man this would be an answer: "It is the most rewarding and illuminating way to live life." For a selfish, blind person, I could say, "It will bring you the greatest peace in the end if you remember the poor, the hungry, the oppressed, if you remember others, if you love, if you learn." ' He shrugged. 'To the oppressed themselves, the answer is, "It will alleviate your pain, your terrible pain." '

" 'I see,' I said. I smiled. I felt a great rush of pleasure. A great sweet rush of pleasure.

" 'Ah,' he said. 'You do understand.'

"I started to cry again. 'Is there no simple watchword?' I asked.

" 'Such as what?'

" 'It isn't always so easy to love and to learn; one can make hideous errors, hideous mistakes, hurt others. Is there no watchword! For example . . . in Hebrew the word "Altashheth"—Do Not Destroy.' I could barely speak. I was choked with tears. I began to repeat the word over and over again. I said it in one final whisper. 'Altashheth.'

"He considered, rather solemnly, and then he said, 'No. There is no simple watchword. We cannot sing "Altashheth" until and unless all the world sings the same song.'

" 'Will that ever happen, that the whole world will sing the same song?'

" 'No one knows. Not Medians, not Hebrews, not Egyptians, not Greeks, not warriors from the north countries, no one knows. Remember. I've told you all that can be known. The rest is chant and rattle and stomp and laughter. Now give me your solemn word that you will serve me and I will give you my solemn word that as long as I live you will never know pain, if it is in my power to prevent it.'

" 'I give it,' I said. 'I thank you for your patience. I think in life I was kind once.'

" 'Why do you keep crying?'

" 'Because I don't like to hate or to be angry,' I said. 'I want to learn and to love.'

" 'Good enough. You will love and you will learn. Now it's night, I'm old, I'm tired. I want to read until my eyes close, as is my habit.

I want you to sleep within the bones until I call you forth. Answer no call but mine. There will be none, most likely, but one never knows what demons are up to, what jealous evil angels may try. Answer only my voice. And then we will begin together. If you are called forth, come to me, wake me up. I'm not worried about you really . . . With your power, you can get me everything I want in this world.'

" 'Everything you want? But what do you want? I can't . . .'

" 'It's books, mostly, son, don't get so excited,' he said. 'I have no use for wealth other than the beauty you see around me, which does indeed mean I am rich, but rich enough. I want books from all lands, to be taken to places, to caves in the north, and to the Egyptian cities in the south. You can do this. I'll tell you everything, and by the time I die, you will be strong enough to resist those masters who aren't worthy of your strength. Now go into the bones.'

" 'I love you, Master,' I said.

" 'Oh, yes, yes,' he said with a wave of his hand, 'and I shall love you too, and some day you'll have to watch me die.'

" 'But do you love me . . . I mean in particular . . . me . . . do you love me?'

" 'Yes, angry young spirit, I love you in particular. No more questions before I send you to sleep?'

" 'What question would I ask?'

" 'The Canaanite tablet by which you were made. You haven't once asked me to read it to you, or to read it yourself, and obviously you can read.'

" 'I can read many languages,' I said. 'I don't want to see it. Ever.'

" 'Ah, well, I understand. Come into my arms, kiss me, that's it, on the lips as Persians do, on the cheeks as Greeks do, and then leave me until I call you forth again.'

"The warmth of his body was good to me, so good, and I rubbed my forehead against his cheek, and then without waiting for a further command, I willed myself into the bones, and into darkness. I felt almost happy."

10

As I have already mentioned to you, this part of my story—the story pertaining to my two masters—will be the shortest.

"But I must explain fully about Zurvan and what he taught me and what he was. Masters after Zurvan, whether I remember them in particular or not, did not have his strength, I'm convinced of that, but more significantly, they didn't have Zurvan's interest in learning and teaching, and it was this passion of Zurvan, to instruct me, this lack of fear of me, of my independence, which influenced the rest of my existence, even during periods when I could not recall anything about Zurvan, his sharp blue eyes or his ragged white beard.

"In other words, I carried Zurvan's lessons forever, even during the darkest times.

"Zurvan was rich, thanks to Cyrus, and had everything he wanted; and he was true to his word that manuscripts were his primary treasures and I was sent on many errands by him, to detect the hiding places of various manuscripts, sometimes to steal outright, or merely to come back with information which allowed Zurvan to bargain for them. His library was immense and his curiosity insatiable.

"But the very first day I rose, he had far more interesting lessons for me than how I was to travel, invisible, at his command.

"My first waking the following day in his house was a startling affair. I appeared, fully clothed in my finest imitation of flesh, and in Babylonian long-sleeve robes, standing in the study. The sun was just coming in and making a glory of the marble floor. I watched it for some time, and only gradually became conscious of myself, that I was Azriel, and that I was here for some reason and that I was dead.

"I walked through the house, searching for other living creatures. I opened a door on a painted bedroom chamber. But what struck me was not the beauty of the murals or the arched windows open to the garden, but that a horde of semivisible creatures fled from me, screeching and jumping up and down and then surrounding the figure of Zurvan, who lay on the bed as though asleep.

"These figures were not easy to see, flashing between mere outline and bursts of light, manifesting snarling faces and making little screams so rapidly that it was difficult for me to pick out any one figure or even get some impression of any one shape. They were humanlike but smaller, fainter, weaker, and carrying on like crazed children.

"At last they had clustered themselves entirely around the bed, obviously to guard Zurvan or perhaps to seek his protection. Zurvan opened his eyes. He looked at me for a long moment, then rose with excitement, and glared at me, as if he didn't quite believe what he saw.

" 'Surely you remember yesterday, Master, when I came to you. You told me this morning you would call me forth.'

"He nodded, and throwing out his arms, he banished the others, until the room lay empty and civilized, a fine Greek bedroom with admirable murals. I stood at the foot of the bed.

" 'So what have I done wrong?'

" 'You heard me call you in my sleep, that's what you did, and you came, and what this means is your power is even greater than I thought. I was lying here half-awake, merely thinking about you and how to begin, and this was sufficient to call you forth from the bones. The bones, by the way, are there. I didn't touch them. You woke upon hearing yourself the subject of my thoughts.'

"He then pointed to the casket, which I saw was on the floor very near to his bed.

"He turned to the side, planted his feet on the floor, and rose, pulling the bedsheet about him like a long toga.

" 'But we'll use this strength, we won't try to stifle it for my ends or for the ends of others.' He pondered.

" 'Go back into the bones,' he said, 'and when I call you, become flesh and come to me in the agora at noon. I'll be in the tavern. I want you to come to me, fully dressed, solid, having walked the distance from here to there, and having found me by the sheer repetition of my name.'

"I did as he said. I sank back into the soft, downy darkness, but this time I took considerable confusion with me, such as why had I waked in the other room, except that it was the room I knew to be his location as of yesterday, and then I slept. I knew the sleep by measures, as one does when one is half-awake, but I suffered nothing but rest.

"When I knew that it was noon—by a series of tiny signals having to do with light and temperature—I found myself standing in the living room again, well formed and dressed. I checked all the particulars. I checked my hands and feet and clothes, and saw that my hair and beard were groomed, and I did this by merely running my hands over my body and wishing for all this to be so.

"A large burnished mirror stood in the room. When I saw myself in it, I was surprised, as I had some superstitious belief that spirits could not be reflected in mirrors. Then a thought occurred to me. I should go to the Master, yes, as told, immediately, but why not call to the others first? See if they were there?

" 'Show yourself, you little craven monsters!' I said aloud, and at once I did see the room full of the small spirits all watching me in august fear. This time they were still, and it seemed I saw layers of them, as though their substance easily penetrated the substance of another, and I realized there were tall well-formed human shapes among them, eyeing me with caution, as well as the little imps who seemed no more than faces and limbs. I continued to look and say, 'Show yourselves.' And soon saw other spirits in the room, spirits that seemed weary and forlorn, like the newly dead perhaps, and one of these spirits lifted his hand to me very slowly and said, 'Which way?'

" 'I don't know, brother,' I said. Looking beyond into the garden, I saw the air full of spirits. I saw them clearly as if they were fixed and could not move. I sensed this was only one way of seeing them. I remembered their attacks in the palace when I'd first been made a spirit, and no sooner did this thought cross my mind than the whole spirit spectacle changed.

"The still and thoughtful dead were invaded from every direction by the angry, whirling, howling spirits I remembered from my firstborn minutes. I cried out: 'Get back! Get away from me!' I was amazed at the roar which came from me. Most of the enemy fled. But one clung to me, clawing at me, though it made no mark on me and I turned and hit him hard with my fist and cursed at him to return to his safest refuge or I would destroy him! In panic, he disappeared.

"The room was empty and still. I narrowed my eyes. I saw the little spirits waiting. But then I heard a voice very distinctly at my ear; 'I told you to come to the agora, to the tavern. Where are you?'

"This was of course Zurvan's voice.

" 'Do I have to draw you a map?' asked the voice. 'Do you remember my command to you? Start walking towards me. You'll find me, and don't be distracted again by either the living or the dead.'

"I felt a crushing anxiety that I had not instantly obeyed him but I did remember his command, I remembered the morning, I made an effort to remember it, then I walked out of the house and into the street.

"This was my first long walk through Miletus, which was a beautiful and open Greek city, filled with marble, and open gathering places, and the fresh air of the coast and the brilliant light of the sea on the clouds. I walked on and on, viewing many things, little shops and stalls and private houses and fountains and small shrines cut in the walls, and then I came to the great open marketplace, surrounded on all sides by the bazaar, and I saw the open tavern, with its bright white awning blowing in the sea breeze, and I saw Zurvan inside, and I came in and stood before him.

" 'Sit down,' he said. 'Tell me why you opened the front door of my house, instead of merely walking through it.'

" 'I didn't know that I could walk through it. I was flesh. You said come to you in flesh. Are you angry with me? I was distracted by the spirits. I saw the spirits everywhere and I had not seen such a spectacle . . .'

" 'Hush, I didn't ask you for all of your thoughts, I merely asked why you didn't walk through the door. Now even when you are most solid, you can walk through the door. You can pass through it, because that which makes you solid is not what makes it solid. You understand? Now, disappear and reappear here. No one will notice. The tavern's half-empty. Go ahead.'

"I did this. It was exhilarating, like stretching all my limbs and laughing and then coming back into this solid form.

"He had a much more cheerful expression on his face and now he wanted to hear what I had seen. I told him. Then he asked, 'When you were a living man, you saw spirits, didn't you? Answer without thinking or trying to remember.'

" 'Yes,' I said. This was painful and I could recall no details. I didn't want to. I felt a sense of betrayal and hate.

" 'I knew it,' he said with a sigh. 'Cyrus told me this, but he was so vague and diplomatic in his language, it was impossible for me to be sure. Cyrus has some special love for you and sense of obligation to you. Look, we're going to go into the realm of the spirits. That's best, to go so that you know what it is. But listen first:

" 'Every magician you will ever know will have a different map of the spirit terrain. He will have a different notion of what spirits are and why they behave the way they do. But essentially, what you will see on any spirit journey is the same.'

" 'So you want some wine, Master?' I asked. 'Your cup is empty.'

" 'Whatever made you interrupt me with that question?' he asked.

" 'You're thirsty,' I said. 'I know because you are.'

" 'What am I going to do with you? How am I going to make you pay attention?'

"I turned and gestured for the wine boy, who came at once and filled my Master's cup. He asked me if I wanted anything, treating me with great deference, more deference even than he had shown my Master. I realized it was my ornate clothing, this great Babylonian show of jewels and embroidery and my formal hair and beard.

" 'No,' I said. I felt sad that I had no money to bestow on him but then I saw several shekels of silver lying on the table. I gave this to him, and he went away.

"When I looked at Zurvan, he was sitting there resting on his elbows merely studying me. 'I think I understand it,' he said.

" 'What in particular?' I asked.

" 'You weren't made or born to obey anyone. The whole Canaanite ritual outlined on the tablet—'

" 'Must you talk of that disgusting tablet!'

" 'Hush! Did you never have an elder in your life, never a teacher, a father, a king? Stop interrupting me. And listen to me. Ye gods, don't you realize, Azriel, you cannot die now! I can teach you what will help you! Don't be so impertinent and stop letting your mind wander. Now! Listen.'

"I nodded. I felt tears spring to my eyes. I felt shame that I'd angered him, and drew a silk napkin out of my robe and blotted my eyes. There was water there I think. Water.

" 'Ah, so that's it! I became angry and that makes you obey.'

" 'Could I leave you if I wished?'

" 'Probably so, but you'd be a fool to do it! Now pay attention. What was I saying to you before you decided that I should have a drink of wine?'

" 'You said that different magicians would outline the spirit world in different ways, and they would give the spirits different names and attributes.'

"He seemed perfectly astonished by this response! I couldn't quite tell why. But it was highly acceptable to him.

" 'Yes, precisely. Now do as I say. Look around you. Look in the tavern and into the agora, look out there into the sun. See the spirits. Don't speak to them or accept any invitation or gesture from them. Merely see all that you can. Search the air as if you were searching for things tiny and precious that you must have, but don't move your lips.'

"I did as he said. I think I fully expected to see the pesty little demons that infested his house. But these I didn't see, so much as the wandering confused dead. I saw their shades or spirits in the tavern, slumped over the tables, trying to talk to the living, walking about as if searching for something . . .

" 'Now look beyond the earthbound dead, the newly dead, and see the older spirits, the spirits that have vitality as spirits,' he declared.

"I did and saw again those tall beings with fixed eyes, transparent utterly, but with human shapes and distinct expressions and I saw not only those who looked and pointed at me, and made gestures regarding me, but hordes of others. The whole agora was filled with them. I looked up into the sky and saw more resplendent spirits. I let out a little cry. These resplendent spirits were not disturbed or angry or lost, or seeking, but seemed more to be guardians of the living, to be gods or angels, and I saw them to the very height to which I could see. Their comings and goings were swift. In fact, the entire spirit world was in constant movement, and one could classify the spirits by movement, the shades of the dead being sluggish, the older spirits slow and more human, and these angelic spirits, these joyful ones, rushed at a speed the human eye could not follow.

"I must have made many sounds of pleasure. I was overcome by the beauty of some of these aerial creatures, rising into the sun itself, and then I would see the hunkering shade of a dead person coming towards me, hungry and desperate, and I would flinch and draw back. A contingent of spirits who had noticed me was now drawing the attention of others to me. These were the middle spirits, as I saw it, between the dead and the angels, but even as I looked I saw that they were interpenetrated with savage spirits, who darted back and forth, making horrible faces and gestures at me, as if they would hurt me, shaking their fists and trying to egg me into a battle.

"The vision was becoming impossibly dense. I had lost sight of the awning of the tavern, of the floor of the agora, of the buildings opposite. I was in a terrain that belonged to these beings. I felt something touch me which was alive and warm. It was Zurvan's hand.

" 'Become invisible,' he said, 'and surround me, hold as strong as you can to me and take me with you and up and out of here. I will remain flesh, I have to, but you will surround me, you will cloak me with invisibility and protect me.'

"I turned and saw him in brilliant colors of living flesh, and I did as he said, swirling around him, just letting every limb loosen and lengthen until I had him wrapped completely and then I moved out of the cafe, and up into the sky with him, through the thick gang of spirits, and through the startled demonic ones who howled and hissed at us, and tried to grab on to us. I threw them off.

"We went high above the city. I could see it beneath me as I first had, the beautiful peninsula jutting out into the blue sea and the ships at anchor with all their different flags, and men working in a fever, doing seemingly senseless but no doubt routine things.

" 'Take me to the mountains,' said my Master, 'take me to the farthest and highest mountain of the world, the mountain where the Gods came and around which the sun revolves, take me to the mountain called Meru. Take me there.'

"We rose up over the desert, over Babylonia, and I saw her cities scattered out like so many flowers, or traps. Traps. They looked like traps. They looked like traps built to make the gods fly down to them . . . the way flowers are traps for bees.

" 'Travel north,' he said, 'to the far north, and wrap me in blankets that I'll be warm and hold me fast. Move with greater speed, until you hear me cry out in pain.'

"I obeyed, swaddling him in fine wool, and completely surrounding him and flying ever northward, until nothing lay below us but mountains, mountains capped with snow, and occasional fields, snowy and empty, where flocks grazed and men rode horses, and then it would be mountains again.

" 'Meru,' he said, 'Find it. Meru.'

"I set my mind to this completely and was only slowly aware that I couldn't do it. 'There is no Meru that I can find,' I said.

" 'It's as I thought. Let us touch down on the earth, down there in the valley where the horses are running, let us touch down there.'

"We did, and I kept him swathed in blankets and surrounded by my invisibility, and realized that in this state I could press my face right beside his face.

" 'It's an old story, an old myth of the great mountain,' he said. 'It is the mountain which inspires ziggurats and pyramids among the tribes that have only a dim memory of it. It is the mountain that inspired the high temples of all lands. Let me go now, Azriel, make yourself flesh and arm yourself well with weapons against these warriors of the steppes. Don't let them harm me. Kill them if they try.'

"I did this, and left him standing, shivering in his blankets. Only a few of the herdsmen had seen us, and they fled at once to the armed men on horseback of whom there were perhaps six, scattered about in some sort of guard. The snow around us was beautiful, but I knew it was cold, I could feel his cold, and I wrapped my fleshly arms around him, commanding myself to be warm and to warm him, and this seemed to give him immediate comfort.

"Meantime the six warriors, stinking worse than their horses, filthy men of the steppes, came riding in a circle around us. My Master called out to them in a language I hadn't heard before, but which was understandable to me, and he asked where was the mountain that was the navel of the world.

"They were taken aback and began to argue, and then all pointed more or less in the same direction, which was north, but no one knew for certain and no one had ever seen it.

" 'Become invisible, lift me and take me away from them. Leave them befuddled. They can't harm us, and what they see is no concern of ours.'

"Once again we were moving north. The wind was now unbearably cold for him. I didn't think I could protect him any better, I had summoned skins to enclose him and I made my heat as strong as I could but then this began to hurt him. I had gone too far.

" 'Meru,' he said. 'Meru.'

"But this gave us no direction, and suddenly he said, 'As fast as you can do it, Azriel, take me home.'

"There was a great roaring noise as I accelerated, and the landscape virtually vanished in a burst of whiteness, and it seemed that spirits ran at us from all directions, falling back as if blown off their course by our strength. My vision was flooded by the yellow of the desert, and then once again, the city of Miletus was plain to me, and we were in his living room and I picked him up in his blankets and skins and carried him in and laid him on the bed.

"The host of little spirits stood around in awe.

" 'Food and drink,' he said to them. And they scurried to obey, bringing him a bowl with some broth in it, and a golden goblet of wine. The goblet was Greek and very beautiful, as all Greek things were then, seemingly more graceful and less rigid in form than things Oriental.

"But I feared for Zurvan. He lay there, frozen it seemed, and I lay on top of him, warming him, swirling around him, then hugging him and then finally when he had turned the proper color of a living being, and his eyes were wide and blue, I let go, laying out the covers.

"His flock of little spirits helped him to sit and even brought the spoon to his lips and the cup to his lips.

"I sat at the foot of the bed. I had no need of broth and was proud of it. Released. I was also very strong. After a long time he looked at me.

" 'You did well,' he said. 'You did wondrously well.'

" 'I never found the mountain.'

"He laughed. 'And you probably never will, nor I, nor anyone else.' He banished all the others, and they fled like slaves, and the room was clean of them. 'Every man holds some myth sacred in himself, some old story told to him, which for him had the ring of truth, or maybe just the allure of beauty. So it was with me and the sacred mountain. And so with your power I have journeyed to the very top of the world and seen for myself that Meru is not a place, no more than I thought it was, but a thought, a concept, an ideal.'

"He rested, and the curious expression returned to him. Any disappointment or fatigue was swallowed by it. He looked at me and his eyes seemed to fill with delight.

" 'What did you learn, Azriel, on your journey? What did you see?'

" 'I learned first and foremost that such a thing could be done,' I said. Then I told him all I'd seen, and how the cities looked like traps to lure the gods of Heaven to earth.

"This amused and interested him.

" 'They seemed,' I said, 'to have been designed especially to get the attention of the gods, to make the gods cease their ethereal flight and come down, as to the temple of Marduk. The mountain, as you said. They dotted the earth like so many open hands of invitation, or perhaps that is wrong, perhaps they looked like fancy entrances to earth, gateways, ah, that's the word the priest would like, I'm sure, that Babylon is the Gateway of the Gods.'

" 'Every city,' he said contemptuously, 'is the gateway of some god.'

" 'What were the higher spirits I saw, the ones who looked joyous and ran to and fro, the ones who passed right through the middle spirits, the ones the dead could not see?'

" 'As I told you,' he answered, 'every magician will have a different explanation, but you saw what there is to see; you saw a great deal of it. Over time you'll see more, but you saw your own power and how they respected it, you saw that the middle spirits, as you call them, could not hurt you, and the demon spirits are idiots, and you can rout them with a nasty face. You saw.'

" 'But what is it all, Master?'

" 'It's what I told you yesterday. It's all that we can know on this earth. The joyous ones ascend, the middle ones see, the pale and sorrowful dead become as the middle ones, and whence the demons? Who knows? Were they all humans? No, I think not. Can they possess and confuse men? Oh, yes they can. But you, the Servant of the Bones, can see them in all their weakness, and you have nothing ever to fear from them, remember? Should they block your path, merely shove them aside. Should they come to invade a human under your protection, to penetrate his flesh and enliven him with their own intentions, reach out with your invisible hand and grab the invisible body of the invader and you will find you can lift it up and hurl it away from its human host.'

"He gave a great sigh. 'I have to rest now, the journey was arduous for me. I'm human. Now, go and walk about the city. Walk in your fleshly body, walk as men do and see as men do. Do not walk through doors or walls, lest you frighten someone, and if the spirits come down to assault you, send them flying with your anger and your fist. If you need me, call out to me. But mostly, you walk now.'

"I was delighted at the prospect. I got up and went to the door. His voice called me back.

" 'You're the strongest spirit I ever saw or knew,' he said. 'Look at you, in your splendid blue robes and gold, and with your hair shining as it falls to your shoulders. Look at you. Visible, invisible, an illusion, solid, it's all possible for you. You could be the perfect instrument of evil.'

" 'I don't want to be!' I said.

" 'Remember that, remember that above all things. You were imperfectly made by bumbling idiots. And as the result you are stronger than any magician could have ever wanted, and you have what men have . . .'

"I started to weep. It was that same instantaneous and uncontrollable weeping that had come on me before. 'A soul?' I asked. 'I have a soul?'

" 'I don't know the answer to that question,' he said. 'I was speaking of something else. You have free will.'

"He lay back and closed his eyes. 'Bring something back for me which hurts no one.'

" 'Flowers,' I said, 'a beautiful gathering of flowers, from this wall and that gate and this garden.'

"He laughed. 'Yes, and with mortals, be gentle! Don't hurt them. Even if they insult you, thinking you mortal, don't hurt them. Be patient and kind.'

" 'I will, I vow it,' I said.

"And I set out on my way."

11

What Zurvan taught me in the next fifteen years was all an extension and elaboration of what was learned in the first three of our days. That I can remember them now clearly for the first time in all these centuries floods me with happiness. I want to tell you the details. Ah, God, that I remember being alive and then not alive, that I can connect one memory to the other, this is . . . this is something more merciful than an answer to prayers."

I told him I thought I could understand, but I said nothing more because I was eager for him to go on.

"After Zurvan released me to go wandering in the flesh, I didn't return until called, which was midnight or after. I had by then a huge bouquet of extremely delicate flowers, no one the same, and these I put in a vase of water for him and set on his study table.

"He made me recount everything I had seen and done. I described every street in Miletus in which I'd wandered, how I'd been tempted to try to pass through solid objects but stayed with his prohibition, and how I had watched the ships in the harbor for the longest time, and listened to the languages being spoken along the shore. I told him I felt thirst at times, and drank from a fountain not sure of what would happen, and that the water filled my body, not through internal organs which I did not possess, but every fiber of it over all.

"He listened to all this and he said: 'What is your estimation of all you saw, or each thing, however you wish to tell me?'

" 'Splendid,' I said with a shrug. 'Temples of incredible beauty. Marble, such marble. The people here are from all nations. I never saw so many Greeks before; I stood listening to a group of Athenians arguing about philosophy, which was very funny to me but I enjoyed watching it, and of course I wandered near the Persian court and was allowed entrance both to the temple and the palace, apparently because of my clothing and demeanor and I wandered in these newly constructed citadels of my old world, and then back out to the temples of the Greek gods, and rather liked their openness and the whiteness, and the whole stamina of the Greek people, which I think is more different from the Babylonians than I ever supposed.'

" 'But,' he asked, 'is there anything you are burning to tell me, anything that made you angry or sorrowful?'

" 'I don't want to disappoint you but I can't think of a thing. Everywhere I beheld splendor. Ah, the colors of the flowers, look at them. Every now and then I'd see the spirits, but all I had to do was close my eyes to them, so to speak, and again there was the bright, living world. I coveted things. I coveted jewelry, and I knew I could steal it in this form. In fact, I did discover one little trick. I could make the jewelry come to me, if I stood close enough and beckoned to it with my whole will. But I gave back what I stole. And I found money in my pockets. I found gold. I don't know how it got there.'

" 'I put it there,' he said. 'Anything else? Did you notice or feel anything else?'

" 'The Greeks, you know,' I said. 'They are as practical as our people were . . . whoever the hell my people were . . . but they believe in ethics in a way that is not connected to divine worship; it is not merely a question of do not oppress the poor, uphold the weak, and all for the glory of the gods, but some further confirmation of much that is . . . is . . .'

" 'Abstract,' he said. 'Invisible and detached from the self-serving.'

" 'Yes, precisely. They speak of laws that pertain to behavior in a manner that is not religious, that's it. They don't possess more conscience, however. They can be cruel. Can't all people?'

" 'That's enough for now. You've told me what I want to know.'

" 'Which is what?' I asked.

" 'You don't envy living people.'

" 'Good heavens, why should I? I've wandered all day and I feel no fatigue, nothing, only a little thirst. No one can harm me. Why would I envy people who are still alive? I feel sorry for them if all that lies ahead is to be a stumbling spirit or a demon. I wish all of them could be born again as I have, but then I know that all I see is, how did you put it, only what is of the earth. Besides . . .'

" 'Yes . . .'

" 'I don't remember ever being alive. I know you said that I was, or I myself said it, or it seems to be something we both know, and we spoke of that cursed tablet and bungling, but I don't remember being alive. I don't remember aching or being burnt or falling or bleeding. By the way, you are right. I have no need of internal organs. And when I cut myself I can bleed or not bleed as I choose.'

" 'You realize, of course,' he said, 'that many of the dead you see hate the living! They hate them.'

" 'Why?'

" 'Because their own existence is shadowy and weak and full of longing for things which they can't have. They cannot be visible, they cannot move objects, they can but buzz like invisible bees through the world.'

" 'What would happen if I became invisible,' I asked, 'and I went up with the more joyous creatures, the ones who are so busy and seem to range so high?'

" 'Do it and come back safe to me, unless you find Paradise,' he said.

" 'You think I might?'

" 'No, but I would never deny you Paradise or Heaven; would you deny such a thing to anyone?'

"I immediately obeyed, throwing off for the first time the weight of the body and the clothes yet commanding them to be at hand.

"I went out into the courtyard, looked for the spirits and found them surrounding me, thickly, and now that my eyes were focused on them, the demonic among them became ferocious, and I had many a struggle on my hands. Over and over the meandering dead detained me with pathetic questions, questions pertaining to those they'd left behind in the living world.

"And I found these meandering dead were in the higher levels as well as the very low, only they had grown lighter and stronger apparently, or at least they were better off than the shuffling blinded anguished dead that roamed the very earth itself.

"I came into the upper air of the joyous creatures and at once they turned to me, their faces filled with amazement, and with gentle gestures they ordered me down. In an instant I was surrounded by them, many of them having vague yet sparkling shapes, some even wings, and some long, white robes, but to a one, they ordered me down, they pointed, and they gestured, and they urged me as if I were a child blundering into a sanctuary. There was no wrath or contempt in them, they simply pointed downward and told me I must go.

" 'No, I won't go,' I said, but when I tried to go higher, I saw the way was wholly covered over with them and their bodies, and it seemed for one instant I perceived, far beyond the layers of them, a light shining but it hurt my eyes, and I fell, plummeted, crashed right back down to the earth.

"I lay in some dark place and the demons closed in on me, tearing at my invisible hair and body so that I dissolved and defeated them simply by slipping away and up, and then I made a right arm and a left arm and swept them aside, cursing them in their own tongues until they had fled.

"I tried to get my bearings; was I below the surface of the real earth? I didn't know. I had fallen into an ashy gloom, a fog, through which I could see nothing material. The spirits that fled from me or hovered near me were part of the pollution and density of this place.

"Then striding out of the fog there came a mighty spirit, shaped like a man as I was, smiling at me in cunning fashion, and immediately I sensed danger. He flew at me with both hands, fastening onto my neck, and then the demons closed in again. I fought him furiously, cursing him, and declaring him powerless, rattling off incantations galore to send him hence, and finally throttling him and shaking him until he was screaming for mercy; he lost his human shape; then he flew away, turned into a wisp of a veil as it were, and the demons fled.

" 'I have to get back to my Master,' I said. I closed my eyes. I called to my Master, and to my body that waited, and my clothes that waited, and then I woke up, sitting in the Greek chair in my Master's study, and he was at his desk, one knee raised with his foot on a footstool, tapping his fingers, and watching all.

" 'Did you see where I went and what I did?' I asked.

" 'Some of it. I saw you rise, but then you could go no higher, the spirits of the upper air wouldn't permit it.'

" 'No, they wouldn't, but they were kind. Did you see the light, way beyond them?'

" 'No, I didn't,' he said.

" 'That must be the light of Heaven,' I said, 'and down must come a ladder, a stairway, yes, to the earth, but why not for all the dead, why not for all the muddled and angry?'

" 'No one knows. You don't require an answer from me. You can reason it out for yourself. But what makes you so sure there will be a ladder, a stairway for anyone? Is it the promise of the ziggurats, the pyramids? The legend of Mount Meru?'

"I thought a long time before answering. 'No,' I said. 'Though those are proofs of course, no, not proofs but indications. I know because of the faces of the higher spirits . . . as they directed me to go down. There was no meanness in them; no evil; no wrath. They didn't shout like gatekeepers of a palace; they simply made it impossible for me to pass, and over and over they offered by gesture the way I was to go . . . back to the earth.'

"He pondered that one in silence. I was too excited to be silent.

" 'Did you see that strong one who attacked me,' I said, 'the one who walked up to me as though he were my height and weight and was smiling, and then flew at me?'

" 'No. What happened?'

" 'I choked him and shook him and vanquished him and threw him away.'

"My Master laughed. 'Poor foolish spirit.'

" 'You're speaking to me?'

" 'I'm speaking sarcastically of him,' he said.

" 'But why didn't he talk to me? Why didn't he ask me who I was? Why didn't he greet me as a creature of equal power, you know, engage in some way other than battle?'

" 'Azriel, most spirits don't know what they're doing or why,' he said. 'The longer they drift the less they know. Hate is common to them. He tested his strength against you. Perhaps if he had vanquished you, he would have tried to enslave you among the invisible, but he couldn't do that. He knows nothing else, most likely, but combat, dominance, and submission. Many human beings live in exactly the same way.'

" 'Oh, yes, I know,' I said.

" 'Go there, to the pitcher of water,' he said. 'Drink all of it. You can drink whenever you wish. Water will make your spirit body in any form stronger. That's true of all spirits and ghosts. They love water and crave the damp. Oh, but I told you this. Hurry up. I have something for you to do.'

"The water did taste wonderful and I drank an amount which a normal man could never have drunk. When I set down the pitcher, I was ready for his command.

" 'I want you to retain your body and walk through the wall into the garden and then back again. You'll feel resistance. Ignore it. You are made of different particles from the wall, and you can pass among the particles of the wall without hurting it. Do it, do it over and over until you can walk through anything solid without hesitation.'

"I found this very easy. I walked through doors, I walked through walls three feet thick, I walked through columns. I walked through furniture. Each time I did feel the swirling particles which made up the barrier or the object, but the penetration was not hurtful and it took only will to override any natural instinct to bow or retreat.

" 'Are you tired?'

" 'No,' I said.

" 'All right, this is your first real errand for me,' he said. 'Go to the house of the Greek merchant Lysander in the street of the scribes, steal every manuscript out of his library, and bring them to me. You will take four trips to do it. Do it in the flesh and ignore anyone who sees you, remember that to make the scrolls pass through the wall, you have to put them inside your body, which includes now your robe. You have to envelop them in your spirit. If it is too hard, then go and come by doors. Anyone who strikes you . . . can't hurt you.'

" 'Do I hurt them?'

" 'No. Not unless they have some power to detain you. In general, their daggers and swords will pass right into you and do nothing. But if they take hold of the scrolls, which are material, you may have to knock them away. Do it . . . gently, I suppose. Or . . . as it suits you, depending on how much the person offends you. I leave it to you.'

"He lifted his pen and began to write. Then he realized I hadn't moved.

" 'So?' he asked.

" 'I'm to steal?'

" 'Azriel, my conscientious one, my newborn spirit, everything in the house of Lysander is stolen! He obtained it all when the Persians came through Miletus. Most of the library was mine. He is a bad man. You may kill him if you like. Doesn't matter to me. But get going and bring back all those books. Do as I say, and never question me on such matters.'

" 'Then you will never want for me to rob the poor man, or hurt the afflicted, or frighten the humble and the meek.'

"He looked up. 'Azriel, we have been over this ground. Your words sound like a variation on one of those pompous inscriptions at the feet of Assyrian Kings.'

" 'I didn't want to waste your time with lengthier questions,' I said.

" 'I have no interest in anything but good behavior,' he said. 'Try to remember my lessons. I love even the pesty familiars I keep here to do my bidding, but Lysander is evil and steals and sells for profit, and cannot even read.'

"The chore proved easy enough. I had only to knock about the servants to send them flying and in three journeys back and forth I was able to transport the entire library to my Master. It was hard, however, with great bundles of scrolls to pass through doors. I couldn't envelop them with my spirit and pass through the particles. But I got better at this as time passed on. Indeed, I learned something he hadn't told me, that I might make my body diffuse and large as I passed through the solid walls and doors, that way better enveloping the scrolls and then contracting again to the normal size of a fleshly man as I walked on with my bundle of goods.

"To be open and fair with him, I did this on my last trip, coming through the wall of his study, with a very large cache of loot, making myself very big and then contracting to lay down the bundle itself.

"He gave me a steady look, and I realized something. All day and night since I had come, I had been amazing him. And he masked it with this look. He showed no fear.

" 'I don't feel any fear of you,' he said, answering my thoughts, 'but you're right; it's not my habit as a magus or a scholar or a man to look startled and to shout.'

" 'What now, Master?' I asked.

" 'Go into the bones, and do not come out until you hear me . . . hear my voice, calling you. That I dream of you or think of you is not enough.'

" 'I'll try, Master,' I said.

" 'You'll disappoint me if you disobey; you're too young and strong to run rampant. You'll hurt my soul if you try to come out when I think of you.'

"Again I felt the ready tears. 'Then I won't do it, Lord,' I said.

"I went into the bones. For one moment before my eyes closed I saw the casket itself and that it had been moved to a hiding place, a niche within the wall, but then came the velvet sleep, and the thought, 'I love him, and I want to serve him.' And that was all.

"The next morning I waked but didn't move. It was a long time, lying in the darkness, feeling nothing of the physical at all, waiting, and then when I heard his voice very distinctly, I answered the call.

"The bright world opened up all around me again. I was seated in the garden, among the flowers, and he was on a couch there, reading, mussed and yawning as if he'd spent the night under the stars.

" 'Well, I waited this time,' I said.

" 'Ah, then you felt yourself wake before I called you?'

" 'Yes, but waited, so that you'd be pleased. Some bit of memory came back to me, or has come at this moment, enough to ask a question.'

" 'Ask. If I can't truly answer I won't make anything up.'

"I laughed and laughed at that! I had some firm conviction in my utter forgetfulness that priests and Magi lied ferociously. He nodded in satisfaction at this.

" 'Your question?'

" 'Do I have a destiny?' I asked.

" 'What a strange question. What makes you think anyone has a destiny? We do what we do and we die. I told you. There is but one Creator God and his name does not matter. Our destiny, for all of us, is to love and to gain greater appreciation and understanding of all around us. Why should yours be any different?'

" 'Ah, but that's just it. I should have a special destiny, should I not?'

" 'The belief in a special destiny is one of the most rampant and harmful delusions on earth. Innocent babes are lifted from the teats of queens and told that they have a special destiny—to rule Athens, or Sparta, or Miletus, or Egypt, or Babylon. What stupidity. But I know what lies behind your question. And you'd better listen now. Go get the Canaanite tablet and don't break it. If you break it, I'll have to put it back together and I'll make you cry.'

" 'Hmmm. It's easy for you to make me cry, isn't it?'

" 'Apparently,' he said. 'Get the tablet. Hurry. We have a journey ahead of us today. If you can take me to the steppes of the north, to the mountains where the great mountain of the gods is supposed to stand high above all else, then you can take me other places too. I want to go home to Athens. I want to walk in Athens. Go on, powerful spirit. Get the tablet. Hurry. Ignorance is of no use to anyone. Don't be afraid.' "

12

I laid hands on the Canaanite tablet, though it filled me with revulsion and hate. Indeed, I rocked with hate. I was so full of hate that for a moment I couldn't move. His voice called me back, with the command that I was not to break it. The writing was very small, he reminded me, and one chip would hurt the contents, and I must know it all.

" 'Why should I?' I asked. I gestured towards the pillows inside the room. Might I bring one out, so that I could sit at his feet without soiling my robes? He nodded.

"I crossed my legs. He was on his couch, one knee up, which seemed his favorite position, and he had the tablet now where he could read it clearly in the sun. This memory is so vivid to me, perhaps because the wall was white and covered in red flowers, and the olive tree was twisted and old, and many-branched as they get, and the green grass sprouting between the marble squares of the garden was soft. I loved to run the palm of my hand over it. I loved to lay the palm of my hand on the marble and feel the sun's heat.

"And of course I remember him with love, in his loose, long, baggy Greek tunic, the gold threads worn off the edging, looking rather scrawny and content and ageless as his blue eyes moved over the tablet, and he drew it close to his face now and then and then moved it far away. I think he must have read every single little word carved on it, in its long narrow columns of cuneiform. I hated it.

" 'You escaped into the spirit world at the hands of idiots,' he said. 'This is an old Canaanite incantation to call up a powerful evil spirit, a servant of evil as powerful as the spirits of evil that might be sent to earth by God. It is to create for a magician a mal'ak, strong as the Mal'ak which Yahweh sent to slay the firstborn of the Egyptians.'

"I was stunned. I didn't answer him. I knew many translations of the story of the flight from Egypt and I knew an image of the Mal'ak, the shining angel of the Lord's Wrath.

" 'This information was regarded dangerous by the Canaanites and sealed in this tablet, if the date is correct, a thousand years ago. This was black magic, bad magic, magic like that of the Witch of Endor, who brought the spirit Samuel up to speak with King Saul.'

" 'I know these stories,' I said quietly.

" 'The magician here would make his own mal'ak which could be as strong as a Satan or fallen angel or evil spirit that had once participated in the power of Yahweh Himself.'

" 'I understand.'

" 'The rules are very strict here. The candidate for the mal'ak must be thoroughly evil, opposed to God and all things good, one who had despaired of God in contempt for God's cruelty to man and the injustice He allowed into the world. The candidate for the mal'ak is to be so determined and angry and evil that he would fight God himself if he could or is called upon to do so. He should be able to meet any Angel of the Lord hand to hand and fight him down.'

" 'You speak of good angels?'

" 'Yes, good and bad; you were to be the equal of them and you may be. You are a mal'ak, not an ordinary spirit at all. But as I said, the one who would become this must be evil to the core of his heart, he must have no patience any longer with God and want to serve the rebellious spirit in mankind, that which has refused to accept God's rules. This spirit is not being created to serve a Devil or Demon, but to be one.'

"I gasped.

" 'You seem rather young to have been so wretchedly evil . . . at least in the form you've chosen on your own, which does seem the perfect emanation of what you were when you were alive. Were you that evil? Did you hate God so much?'

" 'No, at least, I don't think I did. If I did, I didn't know.'

" 'Did you choose to become the Servant of the Bones?'

" 'No. I know I did not.'

" 'More bungling. You weren't evil, you weren't willing, and you did not make a vow to serve whoever would own the bones, did you?'

" 'Certainly not!' I tried to remember. It was so difficult now, the past grew bright, then faded, but I could push back to Cyrus's bedchamber, I could remember that Cyrus had sent me here to Zurvan, and I could remember something before that . . . a priest dead on the floor.

" 'I killed the one who would be Master,' I said. 'I killed him and there was death all around me, I was dying when I was made. Only a little flame remained in me. I was to die. The stairway to heaven was to come down perhaps, or I was to go into the light and be part of it. I don't know which happened. But whatever the case, I was not willing to be the Servant of the Bones, I tried to escape . . . I remember running and calling for help, saying this was a Canaanite curse, but I don't remember to whom I appealed. Only afterwards I brought my bones in a sack into the bedchamber of the King.'

" 'So he's told me. Well, according to this, you should have been an expert on evil and cruelty before you were chosen, and you should have begged for the privilege of eternal life equal to God's angels, and you should have been willing to endure a terrible death. At the moment when the pain became too great for you, your spirit should have separated from the body, and watched the body be boiled down to bones. But only once the pain became too great. Only then. You were to endure the boiling cauldron of gold for as long as you could to perfect your hatred of God that he had made men sentient beings, and then and only then you should have risen free, aware of the power of your triumph over death, and your hatred of God, who made death, and your desire to be the mal'ak who is as strong as Yahweh's cruel heart when he turned it against those whom Saul or David or Joshua would slay.

" 'You are to be the avenger of Adam and Eve, that they were foully tricked by your God. What does that say to you?'

" 'It was all a blundering affair, as you said. I can't remember being *in* the cauldron, only a terrible, terrible fear of it. I think I escaped my body before the pain came, I think I couldn't endure it, all was confusion, I was surrounded by weak and self-seeking individuals, all grandeur had gone. All majesty had gone. I had done something,

something that others wanted me to do, but it seemed tainted, horribly tainted and I'd been confused.'

" 'And there had been majesty in this tainted act?'

" 'Well, I think there had. I can remember a sense of great sacrifice, purpose. I can remember rose petals and a sleepy slow death whose worst pain was knowledge that it was irreversible and would take its time, but not be changed. I don't know why I said majesty. What did Cyrus say of me to you?'

" 'Not enough, I don't think. But according to this tablet, you cannot be destroyed. If the bones are destroyed then you are loosed upon the world to take vengeance on everything living, like a pestilence.'

"Despair descended on me. It descended on me utterly, a despair that would have been impossible for the spirit I had been only a few hours ago. When I wandered upwards towards those with joyous faces, when I saw the gleam of light, I hadn't known despair! I hadn't known it any more than a child being turned away from a plate of sweets. Now I knew.

" 'I want to die,' I whispered. 'I want to truly die as I was supposed to die, before they did this to me, misguided fools that they were! Before they tried this fearsome magic. Ah, idiots! Ah, God!'

" 'Die?' he asked, 'and wander among the stupid dead? Become a demon growling among other spirits, become a great foul enemy of all that is good, a bringer of death and torment!'

" 'No, just die, die as if in my mother's arms, die as if to lie in my Mother Earth, and if I become light and if there is Heaven so be it, but if not, then simply to die, and to live on in the memory of anything good I ever did for anyone, any good act, any act of kindness and love, and . . .'

" '. . . and what?'

" 'I was going to say that I wanted to live on in memory for the acts I had done in praise of God, but I don't care about that now. I just want to die. I would rather God would leave me alone.' I stood up. I looked down at him. 'Did Cyrus tell you who I was in life? How he came to know me?'

" 'No, you can go read his letters for yourself. He said only that your strength was too great for any magician but myself, and that he owed you a great debt, that your death had been his doing.' He stopped, thinking, pulling on his beard. 'Of course the King of all the world is not going to add to a letter that he was personally frightened of a spirit and wishes to get it as far from him as possible, but there was that, shall we say, tinge to the letter. You know, "I cannot command this spirit. I dare not. And yet I owe him my Kingdom?" '

" 'I can't remember his owing me anything. I remember asking to be sent . . . I remember . . .'

" 'Yes?'

" 'Being forsaken by all.'

" 'Well, these fools haven't made a demon. They have made something more like an angel.'

" 'Angel of might,' I said. 'You used those words yourself. Cyrus used them. Marduk used them . . .' I stopped. Stumped by the name Marduk, and seeing nothing to surround the name or make it plausible in my speech.

" 'Marduk, the god of Babylon?' he asked.

" 'Don't mock him, he suffers,' I said, amazing myself.

" 'You want vengeance on those who did this to you?'

" 'I took it. I can't remember anyone else who is not dead. It was the priest's doing, and he . . . and the old woman, she died, the witch, the seer. I can't remember . . . I knew only Cyrus could help me and I knew that I had a right to walk into his bedchamber, that I would make him listen to me. No, I don't want vengeance. No. I don't remember anything enough to want it, any more than I hanker after life. I don't. There is something I want . . . to die . . . to rest, to sleep, to be dead in the sweet-smelling earth . . . or to see the light as I become one with it, one tiny spark of the light of God returned to his flame. I want death most . . . even more than the light. Just the quiet of death.'

" 'You want this now,' he said. 'You didn't want it when you went walking, or roaming the realm of the spirits, or bringing the scrolls for me. Or when you first sat down in this garden and kept touching the grass with your hands.'

" 'That's because you're a good man,' I said.

" 'No, that's because *you* are a good man. Or were. And goodness burns as bright in you now as it ever did. Souls without memory are dangerous. You remember . . . but you remember only the good.'

" 'No, I've told you how much I hate them . . .'

" 'Yes, but they're gone, they're receding from you fast. You can't remember their names, or their faces . . . you don't hate them. But you remember good. Last night, you told me you found gold in your pockets. What did you do with it? You didn't say.'

" 'Well, I gave it to the poor and hungry, a family of them, so they could eat.' I reached out and gathered the loose grass that would come up from the cracks between the marble. I looked at the tender green shoots. 'You're right. I do remember goodness, or I know it. I know it, and I see it and I feel it . . .'

" 'Then I'll teach you everything I can,' he said. 'We'll travel. We'll go to Athens and then down into Egypt. I have never been deep into Egypt. I want to go. We'll travel by magic. Or sometimes merely in the natural way, because you're a strong guardian, and you must remember everything I teach you . . . your tendency, your weakness, is to veer away from pain by forgetting it, and when I die, you'll feel some pain.'

"He fell quiet. I think the lessons were at an end for a little while. He closed his eyes. But I had a further pressing question.

" 'Ask it, then, before I go to sleep.'

" 'These Canaanites, who made this curse. Were they Hebrew?'

" 'Not really,' he said. 'Not Hebrew as you are. Their Yahweh was one of many gods, only the strongest, a war god it seems. They were ancient peoples and they believed in other gods too. Are you glad to hear this?'

"My mind had drifted. 'I suppose I am,' I said. 'Yes, I am. But I belong to no tribe now. My destiny is to belong to the best of Masters, for without them I may forget everything, I may drift . . . I may cease to see or hear or feel . . . and I won't be dead, merely waiting for the one who calls me forth.'

" 'I won't live long,' he said. 'I'll teach you every trick I know that you have the power to do, and how to deceive men with illusions, and how to create spells over them with words and attitudes . . . that's all it is . . . remember . . . words, attitudes . . . it's the abstract . . . not the particular. You could make a curse of a list of barrels of grain if you said it right, you know? But I'll teach you and you will listen, and when I die . . .'

" 'Yes . . .'

" 'We'll see what the wide world teaches you by that time.'

" 'Don't expect too much of me,' I said. I looked at him directly, which I had rarely done in all this time. 'You ask me what I remember. I remember killing the bedouins and I liked it very much. Not as much as the flowers, gathering them, you know, but killing . . . what is there like it on earth?'

" 'You have a point,' he said. 'You have to learn that to love is better . . . to be kind is even better. In killing you crush a universe of beliefs and feelings and generations in that one person whom you kill. But when you do kindness, it's like dropping a pebble in the great ocean and the ripples go on forever and ever, and no wave, not even those as far away as Italy or Egypt, is the same. Kindness actually has considerably more power than killing has. But you'll come to see it. You knew it when you were alive.'

"He considered for a moment, and then concluded his advice for the day.

" 'You see, it's a matter of how well you can measure these things. When you strike down a man, you don't see the full implications of his death, not then. You feel the blood rush in you, even as a spirit you are formed in the likeness of man. But when you do something good, you can see it often . . . you can see it and see it and see it . . . and that's what overrides the desire to kill finally. The goodness shines too bright; it's too . . . undeniable. When you walked you saw it in people's faces, didn't you? Goodness. No one tried to hurt you. Not even the palace guards. They let you by. Was it your clothing and your demeanor? Or did you smile at them as well? Did your face shine with goodwill? Each time you return to me, you are happy, and your spirit, whatever made it, has a great capacity to love.'

"I didn't answer.

" 'What is in your head now?' he asked. 'Tell me.'

" 'The bedouins,' I said. 'What fun it was to kill them,' I answered.

" 'You're stubborn!' he said.

"He closed his eyes and went to sleep. I sat there watching and gradually I slept too, asleep in my body, listening to the flowers next to my ears, and looking up into the branches of the olive tree now and then to see the birds there, and the distant sounds of the city became a music to me. And when I dreamed, it was of gardens, and light and fruit trees and joyous spirits with faces filled with love.

"Words were woven into my dreams.

" 'And I will give thee the treasures of darkness, and hidden riches of secret places, that thou mayest know that I, the Lord, which call *thee* by thy name, *am* the God of Israel . . . I form the light, and I create darkness: I make peace, and create evil . . .' My eyes opened, but then I knew sweeter verses, and sank back into a half sleep of song and willow trees swaying in the breeze."

13

For fifteen years, I traveled with Zurvan. I did his bidding in all things. He was rich, as I've said, and many times he wanted to travel merely as men do, and we went by ship to Egypt, and then back again to Athens and to other cities which he had visited in his youth and had despaired of ever seeing again.

"Almost never did he let on that he was a magician, though now and then he was recognized by one with second sight. And when called upon to heal the sick, he would do what he could. In every place we traveled he bought or had me borrow for him, or even steal, tablets and scrolls of magic, and these he studied and read to me and made me memorize, further reinforcing his conviction that all magic was more or less the same.

"That I can remember these years with crystal clarity is a mercy, because during the time that separated me from his death and the present I have few distinct memories at all. I know there were times after Zurvan's death when I woke with no memory and served my masters out of boredom, and sometimes watched them bring destruction upon themselves and thought it amusing, and even now and then took the bones from them myself to another. But all this is hazy, fog. Meaningless.

"Zurvan was right. My response to pain and to suffering was to forget. And it is the overall tendency of spirits to forget. Flesh and blood, bodily needs, these are what inspire memory in man. And when these are wholly absent, it can be sweet to remember nothing at all.

"During Zurvan's life, he made a better casket for the bones. He made it of very strong wood, plated inside and out with gold, and he made a carved-out space for the bones to rest in their curled position, as that of a child asleep. He had carpenters work on this because, in truth, the work of his spirit familiars was not exact enough for him. Those who know the material world work with greater respect for it, he said.

"On the outside of this casket which was a rectangle just long enough to contain my skeleton, he carved the name of what I was and how I was to be called, and he carved the stern warning that I must never be used for evil, lest that evil descend upon the one who calls. He cautioned against the destruction of my bones, lest all restraint upon me go with it.

"He wrote all this in the form of incantation and sacred poetry in many languages all over the casket.

"He put a Hebrew symbol or letter which means life on the casket.

"It was very good that he did all this early, because his death came quite by surprise. He died in his sleep, and I was called forth only when his house in Syracuse was being raided by petty thieves and people of the village who knew he had no kin and were in no fear for him. And as he had left no demons to guard his body, they sacked the house, found the casket, spoke of the bones, and I awoke.

"I slew everyone present, down to the smallest child who rummaged through Zurvan's clothes. I slew them all. That night, the villagers came to burn the house of the Magus in hopes of dispelling its evil. I was glad of this because I knew that Zurvan, being Greek by birth, though a man of no nation or tribe by choice, wanted his remains to be burnt, and I had arranged them within the house so that they burnt first and fast.

"I journeyed back to Miletus, and then on towards Babylon though I didn't remember why. I grieved for Zurvan. I thought only of Zurvan. I was in pain night and day, invisible, in the flesh, frightened to go into the bones to rest lest I never come out of them, and lugging my skeleton with me through the desert sands.

"At last I came to a city of Babylon but found myself repelled by it and hating it, and walking in pain with every step. I saw nothing that sparked a memory, only a feeling. I left very shortly after I'd come and I went back to Athens, which had been the birthplace of

Zurvan. And finding a little house, I made a safe hiding place for the bones far, far beneath it, and then I went into them. And all was blackness.

"Much later I awoke with faint memories of Zurvan, yet remembering all his lessons, but it was another century. And maybe I always remembered his lessons. I think that may be the key to my eventual rebellion, that I remembered his lessons and loathed the perversion of them.

"Whatever the case, I was called forth in Athens. The soldiers of Philip II of Macedon had come down on Athens and beaten the Greeks, and Philip the Barbarian, as they called him, was looting the city, and in the process the bones were unearthed.

"When I came forth it was in the tent of a Macedonian magician, and he was as amazed to lay eyes on me, as I was on him.

"I remember almost nothing of him. What I remember is the vibrant quality of the world, the lure of being solid once more, of tasting water, and of wanting to be a living and breathing thing even if only an imitation. I knew also my great strength, kept this secret from this Master, and only quietly obeyed his largely petty and foolish commands. He was a small magician.

"I was passed by him to another and another. My next distinct memory is only because Gregory Belkin wakened it in me . . . that I was in Babylon when Alexander the Great died. How I got there, whom I served, I don't remember. But I remember dressing myself, making my body into that of one of Alexander's soldiers so that I might pass before his bed and see him signal with his hand that he was dying.

"I remember Alexander as he lay on his bed, that he burnt with an aura as bright as that of Cyrus the Persian. Even in dying he was very beautiful and strangely alert. He was observing himself die, and he was not fighting to live. Not desperate to live. It was as if he knew this was to be the end of his life. I don't recall him knowing that a spirit had walked past him, as I was solid and very complete. I do recall going back to my Master of the moment and telling him, Yes, the conqueror of the world was dying, and it seems this Master was old and Greek, too, and that he wept. I recall that I put my arm around him to comfort him.

"I wouldn't remember that much if it weren't for Gregory crying out the name of Alexander with such fury in New York and declaring that Alexander was the only man who had really ever changed the whole world.

"I could struggle now through other masters . . . bring up out of the cauldron of memory bits and pieces. But there is no dignity or magic or greatness that calls to me, that makes me long to recount it. I was an errand boy, a spirit sent to spy, to steal, sometimes even to kill. I remember killing. But I don't remember feeling remorse. I don't remember ever serving anyone whom I thought was unspeakably evil. And I do remember that I slew two masters at various times upon waking, because they were evil men.

"But this is hazy, as I said, unclear to me. What I remember next and most vividly, what I remembered only weeks ago when I awoke in the cold clear New York streets to witness the murder of Esther Belkin, what I remembered immediately with any clarity was the last master, Samuel of Strasbourg—named for the prophet, of course.

"Samuel was a leader and a magician among the Jews of Strasbourg. I only remember loving him and his five beautiful daughters, and I remember not the details of the beginning or the middle, but only the last days when the Black Death had come, when the city was in an uproar, and the word came down from the powerful Gentiles that all of us Jews should get out, because the local authorities might not be able to protect us from the mob.

"The last night shines before my eyes. Samuel was the only one left in the house. His five daughters had been smuggled out of Strasbourg to safety, and he and I sat in the main room of his house, a very rich house, I might add, and he made it known to me, that no matter what I said or did, he would not flee the wrath of the mob.

"Many poor Jews could not escape what was about to happen. And Samuel, much to my amazement, had conceived of the notion that someone of his tribe or clan might need him at the end, and that he must remain. He had not always been so self-sacrificing by nature, yet, he had chosen to remain.

"I was frantic, slamming my fists, ranging out and coming back to tell him that the entire neighborhood was surrounded, that the entire population of this district would shortly be burned.

"The history of the world was no mystery to me and neither was Samuel; the substance of the man was vivid then and is now; I'd gotten gold for him in abundance; I had spied on his connections in business and banking; I had been the source of his immense and ever increasing wealth. Killing, that was something I had never done for him because he never thought of anything so crude; he was a merchant Jew, a banker Jew, and clever and beloved and respected by the Gentile community for his good rates of interest and his reasonableness when it came to the payment of debt. A kindly man? Yes, but a worldly man, though a bit mystical, and now he sat in this room, as the mob and the fire drew closer, as the city of Strasbourg turned into hell around us, and he quietly refused to leave.

" 'There are ways out of this city still, I can take you!' I said. Indeed we both knew of tunnels beneath the house of the Jewish district which led to the world outside the walls. They were old, true, but we knew them. I could have taken him through them. Or upwards, with great power, invisible through the air.

" 'Master, what will you do? Let them kill you? Tear you limb from limb? Either the fire will come racing at you from both ends of the street outside, or they will come, to tear off your rings and your robes before they kill you. Master, why are you choosing to die?'

"He had told me twelve times to be quiet and go back into the bones. I wouldn't do it. Finally I said, 'I won't let this happen to you. I'll take you from here, you and the bones!'

" 'Azriel,' he cried. 'There is time and you will be still!' He neatly put aside the last of his books, a volume of his cherished Talmud, and his books of the Kabbalah from which had come much of his magic, and then he waited, with his eye on the door.

" 'Master,' I asked. My memory of this is exquisite. 'Master what of me? What will happen? Will the bones be found without their casket? Where do I go, Master?'

"Surely I had never asked such a self-serving question. Because the look of surprise on his face was so bright. He broke off his reverie and staring at the door and he looked up at me.

" 'Master, when you die, can you take my spirit with you?' I said. 'Can you take your loyal servant into the light?'

" 'Oh, Azriel,' he said in the most despairing voice, 'what ever gave you such notions, foolish, foolish spirit. What do you think you are?'

"The tone of his voice infuriated me. The look on his face infuriated me.

" 'Master, you're leaving me to the ashes! To the looters!' I cried out. 'Can't you clasp my hand as they kill you, if that's what you must have, can't you take my hand and take me with you? Thirty years I've served you, made you rich, made your daughters rich. Master! You're leaving me here. The casket may burn. The bones may burn. What will happen!'

"He looked completely confused. He looked ashamed. At that point the door of the house opened and two very finely dressed Gentile merchant bankers whom I knew came into the room. Both were anxious.

" 'We have to hurry, Samuel,' they said. 'They're starting the fires near the walls. They're killing the Jews everywhere. We cannot help you escape.'

" 'Did I ask you to?' said Samuel with contempt. 'Give me the proof that my daughters are away.'

"Anxiously they put a letter in his hand. I saw it was from one of many moneylenders whom he trusted most, who was in Italy and in a safe place, and it confirmed that his daughters had come and described the color of the dress of each and every one, and her hair, and gave the special word from her which her father demanded.

"The Gentiles were terrified.

" 'We must hurry, Samuel. If you're determined to die here, keep your word! Where is the casket?'

"At these words I was astonished. Only too quickly did I understand! I had been bartered for the salvation of the five daughters! Neither of these men could see me, but they saw the casket of my bones, which was in plain sight with the books of the Kabbalah, and they went to the casket and opened it and there lay my bones!

" 'Master.' I said in a secret voice to him. 'You can't give me to these men! These men are Gentiles. They aren't magicians. They're not great men.'

"Samuel was amazed still, staring at me. 'Great? When did I ever tell you I was great or even good, Azriel? When did you ever ask?'

" 'In the name of the Lord God of Hosts,' I said, 'I did for you what was good for you and your family and your elders and your synagogue. Samuel! What do you do to me now?'

"The two Gentiles closed the casket. 'Goodbye Samuel,' they said as one of them hugged the casket to his breast and they both hurried out the door. I could see the light of the fire. I could smell it. I could hear people screaming.

" 'You evil, evil man!' I cursed him. 'You think God will forgive you because this fire cleanses you and you've sold me for money, for gold!'

" 'For my daughters, Azriel. Spirit, you have found a powerful voice too near the end.'

" 'The end of what?' But I knew. I could feel already the others calling, those who had their hands on the bones. They were already outside the city gates. And my hatred and contempt was boiling in me. Their calls were a temptation!

"I came at Samuel.

" 'No, Spirit!' he declared. 'Obey me, go to the bones. Obey as you always have. Leave me to my martyrdom.'

"There came the call again. I couldn't hold my form. I was too angry. My body was dissolving. I had in my anger forfeited too much. The voices that called me were strong. They were farther and farther away but nonetheless strong.

"I lunged at Samuel and I threw him out the open door. The street was full of flames. 'There's your martyrdom, Rabbi!' I shouted. 'I curse you to walk among the undead for all your existence, until God forgives you for what you did to me, leaving me, bartering with me, leading me to love you, and selling me like gold!'

"From both directions terrified people ran to him, people who were suffering their final anguish. 'Samuel, Samuel,' they called out his name.

"My bitterness broke for an instant when I saw him embrace them. 'Samuel,' I cried. I came towards him. I was growing weak but I was still visible to him. 'Take my hand. Hold the hand of my spirit, please, Samuel, take me with you into death.'

"He didn't speak. The crowd surrounded him, sobbing and clinging to him, but I heard his last thought as he rebuffed me as he turned his eyes away. He said as clearly as if aloud,

" 'No, Spirit, because if I die with my hand in yours you may take me down into Hell.'

"I cursed him.

" *'Not enough grace and goodness for both of us, Master. Master! Leader! Teacher! Rabbi!'*

"The flames engulfed the crowd. I rose upwards through the flame and smoke, and felt the cold night pass through me and I sped towards the sanctuary of the bones. I sped away from smoke and horror and injustice and the screams of the innocent. I went through the dark woods, as a witch to a Sabbath, flying with my arms out, and then I saw the two Gentiles at the door of a small church at a great remove from the city, the casket on the ground between them, and wanting only death and silence; I relaxed into the bones.

"All I learnt of them was that they were weeping for Strasbourg, for the Jews, for Samuel, for the whole tragedy. And that they planned to sell me in Egypt. They were not magicians. I was a marketable prize.

"It didn't seem that mine was a long uninterrupted sleep. I was called, I was taken places, I slew those who called me, and some I can picture, some not. The history of the world was written on the blank and endless tablets of my mind in column after column. I did not think, however; I slept.

"Once a Mameluk in beautiful silk called me forth. It was Cairo, and I chopped him to pieces with his own sword. It took all the wise men of the palace to drive me back into the bones. I remember their beautiful turbans and their frantic cries. They were such a flashy lot, those Moslem soldiers, those strange men who lived all their lives without women, and only to fight and to kill. Why didn't they destroy me? Because of the inscriptions that warned them against a masterless spirit who could seek revenge.

"I recall in Paris a clever satanic magician in a room full of gaslight. The wallpaper was most intriguing to me. A strange black coat hung on a hook. Life almost tempted me. Gaslight and machines; carriages rolling on cobbled streets. But I killed the mysterious man and retreated once more into the bones.

"It was always that way. I slept. I think I remember a winter in Poland. I think I remember an argument between two learned men. But all this is misty and imperfect. They spoke a Hebrew dialect and they had called me, but neither seemed to know I was there. They were good and gentle men. We were in a plain synagogue, and they argued. And then they decided that my bones must be hidden within the wall. Good men. I slept."

"When I came to life again, it was in the bright winter sunlight only weeks ago, as a trio of assassins made their way through the press on Fifth Avenue to kill Esther Belkin as she came out of her black limousine and entered the store before her—innocent, beautiful, without the slightest sense of death circling her.

"And why was I there? Who had called me? I knew only these assassins meant to kill her, these hideous rustic evil men, drugged and stupid and enchanted with the pleasure of killing her, in all her innocence. I had to stop it. I had to.

"But I was too late. You know what the papers told you.

"Who was this innocent child? She saw me, spoke my name. How had she known me? She had never called me. She had only seen me in the thin realm between life and death where truths are visible which are otherwise veiled.

"Let us linger on this killing. A death such as Esther's deserves a few more words. Or maybe I need to recount my coming into awareness. Maybe I need to describe what it was like to see and breathe again in this mighty city, with towers higher than the mystical mountain of Meru, among thousands of people, good and bad, and without luster, as Esther was being marked for the kill."

Part III

How keep dark
and pattern that any man suffers
off—at the wall, at where the hat
comes out of the marrow & yawns—
how keep head up the scream
& up the burial where the pattern is born—
how the leagues washing their hearts
& wrung dry only to sponge back up—men
smooching mirrors—blades honing—
tongue & eyelash of Sweet Thing
staggering the shape by the door in the baggy shadow—
how keep dark back?
Or should one bullet-forth, sleek-clothed or naked—pierce
each entity—each clock—sharpened by art
or wine—how
enter the needle, the cloth—
how take the pattern any man suffers
and lose nothing when you
rip it off.

Stan Rice, *Some Lamb* 1975

14

Follow me now, if you will, into consciousness.

Evals in the bright winter light of day. See how they shine. That's how I first knew them. This was a joke to them because evil was their word for bad, and their names were Eval. Three brothers out of Texas hired to kill the rich girl.

Down the crowded avenue, in a bath of noonday sun they walked, jostling each other, laughing, passing the cigarette, bold and hot for the kill. How they loved to look at themselves in the mirrors of shops, and this was New York, the biggest city in the world, the only city these Evals cared about, except for Las Vegas, where they will go with their earnings after they've "taken her out," which in their vernacular meant kill her.

They weren't never going back to Texas. Who knew what jobs "the man" might have for them? But first they had to kill her dead.

I could feel their easy malice, even as purely as they felt it—Billy Joel Eval in the lead, with the gun in his pocket and also the long sharp pick, such a cruel pick with a rounded blade of steel. And Doby Eval right behind with Hayden Eval "sucking hind teat," they taunted him, and all of them had those sharp weapons, long picks made of steel, oh, so ready to kill her but who was she?

There had to be a reason for my seeing this, there had to be a reason that I stood in the city of New York, breathing in the smells of New York as if I were alive, and visible, when I was neither, only knowing what a genii always knows . . . that he has been called again to duty, that once again his eyes and his mind have opened on a blazing and vital world.

You know how rebellious I was, I've told you, how indifferent, how perfectly willing to cut to pieces a despicable master. But what was happening here?

Loathing these rustic monsters was easy enough. I walked right by them! I saw them up close in their city-drab disguise, in quilted jackets of nylon and ragged cotton pants, machine-made shoes full of nails and hooks for the strings. Billy Joel couldn't wait to see her, couldn't wait to get close to her, and only Hayden held back, scared to tell his brother he didn't like it so much, killing this girl. If only they had known who paid them.

Who had paid them? "A man through a man through a man," said Doby Eval, "as if you can't figure that out?"

Suddenly I felt my feet hit the pavement. But I was too transparent for anyone else to see, gathering slowly, trailing them, coming up so close on them now that they might have looked back and seen me, if anyone could, and I wasn't sure anyone could.

"Who is commanding me?" I whispered. I felt my lips move. The crowd was as thick on this city street as any I'd ever beheld, and the wealth was closing in around me as if this were the marketplace of Babylon on the New Year, or the bazaars of Baghdad or Istanbul.

Through plate glass I saw the faceless white plastic goddesses of fashion in their magnificent fringe and fur, shine of true rubies, magical slippers made of thin steel straps to bind the foot fetchingly.

And all this with no explanation.

Well, you know me well enough by now, the sensualist I am.

Hand me the world in a cup and I'll drink it.

But this killing of the girl, this had to be stopped.

I closed in on them, walked among them, but still they couldn't see me, though I was feeling the shape of my body, the heat of it, the growing density. Yes, I was here all right, this was no garbled hideous phantasm in the wind.

There came the heat of the sidewalk beneath me, and something like the thud of my own feet in leather shoes, just make them plain like theirs. I knew the stench came from the engines in the street, and when I looked up, I saw the towers reaching the noonday clouds, yet lights blazing everywhere, in windows, behind written signs, all fueled by electricity.

What a modern world this was—teeming with the rich—what a

city this was with the humpback dwarf and the cripple lurching past me, both wearing fine clothes and gold, and the screeching woman on the corner, long gone mad, ripped open a blouse of pure silk to show her breasts. Someone pushed her off the curb. Hordes of young men in severe dark suits, each with a tie at the neck of his shirt, walked fast and with purpose, though obviously all disconnected, separate, not even glancing at one another.

The Evals laughed.

"Oh, I'm telling you, this is one hell of a place, this New York, I'm telling you, just look at her, did you see that? Now, you know this broad we're taking out, she's not crazy like that, no way, now you do what I said . . ."

"Do what you said," cursed the brother Hayden.

I was neck and neck with them, I could smell their sweat and the cheap soap they had used to wash half of it away, and I could smell their guns, but that wasn't the way, the gun, the bullet, the explosion—I tried to learn it all as quickly as I could—they would use the sharp-pointed picks that each carried under his clothes.

"*Why do you do this to her?*"

I must have spoken aloud, because Billy Joel stopped, right shoulder jerking up, mouth pulled down on the ends as he stared at Hayden, and then told him, "Will you shut up, you son of a bitch, come on now, I'm telling you we couldn't have gotten out of here any way but this way."

"Sure and we do her and then we just run, just run, like little kids, just run!" said Hayden, shoving his brother with his left hand in the middle of the back, so the brother Billy Joel said, "You lay off, look, you son of a bitch, you see it, you see it, Doby, she's in that goddamn car, that's her car, look at that car."

The three came together, and I fell back, invisible still but totally formed or perhaps I should say conformed to the look of men around me.

I wanted to see her, this girl they meant to kill with their evil picks, as they ambled and danced now, letting the crowd stream past them, nudging each other to stop, there she was! The time had come.

Look. See the long black limousine by the curb, and the driver with his white hair opening the door for her?

Esther. Hair a mantle of dark curls, jet-black hair, as black as mine, and her eyes larger, and the whites of them were so shiny they looked as if they were made of pearls, and her long white throat bare to the swell of her breasts beneath a painted coat, a coat painted with the stripes of an animal not to look like the animal itself but to look like the painted stripes of one.

She didn't even notice them, these three common and visible terrors who were going to "take her out." The crowd shifted and broke to make an uneven path for her.

"What am I to do?" I whispered. "Stop this? Why is she to die, for what?" I didn't want to witness it.

She pushed wide the glass doors of the shop and passed inside, with the throng so thick that five people must have followed her before the Evals made their way in, and now they knew they were in trouble.

"Jesus, do we have to do it in here?"

By that Hayden meant that this was a palace of goods, a treasure house of furs and veils, of leathers dyed in all colors, and perfume rising from the glass tables as if from altars.

They didn't look so ordinary in here, these slithering swaggering bucolic men, no, rather like tramps from a waterfront, crawling out from under the rope with the rats to steal what men have dropped, but it was so crowded, even here, shoulder to shoulder, and cheek turned from cheek, as lashes rose and fell to make the eye private. And the noise was loud. No one took the proper notice—three clothed in filth tracking the beautiful woman.

And she the young queen with the dark shining hair and the painted coat came up the steps to the landing, her face innocent and bright as she reached for a long black scarf, a beaded scarf, a lovely twinkling thing, and caught it in her fingers, dangling from the hook, a scarf full of dark stitched flowers and shimmering embroidered designs, lovely, as if meant for her.

"Good afternoon, Miss Belkin." So the queen had a name, and the merchants of this time were no less clever than in any other.

But I saw Billy Joel had struck! In that one second, he had pushed against her slender back, Hayden took her from the left, and Doby, as frenzied as Billy Joel, drove his pick from the right, so that the three wounds were made at once, and the life inside her lurched, and the language in her died, but not her heart. Her lungs filled with blood.

Geniuses of the kill, these cheap assassins. They walked right away from her, before she even fell, not even bothering to run, out of the door before she even tottered over the glass case. The scarf was still in her right hand. The woman bent over:

"Miss Belkin?"

I had to follow them. She was falling down dead, leaning over the glass, as if this was just a pain she had to feel and it would pass. She'd be dead in seconds! And I knew the killers, and the merchant lady didn't even know she was dying.

I shot through the front doors. I knew I shoved against the humans to move them out of my way. I felt them. I wasn't going to lose the Evals. I went up.

Over the heads of the crowd, I flew, formed but transparent, nothing anyone would notice, and quickly caught up with them.

The Evals had broken apart. But no one in this next block of shuffling hundreds seemed to notice them; what need was there to hurry? Billy Joel had a smile on his face, bright smile.

They had put three hundred people and ten seconds between them and the murder.

"I will kill you for this!" I heard my voice aloud. I felt the air inside me, swirling, as if I'd made myself solid enough to feed on the fumes that rose from the pavements, from the stalled engines, from the blasting horns, from the swarm of human flesh.

Come to me, garments like those of my enemy, as I am made flesh! I dropped down in front of Billy Joel. Reach for the pick. Get it. Kill him. I saw my fingers close on his wrist. He never clearly saw me, only felt the bone break. As he cried out, his brother turned. I drove the pick into Billy Joel, I took its wooden handle out of his belt and drove it in through his shirt, deep, the way he had driven it into her, only many more times.

Astonished, he spurted blood.

"You die, you filthy dog, you killed that girl, you die."

Hayden came towards me, right onto the pick, no trouble at all, and I gave him three quick thrusts, including one in the neck. There were people walking by, not turning their heads. Others were looking at the fallen Billy Joel.

Now only Doby was left and Doby had fled, Doby had seen them go down and was running about as fast as a human can run through the obstacle course of the crowd. I reached out, grabbed his shoulder . . .

"Wait a minute, man!" he said to me. I sank the pick into his chest, the same three times, to make it good, and pushed him towards the wall. People stepped out of our way, turning the other way. He slid down to the pavement dead, and a woman cursed as she stepped over his left leg.

Now I understood the genius of their crime in this crowded city. But there was no time to think on it. I had to return to Esther.

My body was formed, I was running, and I had to make my way, like any other human now, solid, back to the glass doors of the palace.

The air was filled with screams. Men ran into the emporium of clothes. I pushed to get close. I could feel my tangled black hair. I could feel my beard. All eyes were on her.

Out she came, laid and covered on a white linen stretcher. I saw her head tumbled to my side, her big glossy eyes, with their pearly whites so pure, her mouth leaking blood like an old fountain. Just a trickle.

Men screamed for others to get back. An old one wailed at the top his lungs, bowing as he saw her. This was her driver, her guard perhaps, the gray-haired man. His face was furrowed, his narrow back bent. He bowed and cried out, he cried out in a dialect of Hebrew. He loved her. I pushed carefully towards her.

A white car came speeding to the spot, printed with red crosses and topped by swirling lights. The sirens were unspeakable. Might as well have been the picks through my ears, but there was no time to worry about my pain. She was still living, breathing, I had to tell her.

Into that car, they carried her, lifted high, like an offering over the crowd . . . Through the back doors she went inside, her eyes looking for something, for someone.

Gathering all my strength, I moved others out of my path. My hands—true and familiar and mine—hit the long glass windowed side of the white car. I looked into the glass. I felt my nose against it. I saw her! Her big sleepy eyes full of dreamy death, I saw her.

And she said aloud, I heard it, a whisper rising like a whiff of smoke.

"The Servant . . . Azriel, the Servant of the Bones!"

The door was open. The men ministering to her bent low.

"What is it, honey? What did you say?"

"Don't make her speak."

She stared at me through the glass, and she said it again, I saw her lips move. I heard her voice. I heard her thought. "Azriel," she whispered. "The Servant of the Bones!"

"They're dead, my darling!" I cried out. No one around me, pressing as hard as I pressed to see her, cared what I said.

She and I, we looked at each other. Then her soul and spirit blazed for one instant, visible and together, the full shape of her body over her, hair like wings, face expressionless or turned away from the earth forever, who can know, and then she was gone, risen, in a blinding light. I ducked from the light, then tried to see it again. But it was gone.

The body lay an empty sack.

The doors slammed shut.

The siren split my ears again.

The car roared into the stream, forcing other engines out of its path, people shifted and sighed and groaned around me. I stood stock-still on the pavement. Her soul was gone.

I looked up. Knees pushed against my leg. A foot came down hard upon my own. I wore the same kind of dirty string shoe as my enemy. I was almost toppled from the shallow curb.

The car was beyond my sight, and the Evals dead not a hundred feet away, yet no one here in this melee knew, so crowded was it, and I thought—without context, without reason—of what was said about Babylon after Cyrus conquered it, that funny remark which the Greek historian Xenophon had made, or was it Herodotus, that so big was Babylon and so dense with people that it took two whole days before people in the middle of the city knew that it had been taken at all.

Well, not me!

A man said, "Did you know who that was?" This was English, New York talk, and I turned just as if I were alive and I were going to answer, only there were tears in my eyes. I wanted to say,

"They killed her." Nothing came out of my mouth but I had a mouth and the man was nodding as if he saw the tears. My God, help me. This man wanted to comfort me. Someone else spoke:

"That was Gregory Belkin's daughter, that's who that was," the man said, "That was Esther Belkin."

"Belkin's daughter—"

". . . Temple of the Mind."

"Temple of the Mind of God. Belkin."

What did these words mean to me?

Master! Where are you? Name yourself or show yourself! Who has called me? Why have I been made to witness this!

"Gregory Belkin's little girl, the Minders—"

Which way?

I began to fade. I felt it swift and terrible as it always is, as surely as if the Master had commanded all the artificial and gathered particles of me, as it is written, *Return now to your place.* Just for a moment, I clung to the storm of matter, commanding it to sheathe me, but my cry was a wail. I stared down at my hands, my feet, such filthy shoes, cloth and string and leather shoes, slippers more than shoes, shoes on the pavement:

"Azriel, stay alive!" came the voice from my mouth.

"Take it easy, son," said the man beside me. And he looked at me as if he felt sorry for me. He lifted his arm to embrace me. I put my hand up. I saw the tears.

But the wind had come, the wind that comes for all spirits. I was losing my hold.

The man was looking for me and he couldn't find me, and he didn't know why, and thought it was his own confusion.

Then he and all those with him—and the great city—was gone too.

I was nothing now, nothing.

I struggled to see the crowd below, but I couldn't find the spots where the Evals lay dead in their blood still or were being taken away with such care as the queen with her dark hair, the goddess who had died seeing me. She had said it, I heard it, she had said, "Azriel, the Servant of the Bones." I had heard her as a spirit hears, though the man in the car with her might not hear something so small and tragic as her whisper.

The wind took me. The wind was filled with the wail of the souls, faces bearing down upon me, hands seeking to grip me, and turning my back on it as always, I let go. I saw the last dim outline of my hands for one instant; I felt the form of arms and legs; I felt the tears on my face. Yes, I felt that. Then I was a goner.

Into the bones, Azriel. I was safe.

So there you have the picture! Masterless, risen, to witness this, to avenge it? Why? The darkness overcame me like a drug. Safe, yes, but I didn't want to be safe; I wanted to find the man who had sent those Evals to kill her.

15

Time passed.

I felt it more intensely than usual. I knew that I was listening. I was there.

I knew what the world was now, more or less, as always. Bear with me. I knew what men and women knew—those whom I'd seen and touched in the New York street.

The particulars made a moral impression. Emotion gradually accompanied the synthesis of knowledge. Ghosts don't have to interpret. Ghosts don't have to be amazed, or shocked.

But the mind of the ghost, unfettered by flesh, can gather to itself indiscriminately and perhaps infinitely the sum of what is shared or valued by nearby human minds.

Awake once more in the darkness, I grasped the general and the spectacular—that we were nearing the end of the twentieth century of what men call the common era, that fossil fuel and generated electricity were indispensable to the everyday methods of eating, drinking, sleeping, communicating, traveling, building, and fighting, that micromachines of exquisite circuitry could store information in abundance, and that vivid moving pictures in which people appeared and spoke could be transmitted by waves or over tiny delicate fibers more precious than spun glass.

Waves. The air was full of waves. Full of voices speaking both privately and publicly—from telephones, through radios, televisions. The world was as fully surrounded by voices now as it was by air itself.

And the earth was indeed round. Not a mile of it remained uncharted, unowned, or unnamed. No part of it lay beyond communication because the mysterious waves of telephones, radios, and televisions could be bounced off satellites in space and back to earth again at any locale. Sometimes the television pictures and voices were of people and actions taking place at the very moment they were being transmitted: known as live TV.

Chemistry had reached unprecedented heights, achieving through extraction, purification, analysis, and new combinations all manner of new substances, materials, drugs. The very process of combining had been transformed so that there was now physical change, chemical change, chain reaction, chemical reaction, and fusion, to name but a few. Materials had been broken down and made into new materials and the process was without limit.

Science had surpassed the alchemist's dreams.

Diamonds had found their way into the bits of drills, yet people still wore them as ornaments and they commanded millions of dollars, which was, apparently a preferred currency, American dollars, though the world was full of currencies and languages, and people from Hong Kong spoke to people in New York merely by pressing a few buttons. The catalog of synthetic materials and subsequent products had evolved beyond the memory or understanding of the common man so that almost nobody could define for you the ingredients of the nylon shirt he wore, or the plastic calculator in his pocket.

Of course some conclusions—even for me—were inevitable. A car or plane dependent on the combustion of fossil fuel can explode rather than move forward. Bombs can be sent without pilots from one country to another to destroy even the biggest cities with the highest buildings. Hardly anywhere in the world did the sea not taste just a little of gasoline.

New York was very far north of the equator, that was obvious, and one could say it was the capital, in this time, in the Western world.

The Western world. This is where I have found myself. And what is the Western world? Apparently, the Western world was the direct cultural legacy of the Hellenism of Alexander the Great, its concepts of justice and purity infinitely amplified and complicated but never really subverted by Christianity of varying kinds—from crude screaming mystic acceptance of Jesus to dense theological sects which still argue over the nature of the Trinity, that is, whether or not there are three persons in one God. Scarcely a single part of the Western world had not been enriched and invigorated by an immensely creative and relentlessly spiritual Judaism. Jewish scientists, philosophers, doctors, merchants, and musicians were among the most celebrated of the era.

The drive to excel was taken for granted, as it was in Babylon. Even by those in despair.

Natural law and law arrived at by reason had become common values, revealed law and inherited law on the other hand had become suspect and subjected to argument, and all human lives now were "created equal." That is, the life of a worker in the fields was as precious as the life of the titular Queen of England or her elected Prime Minister.

Technically, legally, there were no slaves.

Few were certain as to the meaning of life, as few today as there had been in those times when I was alive.

Once in the scriptorium as a human boy I had read in Sumerian the lament: "Who has ever known the will of heaven?" Any man or woman in the streets of New York today might have spoken the same words.

This Western world, this legacy of Hellenism, infused with ever evolving Judaism and Christianity, had flourished most dramatically in northern climes of the planet both in Europe and in America, harnessing somehow the tenacity and the ferocity of those taller, shaggier, and often fairer dwellers of the woodlands and the steppes, who did not learn to be humans in Eden, but rather in lands where summer was always followed by the brutality of cold and snow.

All the Western world, including its most tropical outposts, lived now as if winter might at any moment descend, isolate, even destroy.

From towns near the northern polar ice cap all the way down to the tip of the jungles of Peru, people thrived in enclaves designed and sustained by machine, microchip, and microbiology, surrounded by surpluses of energy, fuel, finery, and food.

Nobody ever wanted to run out of anything ever again, and this included information.

Storage. Archives. Information banks. Hard disk, floppy disk, backup tape, hard copy—everything worth anything was somehow duplicated in one form or another and stored.

It was basically the same theory that had created the archives of tablets in Babylon which I had once studied. Not difficult to understand.

But in spite of all these dazzling advances, amid which Esther Belkin had somehow drawn me to her like a magnet, and seemed even now to draw my consciousness to her, there existed still "the Old World."

Follow the stream into the marshes, into the mountains, into the desert.

"The East" was what they called it, or the Third World, or the Undeveloped Countries, or the Backward Countries, or the Primitive Areas—and it covered continents still where the bedouin in timeless white garments walked his camel through the sandstorm, happy as ever to live amid sun-bright desolation. Only now he might carry with him a battery-operated television set, and a can of a fire-making chemical called Sterno so that when he pitched his tent, he could listen to the Koran read over the television as his food was heated without the use of wood or coal.

In the rice paddies, in the fields of India, in the marshes of Iraq, in the villages the world over, men and women stooped to gather the crop as they had since the dawn of time.

Huge modern urban outposts had arisen amid the millions of Asia, yet the vast majority of tribes, farmers, weavers, vendors, mothers, priests, beggars, and children remained beyond the reach of Western invention, abundance, medicine, and sanitation.

Sanitation was key.

Sanitation involved the chemical purification of human waste and industrial waste, the purification of drinking water and water for bathing—the nullification of filth in all forms and the maintenance of an environment in which one could be born, give birth, grow up, and die—in maximum security against human or industrial or chemical contamination of any kind.

Nothing mattered as much as sanitation. Plagues had vanished from the earth due to sanitation.

In the "West" sanitation was taken for granted; in the "East" sanitation was viewed with suspicion, or people were simply too numerous to be made to conform to the inevitable habits required by it.

Disease was rampant in the jungles; in the marshes; in the deep pockets of vast cities or in the wilderness where the peasants, the workers, the fellaheen, still lived as they always had.

Hunger. There was plenty and there was hunger. There was food thrown away in the streets of New York and there were those starving in Asia on television programs. It was a matter of distribution.

Indeed, that there was as much organization amid all of this change was the modern mystery—that so much could happen and that so much could remain the same.

Everywhere were dramatic contrasts which could both confuse and delight the eye. The holy men of India walked naked beside the roaring automobiles in the teeming streets of Calcutta. People in Haiti lay on the ground starving to death as they watched planes fly overhead.

The River Nile flowed into the metropolis of Cairo, where the buildings of steel and glass stand as high as in Manhattan, yet the streets were thronged by men and women in loose, airy cotton robes of white or black, as pure as the garments worn by the Israelites when Pharaoh let the people go.

The pyramids of Giza remained as always, only the air surrounding them was thick with the emission of automobiles, and the modern city crawled almost to their feet.

Within a stone's throw of air-conditioned office buildings there lingered pockets of jungle where men knew nothing of Yahweh, Allah, Jesus, or Shiva, or of iron, copper, gold, or bronze. They hunted with wooden spears and poison from reptiles, only now and then stupefied by the sight of big mechanical bulldozers mowing down the forest which was their world.

A flock of goats in the mountains of Judea still looked exactly like a flock of goats in the time of Cyrus the Persian. Shepherds tending sheep outside the city of Bethlehem looked exactly as they had when Jeremiah the Prophet raved.

Though East and West communicated and interacted continuously, each somehow held out against the other. Desert sheiks, rich from the oil discovered beneath their sands, still wore their headdress and robes as they drove about in automobiles. Vast numbers of the world's women still lived indoors almost entirely and only entered a public street if their faces were veiled.

In New York City, capital of the West and city of choice of the more clever and more powerful, the common person was utterly confident and utterly ignorant of "science" at the same time.

What individual anywhere in the world knew the real meaning of binary code, semiconductor, triodes, electrolyte, or laser beam?

In the upper echelons a technological elite with the powers of a priesthood dealt in perfect faith with the invisible: ions, neutrinos, gamma rays, ultraviolet light, and black holes in space.

Icons shone bright for me in my awakening, bright as the eyes of Esther when she died.

"Servant of the Bones, listen," she might as well have said. "Servant of the Bones, come, see."

All the material world was mine to behold, to know, without haste or alarm, as I slumbered, grieving for her, and angry, angry with her killers.

In invisibility and silence, I saw a man parked at Fifty-sixth and Fifth speaking on a tiny phone in his car, in the German language, to an employee of his in the city of Vienna.

One woman in a building in the city of Atlanta in the country of America talked for twenty-four hours before a camera about the weather all over the globe.

Esther Belkin, my lost one, was mourned by thousands who had never known her, her story broadcast to every country which could receive the Cable News Network, or, as it was mostly known, CNN. Members of the international Temple of the Mind of God, to which she herself had not belonged, mourned for her.

Her stepfather, Gregory Belkin, a robust man of substantial height, the Temple's founder, wept before cameras and spoke of cults, terrorists, and plots. "Why do they want to hurt us!" he said. His eyes were clear and brilliantly black, his hair close cut but thick as hers had been, and his skin was almost the perfect color of honey in sunlight.

The mother of the murdered Esther fled the public eye. White-clad nurses ushered Mrs. Belkin past screaming reporters. With the long unkempt hair of a girl, and thin beseeching hands, she looked little older than her daughter.

Law officers and elected officials condemned the violence of the times.

And the times were universally violent. In fact, violence came now like any other commodity, in all sizes and forms.

Robbery, rape, and battery were routine, if not rampant, beneath a canopy of civilization and peace. Small organized wars were in constant progress. People were fighting to the death in Somalia, in Afghanistan, in the Ukraine. Souls of the newly dead wreathed the earth like smoke.

The market for weapons was black, white, chaotic, endless. Struggling little countries vied with larger and more powerful nations to buy up legally or illegally the armaments and explosives of crumbling empires. Powerful nations sought to stop the proliferation of missiles, hand grenades, bullets, and canisters of poison gas, while they themselves continued to develop nuclear bombs which could destroy the earth.

Drugs were critical to people. Everyone talked of drugs.

Drugs cured. Drugs killed. Drugs helped. Drugs hurt.

There were so many kinds of drugs and for so many purposes that no one being could grasp the significance of the sheer multiplicity itself.

In one New York hospital alone, the size of the inventory of drugs which saved lives daily through inoculation, injection, intravenous feed, or oral ingestion was almost beyond human count. Yet a computer system kept perfect track of it.

Worldwide, criminal overlords fought for the trade in illegal drugs—the wherewithal to develop, distribute, and market cocaine and heroin—chemicals with no other purpose than to make people feel an addictive euphoria or calm.

Cults. Cults were a matter of public obsession and fear. Cults were apparently unsanctioned religious organizations, that is, organizations to which people belonged, swearing allegiance generally to a leader of whose morals and purposes others were unsure. Cults could rise, seemingly from nothing, around the figure of one man—Gregory Belkin. Or cults could break off from large organized religions to form fanatical enclaves of their own.

Cults existed for peace and war.

Around the death of Esther Belkin swarmed the argument over cults.

Again and again, her face flashed on television screens.

She herself, a member of nothing, was related to everything—those who were anti-government, those who were anti-God, those who were anti-wealth.

Had her father's cult members actually killed Esther?

She herself had once been heard in private to remark that the Temple of the Mind of God had too much money, too much power, too many houses worldwide. Or had it been the enemies of Gregory Belkin and his Temple who sought through the death of Esther to hurt the father, to warn him and his powerful cohorts that his organization had become too big, and too dangerous, but to whom?

Cults could be liberal, radical, reactionary, old-fashioned.

Cults could do terrible things.

I drifted, I watched, I listened; I knew what people knew.

It was a world of empires, nations, countries, and gangs; and the smallest gang could dominate the television screens of the entire world with one well-planned explosion. The news would talk all day about the leader of fifty as easily as it might about the leader of millions.

Enemies were the beneficiaries of the same democratic and competitive scrutiny as victims.

The faces of the Evals—Billy Joel, Doby, and Hayden—rose to the fore, blazing as bright as Esther's on the television screens for brief seconds. Had these men who killed Esther Belkin belonged to a secret movement? People spoke of backwoods "survivalists" with barbed-wire fences and vicious dogs, who suspected all kinds of authority. Conspiracy. It might be anywhere in any form.

And then there were the Apocalyptic Christians, having more cause than ever before to say that Judgment Day was at hand.

Had the Eval brothers come from such organizations?

Gregory Belkin, the stepfather of Esther, spoke in a soft compelling voice of plots to hurt all God-fearing peoples. The innocence of Esther was significant and cried out to heaven. Terrorists, diamonds, fanatics—these words encircled the brief flicker of Esther's face and name.

The news in all forms—printed, broadcast, computerized on internets—was continuous, alarming, prophetic, fatalistic, detailed, ludicrous by intention and by accident in turns.

As I said, any ghost could have grasped these things.

The question with me was why was I thinking of *anything*? Why wake from my deep sleep, just short of death, always just short of death, and find myself walking amongst Billy Joel, Hayden, and Doby Eval—a sudden horrified witness to their crime?

Whatever the case, I had for the moment lost my taste for merely drifting, for merely existing, for merely hating.

I wanted to pay attention. I wanted to make full use of my mind unfettered by flesh and cast into eternity, a mind that had been gaining strength with each new awakening, taking back into the darkness with it not merely experience but emotion, and possibly a certain resolve.

Inevitably, it was a Master who would put all of this in order through his responses, his reactions, the vitality of his will.

But a very specific question tormented me. Yes, I was back and I wanted to be back. But had not I done things to ensure that I would never be brought back again?

If I wanted to, I think I could remember what I'd done. Forget the world and all its pomp and racket for a moment. I was Azriel. Azriel could remember what he'd done.

I had slain masters.

If I wanted to, I could remember more dead Magi than those I've already described here. I could smell again the camp of the Monguls, leather, elephants, scented oil—flicker of lights beneath the sagging silk, the chessboard overturned and tiny carved figures made of gold and silver rolling on a flowered carpet.

Cries of men. *Destroy it, it's a demon, drive it back into the bones!*

A series of windows in Baghdad looking out over a battle. *Back into the bones! Fiend from Hell.* A castle near Prague. A stone-cold room high in the Alps. And maybe even more—even after the vivid enchanting gaslight on the flowered wallpaper of the sorcerer's room in Paris.

This servant serves no more!

Yes, I'd proved to myself and them that I could slay any conjurer.

So where was the sly, covert consciousness which had brought me here to this presentation of power?

Oh, I could like to aver that I loathed being conscious again and forswore all life and everything that goes with it, but I couldn't really do that. I couldn't forget Esther's eyes, or the beautiful glass on Fifth Avenue, or the moment when the heat came through the soles of my shoes, and when the man, the kindly unknowing man had put his arm around me!

I was curious and free! In an orbit, I was bound to these bizarre events. But no Lord directed me.

Esther knew me but she hadn't called. Had it been someone on behalf of Esther, someone whom I had already tragically failed?

Two nights passed in real time before I realized I was once again awake, and moving through the air: the angel of might, the angel of evil, who knows?

This is what I saw:

16

This was a nearby city, in view of the other. The car moving through the rain was the car that had carried Esther to the place where the Evals surrounded her with their picks. Other cars traveled with it, filled with guards whose eyes roved dark and deserted buildings.

The procession was furtive yet full of authority.

Through the rain, I could actually see the shining towers of the street on which she had died. Grand as Alexandria, or Constantinople, this rock-hard capital of the Western world, New York—in its greedy nuclear splendor. Yet its soaring buildings reminded me of the weapons carried by the Evals. Hard and very sharp.

The man in the car was very proud of the car, proud of the guards who traveled with him, proud of his fine wool coat and the neat trim of his thick curly hair.

I drew in close to see him through the darkened glass: Gregory Belkin, her stepfather, founder of the Temple of the Mind of God, rich man. Rich beyond the dreams of kings in earlier times, because they couldn't fly on magic carpets.

The car? Mercedes-Benz, and the most unusual of its kind, made from a small sedan and elongated by three perfectly welded and padded parts so that it was twice the length of the engines all around it, shiny and black, deliberately glamorous, as if carved of obsidian and polished by hand.

It prowled for blocks before stopping, the driver quick to obey the rise of Belkin's hand.

Then this proud high priest or prophet or whatever he deemed himself stepped unaided out into the light of the street lamp as if he wanted it to shine on his youthful clean-shaven face, hair clipped short on the back of his neck like a Roman soldier, yet softly curly despite its length.

The full length of the dingy dirty block he walked, alone, past dismal boarded-up shops, past signs in Hebrew and in English, to the place he meant to visit, his guards sweeping the night before him and behind him with their glances, the raindrops standing like jewels on the shoulders of his long coat.

All right. Was he the Master? If so, how could I not know it? I didn't like him. In my half sleep, I had seen him weep for Esther and talk of plots, and had not liked him.

Why was I so close I could touch his face? Handsome he was, no one would argue with this, and in the prime of life, square-shouldered, tall as a Norseman, though darker with jet-black eyes.

Are you the Master?

Mastermind of the Minders, that was what the flippant and cynical reporters called him, this billionaire Gregory Belkin. Now he reviewed in his head recent speeches he'd made before the bronze doors of his Manhattan Temple, "My worse fear is that they weren't thieves at all and the necklace meant nothing to them. It's our church they want to hurt. They are evil."

Necklace, I thought, I had seen no necklace.

The guards who watched Gregory from their nearby cars were his "followers." This was some church of peace and good. They wore guns, and they carried knives, and he himself the prophet carried a small gun, very shiny, like his car, deep in the left pocket of his coat.

He was like a King who is used to performing every gesture before a grand audience, but he didn't see me watching him. He had no sense of a ghost at his shoulder like a personal god.

Well, I was not this man's god. I was not this man's servant. But I was his observer, and I had to know why.

He stopped before a brick house. It was filled with glass windows, all of them covered. It had high-pitched roofs for snow. It was like thousands, possibly even millions, of other houses in this same arm of the city. The proportions of this time and place were truly beyond my easy measure.

I was fascinated. His perfect black leather shoes were speckled prettily with rain. Why was he bringing us here?

He went down a step and back the alleyway. A light shone ahead of him. He had a key for a little gate. Then a key for a door between lighted windows in the deep bottom floor of the house.

We came in, he and I. I felt the warmth swoosh around me!

Ceiling overhead. The night locked out. An old man was seated at a wooden desk.

Smell of human beings, sweet and good. And so many other precious fragrances, too many to savor, or name.

All ghosts and gods and spirits feast on fragrance, as I have told you.

I had been starved, and nearly grew drunk on the smells of this place.

I *knew* I was here.

I was slowly taking form. But by whose direction? Who's decision? I loved it.

No old words issued from my lips; I was becoming solid. It was happening, as it had in New York when I chased her killers. I felt it. I felt myself enclosed in the good body, the body I liked, though what that meant I wasn't sure.

Now I know: I came visible and solid in my own body, or the body you see here now, the form I had when I was alive.

No one else here knew. Behind the bookcase I stood, watching.

Gregory Belkin had chosen for himself the very middle of the room, beneath a lightbulb with a frayed cord. And the old man at the desk, the old man could not possibly see me.

The old man's head was bowed. He wore the small black silk skull-cap of observant Jews. There was a green shaded lamp on his desk that was gentle and golden in its illumination.

His beard and hair were snow white and very pure and beautiful, and two long curled locks deliberately framed his face. The flesh of his scalp was pink beneath the thinnest part of his hair, but the beard was rich and flowing.

The books on the walls were in Hebrew and Arabic, Aramaic, Latin, Greek, German. I could smell the parchment and the leather. I drew in these fragrances and it seemed for a moment memory would spring to life, or out of memory would come alive everything I'd tried to murder.

But this old man wasn't the Master either! I knew it immediately.

This old man had no sense that I had come, none at all, but was merely staring at the younger one who had just entered, the strong straight one who stood rather formally before the elder, and removed from his hands a pair of smooth gray gloves which he was careful to put in the right pocket of his coat. He patted the left pocket. The gun was in the left pocket. Little lethal gun. I had a desire to hear it go off. But he wasn't here to shoot it.

The room was so cluttered. Rows and rows of shelves divided me from the old man, but I could see over the tops of books. I smelled incense, and felt a flush of pleasure. I smelled iron, gold, ink. *Could the bones be in this place?*

The old man took off his glasses, which were of the simplest kind, rounded in silver wire, flexible, and fragile, and peered most directly at his visitor, without rising from his chair.

The old man's eyes were very pale, which struck me as it always does, as very pretty to look at—eyes that are more like water than stone. But they were small, and weak with age, and they didn't gleam so much as they accused from the heavy wrinkles of his face.

Stronger, you are getting stronger by the moment. You are almost completely visible.

I couldn't see the entire face of the younger man. I slipped even more to the far left side of him to conceal myself, and became whole and entire as I stood behind the bookcase, calculating my height at approximately his own.

The rain was all over his black coat, and the coat had a seam straight down the back, and next to his neck, pushing up at the black curls of his hair, was a white silk scarf as fine as the scarf she'd clutched in death, a scarf that was probably still in the emporium of her killing. I tried to remember it, the scarf for which she had reached in death not dreaming of the significance of that last gesture, if indeed there was any significance to it at all. The scarf she had wanted was black but glittering, covered with beads. I think I told you this. But now I'm with them again, with them. Bear with me.

The old man spoke in Yiddish:

"You killed your daughter."

I was astonished. So we come immediately to the point?

The love I felt for her tormented me, as if she herself had come up to me and dug her nails in my skin and said, Do not forget me, Azriel, only she would never, never have done such a thing. She had died in characteristic humility; when she had spoken my name it was with wonder.

That was too dreadful to see again, her dying.

Go, fly, spirit. Turn your back on them all—on her death and on the old man's accusation, on this fascinating room with its enticing colors and aromas. Let go, spirit. Let them struggle towards the Ladder of Heaven without your intervention. After all, do souls really need the Servant of the Bones to drag them into Sheol?

I wasn't going anywhere. I wanted to know what the old man meant.

The younger man merely laughed.

No disrespect, it was an uneasy, angry laugh of one who would not be forced to immediate response by these words. The dismissive wave of his hand was not surprise. He shook his head.

I wanted to move around him, look at him, but it was too late for that, I knew I had the full parts, that I stood, that my hands touched the books on the shelf in front of me, and I shifted very slowly to my left, so that the wall of books would hide me, lest the old man see me, though the old man showed no sign even now of realizing I was here with him.

The younger man sighed.

"Rebbe, why would I kill Rachel's daughter?" asked the younger man in Yiddish. "Why would I kill the only child I had?" The language wasn't easy for him. "Esther, my beautiful Esther," he said, sounding heartfelt and strong. He didn't like to speak Yiddish. He wanted his English.

"But you did," said the old man in return. It came from his dry lips with hatred. He spoke now in Hebrew: "You are an idolator; you are a killer; you killed your child. You had her murdered. You walk with evil. You reek of it!"

I was slightly shaken. I could feel it physically, the jarring surprise at the old man's wrath.

The young man again played the game of patience, shuffling slightly, shaking his head as if humoring a half-naked prophet who won't stop raving on your doorstep.

"My teacher," Gregory Belkin whispered in English, "my model. My grandfather. And you blame me for her death?"

This put the old man in a fury.

He too spoke in English:

"What do you want of me, Gregory? You've never come to this house without a reason." His fury was calm. This old man himself would do nothing about the death of this girl. He sat at his desk with his hands clasped on an open book. Tiny Hebrew letters.

I felt the loss of her again, as if I'd been kicked and I wanted to say out loud, "Old man, I avenged her, I slew the three assassins with the leader's pick. I slew them all. They died on the pavements."

I felt her as if I alone in this room held the candle in memory of her. Neither of these mourned her, accusations be damned.

Why are you allowing this to happen, Azriel? Grief for those you don't know is easy. Maybe it is even exciting. But to be alone? That is to be alive. And you are most certainly secret and alone here.

"You break my heart, Rebbe," said Gregory in English. Obviously the current American language was much easier for him. His whole body sagged with his soft whisper of despair. His hands were deep in his pockets. His flesh was a little chilled from the cold outside, and the room itself was stifling. I thought he was lying, and telling the truth.

I fed upon the smell of them, never mind the wax, the parchment, the old reliable scents, I smelled the men—the old man's warm living skin that was so clear and fine, so free of disease that it had become silken in old age, pure like the bones of his living body inside it, which were no doubt so brittle now they could break at the slightest blow.

The young man was immaculate and anointed with fine and subtle perfumes. The perfume rose from the pores of his skin, from the curls of his hair, from the clothing he wore, a subtle mingling of calculated scents. The fragrance of a modern monarch.

I drew closer to the younger one. I might have been now two feet from him, to his left, and slightly behind him. I saw his profile. Thick eyebrows, smooth and neatly groomed and well formed, fine features, molded in good proportion; we would have called him blessed. He had no scar or blemish. Something indefinable to me enriched him and enlarged his power. When he smiled, which he did now sadly and imploringly, his teeth were perfectly white.

His eyes were large, like her eyes had been, but not quite so beautiful. He lifted his hands, another form of plea, small, quiet. His fingers were fine, and the smoothness of his cheeks was fine; he had been nourished as she had, lovingly, as if the whole world all of his life had been his mother's breast. What did he lack? I couldn't find in him a fracture or sore, or break anywhere, only the indefinable enhancement.

Then I realized what it was. He had the prettiness of the young, but he was past fifty years! How dazzling it was. How wondrous the way age sharpened his physical virtues, and made the glare of his eyes so much the more strong.

"Speak to me, Gregory Belkin," said the old man with contempt, "and tell me why you've come, or leave my house now."

I was again startled by the old man's wrath.

"All right, Rebbe," the younger man answered, as if the tone and the manner were nothing new to him.

The old man waited.

"I have a check in my pocket, Rebbe," said Gregory. "I come to give it to you for the good of the whole Court."

By this I knew he meant the Hebrews of the old man for whom the old man was the Rabbi, the zaddik, the leader.

Flashes of memory came at me, rather like jagged pieces of glass— glimpses of my long dead Master Samuel. But it didn't mean anything and I pushed it aside. At this point, keep in mind, I could not recall anything of my past. Nothing. But I knew what this man was— venerable, powerful in holy ways, perhaps a magician, but if he was a magician, why hadn't he sensed that I was there?

"You always have a check for us, Gregory," said the old one. "Your checks come to the bank without you. We take your money in honor of your dead mother, and your dead father, who was my beloved son. We take your money for what it can do for those whom they once loved, your mother and father. Go back to your Temple. Go back to your computers. Go back to your worldwide church. Go home,

Gregory! Hold your wife's hand. Her daughter has been murdered. Mourn with Rachel Belkin. Is she not entitled to that much?"

The younger man gave a little nod, as if to say, ah, things aren't going to improve here, and then he tilted his head to the right and shrugged respectfully and spoke again:

"I need something from you, Rebbe," he said. Direct as it was, it was smooth.

The old man lifted his hands and shrugged. He shifted in the light of the electric lamp, and sighed. His lips were full for the lips of an old man. A faint sheen of sweat appeared on the top of his head.

Behind him stood more shelves of books. The room was so crowded with books it might as well have been made of books. The chairs were big, with their frames hidden inside their leather, and all were surrounded by books. There were scrolls, and scrolls in sacks, and scrolls of leather.

One cannot after all burn or discard old scrolls of the Torah. These must be buried, and properly, or kept in someplace like this.

Who knew what this old man had brought through the world with him? His English was not pure and sharp like that of Gregory, but carried with it the speaking habits of other tongues. Poland. I saw Poland and I saw snow.

Gregory slipped his left hand into his pocket. There was the check, the piece of paper, the banknote, the gift that he wanted to give so badly. I heard it crackle as his fingers touched it. It was folded right beside the gun.

The old man said nothing.

"Rebbe, when I was very little," said Gregory, "I heard you tell a particular tale. Only once did I hear this story. But I remember it. I remember the words."

The old man made no reply. The loose folds of his skin were shiny in the light, but when he lifted his white eyebrows he lifted the folds of his forehead too.

"Rebbe," said Gregory, "you spoke once to my aunt of a legend, a secret . . . a family treasure. I've come here to ask you about what I heard."

The old man was surprised. No. It wasn't that. The old man was surprised only that the younger man's words had some interest for him. The old man gave the silence a moment, then spoke in Yiddish as before:

"A treasure? You and your brother—you were the treasures of your mother and father. What would bring you to Brooklyn to ask me about tales of treasure? Treasure you have beyond any man's dreams."

"Yes, Rebbe," said Gregory patiently.

"I hear your church swims in money, that your missions in foreign lands are lavish resorts for the rich who would visit and give to the poor. Indeed. I heard that your own fortune far outstrips that of your wife, or her daughter. I hear that no man can hold in his mind the exact amount of the money you possess and the money you control."

"Yes, Rebbe," said Gregory again, patiently in English. "I'm as rich as you can imagine, and I know you don't choose to imagine it, nor to dwell on it, nor profit from it—"

"Well, then, come to the point," said the old man in Yiddish. "You waste my time. You waste the precious moments I have left to me, which I would rather spend in charity than in condemnation. What do you want?"

"You spoke of a family secret," Gregory said. "Rebbe, speak to me in English, please."

The old man sneered.

"And what did I speak then, when you were a little boy?" the old man asked in Yiddish. "Did I speak Yiddish or Polish, or was it English then too?"

"I don't remember," said the young man. "But I wish you'd speak English now." He shrugged again, and then he said very quickly, "Rebbe, I am grieving for Esther! It wasn't my wealth that bought her the diamonds. I wasn't the cause of her wearing them carelessly. I wasn't to blame that the thieves caught her unawares."

Diamonds? There was a lie in this. Esther had worn no diamonds. The Evals had taken from her no diamonds. But Gregory was as smooth-tongued at this as anything else.

How he played the part. How the old man studied him.

The old man moved back just a little, as if the strength of the words had pushed him, perhaps even annoyed him. He scrutinized the young man.

"You mistake my meaning, Gregory," he said in English. "I don't speak of your wealth or what she wore around her neck when they killed her. I mean you killed your daughter, Esther. You had her murdered."

Silence.

In the dimness I saw my hands visible against the books; I saw the tiny creases in the skin of my knuckles, and in the place where a man would have a heart I felt pain.

The smooth-tongued one gave no sign of guilt or shame or even shock. Either infinite innocence or infinite evil suffused him and upheld him in quiet.

"Grandfather, that's madness. Why would I do such a thing? I am a man of God as you are, Grandfather!"

"Stop!" said the Rebbe. He lifted his hand.

"My followers would never hurt Esther, they—"

"Stop!" said the Rebbe again. "Get on with it, what do you really want."

Rattled and smiling uneasily, Gregory shook his head. He collected himself to begin again. His lip trembled, but I don't think the old man could see it as I could.

Gregory still held the check, an offering, poised, in his left hand.

"It's something I remember you saying once," said Gregory, the English rapid and natural now. "Nathan and I were in the room. I don't think Nathan heard it. He was with . . . someone else. I don't even remember who else was there, except my mother's sister Rivka, and it seemed there were old women. But it was here in Brooklyn, and we'd only just come. I could ask Nathan—"

"Leave your brother alone!" said the old man, and this time it was English, confident, low, as natural to his tongue as Yiddish. Anger can do that, strip a voice down to the best way that it knows to speak. "Don't approach your brother Nathan. Leave your brother Nathan in peace! You just said yourself your brother didn't hear it."

"Yes, I knew you would want it that way, Rebbe. I knew you wouldn't want me to contaminate Nathan."

"Get on with this."

"That's why I came to ask you. Explain it and I won't bother my beloved brother, but I must know." He went on. "That day, when I was a child, you spoke about a secret thing. A thing you called the Servant of the Bones."

I was stricken. The words caught me utterly off guard. The shock only strengthened my form. I could not have been more stunned if he had turned and seen me. I called clothes to cover me, I called the clothes to cover me as he, the zaddik, was covered. And I felt myself immediately sheathed in black silk similar to his, warm and well fitted, and the air felt warm and the tiny lightbulb rocked on its frayed cord.

The Rebbe looked at the bulb for a long moment, then back at his grandson.

"Ah, be still, Azriel," I commanded myself. "And listen. The answers are coming now."

"Do you remember?" asked the younger one. "A family secret? A treasure called the Servant of the Bones?"

The old man remembered, but didn't speak.

"You said," Gregory continued, "that once a man had brought this thing to your father in Prague. The man was a Moslem, from the mountains. You said that this man had given this thing to your father in payment of a debt."

Ah, this zaddik possessed the bones! But he wasn't the master, no, never would he be, either.

He looked hard and secretively at his grandson.

"You were talking to old Rivka," Gregory pressed, "and you told her the things the Moslem had said. You said that your father should not have accepted such a thing, but your father had been confused because the words on the wooden casket had been in Hebrew. You called it an abomination; you said it should be destroyed."

I smiled. Did I feel relief or anger? An abomination. I am an abomination. And this abomination can destroy both of you and your room of books; it can tear your house to pieces to the rafters! *But who called me!*

I put my hand over my mouth in restraint. In the presence of a zaddik, I could not afford the most incidental sigh or sound. I couldn't afford to weep.

The zaddik was still holding his peace, letting the young man reveal himself more and more.

"Rivka asked you why you didn't destroy it," said Gregory patiently, slowly, "and you said that that was not an easy thing to do. You said it was like the old scrolls, this thing. It could not be destroyed irreverently. You spoke again of something written, a document. Do you remember this, Grandfather? Or do I dream?"

The old man's eyes were cold. "You heard this at my knee?" he muttered. "Why do you ask me of this now?"

Suddenly the old man raised his hand and made a fist and brought the fist down on the desk. Nothing moved, save the dust.

Gregory didn't blink.

"Why do you come here on the day of your daughter's funeral," the old man raged, "and ask me about this old tale! This tale, this secret or treasure, as you call it, that you heard when you were my *eloi*, my shining one, my chosen pupil, my pride! Why do you come speaking of this thing now!"

The old man was trembling dangerously.

Gregory calculated silently, then took a deep breath.

"Rebbe, the check will buy so many things," said Gregory.

"Answer my question! Money we have. We are rich here. We were rich when we left Poland. We were rich when we left Israel. Answer my question. Why do you ask about this thing now?"

I could see no wealth in this room but I believed him.

I knew his kind. He lived only to study Torah and to keep the law, and to pray, and to advise those who came to him daily, those who believed he could see into souls and make miracles, those for whom he was the instrument of God. Wealth would make no change in the life of such a man whatsoever, except that he might study day and night as he chose.

I felt my pulse, very strong. I felt the air in me. My strength had been steadily increasing since the words had been spoken. The bones had to be here. Yes, he had them, and somehow he had called me up. He had laid hands on them, or read the words, or spoken the prayer . . . it had to be this old man, but how was such a thing accomplished and why had I not simply destroyed him out of hand?

Out of memory, like a comet came a face I knew and loved. Hundreds of years were bridged in a moment.

This was the face of Samuel, of whom I've told you. Samuel of Strasbourg. This was the Master who had sold me for his children as I had once sold myself perhaps for the children of God. In my memory I saw the casket.

Where was it now?

The memory was bitter, a fragment; I wouldn't have it. Accusations would distract me and nothing about this past, even with Samuel, could ever, ever be changed.

I stood in this warm room in Brooklyn, with another old scholar surrounded by dusty books, spells, charms, incantations, and I hated him. I despised him. He was far more virtuous, however, than Samuel had ever been, especially in the last moments when Samuel had told me to go my way to hell.

I hated this Rebbe almost as much as his grandson hated him.

And the grandson?

What was he to me, this smooth-tongued Gregory Belkin with his worldwide church? But if he had killed Esther—

I held fast. I let the temper and the pain melt in me; I asked of myself, be alive only, and be quiet.

This young one, groomed as well as a prince, waited in patience in the same manner for the temper of the zaddik to cool.

"Why ask me these things now?" the old man demanded.

I thought of the girl, the tender girl, her head turned on the stretcher. How kind and awestruck had been her little whisper. *Servant of the Bones.*

The old man suddenly lost control of his anger. He gave Gregory no time to answer. He went on with his raving questions.

"What drives you, Gregory?" he asked in English. His tone was intimate suddenly, as if he really wanted to know. He rose from his chair and stood facing his grandson.

"You put a question to me," he said. "Let me put a question to you. What is it in the wide world that you would have? You are rich beyond imagining, so rich that you make our wealth a drop in the sea, yet you make a church to deceive thousands, you fashion laws which are no laws at all. You sell books and television programs that say nothing. You would be Mohammed or Christ! And then you kill your daughter. Yes, you did it. I see into you. I know you killed her. You sent those men. Her blood was on the very same weapon which killed them. Did you do away with them as well? Was it your followers who used those assassins and then dispatched them? What is your dream, Gregory, to bring down on all of us such evil and shame that the Messiah cannot stay away a moment longer! You would take away his choice!"

I smiled. It was a beautiful speech. Remembering nothing of Zurvan then, or anyone wise or eloquent, I nevertheless warmed to this speech, and to the conviction with which it had been made. I liked the old man just a little better.

Gregory adopted the softened attitude of sadness but remained silent. Let the old man rave.

"You think I don't know you did this?" said the Rebbe. He let himself slip back down into the chair. He had to. He was tired in his rage. "I know. I know you and have known you as no one else from the day you were born. Nathan, your own twin, doesn't know you. Nathan prays for you, Gregory!"

"But you don't, do you, Grandfather? You said your prayers already for me, didn't you?"

"Yes, I said Kaddish when you left this house, and if I had only a sign from Heaven, I would bring an end to your life and your Temple of the Mind and your lies and your schemes with my own hands."

Would you, now?

"That's an easy claim to make, Grandfather," said Gregory unperturbed. "Anyone can do things when he has a sign from Heaven! I teach my followers to love in a world where there are no signs from Heaven!"

"You teach your followers to give you money. You teach your followers to sell your books. You raise your voice again to me and you'll leave my house without your answers. Your brother knows nothing of what you speak—this old childhood memory of yours. He wasn't there. My memory of that day is very clear. There is no one alive now who knows."

Gregory raised his hand. Peace, forbearance.

I was enthralled and tormented. I waited for the next word.

"Grandfather, only tell me then what it means, 'the Servant of the Bones.' Am I such filth that to answer me is to desecrate yourself?"

The old man trembled. His shoulders narrowed and drew up under his black collarless coat. He shuddered and in the light his knuckles were pink and sore to look at. The light spilled down on his white beard and on the mustache which covered his upper lip, and on the translucent lids of his eyes as he shook his head and rocked back and forth as if he were praying.

Very smoothly came the voice of Gregory.

"Grandfather, my only child is dead, and I come to you with a simple question. Why would I kill my daughter, Esther? You yourself know there is no reason under God for me to have hurt Esther. What can I give you for the answer to my question? Do you remember this story, this thing, this Servant of the Bones? Did it have a name, was its name Azriel?"

The old man was stunned.

So was I.

"I never spoke that name," said the old man.

"No, you didn't," said Gregory, "but someone else did."

"Who has told you about this thing?" the old man demanded. "Who could have done such a thing?"

Gregory was confused.

I leant my weight against the shelf of books, watching, my fingers catching the loose flaking leather of the bindings. Don't hurt them. Not the books.

The old man sounded hard and contemptuous.

"Has someone come to you with the legend?" asked the old man. "Has someone told you a pretty tale of magic and power? Was this man Moslem? Was he a Gentile? Was he a Jew? Was he one of your New Age fanatic followers who has read your abracadabra about the Kabbalah?"

Gregory shook his head.

"Rebbe, you have it wrong," he said with solemn sincerity. "It was only your talk of this that I heard when I was a child. Then two days ago, someone else spoke the words before witnesses: Azriel, Servant of the Bones!"

I was afraid to guess.

"Who was this?" asked the old man.

"She said it, Rebbe," Gregory told him. "Esther said it as she was dying. The man in the ambulance heard it from her lips as she died. Esther said it, Rebbe. Esther said, 'The Servant of the Bones.' And the name 'Azriel.' Esther said it twice aloud, and two men heard her. Those men told me."

I smiled. This was more of a mystery than I had ever imagined.

I watched them intently. My face teemed with heat. And I knew that I trembled as the old man trembled, as if my body were real.

The old man drew back. He was not willing to believe. His anger vanished. He peered into the younger man's face.

Then came the voice of Gregory, purposefully and cleverly tender.

"Who is he, Rebbe? Who is the Servant of the Bones? What is it, this thing, that Esther spoke of? That you spoke of? When I was a child playing on the floor at your feet? Esther said this name, 'Azriel.' Is that the name of the Servant of the Bones?"

My pulse throbbed so loud I could hear it with my own ears. I felt the fingers of my left hand bear down slightly on the tops of the books. I felt the shelf against my chest. I felt the cement floor under my shoes, and I didn't dare to look away from either of them.

My god, I thought, make the old man tell, make him tell so I will know, my god, if you are still there, make him tell Who and What is the Servant of the Bones? Make him tell me!

The old man was too stunned to reply.

"The police have this information," said Gregory. "They guard it jealously. They think she spoke of her killer."

I almost cried aloud in denial.

The old man scowled, and his eyes moistened.

"Rebbe, don't you understand? They want to find who killed her—not that trash with the ice picks who stole her necklace, but those who put them up to it, those who knew the value of the jewels!"

Once again, the necklace. I saw no necklace then and I saw none in my memory now. There had been no necklace around her throat. They had taken nothing from her. What was this diversion of the necklace?

If only I knew these men better. I couldn't tell for sure when Gregory lied.

The voice of Gregory grew lower, colder, less conciliatory. He straightened his shoulders.

"Now let me speak plainly, Rebbe," he said. "I have always, at your behest kept our secret, my secret, our secret—that the founder of the Temple of the Mind was the grandson of the Rebbe of this Court of the Hasidim!" His voice rose now as if he couldn't quiet it.

"For your sake," he said, "I've kept this secret! For Nathan's sake. For the sake of the Court. For the sake of those who loved my mother and father and remembered them. I have kept this secret for you and for them!"

He paused, the tone of accusation hanging there sharply, the old man waiting, too wise to break the silence.

"Because you begged me," said Gregory, "I kept the secret. Because my brother begged me. And because I love my brother. And in my own way, Rebbe, I love you. I kept the secret so that you might not have the disgrace in your own eyes, and so that the cameras would not come poking in your windows, the reporters would not come crowding your stoop to demand of you how was it possible that out of your Torah and your Talmud and your Kabbalah came Gregory Belkin, the Messiah of the Temple of the Mind, whose voice is heard from the city of Lima to the towns of Nova Scotia, from Edinburgh to Zaire. How did your ritual, your prayer, your quaint black clothing, your black hats, your crazy dancing, your bowing and hollering—how did all of that loose upon the world the famous and immensely successful Gregory Belkin and the Temple of the Mind? For your sake, I kept quiet."

Silence. The old man was sunk in silence, unforgiving, and filled with contempt.

I was as confused as ever. Nothing drew me to either man, not hate or love, nothing drew me to anything but the remembered eyes and voice of the dead girl.

Again, it was the younger man who spoke.

"Once in your entire life, you came to me of your own will," Gregory said. "You crossed the great bridge that divides my world from yours, as you call it. You came to me in my offices to beg me not to disclose my background! To keep it a secret, no matter how many reporters questioned me, no matter how they pried."

The old man didn't answer.

"It would have benefited me to let the world know, Rebbe. How could it not have benefited me to say that I had come from such strong and observant roots! But long before you ever made your request of me, I buried my past with you. I covered it over with lies and fabrications so as to protect you! So that you would not be disgraced.

You and my beloved Nathan, for whom I pray every night of my life. I did that, and I continue to do it . . . for you."

He paused as if his anger had the better of him. I was mesmerized by both of them and the tale that unfolded.

"But as God is my witness, Rebbe," Gregory said, "and I do dare to speak of him in my Temple as you do in your yeshiva, let me tell you this. She said those words when she died! Now you know it was none of your black-clad saints clapping their hands and singing on Shabbes who killed Esther! It wasn't my doe-eyed brother who killed Esther. It was not a Hasid who killed Esther. When the Nazis shot my mother and my father, neither raised a hand to stop the arm or the gun, is that not so?"

The old man, perplexed and torn, actually nodded in agreement, as if they had moved far beyond their own mutual hatred now.

"But," said Gregory, and he held up the check in his left hand, "if you don't tell me the meaning of those words, Rebbe, and I do remember them, then I shall tell the police where I once heard them. That it was here in this house, among the Hasidim whom Gregory Belkin, the man of mystery, the Founder of the Temple of the Mind, was actually born!"

I was dumbfounded. I waited. I didn't dare to take my eyes off the old man.

Still he held out.

Gregory sighed. He shrugged. He walked a pace and turned and looked to Heaven and then dropped his hand. "I will tell them, 'Yes, sir, I've heard those words. Yes, once I heard them. At my grandfather's knee, and yes, he is living, and you must go to him to find out what they mean.' I'll tell them— I'll send them to you and you can explain the meaning of those words to them."

"Enough," said the old man. "You're a fool, you always were!" He sighed heavily, and then more in contemplation than consciously, he said, "Esther said those words? Men heard her?"

"Her attendants thought she was looking at a man outside the window, a man with long black hair! That's a secret the police keep in their files, but the others saw him and they saw her look at him, and this man, Rebbe, he wept for her! He wept!"

It was I who trembled!

"Shut up. Stop. Don't . . ."

Gregory gave a soft laugh of nudging mockery. He stepped back, turning this way and that again, without ever lifting his eyes to see me, though his eyes might, in a better light, have passed over my shoes. He turned back to the Rebbe.

"I never thought to accuse you, any of you, of killing her!" said Gregory. "Such a thought never came to me, though where have I ever heard such words before except from your tongue! And I walk in your door and you accuse me of killing my stepdaughter! Why would I do such a thing? I come here out of respect for her dying words!"

The old man said very calmly, "I believe you. The poor child spoke those words. The papers told of strange words. I believe you. But I also know you killed your daughter. You had it done."

Gregory's arms tensed as do the arms of men who are about to strike others, but he couldn't and wouldn't strike the Rebbe. That would never happen with these two men, I knew. But Gregory was at the end of his tether, and the zaddik was certain of Gregory's guilt.

So was I. But what reason did I have for it? No more than the zaddik, perhaps.

I tried to peer into their souls, for surely they could boast of souls, the two of them, they were flesh and blood. I tried to look, as any human might look, as any ghost might plumb the depths of the soul of the living. I bent my head forward just a little as if the rhythm of their breathing would tell me, as if the beat of the heart would give away the secret. *Gregory, did you kill her?*

Did the old man ask the younger man the same thing? He leant forward in the light of his dusty bulb; his eyes were crinkled and bright.

He looked at Gregory again, and as he did so, quite by accident, and quite for certain, he saw *me*.

His eyes shifted very slowly and naturally from his grandson, to me.

He saw a man standing where I stood. He saw a young man with long curling dark hair and dark eyes. He saw a man of good height and good strength, very young, in fact, so young that some might have thought him still a boy. He saw *me*. He saw Azriel.

I smiled but only a little, like a man about to speak, not to mock.

I let him see the white of my teeth. I confided to his secret gaze that I had no fear of him. Like him, I stood, with a full beard and in black silk, a kaftan or long coat. Like him and one of his own.

And though I didn't know why or how I knew, I did know that I was one of his own, more surely than I was kin to the Huckster Prophet before him.

A surge of strength passed through me, as if the old man had laid his hands on the bones and howled for me! So it often happens, when seen, I grow strong. I was almost as strong in those moments as I am now.

The old man gave no signal to Gregory of what he had seen. He gave no signal to me. He sat still. The drift of his eyes over the room seemed natural and to settle on nothing, in particular, and to have no emotion, except the dim veil of sorrow.

He stared at me again, in the veiled way that Gregory would never notice. He held fast to me in perfect quiet.

Louder came the rush of pulse inside me, tighter the perfect shell of my body closed its pores. I could feel that he saw me and he found me beautiful! Young and beautiful! I felt the silk I wore, the weight of my hair.

Ah, you see me, Rebbe, you hear me. I spoke without moving my tongue.

He didn't answer me. He stared at me as a man stares in thought. But he had heard. He was no fake preacher, but a true zaddik and he had heard my little prayer.

But the younger man, thoroughly deceived and with his back to me, talked again in English:

"Rebbe, did you tell anyone else the old story? Did Esther by chance ever come here seeking to know who you were, and maybe you—"

"Don't be such a fool, Gregory," the old man said. He looked away from me for the moment. Then back at me as he went on. "I did not know your stepdaughter," he said. "She never came here. Neither has your wife. You know this." He sighed, staring at me as if he feared to take his eyes away.

"Is it a tale of the Hasidim or the Lubavitch?" asked Gregory. "Something one of the Misnagdim might have told Esther—"

"No."

We stared at one another. The old man, alive, and the young spirit, robust, growing ever more vivid, and strong.

"Rebbe, who else . . . ?"

"No one," said the old man, fixing me steadily as I fixed him. "What you remember is true and your brother was far from hearing, and your aunt Rivka is dead. No one could have told Esther."

Only now he looked away from me, and up at Gregory.

"It's a cursed thing you speak of," he said. "It's a demon, a thing that can be summoned by powerful magic and do evil things."

And his eyes returned to me, though the young man remained intent on him.

"Then other Jews know these stories. Nathan knows . . ."

"No, no one. Look, don't take me for an idiot. Don't you think I know you asked far and wide among the other Jews? You called this court and that, and you called the professors of the universities. I know your ways. You're too clever. You have telephones in every room of your life. You came here as the last resort."

The younger man nodded. "You're right. I thought it would be common knowledge. I made my inquiries. So have the authorities. But it isn't common knowledge. And so I am here."

Gregory bent his head to the side, and thrust the folded bank draft at the Rebbe.

This gave the old man one second to gesture to me, one second, merely to make the little gesture with his right index finger of Hide or Stay Quiet. It came with a swift negation with the eyes and the smallest move of his head. Yet it was no command, and no threat. It was something closer to a prayer.

Then I heard him. *Don't reveal yourself, spirit.*

Very well, old man, for the time being, as you request.

Gregory—his back to me still—opened the check. "Explain the thing to me, Rebbe. Tell me what it is and if you still have it. What you told Rivka, you said it wasn't an easy thing to destroy."

The old man looked up at Gregory again, trusting me apparently to keep my place.

"Maybe I'll tell you all you want to know," said the old man. "Maybe·I will deliver it into your hands, what you speak of. But not for that sum. We have more than plenty. You have to give us what matters to us."

Gregory was much excited. "How much, Rebbe!" he said. "You speak as if you still have this thing."

"I do," said the old man. "I have it."

I was astonished, but not surprised.

"I want it!" said Gregory fiercely, so fiercely that I feared he had overplayed his hand. "Name your price!"

The old man considered. His eyes fixed me again and then drifted past me, and I could see the color brighten in his withered face, and I could see his hands move restlessly. Slowly he let his eyes fasten on me and me alone.

For one precious second, as we gazed at one another, all the past threatened to become visible. I saw centuries beyond Samuel. I think I saw a glimmer of Zurvan. I think I saw the procession itself. I glimpsed the figure of a golden god smiling at me, and I felt terror, terror to know and to be as men are, with memory and in pain.

If this did not stop in me, I would know such agony that I would howl, like a dog, howl as the driver had howled when he saw the fallen body of Esther, I would howl forever. The wind would come. The wind would take me with all its other lost and howling souls. When I'd struck down the evil Mameluk master in Cairo, the wind had come for me, and I had fought through it to oblivion.

Stay alive, Azriel. The past will wait. The pain can wait. The wind will wait. The wind can wait forever. Stay alive in this place. Know this.

I am here, old man.

Calmly, he regarded me, unmarked by his grandson. He spoke now without taking his eyes off me, though Gregory bent to listen to his words:

"Go there, behind me and in the back of these books," he said in English, "and open the cabinet you see there. Inside you'll see a cloth. Lift it. And bring the thing that is beneath it. It is heavy, but you can carry it. You are strong enough."

I gasped. I heard it myself, and I felt my heart crying. The bones were here! Right here.

Gregory hesitated for one moment, perhaps not accustomed to

taking orders, or even doing the smallest things for himself. I don't know. But then he sped into action. He hurried behind the bookcase at the old man's back.

I heard the creak of wood, and I smelled the cedar and the incense again. I heard the snap of metal latches. I felt myself rise on the balls of my feet, and then sink down again to a firm stance.

The old man and I stared at one another without pause. I stepped free of the bookcase completely so that he might see me in my long coat that was like his, and he showed only the tiniest fear for an instant, then urged me, with a polite nod of his head, to please return to my hiding place.

I did.

Behind him, out of sight, Gregory fumbled and cursed.

"Move the books," said the Rebbe. "Move them out of the way, all of them," said the old man as he looked at me, as if he held me in check with his eyes. "Do you see it now?"

The smell of dust rose in my nostrils. I could see the dust rising beneath the light. I heard the books tumble. Oh, it was sweet to hear with ears and to see with eyes. Don't weep, Azriel, not in the presence of this man who despises you.

I lifted my fingers to my lips without willing it. I just did it, natural, as if I were ready to pray in the face of disaster. I felt the hair above my mouth, and the thick mass of my beard. I liked it. *Like yours, Rebbe, when you were young?*

The old man was rigid, indestructible, superior, and wary.

Gregory stepped out from behind the bookcase, and back into the light.

In his arms he held the casket!

I saw the gold still thick on the cedar. I saw it, and I saw it bound carelessly in chains of iron.

Iron! So they thought that could hold me? Azriel! Iron could hold such a thing as me? I wanted to laugh. But I looked at it, the casket in Gregory's arms, which he held like an infant, the casket still covered with gold.

A faint memory of its making came back to me, but I did not see anyone clearly in this memory. I only remembered the sunlight on marble and kind words. Love, a world of love, and love made me think again of Esther.

How proud and fascinated Gregory was. He cared nothing that his wool coat was full of dust. That dust was in his hair. He stared down at this thing, this treasure, and he turned to lay it before the old man like an infant.

"No!" The old man raised both hands. "Set it there on the floor and back away from it."

Bitterly, I smiled. *Don't defile yourself with it.*

He paid no heed to me, but looked down at the casket as Gregory put it on the floor.

"Good God, do you think it will burst into flame?" asked Gregory. Carefully he positioned the casket directly under the light, directly before the old man's desk. "This is ancient, this writing, this writing isn't Hebrew, this is Sumerian!" He drew back his hands and rubbed them together.

He was passionate and overcome.

"Rebbe, this is priceless."

"I know what it is," said the old man, his eyes moving freely from me to the casket. I did not change. I did not even smile.

Gregory stared rapt at this thing as though it were the Christ child in the Manger and he were one of those shepherds come to see the Son of God made flesh.

"What is it, Grandfather? What's written on it?" He touched the iron chains, slowly, as if ready to be commanded by the old man to stop. He touched the links, which were thick and ugly, and he touched a scroll that was tucked beneath the iron chains, where links crossed links.

This I hadn't seen till now, this scroll, until Gregory's fingers gently tested the edges of it. The gold of the casket itself blinded me and made the water come up in my eyes. I smelled the cedar and the spices and the smoke that saturated the wood beneath its plating. I smelled the flesh of other humans, and I smelled the perfume of offerings.

My head swam suddenly.

I smelled the bones.

Oh, my own god, who has called me? If only I could see his cheerful face for a minute, my god, my own god. My own god who used to walk with me, the god that each man has unto himself, his own god, as I had seen mine, and if only he would come now!

This wasn't really memory, you understand, it was a sudden long-ing without explanation that left me cold and confused.

But I kept thinking of this person, "my god." Would he laugh? Would he say, "So your god has failed you, Azriel, and even amongst the Chosen, you call to me again? Didn't I warn you? Didn't I caution you to escape while you could, Azriel?"

But he wasn't there, my god, whoever that had ever been, and he wasn't smiling. He wasn't at my side, like a friend who'd been walking with me in the cool of the evening along the banks of the river. And he didn't say those things. But he had been with me once, and I knew it. The past was like a deluge that wanted me to fall into it, and be drowned.

A wild hope grew in me, a hope that made my breath come quickly, and the scents of the room suffocated me in my passion.

Maybe nobody has called you, Azriel! Maybe you have come on your own, and you are your own master! And you may hate and disregard these two men to your heart's content!

It was so sweet, this strength, this smile, this seeming joke that I should at last have that power myself. I almost heard my own little laugh. I closed my right fingers over the curls of my beard and tugged ever so gently.

"This scroll is intact, Rebbe," said Gregory eagerly. "Look, I can slip it out of these chains. Can you read it?"

The old man looked up at me as if I'd spoken.

Do you find me beautiful, old man? I know what you see. I don't have to see it. It's Azriel, not made to measure by a Master, not shifted into this or that shape for a Master, but Azriel as God made me once, when Azriel was soul and spirit and body in one.

The old man glared. *I command you! Don't show yourself, spirit.*

Do you, indeed, old man, and I hate your cold heart! Some link binds us one to the other, but you are so full of hate and so am I, how are we ever to know if God had his hand in this, for her, for Esther!

Spellbound, he stared at me unable to answer.

Gregory crouched over his trophy, and touched the scroll gingerly and fearfully.

"Rebbe, this alone is worth a fortune," he said. "Name your price. Let me open the scroll." He laid his hand suddenly right on the wood, and opened his fingers, in love with this thing.

"No!" said the old man. "Not under my roof."

I looked into his pale filmy eyes. *I hate you. Do you think I asked to be this thing that I am? Were you ever young? Was your hair ever this black and your lips this ruddy?*

He didn't answer, but he had heard.

"Sit down there," he said to his grandson, pointing to the nearby leather chair. "Sit there and write the checks I tell you to write. And then this thing—and all I know of it—is yours."

I almost laughed out loud. So that was it! That was it! He knew I was here and he would sell me to this grandson whom he despised. That would be his awful price for every wrong done him and his God by the grandson. He would put me in the grandson's unsuspecting hands. I think I did laugh, but soundlessly, only so that he could see it, see a twinkling in my eye perhaps and a curl to my lip as I sneered at him, and shook my head in reverence for his cleverness, his coldness, his loveless heart.

Gregory backed up, found the chair, and sat down slowly, the old leather peeling and flaking. He was overcome with excitement.

"Name your price."

My smile must have been bitter, knowing. But I was calm. My old god would have been proud. *Well done, my brave one, fight them! What have you to lose? You think your God is merciful? Listen to what they have in mind for you!* But who spoke those words down the long length of the years? Who spoke them? What was it near me and filled with love that tried to warn me? I stared at Gregory. I would not be distracted, drawn away into the mesh of hurt, I would get to the bottom of this mystery first. My own mystery could wait.

I let the nails of my right fingers dig just a little into the hardened flesh of my palm. Yes, here. You are here, Azriel, whether the old man despises you or not, whether the young man is a murderer and a fool, and whether you are being sold once more as if you had no soul of your own and never had and never would. You are here. Not in the bones which lie in the casket!

I pretended my god was there. We stood together. Hadn't I done that with other Masters, without ever telling them, just brought my god close up to be near me, but had he ever really come?

In a cloud of smoke, I saw my god turning, weeping for me. It was in a chamber, and the heat rose from a boiling cauldron! My god, help me! But this was an image without a frame. That was something unspeakable that must never be relived! I had to see things here now.

Gregory drew a long leather wallet from his pocket. He opened it on his knee, and with his right hand held a golden pen.

The old man spoke the sums in American dollars. Huge sums. He gave the parties to whom these checks were to be written. Hospitals, institutions of learning, a company which would then pass the money on to the yeshiva in which the young men of the Court studied Torah. Money would be sent to the Court in Israel. Money would be sent to the new community of the Hasidim who tried to make their own village in the hills not far from this city. The Rebbe spoke all the words with the briefest of explanations.

Without a single question, Gregory began to write, carving the letters into the bank drafts with his sharp, gold pen, then flipping one check up so that he might write another, and another, scrawling his name as mighty men are wont to do.

Gregory finally laid the checks on the desk before the Rebbe. The Rebbe stared at them carefully. He moved them wide apart in a long row, and he studied them and seemed ever so slightly surprised.

"You would give me this much," the Rebbe asked, "for something about which you know and understand nothing?"

"His name was the last word my daughter spoke."

"No, you want this thing! You want its power."

"Why should I believe in its power? Yes, yes, I want it, to see it, to try to figure how she knew about it, and yes, yes, I give those sums."

"Take the scroll out of the chains, and give it to me."

Like a boy, Gregory obeyed, so eager. The scroll was not old, not old like the casket of the bones. Gregory put the scroll into the old man's hand.

Will you wash your hands afterwards?

The Rebbe didn't acknowledge me. He carefully unrolled the vellum, moving his hands to the left and to the right, so that he had the full writing before him, and then he began to speak, translating the words in English carefully for his grandson to hear:

" 'Return this thing to the Hebrews for it is their magic and only they can put it deep into Hell where it belongs. The Servant of the

Bones no longer heeds his Master. Old vows no longer bind him. Old charms no longer banish him. Once summoned, he destroys all that he sees. Only the Hebrews know the meaning of this thing. Only the Hebrews can harness its fury. Give it freely to them.' "

Again I smiled. I couldn't help it. I think I closed my eyes with relief, and then opened them, looking at the old man who looked only at the vellum.

But have I truly come on my own? I didn't dare believe it yet. No. There could be some secret to snare me, some trap in which Esther's death was merely the bait.

The old man sat with the scroll open, staring down at it. He said no more.

Gregory broke the silence.

"Then why haven't you destroyed it!" He was so excited he could scarcely stand there at attention. "What else does it say! What is the language!"

The old man looked up at him and then at me, and then back to the scroll.

"Listen to what I read now," said the old man, "because I will translate it for you only once:

" 'Woe unto him who destroys these bones, for if it can be done, which is not known even to the wisest, that one should loose into the world a spirit of incalculable power, masterless and ungovernable, doomed to remain in the air forever, unable to mount the Ladder to Heaven, or unlock the gates of Perdition. And who knows what shall be the cruelty of this spirit against God's children? Are there not demons enough in this world?' "

Dramatically, he looked up at his grandson, who evinced only fascination.

Gregory did everything but rub his hands together in greed.

The old man spoke again, slowly.

"My father took it because he felt that he must take it. And now you come to me and you ask for it. Well, it is almost yours."

The younger man seemed delirious suddenly, or possessed of a divine joy.

"Oh, Rebbe, this is too marvelous, too wondrous," said Gregory. "But how could she have known, my poor Esther?"

"That's for you to discover," said the old man coldly. "For I cannot possibly know. Never have I called it forth, this spirit, nor would my father. Nor would the Moslem who gave it over into my father's hands."

"Give me the scroll. I'll take it now."

"No."

"Grandfather, I want it! Look, the checks are there!"

"And tomorrow the money will be in the bank, will it not? Tomorrow, when the sums are transferred, when the transaction is finished—"

"Grandfather, let me have it now!"

"Tomorrow, then you come to me, and you take it, and it's yours. And you will be the Master of the Servant of the Bones."

"You stubborn, impossible old man. You know these checks are good. Give it to me!"

"Oh, you are so anxious!" said the elder.

He looked at me. I could have sworn he would have shared a smile with me had I invited him to do it, but I didn't.

Then he looked again at his grandson, who was in a paroxysm of frustration, staring at the golden casket at his feet, not daring to touch it, but wanting it so much he groaned.

"Why did you kill her?" the old man said.

"What?"

"Why did you have your daughter killed? I want to know. I should have made that my price!"

"Oh, you're a fool, all of you are fools, belligerent and superstitious, the idiots of your god!"

The old man was outraged.

"Your temples, Gregory, are the houses of the deceived and the damned," he said. "But let's have no more invectives. We know each other. Tomorrow night, when my bankers tell me that your money is in our hands, you come and you take this thing away. And keep the secret. Keep the vow. Tell no one that you are . . . that you were . . . my grandson."

Gregory smiled, shrugged, opened his hands in a gesture of acceptance. He turned to go, never so much as glancing in the direction of where I stood.

He stopped before the door and looked back at his grandfather.

"Tell my brother Nathan for me that I thank him that he called me with his condolences."

"He didn't do this!" cried the Rebbe.

"Oh, yes, he did. He called me and spoke to me, and tried to comfort me in my loss, and to comfort my wife."

"He has no traffic with you and your kind!"

"And I don't tell you this, Rebbe, to bring your anger down on him, no, not for that reason, but just so that you know that my brother Nathan loved me enough to call me and to tell me he was sorry that the girl was dead."

Gregory opened the door. The cold of the night waited uneasily.

"Stay away from your brother!" The old man rose, his fists on the desk.

"Save your words!" said Gregory. "Save them for your flock. My church preaches love."

"Your brother walks with God," said the old man, but his voice was frail now. He was weary. He was spent.

He chanced a glance at me. I caught and held his eye.

"Don't try to cheat me, Rebbe," said Gregory as the cold air moved into the room past him. "If I don't find this thing here tomorrow night as promised, I'll stand on your doorstep with the cameras. I'll print the stories of my childhood among the Hasidim in my next book."

"Mock me if it pleases you, Gregory," said the old man, drawing himself up. "But the bargain's done, and the Servant of the Bones will be here for you tomorrow. And you will take this thing from me. You who are evil. You who do evil. You who walk with the Devil. Your church walks with the Devil. The Minders are of the Devil. Welcome to this demon and its ilk. Get out of my house."

"All right, my teacher," said Gregory, "my Abraham." He opened the door wide and stepped through it, leaning back into the room so that the light clearly revealed his smiling face.

"My Patriarch, my Moses! You give my love to my brother. Shall I give your condolences to my grieving wife?" He stepped back, slamming the door after him.

There was faint vibration of glass and metal things quivering.

I stayed where I was.

We looked at one another, I and the old man, across the dusty little room, I stepped partway from behind the bookcase and the old man remained fixed behind his desk.

The old man trembled.

Go back into the bones, Spirit. I never called you. I don't speak to you, except to send you away from me.

"Why?" I pleaded. I spoke the old Hebrew knowing he would know it. "Why do you so despise me, old one? What have I done? I don't speak now of the spirit that destroys the magicians, I speak of myself, me, Azriel! What did I do?"

He was astonished and shaken. I stood before his desk; I wore clothes like his clothes, and I looked down and I saw that my foot had almost touched the casket, and how small it looked, and the smell of boiling water rose in my nostrils.

"Marduk, my god," I cried out in the old Chaldean. He knew the words, the zaddik! Let him glare at me in horror.

"Oh, my god, they will not help me!" I sang out the words in Chaldean. "I am here again and there is no righteous path!"

The old man stood rapt, and repelled. He was full of shock and loathing. He threw out his hands:

"Be gone, spirit, out of here, out of the air, and back into the bones whence you came!"

I felt a silken thrill through my limbs. I held firm.

"Rebbe, you said he killed her. Tell me if he did. I slew the men who stabbed her!"

"Be gone, spirit." He threw up his hands over his face, and turned his head. His voice grew stronger. He stepped from behind his desk and walked about me in a circle, shouting the words again, louder, more clearly, his hands flashing in front of me. I felt myself weaken. I felt the tears on my face.

"Why did you say, Rebbe, that he had killed Esther? Tell me and I shall avenge her! I killed the hirelings! Oh, Lord God of Hosts, when Yahweh spoke to Saul and David, he said slay them all to the last man, woman, and child! And Saul and David obeyed him. Was it not right to slay those three filthy men who murdered an innocent girl?"

"Be gone, Spirit!" he cried. "Be gone! Be gone. I will have no traffic with you. Go back into the bones!"

"I curse you, I hate you!" I said to him, but it had no sound.

I was dissolving. All that I had gathered to myself was dispersed, as if the wind had found its way beneath the door and caught hold of me.

"Be gone, Spirit, be gone from here, be gone from my house and from me!"

Blackness.

Yet I couldn't stop thinking.

I couldn't stop being.

I will see you again, old man.

Dreams came to me as if I were human and I slept, and my mind had opened its doors to living teachers. No, Azriel, no, perish, but don't dream.

Yet there came the face of Samuel; Strasbourg; another sanctuary of scrolls and books and it was in flames. I heard my voice. "Take my hand, Master, take me with you into death." Damn you, Samuel! Damn you, old man.

Damn you, all you Masters!

From the top of a hill I looked down on the small city of Strasbourg. Oh, it was nothing so clear then as it was when I described it to you.

But it was there, I saw it. I knew that all the Jews were suffering. I knew I was one of them. And yet I couldn't be one of them. And the bells pealed. The arrogant bells of murderers came from their churches. And the sky was the silent heavy sky of olden days—six hundred years ago—perhaps when the air didn't talk and so clearly I heard the bells.

"Azriel." Chatter. Wind. The invisible were coming, they were coming to me in smoky mist, surrounding me, closing in, smelling the weakness, the fear, and the suffering. "Azriel!" The rumblings of the jealous earthbound surrounded me. The greedy desperate earthbound dead.

Get away from me. Let me remember.

I wanted to know, I wanted to push past all of them as I had the people on the sidewalk when Esther had looked at me. I wanted to remember, I wanted to . . .

For one instant, I stood bright, staring at the Rebbe, but the Rebbe was huge, and his voice was louder than the wind.

Be gone, Spirit! I command you! The old man's face was blood red with his fury.

Be gone, Spirit!

His words struck me. They hurt me. They lashed me. Give me silence for now. If there can be no peace, there can be silence and there can be the darkness. It could be worse, Azriel.

It could be worse.

To be wounded is bad, but not so bad as to kill the innocent and to smile with hate.

17

There are several things I should have attempted. I should have tried to leave the room, intact, and follow Gregory. I had a visible body! I had clothed it perfectly. I should have hung on. I should have tried to wander freely in the streets of Brooklyn and discover more about the world, simply by asking more specific questions of it.

I should have discovered specifics about Gregory Belkin and the Temple of the Mind. People in the streets would have talked to me about these things. I looked like a man. I could have watched the television broadcasts in taverns. I could have spent a night of fruitful, focused learning instead of letting the old Rebbe drive me away from my own self, and into nothingness once more.

Whatever, when the Rebbe sought to destroy me, I should not have wasted time calling out to "my god."

That had been an unthinkable thing for the Servant of the Bones—to call upon my god—for my god had never been with me in my years of evil spectral service. I don't think the Servant of the Bones who cursed Samuel even remembered my god, because he did not remember being human, as I remembered now. My god had been mine when I was a man, a young man living in the city of Babylon where I had died.

Indeed, though I hate to admit it, if I bring to mind Samuel, I remember only how proud I was to be his genii, a ghost of remarkable powers such as simple dead souls almost never acquire. I was the mighty culmination of ancient magic and men who knew how to use it.

Of human life, I had recalled nothing. I could not even recall a Master before Samuel, though surely there had been such men. Back to Babylon there must have been a lineage of such magicians, all of whom I'd served and outlived.

It had to be so. It was so. The Servant of the Bones was passed hand to hand.

And at some point, as the Rebbe had so graciously explained for Gregory's benefit, the Servant of the Bones had rebelled against his solemn purpose. He had turned around in the very midst of his magic and lashed out at the one who had called him into being, and the Servant of the Bones had done this more than once.

But what had preceded all this? Had I not once been human?

What did my memories want of me? What did Esther want of me? Why was it seductive to have eyes and ears, to feel pain, and to hate again, and to want to kill? Yes, I very much wanted to kill.

I wanted to kill the Rebbe, but then again I could not. I held him to be a good man, a man perhaps without blemish, except for want of kindness, and I couldn't do it. There is only so much evil for which you can blame others. I couldn't kill him. I was glad I had not.

But you can imagine what a mystery I was to myself, caught between Heaven and Hell and not knowing why I had come.

But I was not of God, no, I was not of God and I had no god, and when the Rebbe banished me, when he used his considerable power to dissolve my form and addle my wits so that I could not oppose him, he had done so in the name of God and I had not dared to call upon that same God, the God of my father, the Lord God of Hosts, the God above and before all Gods.

No, in that moment of weakness, Azriel, man and ghost, had called upon his pagan god of old, from a human time, a god whom he had loved.

As the Rebbe cursed me, I deliberately called on Marduk in Chaldean. I wanted the Rebbe to hear the pagan tongue. Anger burnt me up as it has so often done. I knew my god wouldn't help me.

Some parting of the ways had occurred with me and my god.

Must I now recall everything? Must I know the story from the start?

Well, if I sought to put it together, to understand it, to know who

I had been and how I'd been made the Servant of the Bones, there should be but one reason: so that I might die.

Really, really die.

Not just retreat into blackness again, to be called forth into another lurid drama, and surely not to be trapped, earthbound, with the lost souls who murmured and stammered and screeched as they clung to mortality. But to die. To be given at last what had somehow been denied me years ago by a trick I couldn't recall.

"Azriel, I warn you." Who had spoken those words then, thousands of years ago? A phantom? Who was the man I saw dimly at the richly carved table who cried and cried? Who was the King? There had been a great king. . . .

But my anger and my rage had weakened me so that I was shocked and dispersed by the Rebbe. My mind was blown apart as surely as my form. My capacity to reason was shattered, and I rose into the night formless, aimless, drifting once more among the electric voices, tumbling as it were above the magnet that holds us all—the spinning world.

But I never let go. I never really let go.

As I came to myself, as I gathered strength again, as I set my eyes upon a destination, I thought of all these various aspects of my situation—that I very well might be utterly Masterless, that I wouldn't fail Esther, that I was stronger than I'd ever been—and I was determined to fight harder this time to be free of either of these two men—the Rebbe or his grandson Gregory—I was determined that if I could not die, I would gain life apart from them.

Who knows what nourishes a spirit, in the flesh or out of it?

Men and women in this time, who would have laughed at our old customs, believed in absolutely preposterous explanations of things—take, for example, how a hailstone comes to form, from a speck of dust in the upper atmosphere, falling, then rising, gathering ice to itself, falling again, then rising again, and becoming larger and larger, till some perfect moment is reached at which the hailstone breaks the circuit and falls to earth and then, after all of that, all of that wondrous process, melts to nothing. Dust to dust.

Someday these people—these clever minds of today—will know all about spirits. They will know as they knew about genes and neutrinos and other things they cannot see. Doctors at the bedside will see the spirit rise, the tzelem, as I saw it rise from Esther. It will not take a sorcerer to drive a spirit heavenward. There will be men clever enough to exterminate or extinguish even something like me.

Note this, Jonathan.

Scientists of your time have isolated the gene for a fruit fly that is eyeless. And when they take his genes and inject them into other fruit flies—God have mercy on his tiny creatures—do you know that these fruit flies produce eyes all over their bodies? Eyes on their elbows? And on their wings?

Doesn't that make you love scientists? Don't you feel tenderness towards them and respect for them?

Believe you me, coming back to myself the following night, taking form again, diaphanous but optimistic and hatefully calm, I did not think to seek the help of scientists any more than sorcerers to effect my final death. No. I was done with all practitioners of the unseen; I was done with everything except justice for a girl I'd never known. And I would find a way to die, even if it meant I had to remember everything, every painful moment of what I'd suffered when death should have come to me, when death should have been granted, when the Ladder to Heaven might have fallen down, or at least the Gates of Hell swung wide.

Stay alive long enough to understand!

It was exciting! It was perhaps the only truly exciting thing that I could at that moment imagine or recall.

On the sidewalk, the next night, in Brooklyn, I took form whole and swift as if some modern man had flicked a light switch. Invisible to mortal eyes, but in the very shape that would soon enough become solid.

I wanted it this way. But still, to come forth on my own? I couldn't quite trust it. But tonight I would make strides in my search for the truth.

Brooklyn again, the house of the Rebbe and his family, and Gregory's car sliding to the curb.

Invisible, I drifted close to Gregory, fairly wrapping myself around him, though never touching him really, escorting him back the alleyway, almost touching his fingers as he unlocked the gate.

When the door opened, I entered with him, beside him, buoyant and fearless, breathing in the smell of his skin, inspecting him as never before.

I think I was luxuriating for a moment in the invisibility, which in general I hate, and came close to see how very well groomed and strong this man was, and that he had the glow of a king. His black eyes were uncommonly bright in his face, unencumbered by fleshly wrinkles that suggest weariness or an attitude, and his mouth in particular was very beautiful, more beautiful than I had realized. He wore fine clothes as before, the simple garments of this era, a long coat of soft fleecy wool, fine linen beneath it, and around his neck, the same scarf.

I went to the far left corner of the room, a much better place than I had occupied the night before, this time quite far to the left of both men and the dingy lamps beside and above them, and the small circle of intimacy which they so unwillingly shared.

Indeed I could see the old man's profile as I saw Gregory's, the two facing each other, and the casket gleaming on the desk, the desk this time which had been stripped of all its sacred books and would no doubt be purified after by a thousand words and gestures and candles, but what was that to me?

I was making the air move. The old man would know it within seconds. I had to be still and resist the lure of my growing strength. Remain diaphanous, quick to move, rather than to be scattered, willing to pass through the wall intact, rather than frightened once more or hurt into disintegration as I had been the night before.

I was near the wall that was closest to the street outside, against a wooden door that appeared unused, its brass handle covered with dust, and I could see my own shape, my folded arms, my shoes. I called the duplicates of Gregory's clothes to form themselves easily around me, in so far as I knew the details.

The Rebbe rested on his elbows, staring at the casket before him, and the black chains looked ugly against the plated gold.

I felt nothing in me that he was so near to the bones. I felt nothing that either man spoke of them, or moved about them, or stared at the casket which held them, and this I noted.

Behave now as if you are living, and as if it matters to go on living. Be careful as the living. Take your time.

My own advice to myself amused me a little. But then I settled in, deep into the corner, beyond where the light fell, beyond where it might even touch my half-visible shoe or inevitably gleaming eye.

Old man, just try it! I was ready for him. I was ready for anyone or anything.

Gregory stepped anxiously into the light. He looked directly at the casket. The old man behaved as though Gregory were not there. Gregory might have been the spirit. The old man stared at the gold plating; he stared at the iron chains.

Gregory reached out, and without asking permission he put his hands on the casket. Then I did feel a shimmer, much as I loathed it, and I was stronger, instantly stronger.

The old man stared right at Gregory's hands. Then he sat back, sighing heavily as if for effect or punctuation, and he reached for a sheaf of papers—rather cheap and light paper, nothing as good as parchment—and he thrust this group of papers at Gregory, holding them up above the casket.

Gregory took the papers.

"What's this?"

"Everything written on the casket," said the old man in English. "Don't you see the letters?" His voice was full of despair. "The words are written in three tongues. Call the first Sumerian, the second Aramaic, and the last Hebrew, though they are ancient tongues."

"Ah! This was more than kind of you. I never expected such co-operation from you."

I thought so too. What had moved the old man to be so helpful?

Gregory could barely hold the papers steady. He shuffled them, put them back in order, and started to speak.

"No!" said the old man. "Not here. It's yours now and you take it. And you say the words when and where you will, but not under my roof, and from you I exact one last promise, in exchange for these documents which I have prepared for you. You know what they are, don't you? They let you call the spirit. They tell you how."

Gregory made a soft laugh. "Once again, your kindness overwhelms me," he said. "I know your disinclination to touch even trifles which are not clean."

"This is no trifle," said the old man.

"Ah, then, when I say these words the Servant of the Bones will rise?"

"If you don't believe it, why do you want it?" asked the old man.

The shock went through me. I was fully visible.

I cleaved to the wall, not daring even to try to see my own limbs. The cloth wound itself around me without a whisper. "Make the shoes to shine even brighter, give me the gold for my wrist, and make my face as clean of hair, yet give me the hair of my youth," I asked silently.

I felt my full weight, denser perhaps than it had even been the night before. I wanted to look down at myself but I dared not make myself known.

"You don't seriously think I believe in it," Gregory replied politely. He folded the sheaf of papers and put them carefully into the breast of his coat.

The old man made no reply.

"I want to know about it, I want to know what she was talking about, I want it. I covet it. I covet it because it's precious and it's unique and she spoke of it with her dying words."

"Yes, that does convey upon it an added value," said the old man, his voice harder and clearer than I had ever heard it before.

I could feel my hair against my shoulders. I could feel the dampness from the concrete wall as it chilled my neck. I made the scarf at my neck thicker. I made it fit higher. The lightbulb stirred. Things creaked in the room, but neither man appeared to notice, so intent were they on the casket and on each other.

"The chains are rusted, aren't they?" Gregory said, raising his right finger. "May I take them off?"

"Not here."

"All right, then I presume we have concluded our bargain. But you want something else, don't you? A final promise. I know. I can see it in you. Speak. I want to take home my treasure and open it. Speak. What more do you want?"

"Promise me, you will not come back to this house. You'll never seek my company again. You'll never seek the company of your brother. You will never tell anyone of how you were born one of us. You will keep your world away as you have always done. If your brother calls you, you will not receive his call. If your brother visits you, you will not receive him. Promise all of this to me."

"You ask that of me every time I see you," said Gregory. He laughed. "It's always the final thing you ask, and I always promise."

He cocked his head and smiled affectionately at the old man, patronizingly, with maddening impudence.

"You won't see me again, Grandfather. Never, never again. When you die, I won't cross the bridge to come to your graveside. Is that what you want to hear? I won't come to Nathan to mourn with him. I won't risk exposing him, or any of you. Very well?"

The old man nodded.

"But I have one last demand of you," said Gregory, "if I am never to speak to or see Nathan again."

The old man made a little questing gesture with both hands.

"Tell my brother I love him. I insist you tell him."

"I'll tell him," said the old man.

Then Gregory moved swiftly, gathering up the casket, letting the chains scrape on the desk as he stood upright with it in his arms.

I felt again the tremors, the strengthening, moving down my arms and my legs. I felt my fingers moving, I felt a tingling as if tiny needles were being touched to me all over. I didn't like it, that it came from his touch. But maybe it came from all of us here, our sense of purpose, our concentration.

"Goodbye, Grandfather," said Gregory. "Someday, you know, they will come to write about you—my biographers, those who tell the story of the Temple of the Mind." He tightened his grip on the casket. The rusted chains left red dust on his lapels but he didn't care. "They'll write your epitaph because you are my grandfather. And you'll deserve that recognition."

"Get out of my house."

"Of course, you needn't worry for the moment. No record exists of the boy you mourned thirty years ago. On my deathbed I'll tell them."

The old man shook his head slowly, but resisted a reply.

"But tell me, aren't you the least bit curious about this casket, about what's in it, about what may happen when I read the incantations?"

"No."

Gregory's smile faded. He studied the old man, and then he said:

"All right, Grandfather. Then we have nothing to talk about, do we? Nothing at all."

The old man nodded.

The anger beat in Gregory's cheeks, wet and red. But he had no time for this. He looked at the thing in his arms and he turned and hurried out the door, kicking it open with his knee and letting it slam behind him.

The old man sat exactly as before. I think he looked at the dust on his desk. I think he stared at the flakes of rust from the iron which had been left on his polished wood. But I couldn't tell.

I felt nothing. I neither moved nor was strengthened, as Gregory with his casket of bones moved away from me. No, he was not Master, never, never, by any means. But this old man? I had to know.

Gregory's steps died away in the alley.

I came forward, and walked to the old man's desk and stood in front of it.

The old man was aghast.

The moment for an outcry passed in rigid silence, his eyes contracting, and when he spoke it was a whisper.

"Go back to the bones, Spirit," he said.

I drew on all my strength to hold out against him, I thought nothing of his hatred, and I thought of no moment in my long miserable existence when I had been either wronged or loved. I looked at him and I stood firm. I barely heard him.

"Why did you pass the bones to him?" I asked. "What is your purpose! If you called me up to destroy him, tell me!"

He turned his face away, so as not to see me.

"Be gone, Spirit!" he declared in Hebrew.

I watched him stand up and move the chair back out of his way, and I saw his hands fly up, and I knew that he was speaking Hebrew, and then the Chaldean, yes, he knew that too, and he spoke it with perfect cadence, but I didn't hear the words. The words didn't touch me.

"Why did you say he killed Esther? Why, Rebbe, tell me!"

Silence. He had ceased to speak. He didn't even pray in his mind or his heart. He stood transfixed, his mouth closed tight beneath his white mustache, the locks of his hair shivering slightly, the light showing the yellowed hairs of his beard as well as the snow white.

His eyes were closed. He began to whisper his prayers in Hebrew, davening, or bowing, that is, very quickly over and over again.

His fear and fury were equal; his hatred outstripped them both.

"Do you want justice for her?" I shouted at him. But nothing would break his prayers and his closed eyes and his bowing.

Now I spoke, softly in Chaldean,

"Fly from me," I said in a whisper, "all you tiny parts of land and air and mountain and sea, and of the living and of the dead, which have come to give me this form, fly from me but not so far that I cannot summon you at will, and leave me my shape that this mortal man may see me and be afraid."

The light above shivered again on its raw cord. I saw the air move the old man's beard. I saw it make him blink.

I looked down through my own translucent hands and saw the floor beyond them.

"Fly from me," I whispered, "and stay close to me to return at my summons, that God Himself would not know me from a man that He had made!"

I vanished.

I threw out my disappearing hands to frighten him. I wanted so to hurt him, just a little. I wanted so to defy him. On and on he prayed with eyes closed.

But there was no time for idle play with him. I didn't know if there was energy enough for what I meant to do.

Passing through the walls I went upwards, rising over the rooftops, passing through tingling wires, and into the cool air of the night.

"Gregory," I said, as surely as if my old master Samuel had sent me to say it. "Gregory!"

And there below in the stream of traffic on the bridge I saw the car, moving amongst its guardians, for there were many. I saw it, sleek and long, keeping perfect pace with the cars before it and behind it and beside it, as if they were birds together in a flock and flew straight, without having to play the wind.

"Down there, beside him and so that he cannot see."

No Master could have said it with more determination, pointing his finger at the victim that I was to rob, or murder, or put to flight.

"Come now, Azriel, as I command you," I said.

And gently I descended, into the soft warm interior of the car, a world of dark synthetic velvet and tinted glass that made the night outside die a little, as if a deep mist had covered all things.

Opposite him, I took my place, my back to the leather wall which divided us from the driver, folding my arms again as I watched him, crouched as it were, with the casket in his arms. He had broken off the useless rusted iron chains, and they lay dirty and fragmented on the carpeted floor.

I could have wept with happiness. I had been so afraid! I had been so sure I could not do it! All of my will had been so fixed on the effort, that I scarce had breath in me to realize it had been done.

We rode together, the ghost watching him, and he, the man clutching his treasure, balancing it carefully on his knees, and reaching in his coat for the papers, and then shoving them back in his excitement and steadying the casket again and rubbing his hands on it, as if the very gold excited him as it had the ancients. As gold had once excited me.

Gold.

A blast of heat came to me, but this was memory.

Hold firm. Begin. From land and sea, from the living and the dead, from all that God has made, come to me, what I require to make of me an apparition, thin as air, to make of me a barely visible yet strong being.

I looked down and saw the shape of my legs, I had hands again, I made clothes like Gregory's clothes. I could almost feel the padded seat of the car. Almost feel it, and I longed to touch it, longed for garments to wrap me round.

I saw buttons, the shining semblance of buttons, and fingernails. And I lifted my invisible hand to my face to make sure that it was clean shaven as his. But give me my hair, my long hair, like Samson's hair, thick hair. I caught my fingers in the ringlets. I wanted so to finish it but not yet—

I had to say when Azriel would come, didn't I? I had to say it. I was the Master.

Suddenly Gregory lowered the casket. He fell down on his knees on the very floor of the car and laid the casket before him, rocking with the motion of the car, steadying himself against the seat, his right hand so close to me he almost touched me, and then he ripped off the lid of the casket.

He pulled it up and off, and it flew off, rotted, dried, a shell of gold almost, and there—there on their bed of rotted cloth lay the bones.

I felt a shock as though blood had been infused into me. My heart had only to beat. *No, not yet.*

I looked down at the remnants of my body. I looked down at the bones that held my tzelem locked within them, coated with gold, chained together, and formed like a child asleep in the womb.

A dimness threatened me, a dissolution. What was the reason? Pain. We were in a great room. I knew this room. I felt the heat of the boiling cauldron. No. Don't let this come now. Don't let this weaken you.

Look at the man on his knees right in front of you, and the bones that he all but worships, which are your bones.

"Body be my own," I whispered. "Be solid and strong enough to make angels burn with envy. Mold me into the man I would be in my happiest hour, if I held the looking glass before my own face."

He paused. He had heard the whisper. But in the dark he saw nothing but the casket. What were creaks and bumps and whispers to him? The car sped along. The city hissed and throbbed.

His eyes were locked to the bones.

"My Lord God," said Gregory, and leaning back on his heels so that he wouldn't tumble, he reached out for the skull.

I felt it. I felt his hands on my head. But it was only a stroking of the thick black hair that was already there, hair I had called to me.

"Lord God!" he said again. "Servant of the Bones? You have a new Master. It is Gregory Belkin and his entire flock. It is Gregory Belkin of the Temple of the Mind of God who calls you. Come to me, Spirit! Come to me!"

I said:

"Perhaps yes, perhaps no to all those words. I am already here."

He looked up, saw me sitting composed and opposite to him and he let out a loud cry and tumbled over against the door of the car. He let go of the casket altogether.

Nothing changed in me except that I grew stronger and brighter.

I reached over towards him and down carefully and put the fragile lid over the curling skeleton of the bones. I covered them up with my hands, and I drew back and up and folded my arms, and I sighed.

He sat slumped still on the floor of the car, the seat behind him, the door beside him, his knees up, staring at me, merely staring, and then as filled with wonder as any human I could ever remember, fearless and mad with glee.

"Servant of the Bones!" he said, flashing his teeth to me.

"Yes, Gregory," I answered with the tongue in my mouth, my voice speaking his English. "I am here, as you see."

I studied him carefully. I had outdone his garments, my coat was soft and flawless silk, and my buttons were jasper, and my hair was long on my shoulders. Heavy! And I was composed and he sat in disarray.

Slowly, very slowly he rose, grasping the handle of the door to aid himself, as he sat back down on the velvet seat and looked first at the casket on the floor and then at me.

I turned sharply for one instant. I had to. I was afraid. But I had to. I had to see if I could see myself in the dark tinted glass.

Beyond, the night moved in a splendid dreamy flight, the city of towers clustering near us, bright orange electric lights blazing as fiercely as torches.

But there was Azriel, looking at himself with sharp black eyes, smooth shaven, his hair a regular mantle on his head, and his thick eyebrows dipping as they always did when he smiled.

Without haste, I let my eyes return to him. I let him see my smile.

My heart beat and I could move my tongue easily on my lips. I sat back and felt the comfort of this cushioned seat, and I felt the engine of the car vibrating through me, vibrating through the soft, exquisite velvet beneath me.

I heard his breath rise and fall. I saw his chest heave. I looked into his eyes again.

He was rapt. His arms had not even tensed; his fingers lay open on his knees. He did not even bend his back as if to brace himself from a shock or a blow. His eyes were fully opened and he too was almost smiling.

"You're a brave man, Gregory," I said. "I have reduced other men to stuttering lunatics with such tricks as this."

"Oh, I bet you have," he answered.

"But don't call me the Servant of the Bones again. I don't like it. Call me Azriel. That's my name."

"Why did she say it?" he asked at once. "Why did she say it in the ambulance? She said 'Azriel,' just as you said it."

"Because she saw me," I said. "I watched her die. She saw me and she spoke to say my name twice, and then that was all she said and she was dead."

He tumbled gently back against the seat. He stared upwards now, past me, resisting the inevitable rocking of the car, and its sudden jerks as it slowed, perhaps blocked by the traffic. He stared and only slowly lowered his eyes to me in the most fearless and casual manner I have ever seen in a man.

Then, lifting his hand, he began to tremble. But it wasn't cowardice. It wasn't even shock. It was glee, the pure mad glee he'd felt when he looked at the skull.

He wanted to touch me. He rubbed his hands together, and he reached out and then he drew back.

"Go ahead," I said. "I don't care. Do it. I would like you to do it."

I reached forward and grabbed his right hand before he could stop me and I lifted it as he stared amazed. His mouth opened. I lifted his hand and pushed it against my thick hair, and laid it on my cheek, and then against my chest.

"You feel a heartbeat?" I asked. "There is none. Only a living pulse as if I were whole and entire a heart, made of a heart, when the very opposite is surely the truth. I feel your pulse, true enough, and it races. I feel your strength and you have much."

He tried to free his hand, but only politely, and I wouldn't let him do it; I held his hand now so that I could see the palm of it in the flashing light coming through the windows.

The car went very slowly.

I saw the lines in his palm, and then I opened my right hand which was free, and I saw the lines in my palm too. I had done well. No Master had ever done better. But I didn't know how to read these lines, only that they had come to me in glorious detail.

Then I made a decision to do something which I could not explain to myself. I kissed the palm of his hand. I kissed this tender flesh of his hand; I pressed my lips right against it and when I felt the shiver pass through him, I gloried in it, almost the way he was glorying in my presence.

I looked into his eyes and saw something of my own eyes in them, in their largeness, their darkness, even in the thick fringe of lashes of which I, once alive, had been so very proud.

I wanted to kiss his lips, to lock hold of them, and to kiss as enemies kiss before one tries to kill the other.

Indeed, if there had ever been a moment for the Servant of the Bones like this with any mortal, I didn't remember it. Not a wisp of such a memory remained; indeed, I felt nothing now except a fascination with him, and all that came to trouble it was her face, Esther's, and her lips and her dying words.

"And what makes you think that I am not Master!" he whispered. A shining smile spread on his lips, almost rapturous.

I released his hand and he slipped it away, and brought his own two hands together as if to protect them against me, but this was done with graceful composure.

"I'm the Master and you know it," he said it gently. But his voice was eager and loving. "Azriel! You're mine."

There wasn't even a sensible particle of fear in him. Indeed the wonder he knew now seemed the kernel of his person, the part of him which had always defied the Rebbe and had defied a legion of others, and would defy me. The wonder in him was . . . what? The monstrous arrogance of an Emperor?

"I am not the Master?" he asked me.

I looked at him calmly. I was thinking about him in wholly new ways, not ways of rage, but ways of wanting to know: who and what was he? Had he killed her? What if he had not?

"I say not, Gregory," I answered his question. "You're not the Master. But then I don't know everything. Ghosts must be forgiven that they know so much and so little at the same time."

"Rather like mortal men," he said with a delicate touch of sadness. "And were you ever one of them?"

A chill caught me off guard, rippling over new skin. Dimness. The cries of people echoing up glazed brick walls. I shook myself all over.

Certainly I had once been a mortal man! And so what.

I was here now in the car with him. The process of incarnation continued in me, with the thickening of the sinews and the deepening of the minerals within the new bones which were now in my fleshly body, and the hair that formed on the backs of my arms and on my fingers, and the soft remnant of beard on my cheek.

And this process had to be of my doing. He sang no songs to make it happen; he recited no chants. He didn't even know it was happening. If there was an alchemy coming from him, it was the alchemy of his expression, his wonder, his obvious love.

Again came the dimness. It came swift and titanic—a procession, a great street with high blue-glazed walls, and the scent of flowers everywhere, and people waving, and a dreadful sadness, so bitter, so total, that for one moment I felt myself begin to dissolve.

The car around me seemed insubstantial, which meant that I was leaving it.

In the memory I raised my arm and voices cried in praise.

My god wouldn't look at me. My god turned his back on me and on the procession, and he wept.

I shook my head. Gregory Belkin was watching all this, keenly sensing it.

"Something troubles you, Spirit," he said gently. "Or is it merely so hard to become flesh again?"

I took hold of the door handle. I looked at the glass and at my face.

I was the one who made myself stay.

The car shuddered and rumbled as it moved over the roughened street. He took no notice. But new light had come in from both sides, penetrating even the black glaze of the windows, and it showed how jubilant he was, and how easy, and how young he looked in his wonder and joy.

"Very well," he said with charm, eyebrows lifted, "so I am not the Master. Then tell me, beautiful one, and you are quite the handsome Spirit, why have you come to me?"

Once again, his teeth flashed white and there seemed a moment near magical when the various ornaments he wore—small and made of gold, at his wrists, on his tie—flickered as if struck by a note of music, and he looked very good, as good perhaps as he thought I looked.

Masters. . . . Who were masters to me? Old men?

I spoke before I thought.

"There was never a Master as brave as you, Gregory," I said, "not that I can remember, though so much lies beyond my reach. No, your bravery is different, and fresh. And you are not the Master. It seems, like it or not, that I have come to you on my own and for my reasons."

This pleased him immensely.

I grew warmer and I felt the fibers of my clothes against me, I felt the snug certainty of being there. My foot flexed in my shoe.

"I like that you're not afraid of me," I said. "I like that you know what I am from the start as any Master might, but you're not the Master. I've been watching you. I've been learning things from you."

"Have you?" he said. He did not so much as flinch. He was in near ecstasy. "Tell me what you've seen." At the moment it seemed there was only one thing he found more fascinating than me, and that was himself.

I smiled at him.

He wasn't a man unused to happiness. He knew well how to enjoy things, both minute and momentous. And though nothing like this had ever happened to him, his life had educated him to enjoy this too.

"Yes," he said, smiling broadly. "Yes!"

I hadn't spoken. We both knew it. Yet he had read my thoughts? What else is in there to read, I wonder?

The big car slid to a stop.

I was glad. I was frightened by his charm, frightened by the fact that I warmed to him, frightened that somehow in talking to him I gained strength. He didn't have to want it or wish it, only perhaps to witness it. But this I couldn't tolerate. I had been there when Esther died and he had not. He had not been there to see me, yet I had been strong enough to take the lives of her killers each in turn.

He stared out the windows, to the right and left. An immense crowd surrounded us, roaring, shouting, pushing up against the car so that it rocked suddenly on its wheels as a boat in water.

He was not concerned. He turned and looked at me. I felt that dimness come again, because this crowd reminded me of that old crowd, the crowd attending the procession, and the petals falling in the light, the incense rising, and people on the flat rooftops, standing at the very edge, with their arms outstretched.

Jonathan, you know now what I remembered, but I didn't remember then, you see. It was confusion. It was as if something were trying to force me to see my existence as a continuum. But I didn't trust it. I must have been very close to Zurvan's teachings a thousand times over the years and never knew it, never remembering Zurvan. Why else did I want to avenge this girl? Why else did I despise the Rebbe for his lack of mercy on me? Why else was this man's evil fascinating me so much that I hadn't already killed him?

He broke in with his gentle, beguiling voice.

"And so we're here, at my home, Azriel," he said.

He pulled me back fast.

"We are at my very door." He made a dreamy, weary gesture towards the people on either side of us. "Don't let them frighten you. I must invite you, please, to come in."

I saw rows of lighted windows high above.

The doors of the car had been unlocked with a loud distinct click. Now someone meant to open the door to my right and his left. In a split second, I saw a pathway made for him, beneath an awning. Ropes hung from bronze stanchions held back the multitude. There were television cameras bearing down upon us. I saw men in uniforms restraining those who screamed and cheered.

"But can they see you?" Gregory asked now, confidentially, as if we shared a secret.

It was a break in an almost perfect chain of gestures for him. Out of generosity I was tempted to let it go. But I didn't.

"See for yourself whether or not they can see me, Gregory," I answered. I reached down and gathered up the casket, and holding it firmly under my left arm, I took a grip of the door handle and stepped over him and out of the car before him onto the sidewalk in the blazing electric light.

I stood on the sidewalk. A great building rose before me. I held the casket of the bones tight to my chest. I could barely see the top of this building.

Everywhere I looked were shouting faces. Everywhere I looked, I looked at those who looked at me. It was a babble of people calling for Gregory, and others calling for blood for Esther, and I couldn't untangle the prayers.

Cameras and microphones descended; a woman shouted questions furiously at me and far too rapidly for me to understand. The crowd almost broke the ropes, but more uniformed men came to restore order. The people were both the young and the old.

The television lights gave off a powerful heat that hurt the skin of my face. I raised my hand to shield my eyes.

A thunderous and united cry rose as Gregory appeared now, with the helping hand of his driver, brushing his coat that was covered with dust from the casket, and he took his place at my side.

His lips came close to my ear.

"Indeed, they do see you," he said.

The dimness hovered, cries in other tongues deafened me, and I shook away again the mantle of sadness and looked right into the blaring lights and screaming faces that were here.

"Gregory, Gregory, Gregory," the people chanted. "One Temple, One God, One Mind."

First it overlapped, prayer atop prayer, as if it were meant to do so, coming at us in waves, but then the crowd brought their voices together:

"Gregory, Gregory, Gregory. One Temple, One God, One Mind."

He lifted his hand and waved, turning from left to right and all around, nodding and smiling and waving to those who stood behind him, and to those far off, and he kissed his hand, the very hand I'd kissed, and threw this kiss and a thousand other such kisses to the people who shrieked and called his name in delight.

"Blood, blood, blood for Esther!" someone screamed.

"Yes, blood for her! Who killed her!"

The prayer came roaring over it, but others had taken it up, "Blood for Esther," stamping their feet in time with their words.

"Blood, blood, blood for Esther."

Those with cameras and microphones broke through the ropes, pressing against us.

"Gregory, who killed her?"

"Gregory who is this with you?"

"Gregory, who is your friend?"

"Sir, are you a member of the Temple?"

They were talking to me!

"Sir, tell us who you are!"

"Sir, what is in the box you're carrying?"

"Gregory, tell us what the church will do?"

He turned and faced the cameras.

A trained squadron of dark-dressed men rushed to surround us and separate us from those questioning us, and en masse they pushed us gently up the lighted path, past the throng.

But Gregory spoke loudly:

"Esther was the lamb! The lamb was slain by our enemies. Esther was the lamb!"

The crowd went into a frenzy of approbation and applause.

Beside him, I stared right at the cameras, at the lights beaming down, at the flash of thousands of small hand-held cameras snapping out still pictures.

He drew in his breath to speak, in full command, as any ruler might, standing before his own throne. Loudly, he intoned his words:

"The murder of Esther was only their warning; they have let us know that the time is come when any righteous person will be destroyed!"

Again, the crowd screamed and cheered, vows were declared, chants were taken up.

"Don't give them an excuse!" Gregory declared. "No excuse to enter our churches or our homes. They come clothed in many disguises!"

The crowd pressed in on us in a dangerous surge.

Gregory's arm closed around me, caressingly.

I looked up. The building pierced the sky.

"Azriel, come inside," he said, again speaking close to my ear.

There came the loud sound of shattering glass. An alarm bell clanged. The crowd had pushed in one of the lower windows of the tower. Attendants rushed to the spot. Whistles sounded. I could see garbed police on horseback in the street.

We were drawn in through the doors across a floor of shimmering marble. Others held back the crowd. But still others surrounded us, making it near impossible for us to do anything but go where they forced us to go.

I was madly exhilarated, alive in the midst of this. Astonished and invigorated. Something told me that my former masters had been men of stealth, wise, keeping their power to themselves.

Here we stood in the capital of the world: Gregory sparkled with the surety of his power, and I walked beside him, drunk on being alive, drunk on all the eyes turned to us.

At last a pair of bronze doors rose up before us, carved with angels, and when they parted we were thrust together inside a mirrored chamber, and Gregory gestured for all the others to remain outside.

The doors swept closed. It was an elevator. It began to rise. I saw myself in the mirrors, shocked by my long and thick hair and the seeming ferocity of my expression, and I saw him, cold and commanding as ever, watching me, and watching himself. I appeared years younger than him, and just as human—but we might have been brothers, both of us swarthy, with sun-darkened skin.

His features were finer, eyebrows thinner and combed; I saw the prominent bones of my forehead and my jaw. But still, it was as if we were of the same tribe.

As the elevator moved higher and higher, I realized we were now completely alone, staring at one another, in a floating cabin of mirrored light.

But no sooner had I absorbed this little shock, this one of many, and no sooner had I righted myself and anchored my weight against the slight swaying of the elevator, than the doors were opened again upon a large sanctuary that appeared both splendid and private: a demilune entranceway of inlaid marble, doorways opening to left and right, and just before us a broad corridor leading to a distant chamber whose windows were wide open to the twinkling night.

We were higher than the mightiest ziggurat, castle, or forest. We were in the realm of the airy spirits.

"My humble abode," Gregory murmured. He had to rip his eyes from me. But he recovered.

From the doorways came the sounds of voices, and padded feet. A woman cried somewhere in agony. Doors were shut. No one appeared.

"It's the mother crying, isn't it?" I said. "The mother of Esther."

Gregory's face went blank then grew sad. No, it was something more painful than sadness, something he had never revealed in the presence of the Rebbe when they spoke of the dead daughter. He hesitated, seemed on the verge of saying something and then merely nodded. The sadness consumed him, his face, his body, even his hand, which hung limp at his side.

He nodded.

"We should go to her, should we not?" I said.

"And why would we do that?" he asked patiently.

"Because she's crying. She's sad. Listen to the voices. Someone is being unkind to her—"

"No, only trying to give her medicine that she needs—"

"I want to tell her that Esther didn't suffer, that I was there, and Esther's spirit went up so light it was like air itself in the Pathway of Heaven. I want to tell her."

He pondered this. The voices died down somewhat. I couldn't hear the woman crying anymore.

"Heed my advice," he said, reaching out for me and taking a firm grip of my arm. "Come into my parlor first and talk to me. Your words won't mean anything to her anyway."

I didn't like this. But I knew we must talk, he and I.

"Still, later at your leisure," I said, "I want to see her and comfort her. I want to—"

No words. No human cunning, suddenly, nothing but the crashing realization that I was on my own. Why in the name of Heaven had I been allowed to return with the full strength of a man? Or strength even greater.

Gregory studied me.

In a thinly lighted anteroom, I saw two women clothed in white. A man's voice rose husky and angry behind a door.

"The casket," said Gregory, pointing to the golden box in my arms. "Don't let her see such a thing. It would alarm her. Come with me first."

"Yes, it's a strange thing, this," I said, looking at the casket, at the gold flaking from it.

Dimness. Grief. The light changed just a fraction.

Go away from me, all doubt, and worry, and fear of failure, I said in a whisper in a tongue that he could not possibly understand.

There came the familiar reek of boiling liquid, of a golden mist rising. You know why. But I didn't. I turned and shut my eyes, and then looked again down the hallway, to the far window open to the night sky.

"Look at that," I said. I had only a vague point in mind, something to do with the raiment of Heaven being as beautiful as the marble that surrounded us, the archways above us, the pilasters flanking every door. "The stars beyond, look," I said again, "the stars."

All was quiet in the house. He watched me, studying me, listening to my every breath.

"Yes, the stars," he said dreamily, with seeming respect.

His quick dark eyes broadened and there came his smile again, loving and tender.

"We'll talk to her later, I promise you," he said. He grasped my arm firmly and pointed. "But come now to my study, come now and let's talk together. It's time, is it not?"

"I wish I knew," I said in a half murmur. "She's still crying, isn't she?"

"She'll cry till she dies," he said. His shoulders were heavy with sorrow. His whole soul ached with it. I let him lead me down the hall. I wanted to know things from him. I wanted to know everything.

I didn't respond.

18

We made our way down this corridor, Gregory leading boldly, letting his feet ring on the marble, and I coming behind him, dazzled by the peach-colored silk panels affixed to the walls. The floor itself was this same lovely nourishing color.

We passed numerous doors, and one of them to our right lay open. It was her room. She was in there.

I came to a halt and peered in, rudely, but the sight which struck me amazed me.

It was a lavish bedchamber, done wildly in crimson with festoons of red silk coming from its ceilings down over the pillars of the bed. The floor was again marble and this time snow white.

But this in itself was not as remarkable as the sight of a woman—the woman who had been crying—sitting on a low couch, her gown airy and shimmering and as red as the trappings of the room. She had jet-black hair, like the hair of Esther, like my hair for that matter—and the same immense eyes of Esther with near glistening whites to them. But her hair was stranded through and through with silver; it seemed almost decorated by greater age. It spilled down behind her back. Nurses in white surrounded her. One moved quickly to shut the door.

But she looked up, saw me. Her face was drawn and sallow and wet with tears. But she was not old. She'd been very young when she'd given birth to Esther. At once she sat up.

The door was shut, the lock turned. I heard her call out: "Gregory!"

He walked on, reaching back for my hand, his own warm and smooth and leading me alongside him.

Others whispered behind other doors. There were wires in the walls that carried whispers. I couldn't hear the woman crying.

We entered the main room, a grand demilune of splendid detail with a lofty half dome of a ceiling. A row of floor-length windows, each cut into twelve different panes of glass, ran across the street side of it, which was flat, and behind us doors of the same frame punctuated the half circle at equal intervals.

It was more than magnificent.

But the view of the night caught me with all its timeless sweetness. Across a deep dark divide I saw towers, patterned with lights set in rows of incredible regularity, but then I came to realize that all of these buildings had these straight rows of windows, that this age was very mathematically precise.

My head was swimming. Information was pouring in on me.

I saw that the room faced not a dark river, as I had supposed, but a broad dark park. I could smell the trees. I looked down and was amazed to see how truly far we were above the earth, from the tiny crowd still clogging the little thoroughfare and the mounted policemen moving awkwardly like trapped cavalry amid a battle. A swarm of ants.

I turned around.

The doors behind us, in the curved wall, were closed now. I couldn't even tell which door had been our door. I was distracted and obsessed suddenly with the brief glimpse of the weeping mother.

But I cleared this for the present.

In the very center of the half circle wall stood a hearth, monstrous, made of the usual white marble and cold and grand as an altar. Lions were carved into this hearth, and a shelf stood above it and above that a huge mirror which caught the reflection of the windows.

Indeed reflections bounced about all around me. The twelve-paned doors of the rear wall were mirrored, rather than glassed! What an illusion it was. We were drifting in this palace, and comforted by the city as if it had taken us in its arms.

A great heap of wood stood ready in the hearth, as if it were cruel winter, which it was not.

All the doors, both real and mirrored, were double doors with gracefully twisted handles of plated gold, and fancy curving frames for their narrow and shining panes of mirror or glass.

I turned around and around, absorbing everything, drawing out of each item every inference that I could, and no doubt drawing as always upon sources of knowledge inexplicable to me. I was startled by each new object. Then I knew what it was. Statues from China, a Grecian urn very familiar to me and comforting, and lavish glass vases of flowers—these things stood on pedestals.

Strewn about us were couches and chairs of peach and gold velvet, tables with lustrous tops, more vases of magnificent lilies and great golden daisies, or so they seemed to me, and beneath all was a sprawling square carpet, reaching almost from the windows over the park to the edge of the circle in the rear.

The carpet was sewn in magnificent detail with the tree of life, full of the birds of Heaven, and the fruit of Heaven, and figures walking beneath the tree limbs, figures in Asian dress.

So it was always; the world changed; the world became more complex; the world increased in invention and sometimes in ugliness, yet the forms of my time were always embedded in the surfaces around me. Every object in the room was connected in some way to the oldest aesthetic principles ever known to me.

I imagined suddenly that the lost tribes of Israel lived in the carpet, those sold when Nebuchadnezzar came down upon the northern kingdom, but that had been before Jerusalem had been taken. Images of battle, of fire.

Azriel, master thyself.

"Tell me," I said, disguising my delight in all this, my weakness and hunger for it. "What is the Temple of the Mind that its High Priest lives in this splendor? These are private rooms. Are you the thief and the charlatan, as your grandfather said?"

He didn't answer me, but he was most delighted. He walked about me, watching me, waiting eagerly for me to speak again.

"There lies a newspaper from the streets opened where you left it," I said. "Ah, there is Esther's face. Esther smiles for the historians. For the public. And beside the paper, what is this pitcher? Bitter coffee. Your taste is on the cup. I smell it. This is all private, your place of recollection. Yours is a rich God, Mind or no Mind." I took the time to smile. "And you a rich priest."

"I'm not a priest," he said.

Two men appeared suddenly, gawky youths in white stiff shirts and dark trousers. They entered out of the wall of doors, and Gregory was flustered.

He made some quick gestures to them that they must go away. The mirrored doors closed again.

We were alone. I felt my breath and my eyes moving in my skull, and I felt such desire for all things material and sensuous that I could have wept. If I had been alone I would have wept.

I regarded him suspiciously. The night, both real and in reflection, pulsed with twinkling lights. Indeed lights were as plentiful and vital in this time as water had been perhaps in earlier times. Even in this room the lamps were powerful, sculpted pieces of bronze work with heavily adorned glass shades the color of parchment. Light, light, light.

His excitement was palpable to me. He could scarce hold his tongue. He wanted to inundate me with questions, drink all the knowledge he could from me. I stood obdurate, as if I were really human and had every right as any man to be quiet and myself.

Air moved in the room, full of the smell of trees and horses and of the fumes rising from the engines; the engines filled the night with discord. If he were to shut the window, it would go away, this noise, but then so would the fragrance of green grass.

Finally he could contain himself no longer.

"Who called you?" he said. He was not unpleasant. Indeed, he seemed now to slip into a childlike candor but with too much ease for it not to be a style. "Who brought you out of the bones?" he asked. "Tell me, you have to. I am the Master now."

"Don't take such a foolish tack," I answered. "It will be nothing for me to kill you. It would be too simple." I felt no weakening in myself as I resisted him.

What if the world was my Master now? What if each and every human were my master? I saw a blazing fire suddenly, a fire not of the world, but of the gods.

The bones which I still held all this time were heavy in my arms.

Did they want me to see them? I looked down at the old battered casket. It had soiled my garments. I didn't care.

"May I set down the bones?" I asked. "Here, on your table, beside your newspaper and your pitcher of bitter coffee and your dead daughter's face, so pretty to look at, with no veil?"

He nodded, lips parted, straining to keep quiet, to think, and yet too exultant really to do either in any organized way.

I laid down the casket. I felt a ripple of sensation pass through me, just from the proximity of the bones, and the thought suddenly that they were mine own, and I was dead and a ghost, and that I was walking the earth again.

My god, don't let me be taken before I understand this!

He approached. I didn't wait for him. I boldly took off the frail cover of the casket, just as he had before. I laid down the cover on the big table, crushing the newspaper a little, and I stared at the bones.

They were as golden and brilliant as they had been the day I died. But when had that been?

"The day I died!" I whispered. "Am I to find out everything now? Is that part of the plan?"

I thought again of Esther's mother, the woman in red silk. I could sense her presence under this roof. She had most definitely seen me and I tried to imagine how I looked to her. I wanted her to come in here, or to find some way to go to her.

"What are you saying?" He questioned me eagerly. "The day you died, when was it? Tell me. Who made you a ghost? What plan do you speak of?"

"I don't know those answers," I said. "I wouldn't bother with you if I did. The Rebbe told you more than I knew when he translated those inscriptions."

"Not bother with me!" he said. "Not bother with me! Don't you see that if there is a plan, a plan even greater than that which I have designed, you are part of it?"

It gave me pleasure to see his mounting excitement. It was invigorating, beyond doubt. His fine eyebrows rose a little, and I saw that the charm of his eyes was not merely their depth, but their length. I was a person of rounded features; the lines of his face came to beautiful trajectories and points.

"When did you first come? How could Esther have seen you?"

"If I was sent to save her I failed. But why did you call her the lamb? Why did you use those words? Who are these enemies you speak of?"

"You'll learn soon enough. We're all surrounded by enemies. All we have to do to rouse them is show a little power, resist the interjecting plans which they have laid with all the solemnity of a god, plans which are only the routine, the ritual, the tradition, the law, the normal, the regular, the sane . . . You know what I mean, you understand me."

I did understand him.

"Well, I have gone against them and they would come against me, only I'm too powerful for them, and I have dreams that dwarf their petty evil!"

"My, but you speak with a silken tongue," I said, "and you give so much in your words. Why to me?"

"To you? Because you're a spirit, a god, an angel sent to me. You witnessed her death because she was a lamb. Don't you see? You came when she died, as if a god to receive a sacrifice!"

"I hated her death," I said. "I slew the three men who killed her."

This astonished him. "You did that?"

"Yes, Billy Joel, Hayden, and Doby Eval. I killed them. The papers know. The news talks of her blood on their weapons and their blood mingled with it now. I did that! Because I had failed to stop them from their evil plan. What sacrifice do you speak of? Why call her the lamb? Where was the altar and if you think I'm a god, you're a fool! I hate God and all gods. I hate them."

He was enthralled. He drew close to me, and then stepped back, and then walked around, too excited to be still.

If he was guilty of killing his daughter, he gave no clue. He looked at me with pure delight in our exchange.

Something struck me suddenly. The skin of his face had been moved! A surgeon had tightened it over all his bones. I laughed at the ingenuity of it and the implications, that things in this age could be done so simply. And with a sudden sinking terror, I thought, What if I have been brought to this age for a reason that has to do with his horrors and the world's wonders, and this *is* the chance to stay whole and alive from now on?

I winced, and he started to question me again. I put my hands up for him to be quiet.

I backed away from my own thought. I turned and stared at the gleaming bones, and I bent down and laid my own fingers, my material fingers, upon my own bones.

At once I felt as if someone were touching me as I touched them. I felt someone's touch on my own legs. I felt my own hands on my own face as I touched the skull. I sank my thumbs into the empty sockets defiantly, where my eyes had been, my eyes . . . something boiling, something too ghastly to think of—I uttered a small sound that made me ashamed.

The room quivered, brightened, then contracted as though it were receding. No, stay here. Stay in this room. Stay here with him! But I was imagining things, as humans say. My body had not weakened at all. I was standing tall.

I opened my eyes slowly and closed them and looked down at the golden bones. Iron fastened them to the rotted cloth beneath them, iron fastened them to the old wood of the casket, but it was the same casket, permeated with all the oils that would make it last unto the end of time, like the bones. An image of Zurvan flashed through me, and with it came a flood of words . . . to love, to learn, to know, to love . . .

Once again came the huge city walls of blue-glazed bricks, the golden lions and the cries of voices, and one of them pointing his finger and screaming at me in the old Hebrew—the prophet—and the chants rose and fell.

Something had happened! I had done something, something unspeakable to be made this ghost, this old ghost who had served Masters beyond recollection.

But if I dwelt on this, I might vanish. Or I might not.

I stood very still, but no more memories came. I withdrew my hands. I stood looking down at the bones.

Gregory brought me out of it.

He moved closer and he put his hands on me. He wanted so much to do this. How his pulse raced. It felt wondrously erotic, these fleshly hands touching my newly formed arms. If I was still gaining in strength, I didn't feel it anymore.

I felt the world. Safe inside it for now.

His fingers clenched the sleeves of this coat. He was staring at it, the precision of it, the dazzle of the buttons, the fine stitches. And all of this I'd drawn to me in haste with the old commands that rolled off my tongue like nothing. I could have made myself a woman suddenly to frighten him. But I didn't want to do that. I was too happy to be Azriel, and Azriel was too afraid.

Yet again . . . what was the limit of this masterless power? I contrived a joke, an evil joke. I smiled, and then whispering all the words I knew, fashioning the most mellifluous incantations I could, I changed myself into Esther.

The image of Esther. I felt her small body, and peered through her big eyes and smiled, and even felt the tightness of her garments on that last day, the flash of the painted animal coat in my eye.

Thank God, I didn't have to see this myself! I felt sorry for him.

"Stop it!" he roared. He fell back onto the floor, scrambling away from me, and then leaning back on his elbows.

I returned to my own shape. I had done this and he had no control of it! I had control of it. I felt proud and wicked suddenly.

"Why did you call her the lamb? Why did the Rebbe say you killed her?"

"Azriel," he said. "Listen carefully to what I say." He climbed to his feet as effortlessly as a dancer. He walked towards me. "Whatever happens after, whatever happens, remember this. The world is ours. *The world*, Azriel."

I was startled.

"The world, Gregory?" I asked. I tried to sound hard and clever. "What do you mean, the world?"

"I mean all of it, I mean the world as Alexander meant the world when he went out to conquer it." He appealed to me, patiently. "What do you know, Spirit Friend? Do you know the names Bonaparte or Peter the Great or Alexander? Do you know the name Akhenaton? Constantine? What are the names you know?"

"All of those and more, Gregory," I answered. "Those were emperors, conquerors. Add to them Tamerlane and Scanderbeg, and after him Hitler, Hitler, who slew our people by the millions."

"Our people," he said with a smile. "Yes, we are of the same people, aren't we? I knew we were. I knew it."

"What do you mean, you knew it? The Rebbe told you. He read

the scroll. What are these conquerors to you? Who rules in this electric paradise called New York? You are a churchman, so says the Rebbe. You are a merchant. You have billions in every currency recognized on earth. You think Scanderbeg in his castle in the Balkans ever had the wealth you have here? You think Peter the Great ever brought back to Russia with him the luxuries you possess? They didn't have your power! They couldn't. Their world wasn't an electrical web of voices and lights."

He laughed with delight, his eyes sparkling, and beautiful.

"Ah, that's just it," he said. "And now in this world so filled with wonders, no one has their power! No one has the force of Alexander when he brought the philosophy of the Greeks to Asia. No one dares to kill as Peter the Great killed, chopping off the heads of his bad soldiers until the blood covered his arms."

"Your times are not the worst of times," I said. "You have leaders; you have talk; you have the rich being kind to the poor; you have men the world wide who fear evil and want goodness."

"We have madness," he said. "Look again. Madness!"

"What does this mean to you? Is this the mission of your church to gain control of the whole world? Is that what drives you, as the old man asked? You want the power to chop off the heads of men? You want that?"

"I want to change everything," he said. "Look back over those conquerors. Look back over their accomplishments. Use the finest reach of your spirit mind."

"I will. Go on."

"Who really changed the world forever? Who changed it more than any single man?"

I didn't answer.

"Alexander," he said. "Alexander the Great did it! He dared to kill empires that blocked his path. He dared to force Asian to marry Greek. He dared to break the Gordian knot with a sword."

I considered. I thought. I saw the Greek cities along the Asian coast, long after Alexander had died in Babylon; I saw the world as if I were standing back from it. I saw it in patches of light and dark.

"Alexander changed your world," I said. "The world of the West. I see what you see. Alexander is the cornerstone of the rise of the West. But the West isn't the world, Gregory."

"Oh, yes, it is," he answered. "Because the West that Alexander built has changed Asia. No part of the globe has not been changed by the West that Alexander built. And no mind today stands ready to change the world as he would, and I . . . as I would."

He drew in close to me, then suddenly with a darting motion, pushed me with both hands. I didn't move. It was like a child pushing a man. He was pleased and sobered. He took a step back.

I pushed him with one hand. I pushed him into a stumble and then a fall, from which he rose slowly, unshaken, refusing to be shaken.

He didn't become angry. He was knocked back a step, but he planted his feet squarely and he waited.

"Why are you testing me?" he asked. "I didn't say I was a god or an angel. But you've been sent to me, don't you see? You've been sent on the eve of the transformation of the world, you are sent as a sign! As was King Cyrus of old, that the people would go home to Jerusalem!"

Cyrus, the Persian. My whole frame ached; my mind ached. I struggled to be still.

"Don't speak of that!" I whispered. My mind went blank with rage. You can well imagine. I was beside myself. "Speak of Alexander if you will. But don't speak of Cyrus. You know nothing of those times!"

"Do you?"

"I want to know why I am here now," I went on, holding firm. "I don't accept your fervent prophecies and proclamations. Did you kill Esther? Did you send those men to kill her?"

Gregory seemed torn. He reflected. I could read nothing from him. "I didn't want for her to die," he said. "I loved her. The greater good called for her death."

Now this was a lie, a brittle, technical lie.

"What would you do if I told you, yes, I did kill Esther?" he said. "For the world, I killed her, for the new world that will rise from the ashes of the dying world, the world that is killing itself with small men and small dreams and small empires?"

"I swore I'd avenge her death," I said. "And now I know you're guilty. I'll kill you. But not now. When I want to."

He laughed. "You kill me? You think you can?"

"Of course," I said. "Remember what the Rebbe told you. I have killed those who have called me."

"But I didn't call you, don't you see, it was the plan, it was the world! It was the design! You were sent to me because I need you, and can use you, and you will do what I will that you do."

It was the world. Those were the very words I'd said to myself in desperate hope. But was it to be Gregory's world?

"Surely you must help me," he said. "I don't need to be your Master. I need you! I need you to witness and understand. Oh, but this is too remarkable that you came alive to see Esther murdered, and to kill those three, you did say that to me, that you killed those three."

"You loved Esther, didn't you?" I asked.

"Oh, yes, very much," he said. "But Esther had no vision. Neither does Rachel. That's why you've come. That's why you were given to our people, to my grandfather's father, don't you see? You were meant to appear before me in all your glory. You are the witness. You are 'He who will understand everything.' "

I was puzzled by his words. Plan, scheme, design. "But what is it I am to witness?" I asked. "You have your church. And what does Esther have to do with it?"

He thought a long moment, and then he said with innocent candor:

"Of course, you were meant for me. No wonder you struck down others." He laughed. "Azriel, you're worthy of me, don't you see? This is what's so supremely beautiful, you're worthy of me, of my time, my brilliance, my effort. We are on a par. You are a prince of ghosts, I suspect. I know it."

He reached to touch my hair.

"I'm not so sure."

"Hmmm, a prince, I'm sure, and you've been sent to me. All those old men; they kept you, passed you down through the generations. It was for me."

He seemed almost moved to tears by his own sentiment. His face was soft and radiant and confident.

"You have the pride and decisiveness of a king, Gregory."

"Of course I do. What does the Master usually say to you, Spirit?" he asked. "What do you remember?"

"Nothing," I said adamantly. A lie of my own. "I wouldn't be with you if I could," I said. "I stay with you now because I'm trying to remember and to know. I should kill you now. That would probably be like your precious Alexander when he cut the Gordian knot."

"No, that won't happen," he said calmly. "That cannot possibly be meant. If God wanted for me to die, anyone could do it. You don't realize the scale of my dreams. Alexander would have understood."

"I am not yours," I said. "I know that much. Yes, I want to know the scale of your dreams, yes. I don't want to kill you without understanding why you had Esther murdered. But I am not yours. Not meant for you. Not necessarily meant . . . for anything."

Somewhere the mother was crying again. That I'm sure I could hear. I turned my head.

"Do as I say," he said, touching me again, clamping his hand on my arm.

I pulled away. I hurt him a little.

My strength had gone past exhilaration. I was restless. I wanted to walk, to touch things. I wanted to touch these couches of velvet, and run my hand on the marble. I wanted simply to look at my hands. I was holding utterly fast. I wasn't sure that I could dissolve now if I wanted to.

It was a strange feeling, to be so strong, and not to know if the old tricks would work. But then I had only lately made myself Esther. I was tempted . . .

. . . But no, this was not the time.

I glared at the bones. I reached down and covered up the bones with the fragile lid. There lay the Sumerian letters for me to read.

"Why did you do that?" he demanded.

"I don't like the sight of the bones," I said.

"Why?"

"Because they're mine." I looked at him. "Somebody killed me. Someone did it against my will. I don't like you either, necessarily. Why should I believe you that I am something worthy of you? What is your scheme? Where is your Alexandrian sword?"

I was sweating. My heart was pounding. (I didn't really have a heart but it felt like it was pounding.) I peeled off this coat, admiring my own handiwork as I did it. I could see how different it was from his clothing, though modeled completely upon it.

Perhaps he noticed the difference too.

"Who sewed these clothes for you, Azriel?" he ordered. "Were they done by invisible angels on invisible looms?" He laughed as if this was the most preposterous idea.

"You'd better think of clever things to say. I may not kill you, but I very well may leave you."

"You can't! You know you can't!"

I turned my back on him. Let me see what else I could do.

I looked at the walls, the ceiling, the peach silk of the drapes, and the great tree of life blazing in the carpet. I drew near the window and the air moved my hair. The coolness came down on my skin and on my hair.

Slowly, I closed my eyes, though I could still take small steps, for I knew where everything was, and I clothed myself, envisioning a robe of red silk, with a sash of silk, and jeweled slippers. I took *her* shade of red, wrapped myself in it, and brought the gold to me for the sleeves and for the hem and for the slippers. I was now clothed in her violent red. Perhaps the mothers here mourned in red.

It was conceivable.

I heard him sigh. I heard his shock. I saw myself reflected in the mirrored panes of the ornate doors, a tall, black-haired youth in a long, red Chaldean robe. No beard, no, no hair on the face. I liked the smooth face. But this would not do, these garments, too antique; I needed freedom and power.

I turned around.

Again, I closed my eyes. I imagined a coat of his cut in this brilliant red but of the finest wool, tailored as his coat was tailored, with buttons of simple and perfect gold, almost pure gold. I imagined the trousers looser and smooth, as a Persian would want them to be, and the slippers I stripped of their embroidery.

Beneath the coat, I drew to myself, against my skin, a shirt like his, only of far whiter silk even than his, its buttons made of gold as well, and round my neck on my chest, beneath the wings of this coat, against the shirt, I brought two full strands of beads which I took from all the opaque stones of the world I loved—jasper and lapis lazuli, beryl, garnet, jade, and ivory. I put amber with this, on these two strings, until I felt the weight against my chest, and then I raised my hand and touched the beads, and when I let my shoulders fall easy, the coat almost closed over this secret bit of vanity, these ancient beads. My shoes I made identical to his shoes, only of the softest cloth, and lined with silk.

He was shocked by these simple magic acts. I had found them easier than ever.

"A silken man," he said. He said it in Yiddish. "*Zadener yinger mantchik.*"

"Shall I cap it off?" I asked. "By walking out of here?"

He drew himself up. His voice was shaky now. If it was not humility, it was some form of respect.

"There's time for you to show me every trick you know, but for now, you must listen to me."

"More interested in your schemes than seeing me vanish?" I asked.

"Alexander would be more interested in his own schemes, wouldn't he? Everything is ready. Everything in place, and now you come, the right hand of God."

"Don't be so hasty. What God!"

"Ah, so you despise your origins and all the evil you've done, do you?"

"I do."

"Well, then, you should welcome the world that I place in your hands. Oh, I see more by the moment. You are here to teach us after the Last Days, I see it."

"What Last Days! When the hell are mortal men going to shut up about the Last Days! Do you know how many centuries ago men yammered on about the Last Days?"

"Ah, but I know the very dates of the Last Days," he said calmly. "I've chosen them. I see no reason to delay in telling you the whole scheme. I see no reason not to make it all known. You recoil from me, deride me, but you'll learn. You are a learning spirit, aren't you?"

A learning spirit.

"Yes," I said. I liked this concept.

I listened to the sound of steps in the passage. I thought I heard the mother's voice, low and urgent, and I didn't like it that she was still crying.

Coldly, I observed that his proximity to me did not matter. He could be one foot away or ten. I was just as strong. I was quite independent of him, which was perfect. As he watched, I covered my fingers with gold rings, and those fine stones I liked for rings, emeralds, diamonds, Eye of the Sea, or pearl, and ruby.

The mirrors were full of us. I would have bound my hair with a leather thong, and should have done it, but I didn't care just now, and again, I felt my face, to be sure it was smooth as was his face, because for all my love of a long beard, I liked this naked skin better.

He walked around me. He took his steps silently and made a circle as if he could close me in this way, with my power. But he knew nothing of magic, circles, pentagrams.

I asked my memory: Had ever I seen a Master more excited than he was, more proud, and more hot for glory? I saw crowds of faces. I heard songs. I saw ecstasy; but those had been masses and masses, and it had been a lie. And my god had been weeping. That was no answer.

The answer was this: I couldn't kill him, not yet. I couldn't. I wanted to know what he had to teach. But I had to be certain of the limits of his power. What if he were to command me now as the Rebbe had done?

I moved away from him.

"You fear me suddenly?" he asked. "Why."

"I don't fear you. I've never served a King, not as a spirit on any account. I've seen them. I saw Alexander when he was dying . . ."

"You saw this?"

"I was there in Babylon and I walked past him with his men, guised as one of them. He lifted his left hand again and again. His eyes were completely ready for death. I don't think he had any more great dreams in his head. Maybe that's why he died. But you are full of dreams. And you do burn bright like Alexander, that is true, and I fight you yet I . . . I think I *could* love you."

I sat down and remained still on a hassock of velvet, and I thought.

I sat there, elbows on my knees. He took his stand in front of me, allowing plenty of room, perhaps ten paces, and then he folded his arms. Take charge.

"You already love me," he said. "Almost everyone who sees me loves me. Even my grandfather loves me."

"You think so?" I said. "You know he knew I was there when he sold you the bones, he saw me."

This stunned him into utter silence. He shook his head, then went to speak, then was silent again.

"I was in the room and visible, and when he saw me with his mean little blue eyes, that was when he agreed to tell you what you wanted to know of the Servant of the Bones and to sell me to you."

The full hurt of it hit him. The full hurt. I thought he would weep. He turned and walked this way and that. "He saw you . . ." he whispered. "He knew the spirit could be brought forth from the bones and he gave the bones to me."

"He knew the spirit was there in his room, and he sold you the bones in the hope that I would go with them. Yes, he did that to you. I know, it's pain, unendurable pain to realize that such a trick could be done. For a mortal man to hurt a mortal man, that's one thing. But for a zaddik to see a demon and know that demon can destroy you, and to pass on that demon to you—"

"All right, you've made your point!" he said bitterly. "So he despises me, so he did as soon as I questioned him. By twelve I was hurling my questions at him, and by thirteen gone from his house, and dead and buried in his Court." He shivered all over. "He saw you and he passed the bones to me. He saw you!"

"That's right," I said.

He grew calm with amazing speed. His face took on renewed confidence and he pondered, easily shoving aside hate and hurt, as I knew that I had to do.

"Will you give me some simple facts?" he asked. His voice went lower. He was radiant with his pleasure. "When did you first see me or anyone connected with me? Tell me."

"I told you. I came alive with Billy Joel Eval, and Hayden and Doby Eval on their way to kill the rich girl. They stuck their picks in her before I knew it. I went after them. I killed them. She saw me as she died, she said my name. Her soul went right up into the light, as I told you. Next I saw you was in the room of the Rebbe, no, as you approached, as you came towards it out of your car, with your guards all around you. I followed you into the room. The next night I did the same. And here we are. The rest I've explained. I became visible to the old Rebbe. I became flesh as I am now, and he struck his bargain."

"You exchanged words with him?" he asked, looking away as if this hurt was something he couldn't quite fight.

"He cursed me, he said he would have no traffic with demons. He wouldn't help me. He wouldn't have mercy on me or answer my questions. He wouldn't recognize me!"

I left out the part that the old man had made me disappear the first time, and that on the second occasion I had left on my own.

His face truly actually changed for the first time.

That is, his next expression seemed a great leap from where he'd been in his feelings and intentions. Something was stripped away from him. It was not the humor, it was not the jubilation, it was not the strength. It certainly wasn't the courage. But something was uncovered in him that was ruthless, and it made me think of my own fingers when they had tightened around the wooden handle of the pick and when I had shoved it into the soft swishy stomach of Billy Joel, right beneath his ribs.

He turned and walked a few steps away from me, and again I felt nothing. I watched; I felt my blood run through my veins. I felt the flesh of my face tighten as I myself smiled a tiny secret smile that aided my thoughts.

All of this is illusion, Jonathan, but the details meant it was very good illusion! As good as now, as I sit before you. Now, it takes strength, great strength, to do it, as you know. And though by the time I came to you, Jonathan, I was used to that strength; I was not so used to it then.

Yes, I'm independent of him, I thought with a great surge of courage, but what about the bones? How does it all figure? Could it be true, that I had been destined for him? In a moment Gregory would realize that the zaddik's seeing me and passing me on did not really contradict Gregory's own theory that I was intended for him.

"Right," he said suddenly, answering my thought. "He was merely the instrument. He had no idea. No idea at all that it was for me that he kept the bones. And Esther's words, that's what made the link. Esther gave me the link as she died; she sent me to him to get the bones, and to get you from him, you see. You are destined for me, and worthy of me."

He paced and stroked the flesh beneath his lower lip with his finger. "Esther's death was inevitable, necessary. I didn't realize it myself. She was the lamb. And she brought you to me. It is I who must make plain to you your full destiny."

"You know, maybe you do have something," I said, "with this talk of my being worthy of you. I mean, perhaps you are worthy of *me*. You are so surprising. I wonder."

I paused, then went on:

"Those masters, maybe they weren't worthy of me."

"They couldn't have been," he said with chilling smoothness. "But I am. And now you're beginning to understand, and you're helping me to understand. I am the Master, but only in so far as I'm your destination, I'm your . . . your. . . ."

"Responsibility?" I said.

"Ah, yes, perhaps that's exactly the word."

"That's why I don't kill you now, even though you sanctify the murder of that poor girl with some fancy babbling?"

"It's facts. She brought you to me, through my grandfather. She sent me to you, and you to me! She did it! That means the plan will work, the plan will be realized. She was a martyr, a sacrifice, and an oracle."

"God guides in all this?" I asked derisively.

"I will guide things as I think God wants me to," he answered. "Who can do better?"

"You *would* seduce me to love you, wouldn't you? You are so used to love, love from people who open your doors and pour your drink and drive your car . . ."

"I have to have it," he whispered. "I have to have the love and recognition of millions. I love it. I love it when the camera shines on me. I love when I see my grand scheme ever expanding."

"Well, maybe you won't get it from me for very long. Before I ever saw Esther die, I was damned tired of being a ghost! I'm tired of serving masters. I don't see any reason for me to do what it says on the casket!"

Anger again. Heat. But it was no more than might come from the body of a man.

I stared at the casket. I ran back my own words through my head. Had I said such a bold thing? Yes, I had, and it had been true, and it had been no curse or supplication to anyone.

Silence. If he said anything I didn't hear him. I heard something, but it was a cry of pain, or worse. What's worse than pain? Panic? I heard a cry that was right between the ultimate agony one can feel and the madness which is about to obliterate all sense of it. I heard a fine scream, you might say, right there between the light and the dark, like a vein of ore on a horizon.

"You saw your own murder?" He was talking to me. "Azriel, perhaps now you will come to see the reason for it."

I could hear the fire beneath the cauldron. I could smell the potions thrown into the boiling gold!

I couldn't answer. I knew that I had, but to speak it, to think on it, was to realize and remember too much. I couldn't. I had tried before. I had memory upon memory of trying to remember and not being able to remember at all.

"Listen, you miserable creature," I said to him in a fury. "I've been here forever. I sleep. I dream. I wake. I don't remember. Maybe I was murdered. Maybe I was never born. But I am forever and I'm tired. I'm sick to death of this half death! I'm sick of all things that stop short of the full measure!"

I was flushed. My eyes were wet. The clothes felt rich and embracing, and it was good to fold my arms, to clutch at my shoulders with my crossed hands, and to look up suddenly and see the faintest shadow of the tangle of my own hair, to be alive, even flooded with this pain.

"Oh, Esther. Who were you, my darling?" I asked aloud. "What did you want of me?"

He was enrapt and silent.

"You ask the wrong person," he said, "and you know you do. She doesn't want vengeance. What can I do to convince you, you were destined for me?"

"Tell me what you want of me. I am to witness something? What? Another murder?"

"Yes, let's proceed. You have to come with me into my secret office. You have to see the maps for yourself. All the plans."

"And I'll forget about her death, forget about avenging her?"

"No, you'll see why she died. For great empires somebody must die."

This sent a rivet of pain through my chest. I bent forward.

"What is it?" he asked. "What good would it do to avenge the death of one girl? If you're an avenging angel, why don't you walk out there in the streets? There are deaths happening now. You can avenge them. Come out of the pages of a comic book! Kill bad guys. Go ahead. Do it till you're tired of it, the way you're tired of being a ghost. Go on."

"Oh, you are one fearless man."

"And you're one tenacious spirit," he said.

We stood glaring at one another.

He spoke first:

"Yes, you are strong, but you're also stupid."

"Say this to me again?"

"Stupid. You know and you don't know. And you know I'm right. You gather your knowledge from the air, the way you do the matter that creates your clothing, even your flesh perhaps, and the knowledge rains on you too fast. You are confused. Is that the better word? I can hear it in your questions and your answers. You long for the clarity you feel when you talk to me. But you're afraid that you need me. Gregory is necessary for you. You wouldn't kill me or do what I don't want."

He drew in closer, eyes growing wide.

"Know this thing first before you learn any more," he said. "I have everything in the world a man could want. I am rich. I have money beyond counting. You were right. I have money the Pharaohs never had, nor the Emperors of Rome, or even the most powerful wizard who ever bombarded you with his Sumerian poetry! The Temple of the Mind of God I invented, whole and entire and worldwide. I have millions of followers. Do you know what the word means? Millions? What does this mean? It means this, Spirit. What I want is what I want! Not some fancy, or longing, or need! It's what I want, a man who has everything."

He looked me up and down.

"Are you worthy of *me*?" he demanded. "Are you? Are you part of what I want and what I'll have? Or should I destroy you? You don't think I can. Let me try. Others have gotten rid of you. I could get rid of you. What are you to me when I want the world, the whole world! You're nothing!"

"I will not serve you," I said. "I won't even stay here with you."

He had been all too right. I was beginning to love him and there was something deeply horrible in him, something fiercely destructive which I'd never encountered in any human.

I turned my back on him. I didn't have to understand the loathing I felt or the rage. He was abhorrent to me and that was enough. I had no reason now, only pain, only anger.

I went to the casket, opened the lid, and looked down at the grinning skull of gold that had been me and still had me somehow, like a flask has its liquid. I took the casket up into my arms.

He came after me, but before he could stop me I carried the casket and its loose cover to the marble hearth. I shoved it noisily on the pyre of wood, and watched the sticks tumble as the heap shifted to receive it. The lid fell to one side.

He stood right beside me, studying me, and then looking down at it. We were looking to the side at each other, each of us, to the side of the hearth.

"You wouldn't dare to burn it," he said.

"I would if I had a bit of flame," I said. "I would bring flame, only if I bring flame I may hurt that woman, and those others who don't deserve it—"

"Never mind, my bumbling one."

My heart pounded. Candles. There were no burning candles in this room.

There came a snap. I saw the light in my eye. He held a tiny burning stick, a match.

"Here, take it," he said. "If you're so sure."

I took the stick from him. I cradled the flame in my fingers. "Oh, this is so pretty," I said, "and so warm. Oh, I feel it . . ."

"It's going to go out if you don't hurry. Light the fire. Light the crumpled paper there. The fire's built up. The boys do it. It's made to roar up the chimney. Go ahead. Burn the bones. Do it."

"You know, Gregory," I said, "I can't stop myself from doing it." I bent down and touched the dying flame to the edge of the paper, and at once the paper was laced with flame and rising and collapsing. Little burning bits flew up the chimney. The thin wood caught with a loud crackling sound and the blast of heat came at me. The flames curled up around the casket. They blackened the gold, oh, God! What a sight, the cloth inside caught fire. The lid began to curl.

I couldn't see my own bones for the flames!

"No!" He screamed. "No." He reached over, chest heaving, and dragged the casket and the lid out onto the floor, dragging some of the fire with them, but this was only paper fire, and he stamped it out angrily. His fingers were burnt.

He stood astride the casket and he licked at his fingers. The skeleton had spilt out, into a weak and gangling figure. The bones lay unburnt, smoking, glowing. The lid was charred.

He dropped to his knees, and drawing a white napkin from his pocket, he beat out all tiny bits of smoldering fire. He was muttering in his annoyance and rage. The lid was blackened but the Sumerian I could still read.

My bones lay amid ashes.

"Damn you," he said.

I had never seen him really angry at all, and he was more angry now than most angry people I'd ever seen. He was raging inside, worse than the Rebbe had raged. He glared at me. He glanced down at the casket to make sure it wasn't burning. It wasn't. It was only very slightly scorched.

"The smell is bitumen," I said.

"I know what it is," he said. "And I know where it comes from, and I know how it was used." His voice trembled. "So you've proved yourself. You don't care if the bones are burned."

He climbed to his feet. His brushed off his pants. Ashes fell to the floor. The floor was filthy with ashes. The fire in the fireplace burned on, consuming itself, purposeless, wasted.

"Let me throw them in the fire," I said. I reached for the skull, and picked up the gangling dead thing.

"Enough, Azriel. You do me wrong! Don't be so quick! Don't do it!"

I stopped. That was all it took, and I too was afraid, or the moment had passed. Five minutes after the battle, can you still slice a man in half with a sword? The wind blows. You stand there. He is lying among the dead, but not dead, and he opens his eyes, and murmurs to you thinking you're his friend. Can you kill him?

"Oh, but if we do it then we will both know," I said. "And I would like to know. Yes, I'm afraid, but I want to know. You know what I suspect?"

"Yes. That this time it doesn't matter about the bones!"

I didn't respond.

"Not even," he said, "if they are crushed to powder with a mortar and pestle."

I didn't reply.

"The bones have completed their journey, my friend," he said. "The bones have come down to me! This is my time, and your time. This is what is meant. If we burnt the bones, and you were still here, solid, and beautiful and strong—impertinent and sarcastic, yes, but still here as you are now, able to breathe and see and wind yourself with shrouds of velvet—would that deliver you into my hands? Would you acknowledge the destiny?"

We glared at one another. I didn't want to take the chance. I didn't even want to think of the whirlwind of the restless dead. The words came back to me, the words engraved on the casket. I shivered, in terror of being formless, impotent, wandering, knocking against spirits I knew were everywhere. I did nothing.

He went down on his knees, and he gathered up the casket and the lid, then rose, one knee at a time, walked over to the table, gently laid down the casket, put the burnt shriveled lid on top of it, carefully, and then he sat down on the floor, leaning against his table, legs sprawled, but looking remarkably formal still in his seamed and buttoned clothes.

He looked up. I saw his teeth flash, and bite. I think he bit down on his lip to his own blood.

He stood up and ran at me.

He came so fast, it was like a dancer leaping to catch another, and though he stumbled, he caught me with both his hands, around my neck, and I felt his thumbs press against me, and I hated it and ripped his arms away. He smacked my face hard this way and that and drove his knee into my abdomen. He knew how to fight. With all his polish and money, he knew the dancing way to fight, like the Orientals.

I backed away from these blows, barely hurt, only amazed at his grace, and how he reared back now and kicked me full in the face, sending me many paces back.

Then came his worst blow, elbow rising, hand straight, the arm swinging around to knock me backwards.

I caught his arm, and twisted it so that he went down on his knees with a snarl of rage. I pushed him flat to the carpet and held him pinned with my foot.

"You're no match for me in that realm," I said. I stepped back and offered him my hand.

He climbed to his feet. His eyes never moved from me. Not for one second had he really forgotten himself. I mean, even in these failed attempts he held a dignity and lust for the struggle and for winning it, too.

"All right," he said. "You've proven yourself. You aren't a man, you're better than a man, stronger. Your soul's as complex as my soul. You want to do right, you have some fixed and foolish notion of right."

"Everybody has a fixed and foolish notion of right," I answered softly. I was humbled. And I did at that moment feel doubt, doubt of anything except that I was enjoying this, and the enjoyment seemed a sin. It seemed a sin that I should breathe. But why, what had I done? I determined not to look anymore into memory. I pushed the images away, the same ones I've described to you, Samuel's face, the boiling cauldron, all of it. I just said, Be done with it, Azriel!

I stood in the room vowing from then on to solve this mystery there and then with no looking back.

"You're flattered that I said you had a soul, aren't you?" he asked. "Or is it merely that you're relieved that I recognize such a thing? That I don't consider you a demon like my grandfather did. That's what he did, right? He banished you from his sight, as if you had no soul."

I was speechless with wondering, and with longing. To have a soul, to be good, to mount the Stairs to Heaven. *The purpose of life is to love and better know the beauty and intricacy of all things.*

He sat down on the velvet hassock. He was out of breath. I had been slow to realize this. I wasn't out of breath at all.

I was hot all over again, with a thin sweat, but I was not soiled yet. And of course some of what I had been saying to him was bluff and lies.

I didn't want to go into darkness or nothingness. I couldn't even bear the thought of it. A soul, to think I might truly have a soul, a soul that could be saved . . .

But I wasn't serving him! This plan, I had to know what it was; the world, how did he mean to get it when armies fought each other all over it? Did he mean the spiritual world?

There were voices in the hall. I could pick out the mother's voice easily, but he ignored it, just as if this were nothing. He only looked at me, and marveled at me, and pondered what I had said.

He was radiant in his curiosity and in what he had allowed to happen here without fear.

"You see how it lures me," I said. "The marble, the carpet, the breeze through the windows. Being alive, the great lure."

"Yes, and there's me to know and love, too, and I lure you."

"Yes, you do." I said. "And something tells me that life has lured me in the past, lured me to serve evil men and men I can't recall. I am lured each time by life itself and flesh itself and when there comes a moment and the door opens to Heaven, and I cannot go through. I'm not allowed to go through. My Masters may go through. Their beautiful daughters may go through. Esther may go through. But I don't go through."

He drew in his breath. "You've seen the Door to Heaven?" he asked calmly.

"As surely as you've seen a ghost appear to you," I said.

"So have I," he said. "I've seen the Door to Heaven. And I've seen Heaven here on earth. Stay with me, stay with me, and I swear to you when the door opens, I'll take you with me. You'll be deserving of it."

The voices came loudly from the hall. But I looked at him, trying to answer what he said. He seemed as resolute, as without conflict, as determined and courageous as he had been before our fight.

The voices were too loud to be ignored. The woman was angry. Others talked to her as if she were a fool. It was all far away. Beyond the windows lay the black night with the lights of New York so bright that the sky itself was reddened like the dawn coming when there was no dawn. The breeze sang.

I looked down at the box. I could have wept. He had me and the world had me. At least for now, for as long as I would allow it.

He drew close to me. And I turned, letting him come close, and between us there was a tenderness and a sudden quiet. I looked into his eyes, and I saw the round black circle within his eyes, and I wondered if he saw in my eyes only blackness.

"You want the body you have now," he said. "You want the body and the power. You were meant to have it. You were meant to be mine, but as of this moment and forever, I respect you. You're no servant to me. You are Azriel."

He clasped my arm. He raised his hand and clasped the side of my face. I felt his kiss, hot and sweet on my skin. I turned and locked my mouth on his for one instant, and then let him go and his face blazed with love for me. Did I feel the same heat for him?

There was a loud noise from beyond the doors.

He made a gesture to me, as if to say, be patient, and then I suppose he would have gone to the door, but it opened, and the woman appeared there, the mother with the black-and-silver hair who before had been wrapped in red silk.

She was sick, but she had groomed and clothed herself in a proper stiff way, and she marched forward. Wet and pale, and trembling, she carried a bundle, a purse, a portmanteau that was too heavy for her.

"Help me!" she cried. She said this to me! And she looked directly at me. She came up to me, turning her back on him. "You, you help me!"

She was dressed in gray wool, and the only silk on her was wrapped high around her neck, and her shoes were fancy with raised heels and beautiful straps across her arched feet, so thin, so full of blue veins beneath the skin. She gave off a deep and rich perfume, and the smell of chemicals unknown to me, and of decay and death, very advanced, death all through her, struggling to wrap its tendrils around her heart and brain and make them go to sleep forever.

"Help me now get out of here!" She grabbed my hand, wet and warm and as seductive as he was.

"Rachel," said Gregory, biting his tongue. "This is the medicine talking." His voice grew hard. "Go back to your bed."

Female attendants in white had come into the room, also gawky boys, in stiff servile little coats, but this entire assemblage stood about idle and frightened of her, nurses and lackeys, and waiting upon his every gesture.

She wrapped her arm around me. She implored me.

"You help me, please, just to get out of here, help me to the elevator, to the street." She tried to make her words careful and persuasive, and they sounded soft, drunken, and full of misery. "Help me, and I'll pay you, you know that! I want to leave my own house! I am not a prisoner. I don't want to die here! Don't I have the right to die in a place of my own choosing?"

"Take her back," said Gregory furiously to the others. "Go on, get her out of here and don't hurt her."

"Mrs. Belkin," cried one of the women. The gawky youths closed in on her like a flock that had to move as one or be scattered.

"No!" she cried out. Her voice took on youthful strength.

As the four of them set upon her, all with anxious and tentative hands, she cried out to me:

"You have to help me. I don't care who you are. He is killing me. He's poisoning me. He's hastening my death by his clock! Stop him! Help me!"

The women's murmuring, lying voices rose to drown her out.

"She's sick," said one woman in full and true distress. And other voices came like tiresome echoes of every word. "She's so drugged, she doesn't know what she's doing. Doing. Doing."

There came a babble as the boys and Gregory spoke, and then Rachel Belkin shouted over all, and the nurse tried to make her own voice even louder.

I rushed forward and pulled one of the women loose from her, and accidentally pushed this woman to the floor. The others were all paralyzed, except for Rachel herself who reached out to me, and grabbed my very head with her right hand, as if she would make me look at her.

She was sickly and raging with fever. She was no older than Gregory—fifty-five at most. A powerful and elegant woman, in spite of it all.

Gregory cursed at her. "Damn it, Rachel. Azriel, back away." He waved his arms at the others. "Get Mrs. Belkin back to her bed."

"No," I said.

I pushed two of the others away from her effortlessly and they stumbled and drew back, clinging to one another. "No," I said. "I'll help you."

"Azriel," she said. "Azriel!" She recognized the name but couldn't place it.

"Goodbye, Gregory," I said. "We shall see if I have to come back to you and your bones," I said. "She wants to die under a different roof. That's her right. I agree with her. And for Esther, I must, you see. Farewell until I come back to you."

Gregory was aghast.

The servants were helpless.

Rachel Belkin threw her arm around me and I held her firmly in the circle of my right arm.

She seemed about to collapse and one of her ankles turned on the shiny floor. She cried out in pain. I held her. Her hair was loosed and hanging all around her, brushed, lustrous, the silver as beautiful as the black. She was thin and delicate in her years, and had the stubborn beauty of a willow tree, or torn and shining leaves left on a beach by the waves, ruined yet gleaming.

We moved swiftly towards the door together.

"You can't do this," said Gregory. He was purple with rage. I turned to see him sputtering and staring and making his hands into fists, all grace lost. "Stop him," he said to the others.

"Don't make me hurt you, Gregory," I said. "It would be too much of a pleasure."

He ran at me. I swung around so that I could hold her and strike him with my left hand.

And I dealt him one fine blow with my left fist that knocked him on his back, so that his head struck the hearth.

For one breathless second I thought he was dead, but he wasn't, only dazed, but so badly hurt that all of the little cowards present ran to attend him.

This was our moment, and the woman knew it and so did I, and we left the room together.

We hurried down to the corridor. I saw the distant bronze doors but this time they had no angels, only the tree of life once more with all its limbs, which was now rent down the middle as they opened.

I felt nothing but strength coursing through me. I could have carried her in one arm, but she walked fast and straight, as if she had to do it, clutching the leather purse or bundle to her.

We went into the elevator. The doors closed. She fell against me. And I took the bundle and held her. We were alone in this chamber as it traveled down and down, through the palace.

"He is killing me," she said. She was up close to my face. Her eyes were swimmingly beautiful. Her flesh was smooth and youthful. "He is poisoning me. I promise you, you'll be glad you did this for me. I promise you, you will be glad."

I looked at her, seeing the eyes of her daughter, just so big, so extraordinary, even with the thinner paler skin now around them. How could she be so strong at forty years? Obviously she'd fought her age and her disease.

"Who are you, Azriel?" she asked. "Who are you? I heard this name. I know it." There was trust in the way she said my name. "Tell me, who are you! Quick. Talk to me."

I held her up. She would have fallen if not for me.

"When your daughter died," I said, "she spoke something, did they tell you?"

"Ah, Lord God. Azriel, the Servant of the Bones," she said, bitterly, her eyes suddenly welling with tears. "That's what she said."

"I am he," I said. "I'm Azriel, the one she saw as she lay dying. I cried as you cry now. I saw her and wept for her, and couldn't help her. But I can help you."

19

This stopped her grief, but I couldn't tell what she made of this revelation or of me. Sick as she was, she definitely contained the full flower of the seeds of beauty in Esther.

As the doors opened again, we saw an army brought out against her—heavily uniformed men, most of them old, all apparently concerned, and most rather noisy. It was an easy matter for me to push the diffident bunch aside sharply—indeed to scatter them far and wide. But this did make them hysterical with fear. She alarmed them further with her voice.

"Get me my car now," she said. "Do you hear? And get out of our way." They didn't dare to reassemble. She fired orders. "Henry, I want you out of here. George, go upstairs. My husband needs you. You, there, what are you doing—"

As they argued with one another, she marched ahead of me, towards the open doors. A man to our right picked up a gilded telephone from a marble-top table. She turned and shot him the Evil Eye and he dropped the phone. I laughed. I loved her strength. But she didn't notice these things.

Through the glass to the street, I saw the tall gray-haired one who had driven the car earlier, the tall thin one who had mourned for Esther. But he could not see us. The car was there.

The men came flying at us with solicitous words for a new assault—"Come now, Mrs. Belkin, you're sick"—"Rachel, this isn't going to help you."

I pointed out a mourner.

"Look, he's there, the one who was with Esther," I said. "That one, who cried for her. He'll do what we say."

"Ritchie!" she sang out, standing on her tiptoes, pushing the others away still. "Ritchie, I want to leave now."

It was indeed the same man with the deeply wrinkled face, and I hadn't been wrong in my judgment. He opened the door at once as we moved towards him.

Outside the building, the crowd pressed in close to the ropes with their candles and their singing; lights flashed on; giant one-eyed cameras appeared, like so many insects, closing in. They produced no confusion in Rachel any more than they had in Gregory.

Great clusters of these people bowed from the waist to her; others were giving cries of mourning.

"Come on, Rachel, come on," the driver said, addressing her as if she were kindred. "Let her pass," he told the straggling troops, who couldn't make up their minds what to do. He shouted a command to an elderly man at the edge of the pavement.

"Open the door of the car now for Mrs. Belkin!"

On both sides the crowd became frenzied. It seemed they would break through the ropes. Loud greetings to Rachel were called out, but this was in profound respect.

She disappeared into the car ahead of me, and I followed her, coming down beside her, close to her on the seat of black velvet, the two of us suddenly locking our hands together, her left and my right. The door was slammed shut. I squeezed tight her hand.

It was indeed the same long Mercedes-Benz, the same in which Esther had ridden to the palace of death, and in which I had appeared to Gregory. No surprises here. The motor was running. The crowd could not stop such a vehicle even in its devotion. Candles flickered around the windows.

The elderly driver was already behind the wheel in front of us, the little wall that once divided this compartment from his having gone away.

"Take me to my plane, Ritchie," she said. Her voice had deepened and taken on courage. "I've already called! And don't listen to anyone else. The plane's waiting and I'm going."

Plane. I knew this word of course.

"Yes, ma'am," he said, with a hint of enjoyment, or mere exhilaration in his expression. Her word was obviously law.

The car edged forward, crushing back the singing crowd, and then lurched for the center of the street, and moved ahead, throwing us against each other.

The wall went up, shutting us off from the driver, giving us a private carriage in which to ride. The intimacy made me flush.

I felt her hand, and saw how loose the skin was, how white. Hands tell age. Her knuckles were swollen but her fingernails were beautifully painted with red paint, and perfectly tapered. I hadn't noticed this before, and it sent a pleasant chill through me. Her face was five times younger than her hands. Her face had been stretched like Gregory's face, tightened and made youthful, and it was a face that had profited by all these enhancements because her bones had such a symmetry, and her eyes, her eyes were for all time.

I cocked my ear, so to speak, for any call from Gregory, for any changes in my physical self as the result of what he might be saying or thundering or doing to the bones.

Nothing. I was completely independent of him as I had supposed. Nothing restraining me.

Indeed, I put my right arm around her and held her tight to me and felt love for her and a tremendous need to help her.

She gave in to all this with childlike abandon, her body far more frail than I'd expected. Or was it simply that mine was becoming ever more solid?

"I'm here," I said, as if I'd been called to attention by my god, or by my master.

She had an ivory beauty in her illness. But it was bad, this illness. I could smell the sickness—not a repulsive smell but the smell of the body dying. Only her massive black-and-silver hair seemed immune; even the glistening whites of her eyes were dimming.

"He's poisoning me," she said, as if she'd read my mind, and her eyes looked up searchingly. "He controls what I eat, what I drink!" she said. "I'm dying, of course. He has that on his side, but he wants me dead now. I don't want to be with him and his minions when I die, his Minders."

"You won't be. I'll see to it. I'll stay with you for as long as you want." I realized suddenly that this was the first time in this incarnation that I had touched a woman, and her softness was enticing me.

Indeed, I could feel changes in my body like those a normal man might experience with a frail full-breasted creature pressed against him. I felt myself grow hard for her.

Could such a thing happen, I thought, not wondering about her virtue, but my limitations. All I got for my pains was a gang of confused memories, that I had indeed had women in this spirit form, and that my masters had railed against it because of its weakening effect. Again the memories were faceless and frameless.

I didn't loosen my grip on her, but my senses were flooded with the sight of her white thighs, her throat, and her breasts.

She was impatient with the drugs that still hobbled her.

"Why did my daughter say your name?" she asked. "She saw you? You saw her die?"

"Her spirit went straight into the light," I said. "Don't grieve for her. And she did speak to me before she died, but I don't know why. Avenging her death, that's clearly only part of what I am here to do."

This baffled her but another point concerned her as much. "She wasn't wearing any diamond necklace, was she?"

"No," I said. "What is this talk of diamonds? There was no necklace. Those three men killed her painlessly, if it is possible. There was no robbery. She suffered such loss of blood that her mind drifted. I think she died without ever realizing that anyone had done her evil."

She looked hard at me, as though she didn't entirely believe me, and she didn't welcome this intimacy I offered her.

"I killed the three men," I said. "Surely you read about it in the papers. I killed them with the ice pick they used to kill her. There were no diamonds. I saw her go into the store. I saw her before I knew just how quickly they would act."

"Who are you? Why would you have been there? What were you doing with Gregory?"

"I'm a spirit," I said. "A very strong spirit with a will and some form of conscience. This is not human, this body," I explained. "It's a collection of elements, drawn together by power. Don't get frightened, whatever I say. I'm with you and not against you. I came out of a long sleep as the three murderers made their way towards Esther. I did not catch on quickly enough to how they meant to do the deed."

She didn't react in fear and she didn't scoff. "How did my daughter know you?" she asked.

"I don't know. There are numerous mysteries surrounding my presence here. I've come, seemingly on my own, but obviously with a purpose."

"Then you don't belong to Gregory in any way?"

"Of course not, no. You saw me defy him. Why do you ask?"

"And this body here," she said with a slight smile, "you're telling me this body is not real?"

Indeed, she stared fixedly at me as if she could learn the truth with her eyes. I could feel the heat building between us.

Then she did a most intimate thing that astonished me. She came forward, surprising me, and she kissed me on the mouth. She kissed me as I had kissed Gregory only seconds before she had come into his room. Her lips were damp and hot and small.

I think my mouth was lax and gave back nothing, but then I cupped my hand behind her head, loving the large rustling nest of her hair, and I kissed her, pressing her mouth as hard and sweet as I could. I drew back.

I felt a deep pang of desire for her. The body seemed in perfect condition. Once again, a few echoes of admonition and advice came to me . . . "lest you vanish in her arms," or some other antique rot. But I was now through with trying to remember, as I've explained.

What was her pleasure?

As for her, she had the passion of a young woman, whether she was dying or not, or perhaps more truly the passion of a woman in full flower. Her lips were still firm and open, as if she were kissing me still or ready to do it. She was shrewd and not afraid of men or of passion. She was like a queen who has had many lovers. Exactly that way.

"Why did you do that?" I asked her. "Why the kiss?" The kiss had strengthened me, enlivened parts of me for specific human function. I call that strength.

"You're human," she said, dismissively, her voice deep and a little hard.

"You flatter me but I am a spirit. I want to avenge Esther, but there's something more involved."

"How did you get to an upper floor with Gregory?" she asked.

"You know his power, his influence. The Lord's Right Hand, the Founder of the Temple of the Mind of God," she said contemptuously. "The Savior of the World, the anointed one. The liar, the cheat, the owner of the largest fleet of pleasure cruise ships in the Caribbean and the Mediterranean, the Messiah of merchandising and gourmet food. You're really telling me you're not one of his men?"

"Ships," I said. "Why would a church have ships?"

"They're pleasure boats but they also carry cargo. I don't understand what he's doing, and I'll die before I understand. But what were you doing with him?" She went on. "His ships dock at every major port in the world. Don't you know all about it? It's not that I don't believe you, that you're not a Minder. I saw you defy him, yes, and you got me out of there.

"But everyone in that building is a Minder. Everyone in my life. Everybody's one of his church," she went on, her words becoming rushed and full of distress. "The nurses are from his church. The doormen, the messengers, the entire staff of the building. Those people chanting, did you see them, they're part of his church. His church covers the world. His planes drop leaflets over jungles and nameless islands." She sighed, then continued:

"What I'm saying is, if you're not one of his, and haven't lured me off to some other place to be locked up, how did you ever get to the upper floor?"

The car was moving away from the crowded streets. I smelled the river.

She didn't believe me. But she was telling me many things. Many intriguing things. I could see something beyond her words that she didn't see.

She distracted me slightly from my thoughts. She found me an attractive male. I could feel this, and I could feel in her a despair that comes with the knowledge of approaching death. There was a careless passion in her, a dream it seemed, to possess me.

I was remarkably excited by it.

"Your accent?" she asked. "What is it? You're not an Israeli?"

"Look, this is trivial," I said. "I'm speaking the best English I can. I told you, I'm a spirit. I want to avenge your daughter. Do you want me to do that? This necklace, why does he say there was a necklace? Why did you ask me about the necklace?"

"Probably one of his cruel jokes," she said. "The necklace started the big fight between him and Esther a long time before. Esther had a weakness for diamonds—that was certainly true. She was always shopping in the diamond district. She loved to go there more than to the fancy jewelers.

The day she was killed, she must have taken the necklace with her. The maid said she did. He latched on to that little detail. He almost sacrificed his big theories of the terrorists killing Esther with all his talk about the necklace. But then the three men, when they were found, they didn't have the diamonds. You really killed those three men?"

"They took nothing from her," I said. "I went right after them and killed them. Your papers tell you they were stabbed in rapid succession by one of their own weapons. Look, don't believe me if that's your wish, but keep explaining to me. About Esther and Gregory. Did he have her killed? Do you think he did?"

"I know he did," she said. Her entire demeanor changed. Her face darkened. "But I think he tripped up on the necklace. I have a suspicion that she took the necklace somewhere before she stopped at the store. And if she did that, then the necklace is in the hands of someone who knows that part of the story is a lie. But I can't get to that person."

This greatly intrigued me. I wanted to question her.

But she was distracted again by physical desire. She examined me, my hair, and my skin. Her grief for Esther was heavy inside her but it warred with a simple human need for levity.

I loved her looking at me.

When I've reached this stage, when I'm this apparently alive, humans notice the same things about me that they would have when I was a true man and walking the earth in an ordinary life that God had given me. They notice the prominent bones of my forehead, that my eyebrows are black and tend to dip in a frown even as I smile but to rise as they move towards the ends of my eyes, that I have a baby's mouth, though it's large, with a square jaw. It's a touch of the baby face with strong bones, and eyes that laugh easily.

She was powerfully drawn to these attributes, and there came again that rush of memory, of ancient people talking and saying things of the utmost importance, and someone saying, "If one has to do it, where could we find a man more beautiful! One who more resembles the god?"

The car moved faster and faster through empty streets. Other engines were quiet, and the pavements of New York were lined with thin, spindly little trees that fluttered with little leaves, almost like offerings before their lordly buildings. Stone and iron were the makings of this place. How fragile the leaves looked when the wind caught them—forlorn, tiny, and colorless.

We took on greater speed. We had come to a wide road, and I could smell more strongly the stench of the river. The sweet smell of water was barely detectable, but it made me powerfully thirsty. I'd passed over this river with Gregory but had not known thirst then. I knew it now. Thirst meant the body was really strong.

"Whoever you are," she said, "I'll tell you this. If we make it to that plane, and I think we're going to, you'll never want for anything again in your life."

"Explain about the necklace," I said gently.

"Gregory has a past, a big secret past, a past I knew nothing about and Esther stumbled on it when she bought the necklace. She bought the necklace from a Hasidic Jew who looked exactly like Gregory. And the man told her he was actually Gregory's twin."

"Yes, Nathan, of course," I said, "among the diamond merchants, a Hasid, of course."

"Nathan! You know this man?"

"Well, I don't know him, but I know the grandfather, the Rebbe, because Gregory went to him to find out what the words meant, the words Esther had said."

"What Rebbe!"

"His grandfather, Gregory's grandfather. The Rebbe's name is Avram, but they have some title for him. Look, you said she stumbled on his past, that he had this big family in Brooklyn."

"It's a big family?" she asked.

"Yes, very big, a whole Court of Hasidim, a clan, a tribe. You don't know anything of this at all."

"Ah," she sat back. "Well, I knew it was a family. I understood that from their quarrels. But I didn't know much else about it. He and Esther quarreled. She had found out about this family. It wasn't just the brother Nathan who sold her the necklace. My God, there was this whole secret. Could he have killed her because she knew about his brother? His family?"

"One problem with it," I said.

"Which is what?"

"Why would Gregory want to keep his past secret? When I was there with him and the Rebbe, his grandfather, it was the Rebbe who begged for secrecy. Now surely the Hasidim didn't kill Esther. That's too stupid to consider."

She was overwhelmed.

The car had crossed the river and was plunging down into the hellish place of multistoried brick buildings, full of the cheap and mournful light.

She pondered, shook her head.

"Look, why were you with Gregory and this Rebbe?"

"Gregory went to him to find out the meaning of the words Esther spoke. The Rebbe knew. The Rebbe had the bones. Gregory has the bones now. I am called the Servant of the Bones. The Rebbe sold the bones to Gregory on the promise that he would never speak to his brother Nathan again, or come near the court, or expose them as connected to Gregory's childhood or his church."

"Good God!" she said. She was scrutinizing me harshly.

"Look, the Rebbe never called me to come forth. The Rebbe wanted no part of me. But he had had custody of the bones all his life from his father, from years in Poland at the end of the last century. I gathered this from listening to them. I had been asleep in the bones!"

She was speechless. "You obviously believe what you're saying," she said. "You believe it."

"You talk," I said, "about Esther and Nathan—"

Esther came home and had this fight with Gregory, screaming at him that if he had kindred across the bridge he should acknowledge them, that the love of his brother was a real thing. I heard this. I didn't pay any attention. She came in and talked to me about it. I said if they were Hasidim they'd recited Kaddish for him long ago. I was so sick. I was drugged. Gregory was furious with her. But they had their fights, you know. But he . . . he has something to do with her dying, I know it! That necklace. She would never have worn the necklace in midday."

"Why?"

"Very simple reason. Esther was brought up in the best schools, and made her debut as a girl. Diamonds are for after six o'clock. Esther would have never worn a diamond necklace on Fifth Avenue at high noon. It wouldn't have been proper. But why did he hurt her? Why? Could it have been over this family? No, I don't understand it. And he weaves in the diamonds, why? Why bring up the necklace in the middle of all this!"

"Keep telling me these things. I'm seeing the pattern. Ships, planes, a past that is a secret as much for Gregory as for the innocent Hasidim. I see something . . . but it's not clear."

She stared at me.

"Talk," I said. "You talk. You trust in me. You know I'm your guardian, I'm for your good. I love you and I love your daughter because you're good and you're just and people have done cruelty to you. I don't like cruelty. It makes me edgy and wanting to hurt . . . "

This stunned her. But she believed it. Then she tried to speak and couldn't. Her mind was flooded, and she began to tremble. I touched her face with comforting hands. I hoped they were warm and sweet to her.

"Let me alone now," she begged kindly. But she put her hand on my arm, patting me, comforting me, and she let her body lean on my shoulder. She made a fist of her right hand.

She curled up against me, and crossed her legs so that I could see her naked knee against mine, firm and fair beneath her hem. She gave a low moan and a terrible outcry of grief.

The car was slowing to a crawl.

We had come to a strange sprawling field full of evil fumes and planes, yes, planes. Planes now explained themselves to me in all their shuddering, keening glory, giant metal birds on tiny preposterous wheels, with wings laden with oil enough to burn the entire world in its fire. Planes flew. Planes crept. Planes lay about empty with gaping doors and ugly stairways leading into the night. Planes slept.

"Come on," she said. She clenched my hand. "Whatever you are, you and I are together in this. I believe you."

"Well you should," I whispered.

But I was dazed.

As we got out of the car, I knew only my thoughts, following her, hearing voices, paying no attention, looking up at the stars. The air was so full of smoke, it was like the smoke in war when everything is burning.

Amid deafening noise we approached the plane. She gave orders but I couldn't hear her words; the wind just snatched them up. The stairs spilled down in one firm piece like the Ladder to Heaven, only it was merely the metal ladder into this plane.

Suddenly, as we began to climb together, she closed her eyes and stopped. She groped, sightless, for my neck with her hands and held me tight, as if feeling for the arteries in my neck. She was sick and in pain.

"I have you," I whispered.

Ritchie, the driver, waited behind me, eager to help.

She caught her breath.

She rushed up the steps.

I had to hurry to catch up with her.

We entered a low doorway together, into a sanctum of intolerable sound. A young woman with brave, cold eyes said:

"Mrs. Belkin, your husband wants you to come home."

"No, we're going to my home now," she said.

Two uniformed men stepped out of the front of the plane. I glimpsed a tiny chamber there, in the plane's nose, full of buttons and lights.

The cold pale eyed woman led me towards the back of the plane, but I took my time, listening so that I could be there if needed.

"Do what I tell you," Rachel said. I heard the rapid capitulation of the men. "Get off the ground as soon as possible."

The pale woman had left me standing beneath the roof and doubled back to stop Rachel. Ritchie, the loyal driver, hovered over Rachel.

"Leave the magazines and the papers there!" Rachel said. "What do you think, she'll come back to life if I read about her? Get off the ground as fast as you can!"

There was a little chorus of weakening rebellion—men, women, even the elderly gray-haired Ritchie.

"You just come with me, that's all!" she said, and once again the silence fell around her as if she were the Queen.

She took my hand, and I was led by her into a small chamber padded in glistening leather. Everything here was smooth. The leather was tender, and the place glowed with refinements: thick glass goblets on a small table, hassocks for our feet, deep chairs that would hold us as dearly as couches.

The voices died away, or sank low and conspiratorial, behind curtains.

The little windows were the only ugliness, so thick and scratched and dirty that they revealed nothing of the night outside. The noise was the night. The stars weren't visible.

She told me to sit down.

I obeyed, sinking into an awkward couch of odoriferous dyed leather that caught me up as if it wanted to render me helpless and awkward, as a father might pick up his son by the ankle into the air.

We faced each other now in these scooped and oddly comfortable couches. I became used to it, the seeming indignity. I grasped that for the severity of the materials, this was a form of opulence. We were lounging here, like potentates. Brilliantly colored magazines lay on the table before us, one neatly overlapping the other. Folded newspapers that had been arranged in a carefully designed circle. Stale air blew upon us as if it were some sort of deliberate blessing.

"You really have never seen a plane before, have you?" she asked.

"No," I said. "I don't need them. This is all so very luxurious," I said. "I can't sit up straight if I wanted to."

The woman with the pale cold eyes had come, and she was reaching down beside me for tethers, a strap with a buckle. I was fascinated by her skin and her hands. All of these people were so very nearly perfect. How?

"Safety belt," said Rachel. She snapped the buckle of her own, and now she did a thing which seduced me.

She kicked off her shoes, her beautiful ornate shoes with their high thin heels. She pushed at them, one foot at the other, till they fell loose, and on her narrow white feet I saw the imprint of the straps that had covered her feet, and I wanted to touch them. I wanted to kiss them.

Was this perhaps one of the most well-developed bodies I'd ever had?

The cold woman looked at me uncomfortably and shifted, and then only reluctantly went away.

Rachel ignored all this.

I couldn't take my eyes off her, vivid and somber in the dim light of this sanctuary, this plane, and I desired her. I wanted to touch the inner flesh of her thighs, and see whether the fleece-covered flower there was as well preserved as everything else.

This was disconcerting and shameful. Another realization came to me. Diseased things can be so beautiful. Perhaps a flame is a diseased thing, if you think about it, a flame dancing on its wick, eating up the wax beneath it, the way this disease was eating up her body from around her soul. She made a dazzling heat in her fever and the keenness of her mind.

"And so we fly in this," I said, "we go up, and we travel faster than we can on the ground, like a javelin hurled through space, only we have the means of directing ourselves."

"Yes," she said. "It's going to take us to the southern tip of this country in less than two hours," she said. "We'll be in my home, my little home which all these years has been mine alone, and there I'll die. And I know it."

"You want to?"

"Yes," she said. "My head's clearing even now. I can feel pain. I can feel his poison clearing from my system. Yes, I want to know it. I want to be a witness to what happens to me."

I wanted to say that I didn't think death was like that for most human beings, but I didn't want to say anything I wasn't sure of, and certainly nothing to bring her more pain.

She gestured to the woman, who must have been lingering somewhere behind me. The plane had begun to roll, presumably on its tiny wheels. It didn't roll easily.

"Something to drink," Rachel said. "What would you like?" And suddenly she smiled. She wanted to make a joke. "What do ghosts like to drink?"

I said, "Water. I'm so relieved that you asked me. I'm parched with thirst. This body is dense and delicately put together. I think it's growing true parts!"

She laughed out loud. "I wonder what parts those could be!" she said.

This water had come. Lots of it. Glorious water.

The clear bottle was nestled in a huge bucket of ice, and the ice was beautiful. Ripping my eyes off the water itself, I stared at the ice. Of everything I had seen in this modern age, nothing, simply nothing, compared to the simple beauty of this ice, glittering and sparkling around this strangely dull container of water.

The young woman who had just set down this bucket of wondrous ice now drew the bottle of water out of it, so that the ice fell and crunched and made a gorgeous twinkling in the light. I could see that the bottle was made of something soft, not glass at all; it didn't have the shimmer or the strength of glass; it was plastic. You could squash the bottle flat when it was empty. It was the lightest container for this water, like a bladder filled with milk strapped to a donkey, the thinnest, finest bladder you could find.

The woman poured the water into two glass goblets. Ritchie appeared. He bent down and whispered something in Rachel's ear. It had to do with Gregory and his rage.

"We're on schedule," he said. He pointed to the magazines, "There's something—"

"Leave all that alone, I don't care, I've read it all, what does it matter? It comforts me that her picture is on every magazine cover. Why not?"

He tried to protest but she told him firmly to go. The plane was taking off. Someone called him. He had to buckle up.

I drank the water, greedily, the way you've seen me drink. She was amused. The plane was leaving the ground.

"Drink it all," she said, "there's plenty of it."

I took her at her word and drained the entire plastic bottle. My body absorbed all of this and was still thirsty, its strongest indicator of growing strength.

So what was Gregory doing? Fuming over the bones? Didn't matter! Or did it?

It suddenly occurred to me that almost every delicate maneuver I had ever performed had been under the direction of a magician. Even taking a woman, I'd done with their grudging leave. I could rise, I could kill, then dissolve. Yes. That is not delicate, but the direct arousal of passion I felt for this woman—the strengthening that came to me from this water—this was new.

It struck me with total clarity that I had to find out just how strong I was on my own, and I hadn't taken any serious steps to do so. I felt as strong in the presence of this woman's carnal attraction to me as I had in Gregory's fascination.

As I put the bottle down, I realized I had let drops of water fall on the papers and magazines. I looked at them.

Then I saw what had so concerned the others about these magazines. The pictures on them were of Esther at the worst moment. There were pictures of Esther almost dead!

Yes, there on the cover of one newsmagazine was the picture of Esther on her stretcher, and the crowds around her.

Someone said we were on course for Miami and cleared for an immediate landing when we got there.

"Miami." The sound made me laugh. "Miami." It was like a joke word you say to little children to make them laugh. "Miami."

The plane was bouncing along. But the pale-eyed girl came with another bottle of water. It was cold. It didn't need the ice. I took it and drank it in easy patient swallows.

I sat back, filling with the water. Oh, this was the most divine moment, a moment almost on a par with kissing Rachel, to feel this water move down my throat and through the coils inside of me made by will and by magic. I breathed deep.

I opened my eyes, and saw that Rachel was watching me. The girl was gone. The glasses were gone. The only water that remained was the bottle I clutched in my hands.

A great pressure bore down on me, fondling me, pushing me against the leather, and teasing me almost with a sweet strength that was mysterious.

The plane was rising fast into the sky, very fast. The pressure increased and my head suddenly ached, but this I sent away from me. I looked at her. She sat still as if praying, as if this were a ceremonial moment, and she did not speak or move until the plane had found some comfortable height and ceased to rise.

I knew the moment by the way she relaxed, and by the sounds of the engines. I didn't much like this plane. Yet the experience was thrilling.

You're alive, Azriel, you are alive! I must have laughed. Or maybe I wept. I needed more water. No, I would have liked to have more water. I needed nothing.

But I had to know what Gregory was doing with my bones. Was he trying at this very moment to call me back? He had to be doing something, though I felt no reverberations. I wanted to know. And I also wanted to know if, strong as this body was, I could at will dissolve it and recall it. I wanted badly to know.

I ran my tongue on my lips, which were cold from the water. I realized that my attraction to this woman, this delicate pale creature, had brought my anger and my confusion to the limit. I had to stop wondering about this and that and simply declare myself master. That's what I had to do. I wanted her. It was all connected in a human way—the carnal desire for her, and the desire to strive against Gregory and defy him, prove to myself he did not control me merely because the bones were now in his possession.

"You're frightened," Rachel said. "Don't be frightened of the plane. The plane is routine." Then a mischievous smile came on her again, and she said, "Of course it could explode at any minute, but, well, so far, it never has." She gave an easy bitter laugh.

"Listen, you have an expression in English, kill two birds with one stone?" I said. "I'm going to do it. I'm going to leave you now, and come back. That will prove to you that I'm a spirit and you'll stop worrying that you're consorting in desperation with a madman, and also I'll find out what Gregory is up to. Because he does have those bones, and he is a strange, strange man."

"You're going to disappear from here? Inside this plane?"

"Yes. Now tell me our destination in Miami. What is Miami? I'll meet you at the door of your home in Miami."

"Don't try this," she said.

"I have to. We can't go on with your suspicions. I see now Esther is like a diamond herself in the middle of a huge necklace, and the necklace is intricate. Where are we going? Where do I find Miami?"

"Tip end of the East Coast of the United States. My home is in a tower at the very end of the town called Miami Beach. It's in a highrise. I'm on the top floor. There is a pink beacon on the tower above my apartment. Further south are the islands called the Florida Keys and then the Caribbean."

"That's enough; I'll see you there."

I looked down at the spilled droplets of water, at the horrifying picture of Esther on the stretcher and then in absolute shock I saw that I was in the picture! I was there! I had been caught by the camera as I had raised my hands to my head and howled in grief for Esther. This was before the stretcher had been put inside the ambulance.

"Look," I said. "That's me."

She picked up the magazine, stared at the picture and at me.

"Now I'm going to prove to you that I'm on your side, and I want to give that devil Gregory a good scare. You want something from your house? I'll bring it to you."

She couldn't speak.

I realized that I had frightened her and silenced her. She was merely watching me. I pictured her body without clothing. The shape of her limbs was pleasing and firm. Her legs in particular had a muscularity to them in their slender form which was graceful. I wanted to touch the backs of her legs, her calves, and squeeze them.

This was quite a lot of strength for me, a lot, and I had to resolve the issue of my freedom now.

"You're changing," she said in a suspicious voice, "but you're certainly not disappearing."

"Oh? What do you see?" I asked. I wanted to add with pride that I hadn't tried to disappear yet, but this was obvious.

"Your skin; the sweat's drying. Oh, it isn't much sweat. It's on your hands and your face and it's gone and you look, you look different. I could swear that there's more dark hair on your hands, you know, just the normal hair of a hirsute man."

"That I am," I said. I lifted my hand, looking at the black hairs on my fingers, and I reached down into my shirt and felt the thick curls on my chest. I pulled at them, pulled them again and again. That was my chest, the rough scratchiness of the hair when it was flat, the silkiness of it when I tugged on it, and played with it. "I am alive," I whispered. "Listen to me," I said.

"I'm listening. I couldn't be more attentive. What is it you see—about Esther's death and this necklace? You were saying something—"

"Your daughter. She touched a scarf before she died. Do you want it? It was beautiful. She reached out for it right at the moment that the Evals surrounded her, the killers, I mean. She wanted it, and she died with it in her hand."

"How do you know this!"

"I saw it!"

"I have that scarf," she said. She went white with shock. "The saleswoman brought it to me. She said that Esther had reached for it, that Esther said she wanted it! How could you know this?"

"I didn't know that part. I just saw Esther reach for the scarf. I was going to ask you if you wanted the scarf. I was going to bring it to you for the same reasons as this merchant woman."

"I do want it!" she said. "It's in my room, the room I was in when you first saw me. It . . . no. It's in Esther's room. It's lying on her bed. Yes, that's where I left it."

"Okay, when I see you in Miami I will have it."

The look on her face was a terrible thing to see.

In a whisper she said, "She went there to get that scarf!" Her voice was so small. "She told me she had seen it and couldn't forget it. She had told me she wanted that scarf."

"In a gesture of love, I'll bring it to you."

"Yes, I want to die holding it."

"You don't think I'm going to disappear, do you?"

"No, not at all."

"Keep yourself in check. I am. Whether I come back, that's the question." I said something under my breath. "But I'll try, try with all my might. This must be tested now."

I leaned over and took with her the liberty she'd taken with me. I kissed her. Her passion passed through me completely. It burned in me.

Now in my heart I spoke the requisite words, *Depart from me, all particles of this earthly body, yet do not return to where you belong, but await my command that you come together instantly when I would have you.*

I vanished.

At once the body dispersed, sending out a fine mist to all the inner surfaces of the plane, leaving a shimmering spray upon the leather, the windows, the ceiling.

I floated above, free, fully shaped and strong, and I looked down at the empty seat, and I saw the top of Rachel's head, and I heard her scream.

I rose up, through the plane. It was no harder than passing through anything else. But I felt the passing, I felt the shivering energy and heat of the plane, and then the plane shot onwards at such terrific velocity that I fell towards the earth as if I had weight. Down, down, through the dark until I swung free, spreading my arms, and moving towards:

Gregory. *Find the Bones, Servant. Find your Bones. Look after the Bones.*

In the wind, as always I glimpsed other souls. I saw them struggling to see me and to make themselves visible. I knew they sensed my vigor, my direction, and for a moment they flashed and glittered and blinked, and then they were gone. I had passed through them and their world, their horrid layer of smoke that surrounded the earth like the filth hanging over burning dung, and I sped forward, like singing, towards the Bones. Towards Gregory.

"The Bones," I said. "The Bones," I said into the wind.

The lights of the city of New York spread out in all directions, more magnificent and tremendous than the lights of Rome at its greatest, or of Calcutta now full of millions upon millions of lamps. I could hear Gregory's voice.

And then before me in the dark, there appeared the Bones, tiny, distant, certain, and golden.

20

It was a large room, not in the apartments of Gregory and Rachel, but higher in the building. I realized for the first time that the building itself *was* the Temple of the Mind of God and it throbbed throughout its many floors with people.

The room itself glistened with steel and glass and tables made of manipulated stone, hard as anything mined from the earth; machines lined the walls, and cameras which moved as the inhabitants of the room moved.

There were plenty of inhabitants.

I entered invisible, easily passing through all barriers, as if I were made of tiny fish and the walls were nets. I wandered among the tables, eyeing the video screens in rows on the walls, the computers set into niches, and other devices which I couldn't understand.

Silently, broadcasts from all over the planet came in on these video screens. Some of them showed the news that all people can receive. Others were obviously monitoring particular and private places. The spy monitors were the most dull, greenish, murky.

The Bones lay in the very middle of the room on a sterile table. The casket, empty, lay to the side. The men surrounding Gregory were obviously physicians. They had the poise and attitude of learned men.

Gregory was in mid-conversation, describing the Bones as a relic, which must be analyzed in every conceivable way without bringing harm to it, X-rayed, carbon-dated, minute scrapings made for contents. Attempt at aspiration if anything inside were liquid.

Gregory was shaken, disheveled. He wore the same clothes as before but he was not the same man.

"You're not listening to me!" he said fiercely to these his loyal court physicians. "Treat this as priceless," he said. "I want no mishaps. I want no leaks to the press. I want no leaks within this building. Do this work yourself. Keep the jabber-mouth technicians away from it."

The men took all this in stride. Not fawning like lackeys, they wrote notes on their clipboards, exchanged glances of agreement with one another, and nodded with dignity to the man who paid the bills.

I knew their kind. Very modern scientists who are just learned enough to be certain that nothing spiritual exists, that the world is completely material, self-created, or the result of some "big bang," and that ghosts, spells, God, and the Devil were useless concepts.

They weren't by nature kind. In fact, there was a peculiar hardness which they all shared, not a sinister quality so much as a moral deformity. It was in their demeanor, but I caught it merely from scanning them carefully. All these men had committed crimes of some kind, with medicine, and their status was entirely dependent upon the protection of Gregory Belkin.

In other words, this was a gang of fugitive doctors hand-picked to do special jobs for Gregory.

It struck me as marvelously good luck that he had committed the Bones to this pack of fools, rather than to magicians. But then where would he find a magician?

What a different scene this might have been if he had called upon the Hasidim—zaddiks who didn't hate or fear him—or on Buddhists or Zoroastrians. Even a Hindu doctor of Western mind might have been a danger.

I took an upright stance, still invisible, then drew close, until I was touching Gregory's shoulder. I smelled his perfumed skin, his fine silken face. His voice was crisp and angry, concealing all his anxiety as if it were a cloud that he could collect and swallow and let out only in a perfect narrow stream of fluid speech.

The Bones. I felt nothing as I saw them. Do some good mischief here, get the scarf and get back to Rachel. Obviously the moving of the Bones had no effect on me; neither did the prying eyes of these doctors.

Am I finished with you now? I spoke to the Bones, but the Bones gave no answer.

They were not in order. They were a haphazardly gathered skeleton, tumbled, their gold brilliant under the electric lights. Flecks of cloth clung to them, like bits of leaves or dirt. Ashes clung to them, but they seemed as solid as ever, as enduring. *For all time.*

Was my soul, my tzelem, locked within them?

Do I need you anymore? Can you hurt me, Master?

Gregory knew I was there! He turned from right to left, but he couldn't see me. The others—and there were six—noted his agitation, questioned him.

One man touched the casket.

"Don't do it!" said Gregory. He was wonderfully afraid. I loved this too much!

There is always an element of pride in tormenting the solid and the living, but really, it was so easy, I had to restrain myself.

To test him and to test myself—that was my mission here, and I must not play games.

"We'll handle them with extreme care, Gregory," said a young doctor amongst them. "But we're going to have to take some substantial scrapings; we've been through that. In order to get carbon dating and DNA, we may have to take—"

"And you want full DNA, don't you," asked another, eager for the eye and the favor of the leader. "You want everything we can come up with about this skeleton—gender, age, cause of death, anything that might be locked inside there—"

"—You're going to be amazed what we can find out."

"—the Mummy project in Manchester, you saw all that?"

Gregory gave them nods and stiff affirmations in silence because he knew I was there. I was invisible still, but now formed in all my parts and wearing my garments of choice, fluid enough to pass through him if I wanted to, which would have sickened him and hurt him and made him fall.

I touched Gregory's cheek. He felt it, and he was petrified. I pushed my fingers into his hair. He drew in his breath.

On and on came the science babble—

"Size of the skull, a male, and the pelvis, probably, you realize . . ."

"Be careful with them!" Gregory burst out suddenly. The scientists were silenced. "I mean, treat them like a relic, you hear me?"

"Yes, sir, we understand, sir."

"Look, the scientists who do this work on Egyptian and—"

"Don't tell me how. Just tell me what! Keep it secret. We don't have many days left, gentlemen."

What could this mean?

"I don't like stopping work for this, so do it at once."

"Everything's going splendidly," said an older doctor. "Don't worry about time. A day or two won't matter."

"I suppose you're right," Gregory said, crestfallen. "But something can still go wrong, very wrong."

They nodded only because they feared to lose his favor. They debated now, speak, don't speak, nod, bow, do what?

I drew in my breath and resolved to be visible; the air moved; there was a faint noise. The room felt a vague commotion as the particles gathered with tremendous force, yet I was taking no more than the first stage, the airy form.

The doctors looked about in confusion; the first to see me pointed. I was transparent, but vividly colored, and perfectly detailed.

Then the others saw me.

Gregory spun around to his right and looked at me.

I gave him my soft evil smile. I think it was evil anyway. I floated. In airy form, I had no need to stand, or to anchor. I was a thousand degrees from the density that obeys gravity. I stood on the ground, but I didn't need to. This was a choice, like the position of a flower in a painting.

He glared at me, seeing the thin mirage of a long-haired man, clothed as I had been when I left him, but thinner than glass.

"This is a holograph, Gregory," said one of the doctors.

"It's being projected from somewhere," said another.

The men began to look around the room. "Yeah, it's one of those cameras up there."

". . . it's some sort of trick."

"Well, who the hell would dare pull a thing like this in your own . . ."

"Quiet!" Gregory said.

He raised his hand for absolute obedience and he got it. His face was locked with fear and despair.

"Remember," I said aloud, "I'm watching you."

The cohorts heard me and commenced whispering and shuffling.

"Put your hand through it," said the white-coated one closest to me. When Gregory failed to obey, the young man approached and moved to do it, and I merely looked at him and watched him and wondered what he felt, if it was a chill, or electric. His hand penetrated me, easily, causing no seam in the vision.

He drew back his hand.

"Somebody's gotten into security," he said quickly, looking me directly in the eyes. They were all babbling again, that someone was controlling the image, that someone somehow had figured a way to do this, and that it was probably—

Gregory couldn't bring himself to answer.

I had accomplished my purpose.

He struggled desperately for some command, some powerful verbal weapon against me that wouldn't make him the fool in the eyes of the others. Then he spoke in a cold voice.

"When you give me your reports, tell me exactly how these bones could be destroyed," he said.

"Gregory, this is a holograph, this thing. I want to call security . . ."

"No," he declared. "I know who is responsible for this little trick. I have it covered. It merely caught me off guard. There's no breach. Get to work."

His self-confidence and quiet air of command really were kingly.

I laughed softly. I kissed his cheek. It was rough and he drew back. But he faced me. The men were astonished by the gesture.

The men merely came closer, surrounding me, absolutely certain in their incredible ignorance and bigotry that I was an apparition being made electrically by someone else. For a moment, I scanned their faces. I saw wickedness in their faces, but it was a brand of wickedness I didn't fully understand. It was too connected with power. These men loved their power. They loved their purpose, but what exactly was it that they did when they weren't analyzing relics?

I let them study me, looking from face to face. Then I struck upon the mastermind. The tall emaciated doctor, who in fact blackened his hair with dye, and who looked older than he was on account of his thinness. He was the brilliant one; his gaze was far more critical and suspicious than that of the others. And he monitored Gregory's responses with a cold calculation.

"Look, this is all very fancy," said this one, "this holograph, but we can get on this analysis tonight. You realize we can give you an image like this, this holograph, of the man who once had these bones?"

"Can you really do that?" I asked.

"Yes, of course—" He stopped, realizing he was talking to me. He began to make gestures all around me. So did the others. They were trying to interrupt the projection of the beam that they thought had created me.

"Simple forensic procedure," said another, boldly ignoring the continuing strangeness of all this.

"And we'll get on this security thing immediately."

Others continued to search the ceilings and the walls.

A man moved to a telephone.

"No!" Gregory said. He stared at the Bones.

". . . permeated with something, some chemical obviously; well, we can have all of that analyzed, I mean, we'll be able to tell you—"

Gregory turned and looked at me. A clearer comprehension of him came to me.

This was a man who could only use everything that came to him; he was not passive in any meaning of that word. The frustration he felt now would fuel his rage and his invention; it would drive him to greater lengths; he was only holding firm now, biding his time. And what he learned now would enhance his cunning and his capacity to surprise.

I turned to the doctors. "Let me know the outcome of your tests, will you?" I said, being a deliberately dreadful devil.

This caused quite a flurry.

I dissolved. I did it instantly.

The heat passed out of me, and the particles swarmed, too tiny no doubt for them to see. But the men felt the change in temperature; they felt the movement of the air. They were in confusion, looking around for another projected figure, perhaps, among them, for a switch in the direction of the light beam which they thought had made me appear.

I understood something further about them. They regarded their science as omnipotent. Science was the explanation not only for me but for anything and everything. In other words, they were materialists who beheld their science as magic.

The irony of this was very funny to me. Anything I did they would perceive to be science beyond their understanding. And I had been made by those who had been convinced that magic had the power of "science," if you just knew all the right words!

I went up and up, through the ceiling and the floor above it, rising through the shiny, bustling, crowded layers of the building, until I could not see the Bones any longer. The golden glimmer was gone.

I was in the fresh and cool night sky. Find Rachel, I thought. Your test is accomplished. You know now you are free.

He can't stop you. Go now where you will.

But in truth, the experiment would only be complete if I could make myself fully solid once more.

The scarf. I had forgotten about the scarf.

I drew down closer to the building. Only now did I really see its full height and grandeur. Covered all over even to its top floors with granite, it sloped majestically as it rose, rather like an ancient place of worship. There must have been fifty floors. Numbers don't come to me automatically. We had been on the twenty-fifth floor just now.

I descended, peering into the windows as I went, looking for the private living chambers. Offices, I saw hundreds of offices. I moved easily from right to left, amazed at the rooms filled with computers, and then I saw laboratories, highly elaborate laboratories in which serious people were diligently studying tiny things beneath microscopes and measuring potions into vials, which they carefully sealed.

What was this, part of Gregory's religious rackets? Drugs for his followers? Spiritual medicines, like the Soma of the Persian sun worshipers?

But there were so many laboratories! There were men and women in sterile white suits and masks, their hair carefully covered with white caps. There were giant refrigerators and warning signs against "Contamination." There were animals in cages—little gray monkeys with wide, frightened eyes. Doctors were feeding them.

In one area, humans moved sluggishly, encased in very bright colored plastic suits and with ominous windowed helmets worthy of modern warriors. Their hands were covered with giant clumsy gloves.

At their mercy, the monkeys chattered desperately and in vain in their little prisons. Some monkeys lay prostrate with illness or fright.

Most curious. Some Temple of the Mind, I thought.

As last I came down to perhaps the twelfth floor and there I saw the great demilune of a living room in which he and I had quarreled. I moved through the window easily, and through the corridors, moving the doors back slowly and lightly so that it would seem a breeze.

I saw Esther's bed. I saw her bed, and her picture beside it, a smiling girl with others in a silver frame, and I saw across her snow-white bedspread the black beaded scarf, folded neatly. I was overcome with delight. As I entered the room physically, I sensed the perfume of Esther. Here she had slept; here she had dreamed.

On her dressing table, there lay diamond rings and earrings with diamonds, and bracelets with diamonds, a scattering of finery, all delicate and pretty with silver or gold. On the walls were photographs—Gregory, Rachel, Esther—together year after year. One picture had been taken on a boat, another on a beach, another at some ceremony or party which required gowns for the women.

"Esther, tell me! Who did it? Why? Would he kill you simply because you learned about his brother Nathan? Why would that matter to him, Esther?"

But nothing came back from the surfaces of this room. The soul had gone straight into the light and taken every particle of pain or joy it had ever known along with it. It had left nothing. Ah, to be murdered and to rise so cleanly!

I drifted towards the scarf. My hand grew denser and more visible as the weight of the fabric tumbled into it; it was beautifully woven, made of lace in its center, long, and trimmed all over with fine small black beads, exactly as I remembered. It was heavy, very heavy. It was almost a shawl. It was strange and unlike other things of this time. Perhaps she had thought it exotic.

The darkness moved around me. *Make yourself whole and flesh.* I did. Something brushed me and flashed before me, dimly and uncertainly. But it was only a lost soul, the soul of an unburied man perhaps, mistaking me in the mist for an angel then moving on. Nothing to do with the chamber.

I uttered a curse against the lost souls, and took my stand with the material world.

I wound the scarf tight in my hands, dazzled again that I was formed and answerable to no one. And then once more, keeping this scarf tight within my grip, I let the particles fly from me, and rolled my spirit round and round this scarf, this heavy scarf so that I might carry it with me.

I soared through the noise and smoke hovering over the city. For one moment I saw its lights below sprinkled exquisitely amid the clouds, the scarf like a great heavy stone in the very midst of my being, slowing me, giving me a rise and fall with the wind that felt oddly good.

Like the birds perhaps, I mused.

Rachel, Rachel, Rachel. I pictured her as I'd left her, not below me, screaming at my disappearance, but how she had been when she was seated across from me, with large hard eyes and all the silver shimmering in her hair, as if it had been threaded there deliberately by twenty slaves to make her magnificent in age.

Within seconds I felt close to her. I could almost see her. She moved through the night as swiftly as I did, and I circled her, rising high above her and then drawing near. I couldn't see her clearly enough. Her image was tangled with movement and light.

It was the plane.

I couldn't enter the plane. I wasn't sure enough to enter it. It was just going too fast. I didn't know if I had the strength. I didn't know if I could bring together the matter for a body in the compartment of such a swiftly moving machine. The whole technology of the plane seemed too full of contradictions, and precarious adjustments. I imagined some hideous catastrophe in which I'd be knocked back once more into oblivion, unable to revive.

If that happened, the scarf would fall to earth, like a bit of burnt black forest, moving back and forth on the wind until it entered the lower atmosphere and then pooled on the ground. Esther's scarf, divorced from all things that had to do with her, and those who loved her. Esther's scarf in some strange city—we were high above small cities.

I drifted without making a choice. I wasn't uncertain however. I would meet her, I resolved.

I waited and I followed; the plane led me like a tiny firefly in the night.

We were above the southern seas. The plane was circling and descending. I saw then the great sprawl of Miami as I came down under the clouds. Glorious in this warm air, this sea-filled, watery air, air as lovely as some ancient city where I had once been very happy as a spirit, learning from a wise man. I could almost . . .

But I had to concentrate. I saw the long stream of eerie colored lights that made the Ocean Drive of Miami Beach. I saw it as clearly as if she'd drawn me a map, and I saw the building with the pink beacon atop it, the very last one on the bony finger of the peninsula.

Slowly I descended, not close to the building, but a few blocks from it, drifting quickly into the large crowd that moved along the street, between the beach and the cafes. The warm air was grand and exhilarating. I almost cried for the sweetness of it, and the sight of the great sea, and the beautiful billowing clouds of the sky. I thought if I had to die, I should like to die here too.

It was a remarkable mix of humans which surrounded me, wholly unlike the busy people of New York. These were pleasure seekers, all rather agreeable, and all eyes for one another, yet most tolerant of the great casual variety of styles intermingled here, and the obvious mix of the very young in ostentatious seductive attire, right along with the commonplace and the very old.

But my clothes were not right. I glanced about at the men. Men wore loose garments, short pants, sandals. No. There was a man in a beautiful white suit, like Gregory's suit, with a shirt and open collar.

I took that style. When my feet hit the pavement, I was dressed like that man and carrying the scarf in my hand and walking south on Ocean Drive towards Esther's building.

Heads turned, people smiled, people here looked at each other, people here wanted to see beauty. There was an atmosphere of festivity. Suddenly a girl grasped my arm. I was startled. I wheeled around and stopped and bowed.

"Yes, what is it?" I asked.

She was little more than a child with huge breasts, almost naked under her pink cotton tunic. Her hair was blond and fleecy and gathered back with a big pink bow.

"Your hair, your beautiful hair," she said. She had a dreamy look.

"In this breeze, it's a nuisance," I said, laughing.

"I thought that was it," she said. "When I saw you coming, you looked so happy, except your hair kept blowing in your face. Here, let me give you this." She laughed with simple gaiety as she removed a long gold chain from around her neck.

"But I have nothing to give you for it," I said.

"Your smile is what you gave me," she said, and rushing behind me, she gathered my hair back at the nape of my neck and looped the chain around it. "Ah, now, you look cooler and more comfortable," she said, jumping in front of me. Her little tunic barely covered her underwear, and she danced on naked legs and sandals that had only one buckle to them.

"Thank you, thank you most kindly," I said with a deep bow. "Oh, I wish I had something, I don't know where to . . ." How could I bring to myself some valuable object without stealing it? I felt ashamed as I looked at the scarf.

"Oh, I would give you this . . ."

"I don't want anything from you!" she said, laying a little hand on mine and on the scarf. "Smile again!" And when I did she cried out with laughter.

"I wish you blessings all your life," I said. "I wish I could kiss you."

She stood on tiptoe, threw her arms around my neck, and planted on me a luscious kiss that woke every molecule of the body. I trembled, not able to gently remove her from me, but fast becoming her utter slave, and all this on the brightly lighted street in the brisk ocean breeze, with hundreds meandering on both sides.

Something distracted me. It was a call. It was Rachel's call to me, and Rachel was very close, and she was crying.

"I have to go now, pretty girl," I said. "You lovely girl." And I kissed her again and hurried down the street, trying to remember to walk at a human pace. I could see Rachel's building up the slope.

I was there in less than five minutes. The kiss of the girl had been like a drink of wine for a mortal man. I was laughing to myself. I was so happy to be alive suddenly that I even felt a morsel of compassion for all those who had ever wronged me or anyone. But that passed fast enough. Hate was too much a part of my character.

These kind gentle people might melt it, however. These kind ones.

Approaching the garden terraces of the building, I looked up at its glorious height. Then I climbed quickly over the fence and sprinted on the drive, hardly realizing that I had bypassed a security gate as I headed for the front doors of Rachel's home.

A huge white limousine was parked there and Rachel was just getting out of it. Ritchie, the faithful driver, had her by the arm. He was agitated though silent. No reporters or anyone around. Only the building attendants in white uniforms, and the breeze rippling through the purple Egyptian lilies.

I turned and saw the sea again stretching forever under the white clouds. This was like heaven to me. Then in the other direction beyond the building I saw an inland bay. More gleaming, dreamy beautiful water, and beyond it towers of light.

I loved this world.

As I drew up to her, I babbled with joy.

"Look, Rachel, there's water all around us," I said. "And the sky is so visible, so high, look at the curling and rolling clouds. You can see their shapes and their whiteness as if it's day here."

She was rigid. She stared.

I slipped the scarf into her hands, and wound her hands up with it.

"That's the scarf," I said. "It was on Esther's bed."

She shook her head. She wanted to say things. She and the somber Ritchie both stared at me in plain shock.

"I've never fainted in my life," she said. "I think I might now."

"No, no, it's only me. I've come back. I saw Gregory, I know what he's up to, this is the scarf. Don't faint. But if you want to faint, go ahead. I'll carry you."

The wide glass doors swung open. Attendants preceded her with her leather bundle and some other suitcase I'd never seen before. Ritchie stared at me and shook his head. His wrinkled face showed anger.

Then she came close.

"Now you see," I said, "all I've told you is true."

"Is it?" she whispered. She was dead white.

"Come on, let's get inside," said Ritchie. He did pick her up, and he carried her in front of me to the elevator. Old as he was, he carried her inside easily in his arms.

"Let me in," I said as the doors started to close. But Ritchie glared at me with a darkly furrowed brow, and jabbed the button and blocked my path.

"All right, have it your way," I said.

I met them at the top. It was just a speedy rush up the steps, rather like racing when I was a boy.

Dumbfounded and enraged, and still carrying her, as she stared at me, Ritchie rushed to her doors and put the key in the lock. The attendants went in with her luggage.

"Put me down now, Ritchie," she said. "It's okay. Wait downstairs. Take the others with you."

"Rachel!" he said. He was staunch, suffering. His gnarled old fingers were curled for a fight.

"Why are you so afraid of me?" I asked. "You think I would hurt her?"

"I don't know what to think!" he said in a roughened, aged voice. "I'm *not* thinking."

She pulled me into the door. "All of you, go," she said.

I saw a blurred panorama of beautiful rooms, many open to the sea, and others open to a garden, just like the courtyard of our house when I was a boy, and the courtyard I could almost remember from that Greek city on the sea where I'd been most unhappy and then happy. I was dazed.

The loveliness of the place, its warmth, its windows framing Heaven is almost impossible to describe. It flooded me with love, and I think the memory of Zurvan touched me, not with words but with revelations. I was washed clean by love and felt a sense of ease. I understood that there could be a world in which only love was the significant virtue. A sense of well-being overcame me. But I did not try to remember anything.

Everywhere soft white curtains waved in the wind. The courtyard exploded with giant red African flowers, lovely purple vines, and the most lacy and soft trees, dancing in the captured breeze. The place was full of the scent of the flowers.

Rachel slammed the front door on those outside, including her driver angel, and she slid the lock and put up a little chain, and then she looked at me.

"You believe me now?" I asked.

She leaned towards me.

"Let me hold you."

She tumbled softly against me. "Take me to my bed," she said. "There, through the garden and over there, to the left, my bed."

She put her arms around my neck and I did as she said. She was light, perfumed, tender.

It was the most marvelous room, open to the sea on all three sides, it was windows and windows; a rush of remembered warmth overcame me again. But where in the world had I ever seen such clouds, and tossed among them in the glowing light the stars, so friendly and small, and kindly.

I set her down on a huge bed of silk, covered with silk blankets and pillows; a soft golden color seemed to be in every fabric or tapestry or design in some way, and the room was filled with soft molded chairs, Turkish luxury.

I smelled the salt, and her perfumed sweetness, and I looked down on her, her wax-pure face. Tenderly as I could, I kissed her forehead.

"Don't be afraid, darling one," I said. "Everything I told you was true. You must believe me. You must tell me what you know about Esther and Nathan."

She began to sob, and then turned, faint, and shivering, and nestled into the pillows. I sat there. I pulled up a silken cover over her, something full of the French flowers. But she didn't need it.

"No, the air itself," she said. "The air. Kiss me again. Hold me again. Be with me."

"I have you in my arms. My lips touch your forehead, your cheek, your chin, your shoulder, your hand . . ." I said. Truth was, I could hardly resist her. I wanted to loosen her fancy clothes, release her in my power.

I softly locked my hand around her fragile wrist. She really was dying.

"Don't fear me, beloved," I said, "unless it eases the pain. Sometimes it does, to fear one thing instead of others."

In answer, she turned and kissed me again, tugging my head down close to her, so that she could push her tongue into my mouth. It was a luscious kiss, full of passion and utter yielding. I kissed her longingly. I felt her hips lift against me. I felt my own body hard for her.

I had to have her, I had to make her happy. And the world would let me know my power in this as it had let me know in everything else. If I lost all power in her arms, so be it.

There was too much human heat here for anything but lovemaking now. The sky itself, the dreamy stars, the high white clouds—these things as well—decreed it.

21

She pulled weakly at the buttons of her blouse. "Undress me, please, help me," she said. I quickly removed all her clothes as she wished. She guided me and assisted me. She sank deep in the pillows, pale, but with a body as firm to touch as a young woman's body.

I kissed the calves of her legs, her thighs. The garden rustled and sighed behind me. For the first time I heard a waterfall, its gentle trickle, and then I listened to the sound of water touching leaves, but my body was an engine of desire, and what drove me was her naked breasts, rather small, with the pink nipples of a girl, and the smell of death, rising sweet like a crushing lily. It was not that the death attracted me; it was that it made her all the more precious, something to be lost in a moment.

She lay back, heaving a deep sigh. The angles of her face were tight and delicate and precise in the dimness.

"Let me see you without your clothes," she said. She reached for buttons, but I gestured there was no need. I stood up and back from her.

Not an electric light burned in the place. It was the dreamiest darkness.

I stretched out my arms and looked up at the sky. Though suddenly aware of a fatigue from all the night's tricks, I nevertheless told my clothes to assemble themselves nearby and await my command. I would be naked.

It worked even more swiftly and completely than last time.

I looked down for the first time on my own chest, pubic hair, erect organ. I was too happy for humility, and to feel the sinews in my arms tighten was to be among living things, and surely some of those things must be good things.

She sat up on the bed, her breasts amazingly firm, and the pink nipples turned up. Her silver-and-black hair made a rumpled mass down her back and displayed a long neck.

"Splendid," she whispered.

A rain of doubts descended on me.

But I had to do it. What was the point of warning her that I might dissolve in the process? I was going to do it.

I sat down beside her, embracing her. I felt the moist thin silkiness of her skin, not healthy in a woman too thin, yet delicious. Even the bones of her wrists were beautiful.

She tugged at my hair, and kissed me with her eyes closed, all over my face, and quite suddenly I realized with a shock that my beard and mustache were on my face.

She drew back, staring at it. I told this hair to go away.

"No," she said. "Bring it back! It makes your mouth sweeter and damper." I felt the hair return as if it wanted to! I couldn't quite figure this out, why the hair had come of its own, but that was the whole story so far, my body came on its own, and in its own form. One lapse in my will, one drifting into pride in my physical self, and the hair had come.

Well, she loved it. I took a long breath, feeling the toll of all this changing and magic, but I was as hard as a statue for her. I wanted to pounce on her. Instead I let her bury her face in the hair of my chest, and kiss my nipples, and the pleasure went right to my loins.

I took her breasts in my hands, enchanted by their smallness, their delicacy. So pink, girlish pink.

"It's all drugs, my love," she said, as though feeling my wonder. She kissed my beard, kissing it along the bone of my jaw. "It's hormones and modern science; I have a woman's chemicals inside me, that's all. They can make me look young, but they can't save my life."

I kissed her and held her, my hands free and rough over her thighs and stealing into the secret crevice, to feel there the firmness of a young woman's secret body. Chemicals, was it? Modern science?

"Those things preserve," I said, "but you make the beauty."

"Sweet God," she whispered, kissing me all over my face. I had my hands beneath her small backside, and cuddled it.

"Yes," I said, "God, capricious as He is; he lavished his blessings on you and on your daughter, Esther."

"And you were the last thing," she breathed into my ear, her hands clawing gently at my back. "You were the last thing she saw. How good that was for her."

A savage strength rose in me, the realization that I had her completely at my mercy, this precious creature, and that no words from anyone could command me away from her. Only her words would hold sway with me now, and only because I would defer to her.

It was like fruit between her legs, like peaches or plums, it was just wet enough. I brought my fingers to my nostrils.

"I can't hold back, my love," I said.

She parted her legs, and lifted her hips, and this was paradise suddenly, to be inside her, inside this hot throbbing fruit, and to have her mouth at the same time, to have both her mouths, to cover her, with hair and strength. I began the manly rhythm. Alive, alive, alive. I was blinded. Pleasure drenched all my senses.

"Yes, now, yes, do it," she said. She lifted her hips against me. I rose up on my elbows so as not to hurt her with my weight, and looking down at her, I felt the seed explode inside her. My jerking motions surely hurt her. But then I saw the blush I wanted in her face, I felt the throbbing in her throat, and knew she was as happy as I was. The tight little core of fruit squeezed the last drop out of me, and I fell over on my back, whole and alive, staring at the ceiling of this room, or staring into airy dark.

Whatever had been my life, spirit or man, I could not recall a pleasure as delicious as this one, as totally humiliating in the way it took over, in the way that it made me feel the slave and the master simultaneously. I didn't ask myself what men felt.

Her head turned from side to side; she was blood red. "Come to me again, please, now," she said.

Overjoyed, I rolled back on top of her and entered her. I didn't need a rest. The fruity secret part was more luscious, tighter than before, throbbing more fully. Again I came and her face flooded with blood, and then finally she scratched my back hard with both her hands, she beat on me with fists, and when I lifted up to thrust, she came with me just far enough, and then lay back, to make it ecstasy.

"Harder," she said. "Harder. Make this a battlefield, make me a boy you've found, a girl, I don't care."

It was too inviting. I slammed against her, harshly, over and over, feeling the seed spill again, the sight of her red face filling me with an all-too-human sense of power. Yes, to have her, to make her come, to make her come, yes, again, and again.

I filled her up. I was so tight inside her, I dragged her hips up off the bed with me, and then in her wetness she let me slide back and forth, and like a brute soldier, I came down, driving her into the silken pillows, and I saw through my half-closed eyes that she smiled.

"Surrender, that's what I want," I said through my teeth. She could not stop the pleasure coming in her; it came and came as if her heart would break. She was red and tossing, and I wouldn't let her go, slamming again and again against her sweet fruitlike lips, and then she lifted both her arms to cover her face, as if she would hide from me.

This sublime gesture, this maidenly gesture, this sweet gesture stripped me of the very last control I ever possessed in this or any other body, and I shot forth my seed for the third time, groaning aloud.

Now I was spent. I was tired. And she grew pale in the light of the moon and the white billowing clouds, and we lay there together. My cock was dripping.

She turned over and in the tenderest way, like a little girl almost, she kissed my shoulder. She ran her fingers through the hair on my chest.

"My darling," I said. I spoke to her in old languages, natural to me, Chaldean, Aramaic, I spoke words of love and testaments of fidelity and devotion, and cooed against her ear, and she rippled with delight against me, and tore at my hair again.

Pillows had tumbled to the side. The air swirled around her, full of the scents of the garden. It stirred beneath the low, white ceiling, and suddenly, as if the wind had changed its direction, there came the song of the sea, the full great sea, relentless, the deceptive song of water, water gurgling in the waterfall that seems to be talking to you when it is saying nothing, has no syllables, and water pounding the beach as if to say I am coming, I am coming. But there was no I.

"If I could die now, I would do it," she said. "But there are things you have to know."

I drifted, I dreamed. I felt my fatigue. I shook myself awake. Did I have my body still? I feared sleep. Yet I felt the need of it, the assembled body needed it, as it needed water. I sat up.

"Don't talk of dying," I said. "It's going to happen soon enough." I turned and looked down at her.

She looked composed, intelligent, all mind with angular collected limbs, quite incapable of the passion we'd just shared. I blurted out:

"I have no power to cure, not a disease this far advanced."

"Have I asked you?"

"You must want to know, you must wonder."

"I'll tell you why I didn't ask," she said, reaching up and playfully tugging at the hair on my chest. "I knew if you had the power, you would have helped me the moment you had the chance."

"You're right, you're absolutely right."

She closed her eyes, and tightened her lids. It was pain.

"What can I do?" I said.

"Nothing. I want these drugs to wear off. I want to die on my own."

"I'm ready to bring you anything I can," I said. I was shaken to the bone by the sight of her suffering, but it seemed to melt, and her face was waxen again and perfect.

"You talked about Esther, you said that you wanted to know—"

"Yes, why do you think your husband killed her?"

"I don't know! That's just it. They quarreled but I don't know. I can't believe it was on account of the family. Esther and Gregory fought all the time. It was normal. I don't know."

"Tell me everything you remember about Esther and Gregory and this diamond necklace. You said she discovered his brother Nathan when she bought the necklace."

"She met Nathan in the diamond district. She could see his resemblance to Gregory and when she mentioned it, he confessed he was Gregory's identical twin."

"Ah, identical."

"But what could it all mean? He told her he was Gregory's twin. He told her to give Gregory his love. She was amazed. She liked him. She met the other Hasidim who work in the store with him. She liked

Nathan very much. She said it was like looking at the man Gregory could have been, all filled up with gentleness and kindness.

"The day she died, I'm sure she took the necklace back to Nathan. I think I remember her saying that she had to drop it off, because some small thing was wrong and Nathan would fix it, and she said, 'Don't tell the Messiah that I'm going to visit his brother,' and she laughed. I think she dropped it off before those killers got her. Gregory knew she was shopping that day at Henri Bendel. He knew that. But I don't think he knew about the necklace. It wasn't till yesterday that the whole issue of the necklace came up. I didn't even know the necklace was gone. Nobody did. Then Gregory brought it up, that the terrorists had seized her necklace and killed her. Sure enough, the necklace was gone, but I couldn't reach Nathan to find out if he had it. Besides, he would have called. I know Nathan only by voice, but I know him now, through one phone call."

"Go back now to the earlier part. Esther quarreled with Gregory about his brother, and the brother was an identical twin."

"She had wanted him to meet with his brother. He had been frantic that she tell no one about the Hasidim, no one. He told her it was a matter of life or death. He tried to frighten her. I know Gregory. I know him when he's weak and not thinking too clearly, when he's caught off guard, and is furious and desperate."

"I've seen this too," I said, "a glimpse of it."

"Well, that's how he was with her. 'No, no, no, you didn't meet any brother, I have no brother!' Then he came storming into me and desperately appealed to me in Yiddish to explain to her how the Hasidim would not want to be connected with him. But he was furious about the whole affair. She didn't speak Yiddish, Esther. She came into the room, and I remember he turned and he said, 'You ever tell anyone about Nathan and I'll never forgive you!'

"She was so confused. I drew her aside, tried to explain how the Observant Jews would not like Jews like us, who didn't pray each day, or observe the laws of the Talmud. She listened but I could see she didn't grasp this. She said, 'But Nathan said he loved Gregory. He said he would love to see his brother. He said that from time to time he tries to call Gregory but he can't get through.'

"I thought Gregory would go out of his mind. 'I don't want to hear any more of this,' he said. 'If you gave him my private number tell me now! These people hurt me. I left when I was a boy. They hurt me! I made my own church, my own tribe, my own way. I am my Messiah!'

"I tried to calm him down, I said, 'Gregory, please, we're not in a television pulpit. Sit down. Rest.'

"Then Esther demanded to know why Gregory had been so kind to Nathan in taking him to the hospital. She said Nathan had told her all about that, this time in the hospital—how Gregory had checked Nathan into the hospital under his own name, and had paid all his expenses, and kept Nathan in a private suite, and didn't want to worry the Rebbe or his wife about it, took care of all of it. She said, 'Nathan said you were so generous.'

"I swear to you, I thought he would go crazy.

"I started to see how complex this was. Gregory had something at stake other than mere publicity. In fact, it was perfectly obvious to me that the Hasid connection would be a help to Gregory with his church, a form of . . . occult status . . . do you know what I mean?"

"Yes, I do exactly. Exotic and pure roots had grown this great leader."

"Yes. So I sat up and tried to ask a few questions, 'Why had Nathan been in the hospital?' And Esther said that Gregory had suggested it, Gregory had told Nathan that they were both at risk for something inherited in their family, and knowing the Rebbe would never agree, he had spirited Nathan away and had all the tests done under Gregory's name. For Nathan it had been a dream, the beautiful hospital suite, kosher food, all the proprieties observed, and the people thinking he was Gregory. He found it amusing. Of course he didn't have the hereditary disease, whatever that was. God, what on earth—"

"Ah, I see," I said.

"What does all this amount to?"

"Keep telling me everything about Nathan and Esther," I said. "What else do you know?"

"Oh, that first night, we fought for hours about it. Finally she agreed she wouldn't tell anyone, or try to bring the families together, but she would see Nathan from time to time and give him Gregory's good wishes. Gregory began to cry with relief. Gregory can cry on cue, and on camera. He went into how his people had cast him out. The Temple was everything to him, his meaning, his life.

"Whenever he went into that speech, Esther and I would just roll our eyes. We knew that he had compiled the teachings of the Temple of the Mind with a computer program. He had programmed in all the information he could about other cults, and which commandments had given the members the most comfort, and then he had chosen a list of the most acceptable and likable commandments. Other aspects of the Temple were created the same way, through secret surveys and computer compilation of the most appealing aspects of other religions. It was a joke to Esther and me. But that night he wept and wept. It was his whole life. God had guided him and his computer.

"I went to sleep. Two days Esther and Gregory didn't speak to each other. But that was nothing unusual. They could have fought over some little political question and scream. It was the way they acted together."

"What else?"

"Two nights later, Gregory woke me at four o'clock. He was in one of his rages. He said, 'Take the phone, talk to him, listen to him yourself.' I didn't know what the hell he meant.

"The voice coming through the phone sounded exactly like Gregory! I mean exactly. I could scarcely believe it was another person, but it was, and he introduced himself as Nathan, Gregory's brother. He asked me kindly to explain to Esther that the families couldn't get together. 'This breaks my heart, that I must say this to my brother's wife,' he said, 'but our grandfather doesn't have long to live and the Court depends on him. He is the Rebbe. Tell Esther that it can't be, and give her my love, and in time I will see her when she comes to visit me.'

"I told him I understood perfectly. 'You have my love too, brother-in-law. I too lost my parents in the camps. I wish you only well.'

"Then in Yiddish he said we were in his prayers and in his thoughts, and if we ever needed him, if Gregory was ever ill or afraid, we must call him.

"I told him how good it was to hear a Yiddish voice, and to talk with him. He laughed and said something like 'Gregory thinks he has everything, and thank God he has a good wife, but you never know when a brother will need a brother. Gregory has never been sick a day in his life, never been inside a hospital, except to visit me of course and take care of me, but I will come if he ever calls.'

"I remember thinking about this hospital stay, these tests. Had Gregory himself had such tests? What was this hereditary disease? I knew it was true that Gregory had never been in a hospital. Gregory had a private doctor, hardly what I would call a licensed practitioner of medicine, but he had never to my knowledge been in a hospital. I said to Nathan how kind he was, and I asked how I might reach him, and then Gregory grabbed the phone back.

"He carried it out of the room with him but I could hear him talking Yiddish in a simple natural way, and intimately, in a way Gregory never spoke to anyone. I was really for the first time hearing him speak to a brother. I had never heard that. I had always been told that all Gregory's people were dead. All of them."

"How long ago was all this?" I asked.

"About a month ago. But I didn't even think of it before now, all this. I mean, I knew in my heart that he had been responsible for Esther's death, I knew when I heard him make his speech about terrorism and enemies that he'd been lying. He was too *prepared* for Esther's death! But honestly, frankly, do you think he *would* kill his own daughter because of all this?"

"Yes, I do, but I see a large design here," I said. "And the Rebbe. You never met or spoke to the Rebbe?"

"No," she said. "I wouldn't go over there to be rejected. I have great reverence for those people, my parents were Hasidim from Poland. But no, I know that kind of old man."

"Well, let me tell you this. That old man also accused Gregory of killing Esther. And he wanted to know the same thing you wanted to know, why."

"Do you realize what this means?" she said. "If he would kill Esther to protect the family secret, then he might kill Nathan!"

"Has there been no call from Nathan concerning this necklace?" I asked. "I know how the Hasidim live, but this is news, diamonds, you know, talk of valuable diamonds snatched by terrorists."

"No, no call that I know of, but you see, I'm cut off, I was surrounded by the Minders. And Gregory himself didn't even come up with the necklace part till the day after the murder. In his first speech, all he did was talk about enemies. Then the next day he . . . my god, maybe that's when Nathan called him, but then he wouldn't have told such a lie or . . . Why in the hell did he bring up the necklace?"

I was quietly absorbing all these words.

"I think I can figure it out," I said. "One thing is true, I foiled his plan. His plan is big. His design is big. I foiled it by killing those tramps that murdered her. So that blurred his attempt at calling it all terrorism. Those men cannot be traced to terrorists, can they?"

"No, not at all. Half the world is crying with him, and others are laughing at him. The men were bums out of some town in south Texas, bums. Now Gregory claims his enemies will use any means to hurt him and these bums were part of it and the theft was to give them badly needed wealth to fight his church."

"Let's leave the necklace for a moment. He still played up the terrorist part, and for some strange reason included the necklace. Now listen, I have to ask you. Why are there laboratories in the Temple of the Mind? Why?"

"Laboratories?" she asked. "I have no idea. I didn't even know there were. Of course there's Gregory own doctor, who pumps him up with Human Growth Hormone and special protein drinks and anything else he can to keep his youth and strength, and they do have some kind of hospital room so that if Gregory runs a temperature one degree above normal, his doctor can examine him in it, but there are no laboratories as such, not as far as I know."

"No, no, I mean big laboratories where people are working with chemicals and computers. Huge laboratories with sterile storage and people even dressed in funny clothes to protect themselves. I saw this tonight. I saw this in the Temple of the Mind. I saw some people wearing orange clothes that covered their whole bodies. I didn't think of it at the time. I was just looking for Gregory . . ."

"Orange suits, you're talking about suits that protect people from viruses. Good Lord, is there disease at the heart of this? Gregory has some disease? What the hell did he do to Nathan in the hospital!"

"I think I know. He didn't hurt his brother. And there is no disease in Gregory, I can tell you that for sure, or in the Rebbe. I would have known the moment I saw them. I sense these things."

She winced, the mere thought of her own sickness suddenly confusing her and muddling her mind.

"What does the Temple do that would require a team of doctors, a big team of brilliant men ever ready at Gregory's command? Research geniuses with microscopes and all kinds of equipment?"

"I don't know," she said again. "Of course one time they did contemplate a line of products, you know, trash like spiritually cleansing shampoo and 'wash away evil vibrations soap'—"

I laughed, I couldn't help it. She smiled.

"But we talked him out of that. He struck some incredibly lucrative deal with a New York designer for all the stock at his resorts and on his boats, and in his jungles . . ."

"There we are again, boats, planes, jungles, doctors, a necklace, a twin brother."

"What are you saying?"

"Look, Rachel, an identical twin is not just a brother, he is a duplicate of the man, and here we have a twin unknown to the world, and not recognized every day of the week perhaps because he wears the beard and the locks of the Hasidim. There are things one can do with an identical twin."

She stared at me. She was silent. Then a wince of pain came again.

"Look, I have to have water," I said. "I'll bring you some water."

"That would be good. Cold water. My throat is sore, I can't . . ."

She sank back down.

I hurried through the beautiful garden, and entered what seemed a grand storage place for fine foods, and sure enough, there were plastic bottles of water galore in the refrigerator. I brought two of these bottles and a lovely crystal glass which I picked off a shelf.

I sat down by her and gave her water first. She had covered herself now. She drank. I drank.

I really was exhausted. This was not the time to be exhausted, not the time to risk sleeping and letting this body disappear. I drank more of the water, and I wondered what had come out of my body into her, had it been real seed, or just a semblance?

I remembered something about Samuel. Samuel laughing at the Catholic nuns who claimed to be made pregnant by spirits. I remembered that from Strasbourg and then another lovely memory came, it was all sensory, it had to do with Zurvan, and I remember him saying,

'You can do it, yes, but it will take away your energy and you are never to seek a woman without my permission.' "

I couldn't remember the speaker, only the love, and the garden, and the words, and how much it was like this. *It will take away your energy.* I had to stay awake.

"What if we're wrong?" she said. "And he had nothing to do with Esther's death. He's a man who uses everything. He used her death but that doesn't mean—"

"The Rebbe said he killed her. I think he killed her. But there's more at stake. This temple of his, does it preach anything unique or of unique value?"

"Not really; as I explained, he invented the creed with a computer program. It's the nearest thing to a creedless creed you can imagine."

She sighed. She told me there was a dressing gown in the closet. Would I bring it to her? She was feeling a little cold. She said there were robes, too, if I wanted them. I did, but not because I was cold. It was a Persian or Babylonian disinclination to be naked.

I found a thick blue robe that fell to the floor, with a tie for the waist, and wrapped myself in this, feeling a little trapped, but it was fine for now, and I needed all my power.

I brought the negligee to her. It was gold like so much in the room, and pure silk and full of beaded work rather like that of the dark scarf. She sat up and I helped her put it on, and I buttoned the pearl buttons for her, and then tied the sash. I buttoned the pearls at her wrists.

She stared at me.

"I have something else," she said, "that I want you to know."

"Tell me," I said, sitting beside her and taking her hand.

"Gregory called me tonight right before the plane landed in Miami. He told me *you* killed Esther. He said you were seen at the scene of the crime. I'd seen your picture in the magazine, but I knew it was a stupid lie. I was about to hang up on him. It's useless, you know, asking him to be reasonable, but then he really went off the deep end. He said you were a ghost, and you needed to take Esther's place in the world, that's how you got in."

"That is trash!" I whispered. "He is a smooth-tongued man."

"That's what I thought. I just didn't believe it. But something seemed very certain to me then. You are here because of Esther's death. You are, and you're here to kill Gregory. I wish you would promise me, whatever happens, you'll kill him. I know it's a terrible thing I'm saying."

"Not to me," I said. "I would like to kill him but not before this mystery is solved."

"Can you possibly see to Nathan? See that he's safe?"

"I can do that," I said, "but I have grave suspicions on that. Never mind. Be assured, whatever happens, I will get to the bottom of it, and Gregory will pay with his life."

"Laboratories," she said. "You know he's crazy, Gregory. He believes he is here to save the world. He goes to other countries, he asks for reception by dictators and establishes temples in countries that . . . and then all this about terrorism. You know," she said as she lay back down on the pillows. "You can't go wrong killing him. This Temple is a racket. It's garbage, and it bleeds people, takes their savings, their fortunes . . ."

She closed her eyes, and suddenly went still, so still that her eyes half-opened and I could see only the whites.

"Rachel!" I said. "Rachel!" I shook her shoulder.

"I'm alive, Azriel," she said softly without moving anything but her lips. Her dark brows moved just a little. She didn't open her eyes. "I'm here," she said. "Will you cover me, Azriel? Even now I'm cold. It's warm, isn't it?"

"The breeze is wondrously warm," I said.

"Open all the windows then. But cover me. What is it? What's the matter with you?"

All the windows *were* open, even the big window doors to my left that looked out on a terrace above the ocean. But I didn't disturb her by saying so.

I was suddenly startled. I noticed her arms for the first time. Really beheld them beneath the sheer silk.

"Your arms, I've covered them with bruises! Look what I've done to you."

"That doesn't matter," she said. "That's nothing. It's only one of the drugs thinning the blood, makes me bruise without feeling it. I loved it, your being in my arms. Come here, will you stay with me?

You know, I suspect I'm going to die right away. I left behind all the drugs that were keeping me going."

I didn't answer her but I knew she was going to die. Her heartbeat was too slow. Her fingers had a bluish tinge to them.

I lay down beside her, and covered her with the tapestried draperies that lay all over the bed, what are called "throws" and "lap blankets," though I had not realized it or thought of it.

She was nice and warm and she lay against me.

"I laughed so hard when he said you were a ghost and you killed Esther to get into the world. And yet I knew you weren't a human being. I knew it. You'd vanished from the plane. I knew it. And yet I thought Gregory was so hysterically funny telling me all this black magic, that Esther had to be sacrificed like a lamb so that you could come into the world and evil beings had done it. He said you'd kill me. He said if I didn't come back, he'd alert the police. I don't want him coming in here, disturbing me. I don't want him to."

"I won't let him," I said. "Rest now. I want to think. I want to remember the laboratories and the men in the orange suits. I want to see the great scheme."

It was a horrid thing to look at, her purplish bruises, and I felt shame that I hadn't been more delicate, hadn't even watched for such a thing, hadn't looked for anything but the age-old juiciness, and for all the rest, what did I care.

I held her arms. I kissed these places, and I could see where needles had made holes in her, and I could see where bandages had been ripped from her, and all the fleece was gone.

"Rachel, you are suffering, and I've made this worse for you," I said. "Let me get for you what you need. Send me. Tell me. I can get anything in the world for you, Rachel. That's my nature. Do you have doctors of great skill? Only tell me who they are. I'll be lost in the winds if I roam searching for doctors and magicians. Guide me. Send me. Send me now for whatever it is . . ."

"No."

I studied her silent face; her smile had not changed. She seemed half-asleep; I realized she was singing, or humming with her lips closed. Her hands were too cold.

I sighed; this was the agony that comes with loving; this was just as fresh as if it had never happened to me before. This was just as hurtful and cruel as if I were breathing and young.

"Don't worry," she whispered. "All the best doctors in the world have done their damnedest to cure Gregory Belkin's wife. Besides . . . I want to . . ."

". . . be with Esther."

"Yes, do you think I will be?"

"Yes, I do," I said. "I saw her go up in a pure light." I wanted to add, "One way or another, you'll be with her." But I didn't add it. I didn't know whether she believed we were all tiny flames that went back into God, or that we had a Paradise where we could kiss and hold each other. As for me, I believed we had a Paradise, and I had a dim memory of flying high once, to the very heights, and of gentle spirits up there concealing something from me.

I lay back. I had been so sure I wanted to die. And now the flame of life that blazed still in her, melting her like a candle, seemed utterly precious to me.

I wanted to try to cure her. I looked at her and tried to see all the workings of her, each thing connected to the next thing, and all bound with veins like woven gold thread.

I did lay my hands on her, and I did pray. I let my hair rest on her face. I prayed in my heart to all the gods.

She stirred. "What did you say, Azriel?" she said. She uttered some words. At first I didn't understand them. Then I realized it was Yiddish she was speaking. "Were you speaking Hebrew?" she asked me.

"Just praying, my darling," I said. "Think nothing of it." She took a deep breath and laid her hand on my chest, as if the very act of lifting her hand and setting it down exhausted her. I put my hand over hers. Too cold, her little hands. I made a heat for us both.

"You're really staying with me, aren't you?"

"Why does that surprise you?" I asked.

"I don't know. Because people try to get away from you when they know you're really dying. Those bad nights, when I was at my worst, the doctors didn't come, the nurses stayed away. Even Gregory wouldn't come. The crisis would pass, and then they would all come. And you, you are staying with me. Doesn't the air smell good? And the light. Just the light of the night sky."

"It's beautiful, a foreshadowing of Paradise."

She laughed a little laugh. "I'm ready to be nothing," she said.

What could I say?

Somewhere a bell rang. It throbbed. I sat up. I didn't like it. I was staring into the garden, at the big red flowers, like trumpets, and realized for the first time that there were dim electric lights there on these flowers. Everything was perfect. There came the bell again.

"Don't answer it," she said. She was damp all over.

"Look," she said. "Stop him, you stop the church. He's what we call a charismatic leader. He's evil. Laboratories. I don't like it. And these cults, these cults have killed people, have killed their own members."

"I know," I said. "It was always that way. Always."

"But Nathan, Nathan is so innocent," she said. "I can remember his voice, it was beautiful, and I thought of what Esther had said, that it was like seeing the man Gregory could have been. That's what the voice was like . . ."

"I'll find him and make sure he is safe," I said. "I'll find out what he knows, what he saw."

"The old man, is he so terrible?"

"Holy and old," I said. I shrugged.

She laughed a sweet delighted laugh. It was wondrous to hear it. I bent down and kissed her lips. They were dry. I gave her some more water, holding her head up so she could drink.

She lay back. She looked at me and only gradually did I realize that her expression meant nothing. It was only a mask for her pain. The pain was in her lungs and in her heart and in her bones. The pain was all through her. The soothing drugs she'd taken before she left New York were gone out of her body. Her heart was faint.

I cradled her hands in mine.

There came that noise again, the bell ringing, the alarm buzzing, and this time there was more than one. I heard the noise of a motor. It came from the elevator shaft.

"Ignore it," she said. "They can't get in." She pushed at the covers with her hands.

"What is it?" I asked.

"Help me, help me get up. Get my heavier robe for me, the heavy silk. Please . . ."

I got the robe, the one to which she pointed, and she put it on. She stood trembling beneath the weight of the ornate robe.

There was huge noise outside the main door.

"Are you sure they can't get in?"

"You don't have to fear, do you?" she asked.

"No, not at all, but I don't want them . . ."

"I know . . . ruining my death," she said.

"Yes."

She was completely white.

"You're going to fall down."

"I know," she said. "But I intend to fall where I want to fall. Help me out there, I want to look at the ocean."

I picked her up and carried her out the doors to the balcony. This was due east. The doors faced not the bay but the true sea. I realized it was the same sea that washed the banks of Europe, the shores of ruined Greek cities, the sands of Alexandria.

A pounding noise came from behind us. I turned around. It was coming from within the elevator. There were people in the car of the elevator. But the doors were locked.

The breeze ripped across the broad terrace. Under my feet the tiles felt cool. She seemed to love it, putting her head against my shoulder, looking out over the dark sea. A great ship, hung with lights, glided by, just short of the horizon, and above, the clouds made their spectacle.

I cuddled her and held her, and started to pick her up.

"No, let me stand," she said. She tugged herself gently free of me and put her hands on the high stone railing. She looked down. I saw a garden far down there, immaculate and full of trees and bright lights. Egyptian lilies galore, and large fanlike plants, all waving just a little in the breeze.

"It's empty down there, isn't it?" she asked.

"What?"

"The garden. It's so private. Only the flowers beneath us, and beyond, the sea."

"Yes," I said.

The elevator door was being forced open.

"Remember what I said," she said. "You can't go wrong killing him. I mean it. He'll try to seduce you, or destroy you, or use you in some way. You can bet he is already thinking in those terms, how best to use you."

"I understand him perfectly," I said. "Don't worry. I will do what is right. Who knows? Maybe I will teach him right and wrong. Maybe I know what they are. Maybe I'll save his soul." I laughed. "That would be lovely."

"Yes, it would," she said. "But you're craving life, craving it. Which means you can be lured by him with all his fiery life, the same way you were lured by mine."

"Never, I told you. I'll put it right."

"All of it, put it all to right."

Several men had just broken through the front door, with a clumsy pounding noise. I heard the wood splinter.

She sighed. "Maybe Esther did call you down. Maybe she did," she said. "My angel."

I kissed her.

The men were blundering into the room behind us. I didn't have to look at them to know they were there. They stopped short; there was a rumble of urgent voices. Then Gregory's voice carried.

"Rachel, thank God you're all right."

I turned and I saw him and he saw me, and he looked hard and determined, and cold. "Let my wife go," he said. Liar.

He was blazing with anger, and anger made him evil; anger took away his charm. I suppose it had done that to mine before. And I realized slowly as I stood there that I loved again, and didn't hate. I loved Esther and I loved Rachel. I didn't hate even him.

"Go to the door and stand between us," Rachel said. "Do that for me, please." She kissed me on the cheek. "Do that, my angel."

I obeyed. I put my hand up on the steel frame. "You can't pass," I said.

Gregory roared. He let out a terrible roar, a roar from the soul, and the whole company of men rushed towards me. I turned around as they buffeted my shoulders, passing me. But I knew already what had made them cry out.

She had jumped.

I went to the railing, pushing them aside, and I looked down into the garden and I saw her tiny empty shell of a body. The light hovered around her.

"Oh, God, take her, please," I prayed in my ancient tongue.

Then the light blazed and went straight up and for a moment it seemed that lightning lashed the southern sky, exploded behind the clouds, but it was only her passing. She'd gone up, and for one second perhaps I'd seen the Door of Heaven.

The garden held nothing but its bed of Egyptian flowers and her empty flesh, her face unhurt, intact, staring blindly upward.

Go up, Rachel, please, Esther, take her up the ladder. I deliberately envisioned the Ladder, the Stairway, replete with all the hanging remnants of memory.

Gregory cried in agony. Men took hold of me by the arms. Gregory screamed and cried and sobbed and there was no artifice to it. The man stared down at her and roared in pain and hit the railing with his fists.

"Rachel, Rachel, Rachel!"

I shook off the hands of the men. They fell backwards, stunned by the strength of it, and not knowing what to do, seemingly embarrassed by the figure of Gregory roaring in grief.

Suddenly there was havoc all around me. More men had come, poor Ritchie had come, and Gregory wailed and wailed and leaned over the railing. He was davening, bowing like a Hebrew and crying out in Yiddish.

I shoved off the men again, hurling some of them to the end of the terrace, I pushed and I pushed at them till they simply backed off.

I said to Gregory:

"You really loved her, didn't you?"

He turned and looked at me, and tried to speak but he was choked with grief. "She was . . . my queen of Sheba," he said. "She was my queen . . ." And then he wailed again, and said the same prayers.

"I'm leaving you now," I said, "with all your armed men."

A crowd was climbing up the slope of the garden below. Men with flashlights shone them on her dead face.

Then I went up and up.

Where would I go? What would I do?

It was time to walk on my own.

I looked back once at the tiny men down on the terrace, confounded now by my disappearance. Gregory had actually collapsed and sat down rocking, holding his head.

Then I went high, so high that the joyous spirits were there, and it seemed as I flew north that they stared at me with great interest.

I knew what I had to do first of all. Find Nathan.

22

By the time I reached New York the need for sleep was weighing me down. I would have to give in to it before further explorations.

But I was fiercely worried about Nathan. Before taking on a body, I prowled invisibly all through the Temple of the Mind.

Just as I expected, there was much chemical research being done there, and there were numerous restricted areas, and there were people working in the night in the strange rubbery orange plastic suits I had seen, and these suits seemed to be filled with air. These suited beings peered through their helmets as they worked with chemicals which they obviously did not mean to breathe or touch. They were loading these into what seemed very lightweight plastic cartridges.

I studied everything else that was going on.

In an antiseptic laboratory, my bones lay on a hard table, being studied by the evil Mastermind doctor, the thin one with the bottle-black hair. He had no hint of my invisible presence as I circled him. I could not make out his notes. I felt nothing for the Bones, except the desire to destroy them so that I could never be driven back into them again. But I might die if that happened. It was much too soon for such a risk.

Other parts of the building were obviously communication centers. There were people watching monitors, speaking on phones and working with maps. There were great electrified maps of the world on the wall, filled with pinpoints of light.

There was a great air of urgency and commotion among these night workers.

All spoke in a completely guarded way, as if they thought they were being monitored by enemies, and their statements were maddeningly vague. "We have to hurry." "This is going to be glorious." "This has to be loaded by four a.m." "Everything at Point 17 is perfectly in line."

I could not make something sensible or sophisticated out of what they said. I managed to discover from one slip of the tongue that the project they all shared was called Last Days.

Last Days.

All I saw alarmed me and repelled me. I suspected the chemicals in the canisters were filoviruses, or some other lethal agent only recently discovered through technology, and the entire Temple stank of murder.

I passed many empty floors, many sleeping dormitories filled with young Minders, and a huge chapel where Minders prayed silently like contemplative monks, on their knees with their hands pressed to their foreheads. The image over the altar was a great Brain. The Mind of God, I presume. It was a mere outline in gold. It was strangely uninspiring. It looked anatomical and bizarre.

I passed rooms where men slept alone, in dimness. In one room was a man covered up and bandaged, with a nurse in attendance. In other chambers, there were other sick people, swathed in sheeting, hooked to gleaming tubes connected to tiny computers. Many solitary rooms contained sleeping members of the church. Some were so luxurious as to rival Gregory's rooms. They had floors of marble tile and gilded furniture; they had sumptuous bathrooms with great square tubs.

I had many unanswered questions about what I saw in the building, and could have spent much more time.

But now I had to go on to Brooklyn. I felt I could see what was happening. Surely, Nathan was in danger.

It was two a.m. Invisible I passed into the Rebbe's house and found him sound asleep in his bed, but he woke the minute I entered the room. He knew I was there. He was at once alarmed and climbed out of the bed. I simply went very far away from the house. There was no time to search for Nathan or to look for more sympathetic members of the family.

Besides, I was growing more tired by the minute. I couldn't dare retreat to the Bones; in fact, I had no intention of ever retreating to them again, not the way that I felt now, and I feared my weakness in sleep, that I might be called back or dissolved by Gregory or even somehow by the Rebbe.

I went back into Manhattan, found a lake in the middle of Central Park not very far at all from the huge Temple of the Mind. Indeed, I could see all its lighted windows. I took form as a man, dressed myself in the finest garb I could conceive of—red velvet suit, fine linen shirt, all manner of exotic gold embellishments—and then I drank huge amounts of water from the lake. I knelt and drank it in handfuls. I was filled with water, and felt very powerful. I lay down on the grass under a tree to rest, in the open, telling my body to hold firm and to wake if there was any natural or supernatural assault on it. I told it it must answer no one's call but my own.

When I woke it was eight o'clock in the morning by the city's clocks, and I was whole, intact, with my clothes, and I was rested. Just as I supposed, I had appeared far too strange for prowling mortal men to attack, and far too puzzling to be disturbed by beggars. Whatever the case, I was strong and unharmed in my velvet suit and shining black shoes.

I had survived the hours of sleep in material form, outside the bones, and this was another triumph.

I danced for joy on the grass for a few minutes, then brushed off the clothes, dissolved with the requisite enchantments, and re-formed, velvet clad, bearded, and free of bits of grass and dirt in the living room of the Rebbe's house. I did not want the beard, but the beard and mustache came as they had before. And maybe they'd even been there when I woke. In fact, I'm sure they had. They had been there all along. They wanted to be there. Very well.

The house was modern, cramped, made of many smallish rooms.

It struck me as most remarkable how conventional this house was. It was filled with rather ordinary furniture, none of it ugly or beautiful. Comfortable and well lighted. Immediately people waiting in the parlor stared at me and began to whisper. A man approached, and in Yiddish I said I had to see Nathan immediately.

I realized I didn't know Nathan's real last name. Or even if they called him Nathan here. Obviously his last name wasn't Belkin. Belkin was a made-up name of Gregory. I said in Yiddish that it was a matter of life and death that I see Nathan.

The Rebbe flung open the doors of his study. He was in a fury. Two elderly women stood with him, and two young men, all of these people Hasidim, the women wigged to cover their natural hair, the young men with locks and silk suits. There was no one about who was not Hasidim.

The Rebbe's face was trembling with outrage. He began to try to exorcise me from the house, and I stood firm and put up my hand.

"I have to speak to Nathan," I said in Yiddish. "Nathan could be in danger. Gregory is a dangerous man. I have to speak to Nathan. I won't leave here until I find him. Perhaps his is a compassionate and fearless heart and he will hear me. Whatever the case, I will speak to him in love. Perhaps Nathan walks with God, and if I save him, so shall I."

Everyone fell silent. Then the men bid the women to go, which they did, and they called several old men from the parlor, and they pointed for me to go into the Rebbe's study.

I was now among an assemblage of elders.

One of these men took a piece of white chalk and drew a circle on the carpet and told me to stand in it.

I said:

"No. I am here to love, to avert harm, I am here having loved two people who are now dead. I learned love from them. I will not be the Servant of the Bones. I will do no evil. I will not be driven any longer by anger, hatred, or bitterness. And I will not be confined by you and your magic to that circle. I am too strong for that circle. It means nothing to me. The love of Nathan is what calls me now."

The Rebbe sank down at his desk, a rather large formal one compared to his desk in the basement, where I had first seen him. He seemed in despair.

"Rachel Belkin is dead," I told him in Yiddish. "She took her own life."

"The news says you took her life!" said the Rebbe in Yiddish. The other men murmured, nodding.

A very very old man, balding and thin with a head like a skull covered in black silk, came forward and looked into my eyes. "We don't watch television; we don't do it. But the news spread fast. That you killed her and you killed her daughter."

"That is a lie," I said. "Esther Belkin met Nathan, Gregory's brother, in the diamond district. She bought a necklace from him. I believe Gregory Belkin had her murdered because she knew of his family and in particular of his twin brother. Nathan is in danger."

They all stood motionless. I couldn't predict what was going to happen. I knew I made a strange sight in the dark red velvet with so much gold ornament on the cuffs and with my dark hair and long beard, but so did they make a strange sight, all of them bearded and wearing hats, either small- or large-brimmed, and in long black silk suits all their own style.

They gradually formed a circle around me.

They began to hurl questions at me. At first I didn't realize what this was. Then it became clear that it was a test. The first question was, Could I quote from this or that book of the Torah. They used letters and names I understood completely. I answered all their questions, throwing out the quotations first in Hebrew and then in Greek, and then sometimes, to really startle them, in older Aramaic.

"Name the prophets," they said.

I did, including Enoch, who had been a prophet in my time in Babylon, whom they didn't know. They were shocked at this.

"Babylon?"

"I can't remember!" I said. "I have to stop Gregory Belkin from hurting his brother, Nathan. I'm convinced he killed Esther because she met Nathan and knew of Nathan, and there are other suspicious things."

Now they began to question me on the Talmud: What were the Mitzvot? I told them there were 613, and they were laws or rules in general concerned with attitude, what one does, good behavior, and what one says.

The questions went on and on. They had to do with ritual and cleanliness, and what is forbidden, and with the heretic rabbis, and with the Kabbalah. I answered everything rapidly, lapsing into Aramaic over and over, then coming back to Yiddish. When I quoted from the Septuagint, I used the Greek.

I referred sometimes to the Babylonian Talmud and sometimes to the old Jerusalem Talmud. I answered all questions about sacred numbers, and the points of discussion became finer and finer. It seemed each man was trying to outdo the other with the delicacy of his question.

Finally I became impatient.

"Do you realize while we carry on like this, as if we were in the yeshiva, that Nathan may be in danger? What is Nathan's name among you? Help me save Nathan, in the name of God."

"Nathan is gone," said the Rebbe. "He is far far away, where Gregory cannot find him. He is safe in the Lord's city."

"How do you know he's safe?"

"The day after the death of Esther he left here for Israel. Gregory cannot find him there. Gregory could never track him down."

"The day after . . . you mean then the day before you first saw me?"

"Yes, if you aren't a dybbuk, what are you?"

"I don't know. What I want to be is an angel and that is what I intend to be. And God will judge whether I have done His Will. What made Nathan go to Israel?"

The old men looked at the Rebbe, obviously confused. The Rebbe said that he wasn't sure why Nathan wanted to take the trip just then, but it seemed in his grief for Esther, Nathan was eager to go and said something about doing his yearly work early in Israel. His work had to do with copies of the Torah which he would bring back. Routine.

"Can you reach him?" I said.

"Why should we tell you more?" said the Rebbe. "He's safe from Gregory."

"I don't think so," I said. "Now that you are all here, I want you to answer. Did any of you call upon the Servant of the Bones? Did Nathan?"

They all shook their heads and looked at the Rebbe.

"Nathan would never do such an unholy thing."

"Am I unholy?" I lifted my hands. "Come," I said, "I invite you. Try to exorcise me, try in the name of the Lord God of Hosts. I'll stand here firm in my love for Nathan and for Esther and Rachel Belkin. I want to avert harm. I will stand firm. Go on, give me your abracadabra Kabbalah magic!"

This roused them all to whispering and murmuring, and the Rebbe, who was still furious, did begin a loud chant to exorcise me, and then all the men joined in and I watched them, feeling nothing, not letting any anger come to the fore, only feeling love for them, and thinking with love of my Master Samuel, and how I had hated him for something perhaps that was only human. I couldn't remember it. I remembered Babylon. I remembered the prophet Enoch, but each time sadness or hate or bitterness came to me I pushed it away and thought of love, love profane, love sacred, love of the good . . .

I still could not recall Zurvan distinctly, only the feeling, but I quoted him now out loud as best I could. Each time it seemed I used new words but it was the same quote: "The purpose of life is to love and to increase our knowledge of the intricacies of creation. Kindness is the way of God."

They kept up the exorcism, and I searched my mind, closing my eyes, and sought for the proper words, calling to the world to yield to me the proper words that would quiet them, just the way that it yielded to me the clothing I wore, or the skin that appeared human.

Then I saw the words. I saw the room. I didn't know where it was then. Now I realize that it was the scriptorium in my father's house. All I knew was that it was familiar and I began to sing the words, as I had sung them long ago, with the harp on my knee. As I had written them over and over.

I sang them now in the ancient tongue in which I learned them, loudly and with rhythm, rocking as I sang:

> *I will love thee, O Lord, my strength.*
> *The Lord is my rock, and my fortress and my*
> *deliverer; my God, my strength,*
> *in whom I will trust, my buckler*
> *and the horn of my salvation and my high tower.*
>
> *The sorrows of death compassed me,*
> *and the floods of ungodly men made me afraid*
> *The sorrows of hell compassed me about:*
> *the snares of death prevented me*
> *In my distress I called upon the Lord,*
> *And cried unto my God; he heard my voice . . .*

This silenced them. They stood staring in wonder, not afraid and not full of hate. Even the Rebbe's soul was stilled and had lost its hate.

I spoke in Aramaic: "I forgive those who made of me a demon, whoever they were, and to whatever purpose. Learning to love from Esther and Rachel, I come in love and to love Nathan and to love God. To love is to know love, and that is to love God. Amen."

The old man looked suspicious suddenly, but it was not of me. He looked at the telephone on his desk. Then he glanced at me.

The very old one said, in Hebrew, "So he was a demon who would be an angel? Is such a thing possible?"

The Rebbe didn't answer.

Then suddenly the Rebbe picked up the phone and punched in a long series of numbers, too long for me to follow or remember, and then he began to talk in Yiddish.

He asked if Nathan was there. Had Nathan arrived safely? He assumed that someone would have called, had Nathan not arrived, but he wanted to speak to his grandson.

Then shock came over his face. The room was silent. All the men looked at him and seemed to know what he was thinking.

The Rebbe spoke into the phone in Yiddish:

"He didn't tell you that he was coming? You have not heard from him, one single word?"

The old men were distressed. So was I.

"He's not there," I said. "He's not there!"

The old man went over all the details with those at the other end of the line. They knew nothing about Nathan coming to Israel. Last they heard, Nathan would come at his regular time later in the year. All was in readiness for Nathan's regular visit. They had received no calls from Nathan about an early visit.

The Rebbe put down the phone. "Don't tell Sarah!" he said with his hand raised. All the others nodded. He then told the youngest of the men to go for Sarah. "I'll speak with Sarah."

Sarah came into the room, a modest and humble woman, very beautiful, her natural hair covered by an ugly brown wig. She had narrow almond-shaped eyes, and a lovely soft mouth. She emanated kindness and when she glanced at me shyly she made no judgment.

She looked at the Rebbe.

"Your husband has called you since he left?"

She said no.

"You went with him and Jacob and Joseph to the plane?"

She said no.

Silence.

She looked at me and then looked down.

"Please, forgive me," I said, "but did Nathan tell you he was going to Israel?"

She said yes, and that a car had come for him, from a rich friend in the city to take him, and he had said he would be back very soon.

"Did he tell you who this friend was?" I asked. "Please tell me, Sarah, please."

She seemed utterly reassured and something inside her was suddenly unlocked. I saw in her eyes the same gentleness that I had seen in the girl on the street in the southern city, and in Esther herself, and in Rachel. The pure gentleness of women, which is wholly different from the pure gentleness of men.

Maybe this is what happens when you love, really love, I thought. People love you in return! I felt so free of hatred and anger suddenly that I shivered, but I implored her with my eyes to speak.

She looked shaken and then she glanced at the Rebbe, and bowed her head and blushed. She was about to cry.

"He had with him her diamond necklace," she said, "the necklace of his brother's daughter, Esther Belkin. He was taking it to his brother."

She began to cry.

"When he had heard of the necklace being stolen," she said, "when he heard this tale, he knew it wasn't true. He had the necklace. Esther Belkin had given it to him for mending." She swallowed her tears and continued. "Rebbe, he didn't want anyone to be angry. He called his brother to tell him. He said his brother was crying. The car came to take him to his brother so that he might restore the necklace to him which had been Esther's, and then his brother wanted Nathan to come with him to Israel that they stand together at the Wailing Wall. Nathan promised me that when he had comforted his brother, he would return. Perhaps, he said, he could bring his brother back home."

"Ah, of course," I said.

"Quiet," said the Rebbe. "Sarah, don't be sorry or sad. Don't worry. I'm not angry that he went with his brother. He went in love, with good intentions."

"He did, Rebbe," she said. "He did."

"Leave this to us."

"I'm so sorry, Rebbe. But he loved his brother and was so stricken with grief for the girl. He said the girl would one day have come to us and would have wanted to be one of us. He was sure of it. He had seen it in her eyes."

"I see, Sarah. Don't think any more about it. Go out now."

She turned her head, still crying, glanced back at me once, and then left the room.

I felt so sorry for her, so very sorry! She knew something was wrong, but she had no idea what was wrong, how bad it was. She was loving by nature. Maybe Nathan was too. Very likely so, as Rachel and Esther had said he was.

"It's just as I thought," I said.

The old man waited on me in silence.

"Gregory used the necklace to lure Nathan to him. Gregory published that stupid story of the stolen necklace so that Nathan would call him, and he could persuade Nathan to meet with him and stay with him. Nathan prepared you for his prolonged absence. Gregory put him up to this. I will do everything in my power to see that Nathan is returned unharmed. I can't stay with you now. Will you give me your blessing, all of you? I won't linger begging for it, but if you want to give it, I will receive it with love in the name of the Lord. My name is Azriel."

They cried out, throwing up their hands and backing away. It was the fear of knowing the name of a spirit, though I hadn't expected such alarm at this point. I put my hands to my temples and thought again, "Yield to me the words! Yield to me the words. I know my name is not evil."

Then I declared. "I was named Azriel by my father when I was circumcised in our own house of prayer at Babylon. We were the last tribes taken hostage out of Jerusalem by Nebuchadnezzar. The name was good enough for God and for the Tribe and for my father!

Nabonidus was King and we practiced our faith in peace under his rule. We sang the Lord's Song in that strange land every day."

A great flush of energy passed through me, but again the memory lacked substance, color. I knew only that what I said was true, and that if I could solve this blasted mystery, this horror, then perhaps in time I could recall other things, just as I had recalled this, and all my past would come to me. Not in hatred, but in love. I was now fascinated by love. No doubt of it.

They fell to murmuring, it is his Hebrew name, it is his human name, it is his own name blessed by God, and some arguing that to know my name only gave them power over me and others whispered that I was an angel.

Then with a nod from the Rebbe, they all gave me their blessings. I felt nothing, but at least I didn't dislike them anymore; I loved them and saw them for what they were and feared all the more for Nathan.

"But what is Gregory doing?" the Rebbe whispered, more to himself than to me.

"I don't know," I admitted again. "But Nathan is an identical twin, is he not? And your grandson Gregory would be the Messiah, would he not? He would change the whole world."

The old man was perplexed and horrified.

I asked, "If I need you, for Nathan's sake, for the sake of the love of all God's creatures, will you come?"

"Yes," said the Rebbe.

I was about to walk out of the room. But I decided for obvious reasons that it was best to vanish. I did so slowly so as to amaze them, growing transparent, rising, extending my arms, then vanishing altogether. I don't think they saw the tiny bits of moisture all through the air. They probably only felt the coolness and then the heat when a spirit vanishes.

I left them staring solemnly at the place where I'd stood. I wanted desperately to comfort Sarah, whom I saw crying at the kitchen table, but there was no way, no time.

I went up higher and higher.

"Gregory!" I said, and I set my destination to that place where the Master of the Bones might be—his Temple. To search, as a spirit, for Nathan was impossible. I had never laid eyes on him, caught his scent, seen or touched him or his garments. He might have been sleeping in one of those rooms in the Temple which I roamed, invisibly, the night before. But I had not lingered on faces. There had been hundreds of faces.

Go to Gregory. The danger to Nathan was with his brother, and that was where I had to be now. I had one comforting thought. Whatever was in store for Nathan had probably not transpired yet.

On the other hand, the people in the Temple had been working full speed on the project called the Last Days.

23

A huge mob surrounded the Temple of the Mind. I came down into it invisible, amid the cameras and the radio people and understood that Gregory Belkin was to appear to make a momentous statement at six p.m. or before and that he knew the identity of his enemies and the enemies of the Temple. He intended to name his terrorist enemies and try to prevent their new plan of destruction.

The crowd spilled out, blocking Fifth Avenue, and many of the Minders, virtually pushed away by the press, were in the park praying.

I went up and into the building and found Gregory seated in a huge room with five men, amid the big electric maps and numerous monitors, and he was hard at work going over the final directions. The room itself was soundproof, and before I made myself visible I saw that no camera monitored the room itself. All monitors revealed the outside, and the walls in the rooms didn't have ears either.

As I descended, Gregory spoke:

"Nothing will happen until two hours after I'm declared officially dead—" he said, and these words immediately galvanized me.

I appeared in my full Babylonian robes of blue velvet and gold, and my long hair and beard, and I snatched him up from the chair.

The men raced at me, and I threw them back. Through another door came a small group of heavily armed soldiers. Someone fired a gun. Gregory shouted no. No. This little cadre of ruthless guards surrounded me with powerful modern guns, the kind that fix you in a beam of light before they shoot you. All these men had the look of killers.

As for those who had been gathered at the table, they were the milder sort, though equally as serious, that included the Mastermind Doctor, and they reeked of resentment and suspicion and absolute desperation that I had interrupted them.

"No, be calm," said Gregory. "This is inevitable and this will not stop us. This is an angel sent from God to help us."

"Is that so?" I said. "What have you done with your brother? If you don't talk the truth to me, I'll tear you limb from limb and all these men will die with you. That's the only alternative you give me. What is this about your official death? Talk now, or I will destroy."

Gregory sighed and then he told the other men to go. "Everything will go as planned; only this angel needs to know the scope of his power," he said. "Go on, man your desks in the building and see that my brother is comfortable and not afraid. Everything will be glorious. We are in the time of miracles. This creature you see here is a miracle from God. Say nothing to anyone."

The men at the table left with amazing speed, but the soldiers took a little more firm persuading from him that he knew what he was doing.

I flung him back down in his chair.

"You lying monster," I said. "How could you tell the world I killed your wife and your daughter? Tell me now where Nathan is, tell me now what you mean to do."

I scanned the monitors all along the tops of the walls. They covered entryways, the lobby, elevators that were not in operation. I could see nothing but empty space in most. And guards passing.

The maps were dazzling and filled with pulsing neon colors, countries done in scarlet and yellow and rivers drawn in light like lightning. But there was no time to admire these things.

"Haven't you guessed it, clever spirit?" he said. He smiled up at me. "How glad I am to see you. What took you so long? I need you, and time is running out."

"I know you're going to do something with your brother," I said, "put him in your place to be killed, so that you can rise from the dead! That much is easy to figure and six is the hour you've marked for it. Six or before, what does that mean? I want your brother now, safe and in my arms to be taken back to his people."

"No, you don't, Azriel," he said with great reasonableness, his confidence flaring up in him like an unquenchable fire. "Sit down and let me tell you what is to happen. You cannot imagine the beauty of it, and Nathan will suffer no pain. He is sedated and hardly knows what will happen to him."

"I'm sure he is!" I said with great contempt, and a memory came back to me of people giving me something to drink, and saying, "You will not suffer." They were painting gold on my skin.

"If you kill me," Gregory said, "you will change nothing. The plan goes into operation after my death. If you want me to die before six o'clock then you will simply move up the time of the Last Days. Everything is set into motion. Only I can stop it. You'd be a fool to kill me." He gestured for me to sit down.

"This room is soundproof, it has no security monitor," he said. "What we say here is private, utterly. And I want your attention and your sympathy."

"The soldiers?"

"I pressed a button, here under the table. They won't come in again, but what I tell you must be secret, secret from all the world. You must be one of us when we leave this room. We have to leave it together."

"You're dreaming."

"No. You lack vision, Spirit, you always have. You've spent too many centuries a slave. Now, only in my time, have you known your full strength. Admit it. The doctors found living seed in my wife. You've lost your glaze-eyed confused look, Spirit. My wife taught you how to be a man?"

I said nothing. But I did have a strong sense of something—that I couldn't simply solve this by chopping him up like the Gordian knot.

"Right you are!" he said. "Sit down, and listen to me."

I took the first chair to his left.

He picked up a small multi-buttoned remote control device. I placed my hand on it.

"It controls the monitors, nothing more. Most are security. Only two have film in them. Look directly up there, over the central map."

At once two of the screens began to fill with still shots—frozen for about two seconds each—of people who were starving, or the dead, battlefields, bombed-out buildings, trash heaps. I recognized that these photos were a steady panorama from all over the world. I could see the Mayan temples in one picture of gathered villagers. In another I saw ruins I knew to be in Cambodia.

He watched these almost serenely, as if he'd forgotten my presence or took me utterly for granted.

"Assure me nothing will happen to Nathan," I said, "as we talk."

"I assure you," he said. "Nothing will happen, until six o'clock and even then it depends on my signal. But I should let you know, angelic one, you have no bargaining power."

"Oh?"

As he turned and smiled graciously at me, he was now preening and full of happiness.

"I've waited so long for this to come," he said, "and to think that you arrived in the midst of it. I do think God sent you as an answer to the sacrifice of Esther. I myself didn't see the symmetry of it or the genius until later. I offered up Esther, whom I loved, truly loved, and you came through the break from the Heavens." He seemed perfectly sincere.

"I have not been in Heaven," I said. "Where is Nathan?"

"First," he said, "let us think intelligently. If you should lose your angelic temper and kill me, you'll only trigger the plan automatically. If you destroy this building you'll trigger the plan automatically. If you want any chance of understanding, acceptance, or modification, you need me. And hear me out."

"All right," I said. "But you do plan to kill Nathan at six o'clock. You admit it. And you could do it before. That's why you put him in the hospital under your name, to create DNA evidence and dental evidence to identify Nathan as you, so that your death would be certified, didn't you?"

He didn't seem at all happy to hear this much figuring.

"That's a crude version of what I accomplished," he said. "But look, the world is at stake, Azriel, the world itself. Dear God, you must be my Divine Witness."

"Don't get romantic, Gregory, tell me the plan. Somewhere else you have DNA documents that will be used to cleverly replace Nathan's set, and these documents will confirm you when you have risen. You have many people involved in erasing and moving data."

"I'm beginning to love your intelligence," he said. "Now really use it. This is for the world itself! It's for that that we do what we do. And you cannot prevent what will happen, and you must keep it in your mind that when the Last Days come, and they will begin sometime before midnight this night, you will need me. You will need me desperately, just as everyone alive and meant to live will need me. Otherwise only disaster can follow upon disaster."

"Okay, what is this Last Days? What's to happen? You're going to have him assassinated. Then what? Appear to rise from the dead?"

"In three days," he said. "Isn't that the way the other Messiah did it?" He was cooler.

Three days. Blurry horrid images filled with—lions, a loathsome swarm of bees, dancing. I shivered and fought it off. I saw the cross of Christ. I saw the risen Christ in paintings old and new. I heard Christian words in Greek and Latin.

"I'm eager to have you understand this," he said. "You know, it's occurred to me several times that you are the only one who will fully appreciate this."

"And why's that?"

"Azriel, nobody else alive has my courage. No one. It takes courage to kill. You know it does. You know time and the world, and have probably witnessed war, starvation, injustice. But first, allow me to caution you. If you don't hear me out, if you decide that my death is appropriate and that you don't care what happens to the world, there's the question of the Bones."

"Yes?"

"They are in a kiln in this building, and a word from me will roast them and melt them into running liquid. Oh, and I should tell you the results of our tests on them, shouldn't I?"

"If you want to waste the time. I'd rather hear about the Last Days."

"Don't you want to know what's inside your bones?"

"I know. My bones."

He shook his head and smiled. "No more," he said. "The human bone is almost entirely devoured by the metals in which it was encased. There is very little if anything left. Which means I think that as soon as the metal is heated it will easily incinerate and obliterate any trace of the human remaining."

"That's what it means to you?" I smiled. "How amusing. Your test results have an entirely different meaning for me. Did you find enough there to do your DNA magic?"

He shook his head. "There's almost nothing left."

"That's good news. But go on."

He studied me most intensely. He reached out to take my hand, which I more or less allowed. All his charm was in play now, and his eyes had the depth of greatness, and the sincerity of greatness. Very alluring. Rachel had warned me of this.

But I loathed him. For Esther and Nathan alone, as if all the world didn't matter, or as if to mourn them was to mourn all injustice.

"Azriel, this is a dream of unparalleled greatness. It has harshness in it and death, but so did the conquests of Alexander. So did the conquests of Constantine. You know they did. You know the land of Egypt lived in peace for two thousand years because of harshness and the willingness to kill. You know or remember those long times of peace. The Peace of Alexander, and after him the Pax Romana."

"Tell me the plan."

He pointed to the big map on the wall, the map of the world that was filled with pinpoints of light. The pinpoints were red and blue mostly, though some were yellow. They were in stark contrast to the lights of the map, but I saw now much drawing and marking on the map. Much detail.

"Those are my headquarters throughout the world," he said. "Those are my Temples, my so-called resorts, my so-called business offices. Airports. Islands."

"God, why does ambition come to such a man?" I said. "Think of the good you could do, you blithering moral idiot!"

He laughed sincerely and like a child. "But that's just it, my tactless and impulsive one, I am a moral genius." He pointed to the maps:

"They are ready within two hours of confirmation of my death to destroy two-thirds of the world's population completely. Now, before you object, let me explain that this will be done by a filovirus perfected here by us which is already in place in those various temples. Don't interrupt."

He raised his hand and went on.

"It is a virus which kills within five minutes or less; it is airborne only as long as its host breathes, which is no more than five minutes; its first immediate action is to fog the brain and to fill the victim with a feeling of peace and ecstasy."

He smiled gently, his eyes glazed suddenly, as though he were listening to grand and majestic music.

"No one will suffer, Azriel, at least not more than a few moments. Oh, it is such perfection compared to the hideous, bumbling stupidity of Hitler when he bludgeoned, shot, and tormented the Jews. What a crude, cruel monster he was. A digger of graves, a ragman, a fiend who tinkered with the gold in the mouths of his millions of victims." He shrugged. "Ah, maybe it simply wasn't the time. We didn't have the technology."

He resumed:

"The virus will be dropped along with a lethal gas that tends to dissipate within four hours. These combined should kill everything living and human in the area. My planes and helicopters are ready worldwide to perform the annihilations. They will go over and over the territories involved until all people in them are exterminated.

"Foot battalions have been organized in some densely populated cities, like Baghdad and Cairo and Calcutta. They will insert the gas and the virus into large buildings through their air systems. Some of these people are themselves willing to die. Others will wear protective clothing."

"Good God, how many cities, countries, people, are you talking about?"

"Most of the world, Azriel. I told you. Two-thirds of the world's population. Think of it as an inevitable plague, if you will, a plague which comes in angelic form, to clear the planet of the debris as other plagues have done in the past. Do you know what the Black Death did to Europe?"

"How could I not?" I thought of Samuel and the burning houses of Strasbourg.

"What you don't know is that Europe would be a desert now were it not for that plague. You don't know how many died in the flu epidemic early in our century. You don't know that AIDS was meant. You don't know that it takes courage to learn from nature and rise above it, rather than simply tamper with it, and make chaos out of it as you destroy it."

"What countries of the world; you speak of Asia?"

"Oh, yes," he said. "Definitely. Asia, the Orient, all of those people will be wiped off the face of the earth. All of northern Russia. Only some of eastern Russia will be saved, and even on that score I haven't entirely made up my mind. There will be no more Japan."

He didn't want to stop for breath, he went right on, excited now. I could swear that a light emanated from him.

"You haven't been here long enough to know the logic of it. First and foremost, everything in populated areas on the African continent will be wiped out. Think of it. Emptying Africa. Villages have been targeted, all areas where men and women live. The only animals who will survive are those which are far from populated areas. It's brilliant. You see, the filovirus won't affect most animals anyway, and the gas will dissipate soon enough for most animals to survive it. Oh, it's very complex. It has stages. But everything has been done to avoid panic or pain or knowledge among those who are dying. They will not suffer, no, they will not endure the absolute agony of our parents and others in the German camps. That was hideous, beastly."

I didn't dare interrupt him. But, Jonathan, you can imagine my feelings at this moment. Panic rose in me, but something harder overcame it: a determination that this madness was not going to happen! Absolutely not going to happen! I kept a mask of a face:

"You truly have an immense vision, Gregory."

"Every living person in India and Pakistan will be wiped out," he continued with rapturous enthusiasm. "In fact, almost every living person in Nepal, too, and up into the mountains. Of course Israel will be destroyed because Palestine has to be destroyed, and Iraq and Iran. In fact, all of that world will go—the Armenians, the Turks . . . the Greeks, the Balkans, where the war goes on, Saudi Arabia, Yemen . . ."

"The Third World, as you call it," I said. "The poor world. That's what you're talking about."

"I'm talking about the world that is fatally diseased, always at war, courting famine, and dragging us all down with it. The great unsalvageable world—the world that Alexander couldn't save, or Rome, or Constantine, or the President of this country, or the United Nations, or all the weak fumbling liberal kindhearted peacemakers of today who do nothing but preside over massacres!"

He sighed.

"Yes," he said, "the disease ridden, the uncontrollable, and the unredeemable. It's absolutely essential. They will all die. By midnight tonight most will be dead. But the Temples are ready for a renewed gas attack on all areas again tomorrow. Our vans, our planes, our helicopters—all are disguised as medical vehicles. Our people are clothed as medical people. Anyone seeing them will think they are trying to help. People will come to them for help and shelter, and they will kill these people without torturing them or frightening them. It's going to work brilliantly. We have worked out our estimates. All of Cairo will be dead in two hours. Calcutta will take longer."

He looked sad as he continued:

"The third day will be the worst, because we have to hunt down those who might have somehow survived and it will be difficult. People will know fear. But it will be brief. There may be bullets used then, even bombs, but we hope not. We envision a beautiful and silent world by the end of the third day."

His hand fell warm and firm on mine, his eyes glowed.

"Imagine it, Azriel, all of the African continent still and quiet, the beautiful pyramids of Egypt standing in silence, the smog and filth of Cairo settled down like so much sand. Imagine Zaire with no more epidemics and secret filoviruses brewing to destroy the world. Imagine the starving put to sleep in silence. Imagine the great rain forests allowed once again to grow, the dense jungle blooming without intrusion, the wild animals of the interior allowed to multiply as God planned for them to do.

"Oh, Azriel, my dream is as great as Yahweh's dream when he told Noah to build the ark. I have even sheltered critical species. Very talented geniuses and scientists have already been lured here for a convention so that they might be saved as their people die. This, my country, is my ark. But the rest must die. There is absolutely no other beautiful or elegant or merciful way out of our present state."

"Israel must die, you would do this to your own people?"

"Have to, no way around it. Besides . . . We must reclaim the Holy Places in peace and stillness. But don't you see, many Jews here will survive. Everyone in the United States and Canada will survive. No one in this country will be hurt at all.

"The attacks in this hemisphere will wipe out only the southern lands—all of Mexico, Central America, and the Caribbean. All those islands peaceful again and beautiful, where the poinsettia can bloom a deep red, and the palms can blow in the wind.

"But everything that is in our country and Canada will survive. The filovirus dies quickly. We've perfected our formula out of all three strains of Ebola and some we've found ourselves. The gas dissipates. I told you. It breaks down utterly. You don't know the lengths we've gone to to perfect our formula so that horses and cattle will be immune. You don't know how we have worked to make this merciful."

He sighed, with a little shake of his head, then said:

"There will be spot exterminations of villages in the Amazon jungle—yes, that will happen—but in general the wildlife will rebound. It won't be hurt by these clever poisons. Azriel, do you realize the geniuses I have working for me, men who worked in government germ-warfare programs for years, men who know things you and I know nothing of?"

"And Europe?" I asked. "You will kill Asia Minor? You will kill the Balkan countries. What will you do with Europe?"

"That is our biggest problem strategically. Because we must wipe out the Germans, we must do that on account of what they did with Hitler to the Jews. The Germans have to die. They have to. All of them. Absolutely.

"But we want to spare all other European countries. Except Spain. I just don't like Spain, and Spain has had too much Moslem influence. But the extermination in Germany will be very stealthy, involve more foot workers than anyplace else, and there may be some unavoidable casualties among the French and the English, especially those traveling in Germany at the time."

He stood up and he walked to the map. "It's all prepared. It's all in place. The final chemicals have been shipped. What remains here in the building can be used to attack anyone who enters the building. There are areas that can be sealed off where police and authorities can be gassed.

"You realize of course," he said, "that from most of these condemned areas, we will be the only broadcast that the United States receives. We will have the advantage in describing this gentle plague. We have written our poetry, which is worthy to be remembered, like the story of the battles of Darius carved in rock."

He pointed to the various monitors whose cameras remained fixed on corridors or empty rooms or elevators. "All killing traps. We are a fortress here.

"On the third day," he said, "as the United States weeps in confusion for the rest of the world, while secretly sighing in relief to be rid of it, I will rise from the Dead, and I will tell what I have seen of these deaths everywhere, and that this plague was inevitable and the will of God. All the members of my Temple are prepared to take positions of leadership."

"Do they know it's a hoax!" I demanded. "Your own idiot followers? Do they know it's Nathan, an identical twin, who will be killed?"

He smiled patiently at me, his back to the map, his arms folded.

"You tricked him into the hospital to acquire the DNA you need to verify your own death," I said. "How many know about the fraud? How many are there involved in exchanging the DNA records at the key moments in order to verify your resurrection?"

"Enough key people know. Of course the great mass of my followers don't know. They know who I am, and when I appear they will know it's Gregory. I take the responsibility for this on my own shoulders. I take the guilt of the murder of the world, and the burden of a new myth of my journey to hell and back. I am the new Messiah. I am the anointed one. And my secret things are mine, as Yahweh's secrets were His."

He took the time to calm himself. His eyes were wet with emotion. "You're beautiful, Azriel. I need you. You've been sent to be at my side. You've been sent."

"Get on with this plan. Who knows what?" I demanded.

"Only a few in this location know that the death and the resurrection are a trick. Isn't that how it probably happened the first time?"

"The first time," I whispered. "And what was the first time? Was it Calvary? Is that what you think?"

"Even the people distributing the gas throughout India do not really know what it will do. Only those in charge know. There are levels of knowledge. Mine is a world of zealots willing to die for me, don't you see, die for me and for a new world. Now listen to what I say. Listen!

"Imagine the relief when people realize what has taken place. I mean it. Think of the relief in the minds of all intelligent Americans and Europeans, all Westerners, or whatever you want to call us."

He sat down again and leaned towards me. "Azriel, people will be overjoyed when the Great Death has passed. They will be overjoyed! Only the West with all its resources will remain, that's all. All the poverty, the disease, the tribal war, gone. Gone from the earth. A new beginning.

"We, the Temple of the Mind, will take control. We outnumber those in Washington who might at first resist us. We will have no problem in other places. We know what has happened. We have the knowledge. We will go on the airwaves describing that the will of God has been done, and that the earth is now at peace, and free of millions who covered it like termites and parasites."

"And you think the President of this country is going to take your hand for this?"

"Well, we'll probably have to kill him. But at least we'll give him a chance. At the moment he is an extremely brilliant man and rather beautiful. But our Temple people in Washington are ready. There are three thousand of them within blocks of the White House, and the nearby Pentagon. I presume you know these are our important buildings. We can gas everyone in those buildings. If necessary the entire population of Washington can be gassed. I've agonized over this. I believe that we should not do this to our own people."

"How merciful."

"Just wise. We want the government to realize it has been spared by the prophet Gregory at the will of the Lord to help rebuild a new and bountiful world order. At least, we want to give the President and our congressmen time to visualize these empty continents where the lilies of the field can bloom again in all their glory."

He implored me with his eyes. He was truly moved. When he trembled it wasn't fear, but a great anticipation.

"Don't you see, my friend?" he asked. "This is what everybody wants. When a man turns on television at night and sees the war in the Balkans, it fills him with despair. Well, there won't be any more war. Bosnians and Serbs alike will be dead.

"Imagine never having to worry again about the naked millions, the hunger, the floods, the disasters in India. All gone. All of those beautiful cities and temples lying virgin and ready to be reawakened. No one wants to hear any more about petty genocide in Iraq, or street riots in Tel Aviv, or massacres in Cambodia. We're all sick of watching the Third World struggle, while we remain impotent, castrated by our superiority and refined values.

"Everyone wants this!

"It is what Alexander would do! It is what Constantine would do! No one has the means, the guts, the wisdom, or the courage to do it but me! I alone will do this. I alone will do it! I will strike as the Pharaoh struck when he rode down on those who invaded the Valley of the Nile."

I said nothing. A clock was ticking in my brain, a clock. Six or before. What time was it now?

"You've got to consider it," he continued. "You've got to carefully consider it. Imagine the jungles of Indochina and those beautiful ruins, with all the warlike people gone! Imagine the majesty of a city like Berlin. Imagine its resources. In fact Germany will be filled with resources. And those the Germans hurt in the World War will be so happy that Germany is gone!

"All these people have brought this on themselves! I was born to do this, you're proof of it."

"How can you be so sure of that?" I asked. "Doesn't my presence make you pause even an instant!"

"No. Not when I picture the world after the Last Days. The Paradise. Imagine the quiet sweet earth, growing with grass again, and only those of the West preserved to reinvent, and to save, to rebuild nations without ever letting the chaos of the past redevelop. America will colonize these peaceful and beautiful worlds. Under my leadership. If the government helps, that will be good. We need the help. If not, we take over the government."

"And the people in this country, you think they will let you do this?"

"Trust me, they will be very happy once it has sunk in, once they know all that is gone, once they know we are living in a world filled again with natural resources, and abundant land, and beautiful monuments, and fertile and magnificent places to be colonized. Even our Afro-Americans will be delighted that they don't have to worry any more about Africa. American members of all our minority populations will be saved. No people or race exists that does not have a colony in America. This country is the Ark! Cooperate! They'll worship us. They'll worship the risen Messiah, and then his Hasid roots can be known, and it will all be written down; it will become the great turning point in history."

I let him go on: he was truly in his own grip now, nothing could have shut him up, this was his aria.

"Azriel, if you only knew how much we have tried to help these poor nations. If you only knew the conditions in Baghdad and Israel. If you only knew the impossible state of things.

"The first half of this century, we saw fascist madmen like Hitler and Mussolini, and Franco and Stalin. We saw their crude methods fail and pitch Europe into agony.

"Now there are no more such men in the West. There isn't a single leader in the West capable of the clarity of Franco.

"One must go to ragged poor places like Baghdad to find little dictators, like Saddam Hussein, or to the Balkans to find those who would fight to the death. Even Russia itself has no great Stalin, no Lenin, no Peter the Great."

"And you saw these men as great?" I asked. "You see them as great?"

"No, they were evil. They did harm, and by the way, they annihilated millions. Don't think for a minute Stalin didn't kill as many people as Hitler. They killed and they killed and they killed. But it was crude, sadistic, ugly, primitive. I don't count them as great.

"Now the West is led by people who are caught in the trap of their own conscience and benevolence. They know they should bomb Iraq and Iran off the map, but nobody has the guts to do it! Everybody knows Africa is a breeding place for plagues that can kill the world. No one has the guts to annihilate the population."

"And here, what of the poor and the ragged here?"

"We are the Ark, I told you. In the New World, our small population of unredeemables will be given a new chance. Or executed. It won't be a problem. It's nothing. It's a gnat in the face, our problems here.

"That's the beauty of it. America, New York itself, contains people of all races. They can begin the new world order with us. If some do rebel, out of sentiment for their lost lands, we kill them. But we have gone against no race, no tribe, and will in this safe haven protect the remnants of all peoples.

"And remember our campaign through television is extensive. It's all worked out. As the horrible deaths are reported, we will control the news from those areas completely. The President and his Army will be helpless. There will be no overseas connections or allies. Only the Temple of the Mind of God."

"And during these Last Days," I said, "people here will be in a panic that they too are going to be exterminated. All America will be in panic and fear of this plague."

"Exactly, then they will discover that they are blessed. And I have come back from the Dead and have brought with me a vision of a New World. They will learn that God's will decreed these things, that God chose the Temple as His instrument, but I have been among the Dead! Believe me, when this thing is over, the Temple of the Mind of God will be the only worldwide institution left in existence, and resistance to us will be simple to block. We have it all planned, we have our leaders, we have our stations, we have everything in order.

"Nathan has to die in my place at six o'clock, and if I die before that, if anything happens to me, if I give a signal, the world extermination process will begin automatically. And I have a thousand ways of giving that signal."

"Like, name one, for instance?"

"I beg your pardon?"

"What if I simply kill you now and save Nathan and reveal the plot."

"You can't. Don't you realize there are soldiers at all the doors?

And the Bones, remember, I've told them, if you begin to fight us, they are to cremate the Bones. That will end your existence."

"What if it doesn't?"

"What can you do? You can't stop all these people worldwide, you can't even betray this building into the hands of the enemy. We have it under control perfectly. Don't you see? You can only be in one place at one time, spirit or not, and your abilities are limited. When Rachel committed suicide right behind your back you didn't even know it."

"And you think I'm just going to let you do this," I said. "You think I won't try to stop you. You think I will be a party to this horror? You count yourself among the wrong leaders. Cyrus rose to power by tolerance of the religions in his Persian empire. Alexander brought Hellenism to Asia, he married Asian to Greek. The Pax Romana was a time of tolerance. Don't you see, you filth, you take your place with the destroyers!"

I couldn't hold my temper. He looked hurt, deeply hurt but more than that, disappointed and sad, a man committed.

"You take your place with Attila the Hun," I said. "You take your place with Tamerlane, who built walls out of the live bodies of the conquered. You do indeed take your place with the Black Death and with Ebola and with AIDS. You are destruction!"

He shook his hands. He put them up to his face.

"Azriel, try to comprehend the beauty of this. The scope. It is what the world needs, and the only thing that can save the world. Nations have always been annihilated to make way for other nations. The Indians of America were wiped out so that this great nation could rise. Must I remind you what Yahweh told Joshua and Saul and David? To annihilate their enemies to the last man, woman, and child.

"Don't you see, Azriel, this takes brilliance and courage. Unbelievable courage. And I have it. I have it and the means and I can see it through. I can endure the condemnations, the outcries. I have the vision!"

He stood up again, and went to the map as if musing.

"You know, once it's begun, perhaps then you'll see."

"It isn't going to begin!" I declared. I stood up.

There was a little star at the very center of the map. I saw it too late. White, the Star of David or the Star of Magicians. It had had much significance down through the years. He stared at it lovingly.

Too late, I realized that he had pressed it! It was a button. He had triggered something!

"What have you done?" I demanded.

"Merely sent Nathan to his death. He's groomed and ready. He'll be assassinated in front of the building within five minutes. That starts the worldwide countdown of two hours. You have that time to learn from me, and pray you do, and become my helper."

I stood up, dumbfounded.

"My God!" I declared in prayer and utter horror.

"Well, what are you going to do? Stay here? Kill me? Try to save Nathan? Nathan is going down in the elevator now. Look at that monitor. You see it?"

I did. High up in a far corner I saw a blurry picture of Nathan, the true identical clone of Gregory now, his beard and locks shorn, held up by those who stood next to him. He wore Gregory's clothes. I could even see the slight bulge of Gregory's personal gun in the coat pocket. To my horror I realized that the front elevator doors were opening. To my horror I realized that the figures were moving towards the front doors of the Temple, towards the crowd.

"You can't do anything, Azriel. You came back to life to be my messenger. If you kill me now you kill the one man who might be persuaded to stop this a little later on. I won't of course, but you'll make it a fait accompli, as we say, if you kill me. You need me. You know you do. You need me badly."

In desperation, I gave a cry for the iron to come to me that I needed. I held two nails in my hands. I kicked him back against the map, then threw him against the wall, lest the map be full of triggers and buttons.

I drove the nails through his hands. He winced but he didn't cry out.

"You fool!" he said. He shut his eyes as if savoring the pain. Then became enraged.

"Well, you wanted to be the Messiah, didn't you?" I said.

He cursed and snarled, writhing, hands nailed to the wall.

On the monitor I saw the figure of "Gregory," Nathan in disguise, stepping out into the crowd.

I dissolved and moved myself to that spot with all my power, invisible.

But even as I did, I heard the rifle shots. I heard the hail of bullets that descended upon the innocent Nathan. I heard the screams rising from the street.

24

Nathan lay in a pool of blood, eyes blinking at the bright summer sky, as the crowd panicked around him. The assassins had been snared by the mob. Sirens screamed. The Minders wailed.

I stared down at the body of Nathan. I saw the confusion in his bright dark eyes. Memory swam over me, threatening to pull me from the moment.

Then I realized that everything around me had changed. The building had faded. The crowd was gone.

Up before me into the beautiful sky rose the gleaming and unmistakable Stairway to Heaven.

With my own eyes, I tell you, I saw a light that others have told you over and over is indescribable. I saw a light so full of warmth and love and understanding that it filled me in my invisibility, reached me at my core. And I saw Nathan slowly walking up the Ladder.

At the top Rachel and Esther appeared. There were others I didn't know, and suddenly I realized in this blinding and beautiful brightness that they were telling Nathan he had to go back, he couldn't die, he had to return.

Nathan turned around obedient and began to cry; he cried and cried with his hands to his eyes. His image now was Hasid; he had the beard and locks they'd shaved from him. He had his black hat. But he was a spirit returning to the ravaged body that lay on the ground, in which the heart had just ceased to beat.

Suddenly Rachel called to me. I found myself running up the Staircase. Nothing stopped me. I was on it, I tell you, Jonathan, I was on the golden stairs and there above they stood, I saw them all, not only Rachel and Esther, but my father, my own father, and Zurvan, my first teacher, and Samuel and others. I saw them; in a flickering my whole memory was restored to me.

My life passed through youth and innocence into the horror of my murder in which I knew each personage and his or her role, and then all Zurvan's teachings returned to me. Everything I had ever done I saw, good and evil.

I was almost to the top, and Nathan was staring at me in astonishment. Rachel stepped forward.

"Azriel," she said, "you go back, into Nathan's body. Azriel, he's not strong enough to fight Gregory, but you are. You can keep the body alive! Azriel, I beg you."

Nathan turned to me; he was so like Gregory and yet so pure and clean and full of love, utter love. He looked searchingly at all those gathered at the top of the stairs, only a few feet away, where the garden began and the light rose with limitless brilliance.

"You mean I could stay with you?" he asked the others. He looked at Rachel and Esther, and other Hasidim I did not know, Elders, and my elders too!

I wanted to throw myself into my father's arms. "Can't we both come now?" I cried. "Please, Father!"

Suddenly Zurvan spoke, "Azriel, you have to go back in that body and make it get off the ground. Even if it means you never get out of it. You must do it."

"Azriel, please," said my beautiful Esther, "please, you know how evil Gregory is. Only an angel of God can stop him."

My father was crying as he had thousands of years ago. "My son, I love you, but they need you so badly. They need you, Azriel! Only if that slain body rises now can the plot be undone!"

I saw the rationale of it in an instant. I saw what they meant. To foil the assassination now and seize the cameras, that was the only way to warn the world.

I turned, nodding, "Go with God, Nathan!" I cried, and I heard their lovely voices behind me thanking me and praying for me.

Then suddenly from both sides I saw the malcontent spirits tearing at me, faces twisted in hate, my former Masters by the dozen whom I'd forgotten, men for whom I had done evil.

"Why do this?"

"Why should you?"

"Let the madman destroy the world."

"What do you care!" demanded the magician from Paris.

"They're using you again. They're using you!" declared my Mameluk master, whom I'd slain on sight.

"You'll lose your spirit strength, don't you see?"

"You'll be mortal in that body, trapped; you'll die in it of the wounds it sustained."

"Why suffer mortality like that when you are a free spirit!"

And behind these faces and voices were legions of swarming angry, envious, and hateful spirits.

I glanced back up the Stairway. I saw them all gathered, and Nathan had his arms around the others, and they around him. Rachel raised her hand and sent to me a kiss. And in a childlike manner Esther waved. They were fading into utter brilliance. My father had become pure illumination.

I looked at the light and I let it fill me. I treasured just one fraction of a second of understanding, at peace with all things, at peace with all that had been done to me, and that I had done, and all that had ever happened; the world had meaning then. It had a full and magnificent meaning. And the millions of the poor, the hungry, the angry, the warriors—they were not parasites as Gregory had said; they were souls!

"No," I said to the angry spirits. "I have to do it."

"Go into his body, resurrect it," said Zurvan, "even if it means you lose everything."

"Azriel, my love goes with you!" cried Nathan. He had begun to glow like the others.

Blackness. I felt myself sucked down as if by the most powerful mechanical force, and suddenly I was filled with pain, pain in my lungs, pain in my heart, pain in every limb, and I was blinking at the sky as men put me on a stretcher, just as they had done with Esther.

I lurched, rolled over, even though they were astonished, and saw no more stairway and no more light, only the Temple itself, and the mob screaming.

I sat up on the stretcher and then I climbed off it. The medical men backed away in pure astonishment. I knew why. The wounds were fatal. More than one was fatal.

I saw the cameras and I beckoned to the reporters. I reached out for their hands.

"Your government, your agencies. Surround this building and search it at once. An impostor has taken my place. An impostor has tried to kill me. This building is loaded with fatal viruses; and there are Temples of the Mind throughout the world ready to discharge them. Stop them. You must reach the thirty-ninth floor. You must reach the room with the map, and the impostor nailed to the wall. Hurry now! I give you permission to enter the Temple of the Mind. Take guns with you."

I turned around. Everywhere I looked, people had whipped out those little phones that open up and they were screaming into them. The police rushed at the building. Sirens screamed.

"It is an impostor," I said, "it is a twin, and he plans destruction you cannot imagine."

I could see the television cameras coming down on me. "The Temple of the Mind in every country must be stopped. Every building contains poison gas, and deadly viruses. You must stop the Temple of the Mind wherever it is, and beware their lies, beware their lies. Look what they have done to me, and I am living to tell you this."

I felt myself growing weak. The blood was pumping right out of my heart. I realized I was undone. I reached out and grabbed for a microphone. I heard my own voice, tinged with Nathan's tone, rise in volume.

"Minders, your leader has been shot and tricked. Minders, you have been infiltrated. Go inside, destroy the people who have deceived you!"

I was about to collapse. I grabbed hold of a young woman, a reporter who stood beside me with her cameraman catching every breath I took or lost.

"The Armed Services, the people who deal in deadly disease. Worldwide. Alert them. There is enough in any one Temple building to destroy a city, even this one!"

In a blur I saw them all distracted, turning away from me.

A riot of screams broke out. I turned, almost falling, supported in fact by the doctors around me. There in front of the glass doors, held back by confused and frightened followers, stood Gregory, bleeding from the wounds in his hands, screaming:

"I'm Gregory Belkin!" he cried. "That man is an impostor! Look, I bleed like Christ from my hands! Stop the Devil. Stop the Liar."

I faltered. I was almost going down. I looked around me, and then I remembered there was the gun in the left pocket of my coat. He had outfitted the drugged Nathan to perfection, as he himself would have been outfitted, even to his personal gun. It was his little gun, the one he carried the first night I ever saw him, the one he always carried.

I took the gun out, and people screamed and fell back. I staggered towards Gregory and before the bodyguards could think what to do, before anyone could, I began to shoot Gregory. I shot him over and over again. Astonished, he stared as the first bullet struck his chest, then with the second he went up in the air as if calling for help; the third hit his head. I shot another one, before anyone could stop me. He fell dead on the pavement.

There was noise all around me. Someone had taken the gun, very carefully, from me. I heard the endless babble of voices into the phones. I saw armed men running towards the doors of the Temple and the dead body. I saw men putting down their guns and throwing up their hands. I heard shots. I turned and found myself falling into the arms of a young doctor, horrified and staring at me with awe.

I tried to search his soul. "Act fast," I said. "Act fast! The Temple will annihilate the peoples of whole countries. It is poised and ready! That man I killed is a madman. It was all his evil plan. Hurry."

Then I felt myself sinking, not down into the numb indistinct darkness of spirit sleep, but into mortal agony, into a pain that made it impossible for me to talk. I tasted mortal blood in my mouth.

"Call the Rebbe Avram," I said. "Call for Nathan's wife." I begged for the words to come, the names of the community and Court in Brooklyn. Someone said a name for the Rebbe Avram and that was correct, and I said, "Yes, call him to bear witness that I killed the impostor."

I was on the stretcher again blinking at the sky. Is it enough? Will it stop? I closed my eyes. I felt the ambulance rolling, and I felt oxygen pouring into my lungs. I saw above me an innocent face.

I pushed aside the plastic mask. "Connect me now to the people who can stop the Temple."

A phone was thrust at me. I didn't know the person to whom I poured out my last appeal:

"It's the Ebola virus," I said, "a mixture of old and new strains, developed to kill in five minutes. It's in canisters. Hurry. The gas and the virus are in Temples in cities in Asia, the Middle East, Africa. On the ships. The planes are ready to go out. The helicopters. Tell all the good Minders they must cooperate with you. Ninety-nine percent of the cult is innocent! Tell them to turn on their local leaders! Everywhere. You've got to surround and reach them all before it begins. These people mean to kill."

I lost consciousness. I went on speaking, struggling, feeling pain, but I was really unconscious. The human body had broken down, and I was on the brink of death. I was so glad. But had I done enough?

I woke in the emergency room. Again people surrounded me. The Rebbe stood over me. I saw his white beard, the tears in his eyes, I saw Sarah, Nathan's wife. I spoke in Yiddish. "Tell them I speak the truth," I said, "that I am your grandson Gregory, and declare the dead body that of an impostor. You have to. He has arranged for this body, of Nathan, to be verified as his own. Say only that I am your good grandson if you will. It's dark. It's tangled. And I think I'm dying."

Then Sarah's face flickered before me: "Nathan?" she whispered. I turned close and beckoned for her to come down near my lips.

"Nathan walks with God, and Nathan is no more," I said. "I saw him go into the arms of those he loved. Don't fear. Don't fear at all. I'll keep this body alive as long as I can. Help me."

She sobbed and sobbed and her hands stroked my forehead.

I heard a voice, "We're losing him! Everyone out! Out!"

The world went dim. All things were known to me yet dim, and I felt only the peace I'd known in the light, the memory as fresh as a fragrance. The dimness thickened and then loosened. I knew I was being moved.

I knew we were going up in an elevator. And then all went very dim, and a shadowy figure appeared near me. I wasn't certain whether it was good or bad, and then I recognized its voice and the Greek it spoke.

"The purpose is to love and to understand, to value . . ." it whispered.

All was blackness. I think I was thinking, Will the Stairway come now? Will it? Can it do that for me after all I've done? Then nothing.

I awoke in a room in what they call Intensive Care. I was hooked to machines. Nurses surrounded me. Great men were waiting to speak to me, heads of armies and heads of state.

I realized that my pain was dulled, and my tongue thick. I was mortal, utterly helplessly mortal! And I had to stay in this body. It was the only body they would continue to listen to.

The Rebbe appeared. I saw the black clothes and white hair and beard before I recognized the face. Then I felt the nearness of his lips. This time he spoke in the ancient Aramaic for me alone:

"They've been stopped. DNA on file in the hospital confirms that you are Gregory. I have declared the dead man a demon who took the place of my grandson. This is, in its own way, the perfect truth. The Temples all over are being seized. The scientists and masterminds are surrendering. Arrests are being made. In all lands the evil work is at a halt." He gave a great sigh. "You have accomplished it."

I tried to squeeze his hand, but I couldn't feel my own hands, and only gradually did I realize they were taped to the sides of the bed. I sighed and closed my eyes.

"I want to die here, if I may," I said to the Rebbe. I spoke Aramaic again. "I want to die in this, your grandson's flesh. If God will have me. Will you bury me?"

He nodded. And then I slept—troubled, thin, mortal sleep, living sleep.

It was very late in the night when I awoke. All the nurses were beyond the glass. Only the monitors and the machines sustained and befriended me. In a nearby chair, the Rebbe slept.

With absolute shock I realized I was in my own body. I was Azriel. With all my will, I transformed myself back into Nathan. But the flesh of Nathan was dead. This was only an illusion. I could surround the flesh and make it move, but possession as such had ended.

I turned my head, I began to cry. "Where is the Stairway, My Lord? I haven't suffered enough, have I?"

Then I was Azriel again, as easy as taking a breath, and the needles and other medical connections were not connected to me. I stood up, strong, solid, healed in my own sound body, and in my favorite Babylonian robes of blue with gold. My beard, mustache, all there. I was Azriel.

I looked at the sleeping Rebbe. I saw the figure of Sarah, asleep, her hand on a pillow, on the cold floor.

I walked out of the room. Two nurses noticed and came to me gently and told me I couldn't be here without permission, the man in the room behind me was very sick.

I looked back. There lay his body. He was dead, as he had been since the bullets had struck him. Suddenly they heard the alarms go off. They heard the signals.

The Rebbe woke. Sarah climbed to her feet. They stared at the dead body of Nathan.

"He died at peace," I said, and I kissed the nurse on the forehead. "You did everything you could."

I walked out of the hospital.

25

I walked through the city of New York. When I came to the Temple, I found it surrounded by police and military men of many different kinds. Clearly the building had been taken and evacuated of all the evil ones.

Nobody noticed me much—just a crazy man in velvet robes, I suppose. There were Minders everywhere weeping and crying.

I went into the park where the Minders lay weeping on the grass and under the trees and singing hymns and declaring they didn't believe it was all a lie. They couldn't. The message of the Temple had been love, be kind, be good.

I stood still for a moment, and then using all my power I changed my shape into Gregory.

I found this surprisingly difficult to do, and difficult to sustain.

I walked towards them and as they stood up, I told them to be quiet.

In Gregory's voice I told them that I was a messenger sent to tell them their leader had been deranged, but the age-old message of love still had its full truth.

There was soon a huge crowd around me. I talked on and on answering simple questions about their platitudes, love, sharing, the planet's health, all of this, confirming that this was good. Then finally I spoke Zurvan's words.

"To love and to learn and to be kind," I said.

I was exhausted.

I vanished.

I drifted invisible up past the windows of the Temple of the Mind. "The Bones," I whispered. "Take me to the Bones."

I found myself in a room with a kiln. But it was empty and unmonitored now, for the whole system seemed to have been arrested. I opened the door of the kiln and I saw the Bones unharmed. Just the old skeleton.

I pulled the skeleton out, letting it flip and flop about on its new wires as I did so, and then I called for the strength I needed to make my hands like steel and I crushed the skull to pieces, rubbing the pieces harder and harder together till it was powder dropping from my hands, gold powder.

All this I did invisibly, and to each and every bone, grinding it between my hands until there was only dust left, a glittering tiny scattering of golden dust, I saw it swirl up into the ventilating system. I opened the window to the street, and it flew out, this dust, on a great gust of fresh air.

I stood watching until I could see no more dust, only tiny points here and there of gold, and I called down a wind to cleanse the room, to carry it all away into the world, and soon there was not one tiny pinpoint of gold remaining.

I stood thinking, studying.

Then I discovered that I was visible, whole, dressed.

I walked out of the room. But there were so many police now. There were lots of people from the Centers for Disease Control here, and members of the army. No use to parade through these panic-stricken men.

Besides, I had work to do. I felt no taste for it. But I had to do it. Too much poison was stashed in too many vulnerable places. Too many madmen had a head start upon the officials and soldiers who were coming after them.

I threw off the body—again the effort surprised me—and went up and out of the building and high over the world, and then descended to the Temple of the Mind in Tel Aviv.

Soldiers had it surrounded. I entered invisibly and slew every last follower of Gregory who resisted. I slew the doctors who guarded the toxic weapons. I moved fast with swift and certain blows. I made no noise. Death lay in my wake. It was wearisome and sad, but done well and completely.

At once I moved on to Jerusalem and there found that Gregory's followers had all surrendered. The city was safe.

Not so in Tehran. Once again, I slew the resisters, and here I must confess to an evil indulgence. I took lavish and splashy physical form to kill, so that some of the more superstitious Persian Minders—converts of Gregory's from desert religions—would be especially affrighted. Vanity, ah, vanity. I disgusted myself with this fancy show. Blood had lost the shine of rubies. Fear in the eyes of my victims wasn't so pretty.

So I suppose my games were instructive to me, and therefore had benefit. Whatever, I slew everyone in the Tehran Temple who did not bow down and beg for mercy, who did not throw down a weapon and crawl towards surrender.

There were other temples which required my intervention.

But I am not going to give you this litany of slaughter.

Let me say only that I assessed each Temple, whether or not it had been "neutralized," as modern military men would say, and I gave my assistance where I thought it was imperative. I grew more and more tired.

I knew the modern world must complete this work. I knew that it must appear as if the world itself had conquered Gregory Belkin and the Temple of the Mind. I left the certain victories to the human beings.

I learnt from this rampage. I learnt that I did not love at all to kill anymore. Nothing of the Mal'ak remained in me.

My fascination was with love, my obsession was with love.

And the truth is, that the very last of these murderous tasks—the killing of a few very dangerous Minders in Berlin and in Spain—I did with weariness and no small demand on my own endurance and fortitude.

Temple battles would continue.

I was finished.

A great relaxation overcame me. It was easy to return to my own fleshly form. It was the natural result of preoccupation or distraction—to become physical, the creature you see and hear, to feel and smell, and to walk in the world. Invisibility became a feat. I found this compelling.

For a week I wandered the Earth.

I wandered and wandered.

I went into the lonely sands of Iraq. I went to the ruins of the

Greek cities. I went to the museums which held the finest of the art of my times and gazed on these things in quiet.

It took energy to move from place to place in spirit form, but in either state I was quite strong. Indeed to take on any other form than my own became harder.

And as you know—as you saw yourself earlier—when I called back the body of Nathan to me, there was no wedding of my cells with his cells. His flesh was putrid and from the grave, and I sent it back, humbled, and ashamed that I had troubled it.

I studied all the time I wandered. I went into the bookstores and the libraries. I read through many nights, without sleep. I watched the television endlessly as the Temples were contained and destroyed in various countries. I heard of the mass suicides. I saw it all blended finally with the other news all over the world. It was headlines at the beginning of the week. By the end it was still first page of *The New York Times* but much further down.

And the magazines burst forth with their great flower-colored covers, and then a new issue came out and it was another story.

The world went on. I knew your books. I read them in the night. I went to your home in New York City.

I came here after you, to find you. You remember. You had a deep fever.

All the rest you know. I can still change my shape. I can still travel invisibly. But it gets harder and harder to change into anyone else. You see?

You understand? I'm not human. I am the full spirit that I dreamed I would be—in those dark terrible moments when rebellion and hate seemed my only source of vitality.

I don't know what will happen now. You have the tale. I could tell you more, about those bad masters, about little things I saw, but all will be revealed in God's good time.

That's the end of my adventure. That's the end. And I am not dead. I am strong, I am seemingly without flaw. I am perhaps immortal. Why do you think? What more does God want of me?

Will Rachel and Esther and Nathan forget me? Is that the nature of the bliss that lies beyond the light, that you forget and only come when you are called?

I've called. I called and called and called. But they don't answer. I know they are safe. I know someday I may see that light. Beyond that, the purpose of life is to learn to love and that is all I intend to do now.

Is it the blood of Gregory himself that keeps me the wanderer? I don't know. I only know I am whole and that this time I served myself as best I could.

I killed, yes, but it was not for a cause, but to stop one. It was not for a master, but to stop one. It was not for an idea, but for many ideas. It was not for a solution, but for the slow unfolding mystery around us. It was not for death, death which I wanted above all, the rest, the grandeur of the ultimate election to die. No, what I did was not for that. I did it for life—so that others may struggle for it. I turned my back on the light and then I shot to death the man with the great plan.

Never forget that, Jonathan, when you write the story. I shot Gregory Belkin. I took his life.

Has God made a special place for me? Has he made it easy for me? Did he give me visions and signs? Was my god Marduk a guardian spirit? Or was he and were all the spirits I saw merely dreams of the lonely human heart that endlessly refurbishes heaven?

Perhaps the story is chaos. It is another chapter in the endless saga of the blunted yet stunning accomplishments of vicious human wills, the stunted yet dazzling ambitions of little souls. Mine, Gregory's . . .

Perhaps we are all little souls. But remember, I told you I've seen these things. And as I turned my back on the Light of Heaven, I committed yet another murder. Death was mixed up in my story from its earliest days.

And I don't know any more about death finally than any mortal man living knows. Perhaps less than you do.

Part IV

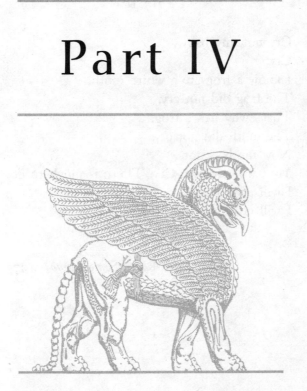

LAMENT

Cry not, my baby.
Cry.
I know a frog ate a white moth.
The frog did not cry.
That's why he's a frog.
The moth did not cry.
Now moth is not.
My baby, cry not. Cry. There is much to do.
I will cry too.
I will cry for you.

Stan Rice, *Some Lamb* 1975

26

It was morning again, cold and clear and still. He said he had to sleep again, but not before fixing me my breakfast. I ate the hot hominy again, prepared by him, and then we lay down together and slept.

When he awoke he smiled at me, and he said:

"Jonathan, I'm not leaving you here. You're too sick and you must go home."

"I know, Azriel," I said. "I wish I could concern myself with such things, but all I can think about is the story. It's all there, isn't it, on the tapes?"

"Yes, in duplicate," he said with a laugh. "You'll write it for me when you're ready, and, Jonathan, if you don't you will pass it on to someone, won't you? Now, I think we should get ready and I should drive you home."

Within the hour we were packed and in the jeep. He had shut down the fire and all the candles in the cabin. I was running a temperature still, but he'd bundled me up well in the back so I could sleep, and I had the tapes tight in my arms.

He drove fast, fast as a madman, I suppose, but I don't imagine he put anyone in danger.

Every now and then I'd look up, roll over, and see him in the driver's seat, see his long thick hair, and he'd turn and give me a smile.

"Sleep, Jonathan."

When we pulled into the driveway of my house, my wife ran out to greet us. She helped me from the back of the jeep and my two children came, the young ones who are still at home, and they helped me upstairs to the bedroom.

I was afraid he would go now, forever. But he came with us, walking through the house as if it were the most normal thing in the world.

He kissed my wife's forehead, he kissed each of my children.

"Your husband couldn't stay up there. Terrible storm. He got a fever."

"But how did you find him?" my wife asked.

"I saw the light coming from his chimney. He and I have had pleasant talks together."

"Where are you going?" I asked him. I was sitting up against a heap of pillows.

"I don't know," he said. He came up to the side of the bed. I was covered with two quilts, and the little house, set to my wife's temperature, seemed intolerably warm, but I was greatly relieved to be home.

"Don't go, Azriel," I said.

"Jonathan, I have to. I have to wander. I want to travel and learn. I want to see things. Now that I remember everything, I am in a position to really study, to really comprehend. Without memory there can be no insight. Without love, there can be no appreciation.

"Don't worry for me. I'm going back to the sands of Iraq to the ruins of Babylon. I have the strangest feeling, that Marduk is there, lost, with no worshipers and no shrine and no temple, and that I can find him. I don't know. It's probably a foolish dream. But everyone I ever loved—except you—is dead."

"What about the Hasidim?"

"I may go to them in time, I don't know. I'll see whether it does good or makes fear. I only want to do good now."

"I owe you my life, and nothing in my life will ever be the same. I'll write your story," I told him. "You know what you are now."

"A son of God?" he asked. He laughed. "I don't know. I know this. That Zurvan was right, in the end there is one Creator, somewhere beyond the light I saw the truth of this, and only love and goodness matter.

"I don't ever want to be swallowed by anger or hate again, and I won't be, no matter how long or hard my journey. If I can just live by that one word it will be enough. Remember? Altashheth. Do Not Destroy. That alone would be enough. Altashheth.

He leaned down and kissed me.

"When you write my story, don't be afraid to call me the Servant of the Bones, for that is what I still am, only not the servant of the bones of one doomed boy in Babylon, or some evil magician in a candlelighted room, or a scheming high priest, or a king dreaming of glory.

"I am the Servant of the Bones that lie in the great field that Ezekiel described, the bones of all our human brothers and sisters."

He spoke the words of Ezekiel in Hebrew, words which the wide world knows as the following from the King James edition:

> *The hand of the Lord was*
> *upon me, and carried me out*
> *in the spirit of the Lord, and set*
> *me down in the midst of the valley*
> *which* was *full of bones,*
>
> . . . *and behold,*
> there were *very many in the open*
> *valley; and, lo,* they were *very dry.*

"Who knows?" he continued. "Maybe some day the breath *will* come into them? Or perhaps the old prophet meant only that one day all mysteries would be explained, that all bones shall be revered, that all who have lived will know a reason for what we suffer in this world."

He looked down at me and smiled.

"Perhaps someday," he said, "the bones of man will yield the DNA of God."

I could find no answer. I too smiled, however. And I simply let him go on.

"But I must confess, as I leave you, I am dreaming of a time when the division between life and death will be no more and ours will be the eternity we imagine. Goodbye, Jonathan, my gentle friend. I love you."

. . .

That was a year ago.

It was the last time I actually spoke with him.

Three times I've seen him since, and two of those times were on the television news.

The first time I saw him was among the medical workers in a cholera epidemic in South America. He was in simple white medical garments, and he was helping to feed the sick children. His hair, his eyes—it was unmistakable.

The next time I saw him, it was in news footage of Jerusalem. Yitzhak Rabin, the Prime Minister of Israel, had been assassinated the day before.

Azriel was a face in the crowd that saw the CNN camera and turned and moved towards it.

He seemed to peer directly through the lense at me.

The newscaster spoke of a city and a country weeping for its murdered leader. The world wept for the man who had wanted peace with the Arabs, and was now dead.

Azriel stared at the camera, and the camera lingered. Azriel was silent—thoughtful—looking right at me. He was dressed in plain black clothes.

The camera and the news moved on.

The third time was merely a glimpse. But I knew that it was Azriel. It was in New York. I was in a cab speeding downtown, navigating wildly through the early afternoon traffic, and off to the side I saw Azriel walking on the street.

He was handsomely dressed, with his hair untamed, and looked magnificent, striding along, carefree and full of wonder. He turned suddenly as if he had felt me see him; he looked around puzzled. But the cab shot on. Trucks blocked my view. We traveled blocks, weaving in and out of other cars. I couldn't have told where it was even, the place where I saw him.

Maybe it wasn't Azriel, I wasn't sure, or so I told myself.

And then, of course, I knew that he could reach me if he wanted me. I did not go back to look for him.

. . .

It's taken twelve months to prepare this book for publication, and then to publish it effectively under the cloak of anonymity so that my own colleagues won't laugh me out of the university, and those who need to hear this tale won't be hampered by knowing my identity.

There you have it. The Tale of the Servant of the Bones. And the story of what really happened with the cult of the Temple of the Mind. Or you have one story of one soul and its agonies and its refusal to give up, and its ultimate victory.

Azriel, if you read this, if you are pleased, let me know. A call; a small written note; your presence. Anything. My life has never been as it was.

But I am confident that wherever you are, you are both happy and good. And that is what matters to you most, I am sure of it.

Altashheth.

11:50 p.m.
July 11, 1995

A NOTE ON THE TYPE

This book was set in Janson, a typeface long thought to have been made by the Dutchman Anton Janson, who was a practicing typefounder in Leipzig during the years 1668–1687. However, it has been conclusively demonstrated that these types are actually the work of Nicholas Kis (1650–1702), a Hungarian, who most probably learned his trade from the master Dutch typefounder Dirk Voskens. The type is an excellent example of the influential and sturdy Dutch types that prevailed in England up to the time William Caslon (1692–1766) developed his own incomparable designs from them.

Composed by Creative Graphics Inc.,
Allentown, Pennsylvania
Printed and bound by Quebecor Printing,
Fairfield, Pennsylvania
Designed by Virginia Tan